Laura Black
Glendraco

Pan Books London and Sydney

D1396005

First published in Great Britain 1977 by Hamish Hamilton Ltd
This edition published 1978 by Pan Books Ltd,
Cavaye Place, London SW10 9PG
© Laura Black 1977
ISBN 0 330 25381 6
Made and printed in Great Britain by
Cox & Wyman Ltd, London, Reading and Fakenham

one

I sat in my bedroom, waiting for a knock on the door, while downstairs they were deciding my future.

The low sun sent a flood of dusty golden light into my room, for it was an early evening in May in the year 1860, and my window faced to the west. The sun held me in the window, although there were a dozen things I should have been doing. Most urgently, there were worsted stockings to darn, and a chapter of the Book of the Prophet Jeremiah to be learned by heart. My grandmother would demand to see the stockings, and my grandfather would demand to hear the chapter. If I sat idle for another second in the evening sunlight, I was sure to be in dreadful trouble later.

Yet still I sat in the warm, dusty golden glow, feeling unable to move. I sat idle, fingers that should have been busy with the darning-needle laced about my knees, eyes that should have been bent to the Bible turned to the western sky. Idleness was, of all sins, the one that filled the God of my grandparents with the most unrelenting rage. Every day of the seventeen years of my life, this grim gospel had been preached to me. It was Satan who found mischief for idle hands, who fought an unceasing battle in my heart with God, the Prophet Jeremiah, and my grandparents.

It was dreadful to think how often he won.

As he was winning now, holding me motionless and tense in the evening sun. The sunlight was dusty from the streets and chimneys of Edinburgh: but beyond the wilderness of granite buildings there were huge bare hills and empty glens and rushing rivers. I had never seen them. My grandparents had no regard for solitary places. But the horizontal sun seemed to be trying to pull my heart out over the rooftops to a wild distant place of crying birds and sweet cool winds.

I sat idle because of the sunlight, and because my mind was full of suffocating curiosity. What were they saying downstairs, my grandparents and their mysterious visitor? It was myself they were discussing, that I knew. It was my future they were discussing, that I knew. Little Janet the under-housemaid had slipped upstairs to tell me so, my single ally in the house, the one other rebel.

Unseemly curiosity ranked almost with idleness in the long list of sins with which Satan tempted girls like me. All useful knowledge, said my grandfather, was to be found in the Bible and in his law-books. If the Lord had intended us to know more, the Bible would have told us more. If the Lord had intended me to know what they were saying downstairs, He would have turned me into a fly, and sent me to sit on the parlour wall where I could listen. A female of good sense and strict moral principles would have been content to wait to be told what they were deciding: but I was *not* a female of good sense, or even, as I was so often warned, of moral principles. I did not want to wait to be told. I wanted to know now.

Besides, there was always the awful possibility that my grandparents would refuse to tell me anything. There was a great deal they refused to tell me. There were subjects they would never discuss. I was surrounded by locked doors, of which they had hidden the keys, by windows kept closely shuttered, and books that could not be opened. Sometimes my head almost burst with questions: but there were very few answers. Once, long ago, at dinner, I asked about my other grandfather, my father's father. I knew that he was James Drummond: that was all I knew.

My Strachan grandfather, my mother's father, said, 'The subject will not be discussed in this house, on this occasion or any other.'

He closed his mouth like a rat-trap, and we finished the meal, as we usually did, in silence.

When I was small, I sometimes repeated such questions, so burning for the answers that I ignored the gathering frowns and the frightening silences: then I would be beaten and sent hungry to bed, for impertinence, for disobedience, for idle chatter. Then, sometimes, I entirely lost my childish temper – I screamed, and flailed out impotently with small fists. The consequences were terrible – beatings, bread and water, and the Minister coming to cleanse me of the devil which possessed me. I hated his interminable droning prayers much more than I hated the cane.

When I grew up I learned discretion; but nothing cured my curiosity. I wanted to know who I was and where I came from: but 'The subject will not be discussed in this house.' There was something to be bitterly ashamed of, it seemed, some secret too dreadful to be mentioned. Is it any wonder that I wondered?

And is it any wonder that, as I sat with my fingers laced about my knees in the dusty golden sunshine of evening, I was consumed, all over again, with curiosity?

It had been so very odd, such a break in the rigid routine of my grandparents' household. The closed carriage drew up in George Square, near our house. I could not see, from the parlour window, who was in it: but I saw the liveried footman run to the door and ply the knocker. Old Carstairs, the parlourmaid, creaked presently into the room, and whispered importantly to my grandmother. My grandmother looked first astonished, and then alarmed, and then grimly ready for battle.

She said to Carstairs, 'Inform your master. Request him from me to interrupt his work to entertain her ladyship.'

This was amazing in itself. When my grandfather retired to his study to read the documents he brought home in fat, dusty deed-boxes, nothing was permitted to disturb him. It was one of the rules of the house, like the rule against intoxicating beverages, and that against playing profane music on the Sabbath. Yet now he was interrupted, summoned to the parlour to entertain a visitor. Who was this 'ladyship' whose arrival caused so dramatic a breach of the law?

I was agog to know: but my grandmother turned to me and said, 'Christina, you will go immediately to your room, and stay there quietly. You have many things to occupy you usefully. I shall send for you later if her ladyship desires to see you.'

'Yes, Grandmamma.'

I took up the worsted stockings which I had been about to darn, and climbed the two floors to my bedroom.

Some twenty minutes later Janet slipped in.

'Oh, Miss! Sic a grand leddy! Diamonds as great as a whaup's eggs! I creppit by the door, an' heard her say – "The lass has a richt to be askit. I'm offerin' the lassie a hame an' a future, an' she has the richt to be askit!" It's yoursel' she was meanin',

Miss Kirstie! What cud be the hame an' the future? You'll no' be leaving?'

'I don't know, Janet,' I said. 'I don't know anything.'

A home and a future? Me? Offered by a grand lady with diamonds as big as a curlew's eggs?

The minutes crawled by. The sun began to go down in a tumult of purple clouds beyond the Edinburgh rooftops. I could bear it no longer. I opened my door as softly as I could, and started on tiptoe down two flights of stairs.

I kept a sharp eye out for the servants, for they were all, except Janet, old and dour and rigidly pious. They had all, always, reported me to my grandparents for things I had done, or things they thought I had done, or things they suspected I would have done if they had not been by to stop me. They were eyes and ears, silent spies; they were prosecuting attorneys in the household's criminal court.

The courtroom, of course, was my grandfather's study. Heaven knows how many hundred times I was summoned, and stood facing my grandfather across the deeds and documents on his desk. The room was dark, all browns and blacks; there were shelves of calf-bound legal books, heavy mahogany furniture with blackish leather upholstery, and a sombre painting in a blackened frame of a Covenanting worthy with a face as grim as my grandfather's. Carstairs or some other old woman would report that I had stolen a slice of cake from the kitchen; or had looked as though Satan were tempting me to do so.

I was always found guilty, convicted, punished; if I lied I was disbelieved, and if I told the truth I was disbelieved.

I was sure the servants wanted me punished. I was sure they gained a cruel satisfaction in earning me a whipping. I was sure I saw a gleam of joy in those hard pale eyes, the twitch of a smile on those pinched, psalm-singing mouths: signs of pleasure which they never otherwise showed at all. I hated them.

Now I was a woman, approaching eighteen, marriageable. It made not a particle of difference. To those pitiless old women I was still a wicked child; they still spied on my every movement, and reported me to my grandparents. I was more of a prisoner than a poor hungry thief caught by the police in the wynds.

What did I want? To be kissed on the mouth by a man, as little Janet told me she had been? Yes, I dreamed of that. To run, for all my skirts and floor-length petticoats, like barelegged tinker-girls on the sands at Portobello? Yes, and to ride a galloping horse, like the jockeys on Musselburgh racecourse: but of course I had never been allowed so much as to see the races. To strip off all my modest and stuffy clothes and plunge into the waves of the sea; to walk across a bare hilltop where wild birds shouted ... Truly I could not picture a millionth of the things I wanted: but they all answered to the same name: 'Freedom'.

One other thing I wanted, that May evening. I very badly wanted to know what they were saying about my future in the parlour.

The upper stairs were dark, and smelled of beeswax polish. They were uncarpeted; some of the stairs creaked. I came down slowly, treading delicately, listening for voices or movements of the servants who spied on me. I came down to the landing of the main bedroom floor. I stopped and listened intently; there was no sound except the thudding of my heart. The servants were all at their stodgy meat-tea, being waited on by Janet, who would get what scraps she could after the others had finished.

I tiptoed on down the wider, carpeted stairs to the lower landing. Here were the parlour and my grandfather's study, the two places where the unhappiest hours of my life had been spent.

Still there was nothing to be seen or heard. I crept towards the parlour door.

I was nearly eighteen: but still I crept towards the door like a child, and I was frightened like a child of being seen by a parcel of elderly female servants. I would be punished anyway, for not darning my hated worsted stockings, for not learning my chapter of the Prophet Jeremiah. If I were seen, I would be punished for disobedience, for leaving the room in which I had been told to wait; I would be punished for eavesdropping, and for the sin of immodest curiosity.

Yet it was my future they were discussing.

I could hear a low, grumbling monologue from beyond the parlour door. It was my grandfather's voice. He generally expressed himself at enormous length: perhaps because he was a lawyer, a Writer to the Signet; perhaps because he had lived all his days in the shadow of the Kirk, used to its interminable prayers and sermons. I could not make out a word he said: but I knew the tone so well. He was laying down the law – the law of Scotland, or the joyless law of the Free Kirk, or his own law. They were all one in his mind. There was no answer to his pronouncements, no appeal from his judgements. He had decided about my future, and he was giving his decision. The mysterious visitor – for all she was a ladyship, and had diamonds as large as eggs – would have to accept it without argument.

I was astonished, therefore, when a high, arrogant voice cut in on my grandfather's oration. His own wife would never have dreamed of interrupting him.

The visitor said, 'I understand your position, Mr Strachan. You may believe that I am aware of the sincerity of your motives. There is no need for you to take any more of my time, or of your own far more valuable time, in repeating yourself.'

I gasped. The visitor had a commanding voice which bespoke a commanding personality: but *no one* spoke like that to my grandfather.

He began rumbling a reply, but she broke in again. 'Give me the credit I am giving you, Mr Strachan. We may not see eye to eye on all points, but I will thank you to give me as much credit for the seriousness of my feelings as I give you for the high-mindedness of yours.'

Rumble and grumble from my grandfather, and a thin echo in the voice of my grandmother.

The visitor said again what Janet had heard her say: 'The child has a right to be asked. The offer I am making may be refused, but I will not consent to your granddaughter not knowing that it has been made.'

I was completely puzzled – confused, worried, excited. I had a right to be asked – asked what? An offer had been made. Of a home, a future? I was to be told the offer had been made – the imperious visitor was insisting on that. But the offer might be refused – might already have been refused by my grandparents – refused on my behalf, for the good of my wretched soul, without reference to my own yearnings . . .

'Miss Christina!' said a shrill voice behind me, vibrant with outrage.

It was Carstairs, the parlourmaid, most stone-faced and stone-hearted of all the grim old servants. She had prowled silently up from the kitchen or the housekeeper's room. Perhaps she had been hoping to catch me disobeying my grandmother's commands; there was no mistaking her satisfaction that she had succeeded.

'Wad ye listen at doors?' she went on, scandalized. 'For verra shame!'

The door of the parlour flew open. There stood my grandmother, whose ears were attuned to every sound in the house. She had heard Carstairs's horrified voice over the argument in the parlour. I was caught indeed.

'I instructed you to stay in your room, Christina, until I sent for you.'

'I stayed there as long as I could bear it, Grandmamma.'

'Wilful disobedience,' said my grandfather, 'has never been countenanced in this house, and we are not now disposed to relax into tolerance of wickedness.'

'Stuff,' said the high arrogant voice I had heard so clearly from the landing. 'I expect she was eaten with curiosity. Come in, child, and let me look at you.'

The lady was sitting with her back to the window, so I could not immediately see her clearly.

I came into the room and curtseyed.

As I came forward, full into the evening light from the window, the visitor made a sudden and startled movement. There was no mistaking it. Something about me, about my face, gave her a shock, filled her with momentary astonishment.

'I have the honour to present to your ladyship my granddaughter Christina Drummond,' said my grandfather.

'I would have no need to be told her surname,' said the visitor softly. 'The resemblance is most startling.'

A frown, his blackest frown, darkened my grandfather's face. My grandmother's mouth compressed itself into a thin line of intense disapproval.

Resemblance? To whom?

The visitor answered the question which must have shown in my eyes.

She said to me, with a slight smile, 'I always thought it so great a pity that your grandfather never had a daughter. I am speaking of course of your other grandfather, of James Drummond, whom I knew. A daughter of his could hardly have failed to be a beauty. Well, the blood is strong. Your grandsire has stamped his stock, as we say of the racehorses. In this one regard at least, dear child, you are fortunate in your inheritance.'

I fortunate? Fortunate to resemble my never-to-be-mentioned Drummond grandfather? I a beauty?

I could see myself, from where I stood, in a gilt-framed French looking-glass over the fireplace. It was a pretty glass, a most unlikely thing for my grandparents to own. Edinburgh houses were full of beautiful things, but not their house: it seemed to me they chose chairs for discomfort, pictures for gloom, and everything else for inconvenience. But their daughter, my mother, had sent them the looking-glass from France, and I suppose it was in her memory that they still had it hanging in the parlour.

I could see myself from where I stood, when I straightened after my curtsey. I saw the face I had always had, the face I had grown glumly resigned to, remarkable only for being wrong in every way. What a shame it was, my grandmother so often said, that I inherited my face from my father instead of my mother. I did not clearly know, except by reference to myself, what my father had looked like – he died just before I was born, and there were no pictures of him in the house. I never saw my mother either, for she died giving birth to me, here in her parents' house, but I knew her face well from the pictures they cherished: a serene face, prettily round and dimpled, very fair in colouring. If I had been lucky, I would have looked like her. But, as I was brought up to understand, fortune was unkind to me, and I had instead my father's face and colouring.

My father's face; and my grandfather's: the Drummond whose name was on no account to be spoken.

I a beauty?

I saw a skin which my grandmother said was far too pale, cheekbones which were too high, eyes which were too large and

12

dark, eyebrows which were too strong and straight, and hair, worst of all, which was dark red. With better fortune, my grandmother said, I would have had a high healthy colour, a round and dimpled face, eyes of modest pale grey or blue, unemphatic eyebrows in a feminine arch, and, most of all, my mother's flaxen curls.

I a beauty?

I had been brought up to believe that I was accursed in my face. And with the face I inherited from my father's family, I inherited so much besides; the wildness and wantonness, the furious temper, the impatience and dissatisfaction, which set me at war with my world. Carstairs often said so.

In person, also, I fell deplorably short of what might have been hoped and expected. My grandmother would have liked me to be blessed with my mother's soft fullness, the generous and feminine figure which the drawings of her showed. But I was obstinately slim. Carstairs said I was no better than a scrawny boy. In fact I swelled out, at hip and bosom, a good deal more than was revealed by the clothes my grandmother chose for me: they revealed nothing, those thick stuff gowns! My legs were slim, without the swelling calf and dimpled knee which I was told my mother had had; my arms were slim, and my wrists and hands. Not that these deformities were of much account: for the way my grandmother dressed me for modesty, my arms and shoulders were as invisible as my legs and bosom.

I a beauty? Could it be so?

'Will you be staring at yourself all night, Christina?' asked my grandfather, whose face had not lost its ominous, ill-tempered frown. 'What will her ladyship think of you?'

'I beg her ladyship's pardon,' I said. 'I was wondering what my father and grandfather looked like.'

'All the Drummonds of your family,' said her ladyship, 'looked like fallen angels.'

This was too much for my grandparents, even from a visiting ladyship. My grandfather sucked in his breath, as he did at the language of the fishwives in the square; my grandmother's mouth became so thin a line that she might have had no lips at all.

Carstairs brought in a lamp, and placed it on a table near

her ladyship. For the first time I could see the visitor's face clearly, since until then it had been silhouetted against the evening sky.

I had never seen a face so full of contradiction, so much at odds with itself. She was very old – perhaps ten years older than my grandmother, a few years older even than my grandfather – and there were deep lines etched about her eyes and on her forehead. Yet her grey eyes had the clarity and impudence of a child's. The lines on her brow spoke of frowns, of the high commanding temper I had heard in her voice; but there were lines round her mouth that spoke of laughter. Her nose was narrow and high-bridged; it put me in mind of the beak of a predatory falcon, or the prow of a raiding Viking ship: it was a warrior nose, a fierce piratical nose. Yet her mouth had a soft and sensuous curve, gentle, vulnerable, pleasure-loving. Her hair was thick and perfectly white, her eyebrows black.

I had not the knowledge to appreciate the magnificence of her clothes. They were not such as my grandmother wore. I could see that Janet was right about the diamonds: a ring, and two matching brooches at her collar.

She smiled at me a second time. The smile lifted the corners of her mouth like the ends of a recurved longbow; it was a smile of great sweetness, a most rare thing in my grandfather's house.

She turned to my grandfather. 'Mr Strachan,' she said, 'I hope you will agree with me that the child's curiosity was forgivable. I myself would have had my ear stuck fast to the keyhole. I trust Christina will not be punished as a consequence of my calling here. Come, will you promise me?'

Her ladyship's smile made not the least impression on my grandfather, nor the appeal she made, in a gentler voice, on my behalf. He was not given to being softened by smiles, nor to listening to appeals.

He said, 'Your ladyship must excuse me from making any such promise. Neither wilful disobedience nor deceitful eavesdropping are to pass unchastised in this house.'

'You will not spare the rod, Mr Strachan?'

'I will not.'

She glanced at me quickly. What I saw in her eyes gave me a

jolt of astonishment, and joy, and hope. I saw pity. I saw regret, and apology that she had not saved me from punishment. But far beyond that, I saw complicity, fellow-feeling. I saw, and it filled me with wonder, a rebellion like my own.

I wanted to go with her, whoever she was, wherever she was going.

Turning to my grandfather, she said, 'You do undertake at least, do you not, to inform the child of the offer that I have made to her?'

'Your ladyship's offer has been refused.'

'You have made that abundantly clear, Mr Strachan.'

I burst out, for I could not contain myself, 'What offer?'

'Leave the room, Christina,' snapped my grandmother. 'We will not tolerate pertness.'

'You will come to my study when I send for you,' said my grandfather.

I curtseyed to her ladyship and left the room quickly. I did not want them to see my tears of disappointment and rage.

They would not tell me who her ladyship was.
They would not tell me what her offer was.

They told me instead what my punishments were to be, and what my future was to be.

The punishments were nothing. I could endure a beating. But the future was unendurable.

I was to marry Findlay Nicholson, soon after my eighteenth birthday. Our betrothal was to be announced almost at once.

Findlay was the son of Dr Nicholson. They lived on the other side of George Square, in a house identical to my grandfather's on the outside and almost identical inside. Dr Nicholson, like my grandfather, was an Elder of the Kirk. Though twenty or more years younger than my grandfather, he seemed the same age, owing to his utter solemnity, the rigidity of his views, and the length at which he spoke on the very few subjects he was prepared to discuss at all. I did not hate him the worst of our neighbours, because I hated his son Findlay more.

I had known Findlay all my life. He was some years older than

15

myself – a spotty schoolboy at the High School when I was a young child, a pudgy student at the University when I was in the schoolroom. He followed his father into medicine; recently qualified, he had joined his father in partnership.

He was fat and pasty. He was a supremely dutiful son. His lips were always wet; I imagined that the palms of his hands were wet likewise. I could never think of him without shuddering.

I had been aware for months that he followed me with his eyes. (They were pale, prominent eyes, exactly like his mother's.) When I walked in Princes Street Gardens, prim among the prim tulips, taking the air with my grandmother, or convoyed by Carstairs in a rusty bonnet, Findlay would watch me as I moved, half hidden behind a clump of lilacs or a privet hedge. Often a high blustery wind lashed down Princes Street, and through the gardens, twitching off the hats of men and thrashing at the skirts of women. Fine ladies wore great hoops, which were caught and swung by the wind; but not my grandmother or I, for our principles forbade display; when the wind plucked at my skirts I was aware of Findlay's globular eyes fixed to the swirling hem, hoping for a glimpse of my legs. He seemed to me that sort of man, as full of furtive desires as a rotten potato of maggots. His eyes made my skin crawl.

He hardly ever spoke to me. He never made any attempt to touch me. I might have liked him better if he had: except I was sure his hands would be so damp.

A week after the old lady's visit, I was called to my grandfather's study.

'The decision has been taken by Dr Nicholson, his excellent son, the Minister, and ourselves,' said my grandfather. 'It is a suitable connection, and better than some aspects of your past character and conduct could have led us to hope you would contract. The Nicholson family temper strict principles with Christian charity. I trust you will show gratitude as well as obedience.'

At family prayers that night – the three of us, and all the servants – the Lord's blessings were asked for my betrothal; and in a long extempore prayer my grandfather besought the Lord to humble my proud heart, teach me obedience and meekness, lead my erring feet in the narrow path of duty, and make me a fit wife for an Edinburgh physician.

I could not speak. I could not think. I was numb. I went to bed, two hours after hearing my future, unable to grasp what they were doing to me.

The following evening I said to my grandfather, 'Was this decision already taken when her ladyship came? Was that why you refused her offer?'

He paused before replying. I knew that, if he replied, he would tell me the exact truth.

He said, 'No. When her ladyship favoured us with a visit, the matter had been extensively discussed, but no firm decision had been taken.'

I nodded, remembering. The elder Dr Nicholson had come several times to our house in February and March; he had long conferences with my grandfather in his study. I thought nothing of it. It might have been my grandfather's health they were discussing, or the doctor's legal affairs, or the business of the Kirk. My grandfather returned these visits. Both he and Dr Nicholson had conferences with the Minister. These meetings extended into May. I still thought nothing of them, nor linked them to the peeping eyes of Findlay Nicholson.

I could see now that they had a lot to discuss, and two things above all. One was my unsatisfactory character – perhaps my shameful ancestry. The other was the size of the settlement. Dr Nicholson and my grandfather, usually allies, would have taken opposite sides about the settlement.

I said, 'May I ask a further question, Grandpapa?'

He told me that I might.

I said, 'Was it the other way about? Did you come to this decision about – Findlay and me – because the lady came? Because of the offer she made?'

He did not answer this question directly, but said, 'Influenced wholly by concern that your life should be lived henceforth according to the precepts by which we have endeavoured to rule it heretofore, and guided by anxious prayer, we have concluded that this union will place you in a useful and virtuous situation, rather than one fraught with temptation and luxury.'

This answer – like many of my grandfather's remarks – needed teasing out, like tangled darning-wool, before I could quite make sense of it. I straightened it out in the end. They were marrying me to Findlay to prevent any possibility of her ladyship's offer being repeated, or any other offer like it.

They were shutting me up for life, for the good of my soul, with Findlay's bulging eyes and wet lips and palms.

And they were buying the Nicholsons' consent with my dowry.

All this I understood in my mind, but my heart and body were still numb. I was not yet *feeling* a response to what they told me.

I spoke once to a boy who had broken his arm playing football. He said that he knew his arm was broken – they told him so, and he could see that it hung oddly – but for some hours he felt nothing. Then it came to life, and hurt him very badly.

That night, in my narrow bed, I came to life. I writhed at the thought of sharing a bed with Findlay; I felt corrupted and dirty at the thought of his touch.

In the small hours, exhausted but still sleepless, I tried to ask myself sensible, grown-up questions. Was I being unfair, childish, ridiculous? Would I not grow to value Findlay's piety and prosperity, his honesty, respectability, success? Could I not resign myself? Overcome my prejudice? Suffer his embrace, if not precisely enjoy it?

Dawn came pale through the window; and with the sleepy brawling of the sparrows in the trees of the square came the answer – No! No! No!

It was disgusting, it was horrible, it was not to be borne.

I climbed out of bed and looked at the dawn. With my elbows on the window-sill I rehearsed the speech I would make to my grandparents: 'I am truly sorry to go against your wishes in anything, and it is in no spirit of perversity that I do so. My brain cannot control my feelings, and I confess to an unconquerable aversion to Findlay Nicholson. I detest him, the thought of his embrace makes me feel ill, the thought of his hands ...' No – I must above all things be reasonable, convince them that I was incapable of marrying Findlay ...

They could scarcely force me to the Lord's Table with Findlay. They could not command my tongue, if my tongue said 'No' during the ceremony ...

This comforting line of thought died as dawn faded into full day. They *could* force me into this. They had come to the decision slowly, gravely, solemnly, with prayer, with the concurrence and support of the Minister. They would not change their minds because I raised some girlish objection. They could and would force me, because they would have the terrible iron certainty that they were right.

Like every Scottish child brought up in a Free Kirk household, I had read the stories of the Saints, the Covenanting Martyrs. Sacrifice was glorious. Life was not for pleasure but for worship and obedience. My own desires were nothing, when weighed in the balance against my duty. My highest destiny was to do my duty. All my objections were the voice of Satan whispering against the call of duty.

When Janet called me down for prayers and breakfast, I realized that there was only one thing I could do.

I would run away.

After breakfast, pretending to sew, I gave up the plan in despair. I had a few pennies in my purse. I could get an omnibus in Princes Street, and go some way towards Leith or Granton – and then what? I knew nothing, nobody. My only education was in housekeeping; I played the pianoforte badly and did water-colour sketches worse.

Having run away, where could I run to then, but back home?

In the middle of the morning, from the parlour window, I saw the fishwife cross the square to our door. It was Jennie Ross, the usual woman who came to us and to our neighbours, a big healthy woman as strong as a strong man, with her skirt kilted up over her bright striped petticoats, her legs and feet bare, her basket of herrings or haddies strapped to her back. She had walked up from the Firth in the morning, shouting and singing with her friends; after a day at the doors of houses and shops, she would stride back unburdened, a little richer, to pass the evening and night exactly as she wished.

I had heard from our servants that the fishwives played golf and even football; that they drank whisky; that their songs were more licentious even than their speech, and their behaviour more licentious than either. Jennie Ross was said to be more respectable than most; otherwise she would not have been allowed near our door. She did not look respectable to me. She looked magnificent.

Jennie Ross came up the area steps from the kitchen door, having sold or not sold some of her wares to the household. Glancing up, she saw me at the window. She waved cheerfully, shouted something I could not understand, roared with laughter, and strode away, barefooted, like a healthy savage.

Ah God, how I envied her!

Findlay Nicholson came to call, his hat as tall as a factory chimney above the pasty pudding of his face.

He took my hand, and pressed it.

His palm was wet. It felt like one of the fishes in Jennie Ross's basket.

'I wish ye happy, Miss Kirstie,' said Janet dubiously.

I nodded dully. I could think only of Findlay's cold damp hand, and his pale eyes, fishlike too, glancing furtively at my bosom.

I thought of other eyes that had struck me: clear, childlike, impudent eyes in an old face.

'Janet,' I whispered, 'what is the name of the old lady who called here ten days ago?'

'I dinna ken, Miss, but mebee Miss Carstairs wull gi' us it.'

'Ask her, Janet! But don't tell her I want to know.'

'Ay. Did ye see the stanes she wore at her breastie? Losh! I never saw the like.'

An hour later Janet whispered to me: 'She'll no' tell, Miss Kirstie. But I haird her hain' a crack wi' a frien'. She mentionit the name – boastin', ye ken, about the grand folks we'll hae as veesitors here.'

'Yes? Go on, please go on!'

'Ay, weel! She'll be ca'd the Countess of Draco.'

A countess? I had had no idea that we had entertained a member of the high aristocracy. I had imagined her the wife or widow of a knight, like some of the advocates and industrialists my grandfather knew; perhaps of a Law Lord.

Draco meant nothing to me. I had never, to my knowledge, heard the name.

'She'll bide,' said Janet,'in a great cassel in a glen. They ca' it Glendraco.'

And then there was the faintest and most distant tinkle of a bell in my memory. Was it something I had read? Something I had learned at school? Something a servant had whispered behind my back?

I could not suppose that Countess or Castle had the smallest connection with me. Yet she had come here. She had made an offer. As a result of which I was bound to Findlay Nicholson.

'But she's no' at her cassel the noo,' said Janet, full of what she had learned from Carstairs's servants-hall snobbery. 'She bides at Lucksie, wi' a duke. Wull a duke be grander yet, Miss Kirstie? Higher than a countess? Is't possible?'

Everyone in Edinburgh had heard of Lucksie – even I, who knew almost nothing about anything. I knew it was an immense new palace, built by some great man; I knew that it was not far from the city.

There were atlases and gazetteers in the parlour. I stole time from my stitching to look at them. I nearly cried out in triumph: for Lucksie was a bare four miles from Edinburgh, on the Dalkeith road, near Gilmerton. From that road I had seen great grey towers, rawly new-built, above the trees on the further slope of a hill. I had supposed it a prison or barracks, but it was Lucksie Castle, built on the site of an old peel-tower, the new seat of the Duke of Renfrew.

I counted the pennies in my purse. There were seven of them; not a noble sum, but enough to carry me, by one means or another, to Lucksie.

Findlay called again, to take me for a walk in the Gardens. Our betrothal was about to be made public; there could be no harm, even in my grandmother's eyes.

Findlay treated me in a new way. He was proprietorial. His voice was as unctuous as ever, but it had a new teaching note in it. He was starting to try to improve me.

'There, Christina,' he instructed me as we waited to cross

Princes Street, 'is, as you may know, the new building of the Life Association Offices, completed only last year, and said to be the handsomest and most commodious commercial building in Scotland.'

I nodded submissively, foreseeing a lifetime of such lectures. A three-horse omnibus trundled by; I wanted to push Findlay under it.

The wind gusted down the street, pressing my clothes against my body, so that my skirts were moulded to the form of my thighs and hips. Findlay's eyes flickered up and down me; he looked as though he wanted to lick his lips.

Then another gust of wind, a blessed gust, plucked his tall silk hat off his head, and sent it bowling merrily down the street.

Findlay gave a wordless cry, and set off after his hat. I had never seen him run before; he was not built for running, and seemed to get no enjoyment out of it.

I was forgotten. Until he caught his hat, he would have no thought for me at all. His hat went faster than he did, sometimes rolling like a hoop, sometimes bouncing. It bounced into Castle Street, and still bounced on, Findlay in panting pursuit. Findlay was by no means the only man chasing a hat in Princes Street that day; he was just the ugliest.

I lost sight of him behind a baker's cart.

I thought as fast as I could, as clearly as my intense excitement allowed. If ever there was a moment to escape, this was the moment. My grandmother would not expect us back for an hour. Findlay would catch his hat eventually – or, more likely, someone would catch it for him – and he would come back to look for me. He would guess I had gone on into the Gardens, and go there to search among the nursemaids and children and flirting couples. Sooner or later, in a dreadful flurry, he would come back to George Square and report that he had lost me; probably he would expect me to have returned already.

Only then would the hue and cry be raised: and by then I would be miles away.

I saw the omnibus turning up the Mound. It was going in the right direction. But it was too far away for me to catch; there would be another presently. I looked the other way, towards

Castle Street, to see if another was coming. I did not see an omnibus; what I saw was Findlay, his hat restored to his head. His mouth was open; he looked dishevelled, exhausted, and angry at his loss of dignity; he was marching back to the corner where he had left me.

I looked left again. The omnibus, which had been blocked by a cart, was trundling into motion again. Findlay had not yet seen me.

I ran, faster than Findlay, not caring what anybody thought. I ran into the wind, buffeted by it, thinking of nothing except catching the omnibus, wildly excited that my escape had begun. I clutched my own hat as I ran, or I would have lost it, in spite of pins; my basket hit against a portly gentleman, who turned angrily, but laughed instead when he saw me. I was laughing myself with excitement.

I caught the omnibus a few yards up the Mound, and sank, panting, triumphant, on to the wooden seat. I could feel my hair coming down at the back from the tight knot my grandmother thought modest: and I knew my face was crimson.

Two facetious gentlemen in fancy waistcoats congratulated me on my turn of foot. I tried to stare at them freezingly, but I was panting too hard to be dignified; and much to my own surprise I burst out laughing. They laughed too. They were very friendly – perhaps too friendly. I suppose it was immodest and unseemly of me; certainly my grandmother would have been appalled. I had never, of course, been on an omnibus by myself before – and never, never laughed out loud with flashily-dressed 'sporting men'. I was behaving like Jennie Ross the fishwife.

Heaven knows who or what they thought *I* was. Luckily, perhaps, they got off the omnibus in Teviot Place, after a quarter of a mile.

The conductor was an altogether sterner personality. He asked me disapprovingly where I was going; I said as far as possible along the Dalkeith road. Then I rummaged in my basket for my purse.

I had no purse. I had dropped it while I ran. I was penniless. The conductor did not believe my tale. No one in the omnibus believed me. No one offered to lend me sixpence. I felt myself blushing furiously, angry and humiliated. It was such a little

23

thing, to drop a purse as I ran, yet it had got me into this horrid situation of being stared at, and disapproved of, and disbelieved, by a dozen frowning strangers.

They made me get off the omnibus, still with almost four miles to go.

For a second – no, for a fraction of a second – I considered creeping back to George Square, with a story about losing Findlay in the crowd. Then I thought of – everything – and started walking to Lucksie.

People looked at me curiously. I stared back as arrogantly as I knew how.

I walked fast, enjoying myself, but envying the bare feet of Jennie Ross. Every stride was taking me further away from George Square, and Findlay, and my detestable future; nearer to Lucksie and the Countess and a different future. What was it my grandfather had decided to protect me from? 'A life fraught with temptation and luxury.' Towards just such a life I was headed.

I found myself walking a little slower, a great deal slower, as I pictured my arrival at the Duke of Renfrew's new palace. There would be, I imagined, some kind of enormous portico. A footman would answer when I pulled the bell-rope. I would ask for the Countess of Draco.

Would I? Dared I? If I dared, would they so much as let me in? I was an ignorant little nobody, from a drab professional household, dowdy, dusty, windswept, a scarecrow. Was I truly going to beat on the door of a duke?

Yes, I told myself firmly, I was.

If only because I now had no choice. After nearly an hour of walking my boats were well and truly burnt.

I saw the familiar grey towers at last, rising monstrous above the treetops. A little further on, I came to a pair of lodges, each like a small castle, each with a neat garden. Huge wrought-iron gates, gilded and full of heraldic animals, stood wide open. I walked through. No one challenged me, but a woman in one of the gardens nodded and smiled. I took her to be the lodge-keeper's wife; I smiled back nervously. I found myself in a long, dead-straight avenue of newly planted trees. At the end of the avenue I glimpsed what looked like a huge grey cliff: it was the side of the castle, still a long walk away.

I suddenly felt very tired, and my feet hurt dreadfully. I knew I must look like a tinker who had slept for a month under a hedge.

But this was no time for collapse, or self-pity, or self-consciousness. Going forward was a horribly alarming prospect; going back was stark impossibility.

A closed carriage came slowly down the drive, drawn by a pair of heavily built grey horses. I stood aside to let it go by. The coachman glanced at me without interest, the footman beside him with raised eyebrows, the groom behind with a grin. The windows of the coach were curtained, so that I could not see who was inside.

To my astonishment, the lodge-keeper's wife in her garden curtseyed to the back of the coach, although nobody inside it could possibly have seen her.

She looked in my direction, and saw the surprise on my face. She laughed, and said, 'Ay, it's daft-like to bob at a body's back, but her leddyship desairves ony salutation folk can gi' her.'

I was impressed that anyone should inspire such respect, especially as Lowland Scots are not an obsequious breed.

'Whose carriage is it?' I asked. 'Who is inside?'

'The Dowager Countess o' Draco, the guid God keep her. She bided wi' his Grace twa-three weeks, but she's awa the day to her ane place. I dinna just ken where she gangs, but it's a gey lang step for an auld body.'

My legs suddenly gave way beneath me. I was too tired to stand; I was overcome with utter despair. I collapsed on the mossy ground under a tree, and burst into tears.

two

She was going home, a long way away. It was somewhere no railway went near, or she would never have been travelling in a carriage. That meant it was probably somewhere in the Highlands. Even with a purseful of guineas, how could I travel alone into the Highlands?

I had not got a single penny piece, and there was no one in the world I could beg or borrow from.

Of course I could find out where Glendraco was; but for all the chance I had of getting there, it might as well have been on the dark side of the moon.

I would never see her. Without her, I would never escape. Findlay's lips and hands and improving lectures would fill the rest of my life.

And now I must walk four miles home, and face my grandparents. There was no alternative, none, except to stay here and die.

And that, wretched as I was, I was *not* yet prepared to do.

I heard hoofbeats and wheels. I looked up, blubbering still, ashamed to be seen in such weakness. The lodge-keeper's wife had come out of her garden and crossed the avenue to assist me: and as she reached me a gig turned off the road into the avenue.

'Why, wha' ails the lassie?' cried the woman.

'I'm so tired,' I said. 'And I've had a shock. It's nothing. I am quite well really—'

The gig had drawn up. Ashamed of my tears, of my whole tattiebogle appearance, I turned away quickly to hide my face.

A man's voice, a pleasant voice, said, 'Can I be of any assistance?'

'No, thank you,' I said, as steadily as I could. 'I wish only to be left alone, if you will please drive on.'

But the dignity of my reply was quite ruined by a hiccup.

And then, suddenly, such a wave of renewed misery flowed over me that I lowered my face to the ground again and the tears poured out of my eyes. For I thought of walking all the way back, and facing my grandparents, and marrying Findlay. I felt the woman's hand patting my shoulder. Then I heard the man jump down from his seat. Very shame made me sit up. I found a large and beautiful silk handkerchief held under my nose. Gratefully I took it, and dabbed at my eyes and cheeks.

I said, 'Thank you, sir. I am not usually as weak and stupid as this.'

'I find it hard to believe,' said the pleasant voice of the gentleman, 'that I cannot be permitted to help you in any way.'

'Whisht, ma lord,' said the lodge-keeper's wife, 'tak' the young leddy up in your wagon an' drive her where she'd gang.'

'That had occurred to me,' he said drily. It seemed he was a lord. He certainly sounded like one. 'My horse, my, er, wagon, and my humble self are all at your service, ma'am.'

'You are very kind, sir,' I managed to say. 'But I do not think it would be proper for me to travel alone with you.'

'Very correct,' he agreed, with a smile in his voice. 'But is it so *very* proper to be lying in floods of tears, unchaperoned, beside the Duke of Renfrew's avenue?'

'I couldn't help it,' I explained. 'It was – force of circumstance.'

I still felt crushed by disappointment, I still felt overwhelmed by despair; but I recovered enough to look up at the pleasant-sounding Lord. He looked as he sounded. He was a tall, powerful man of about thirty-five; he had thick, curly light-brown hair and side-whiskers, blue eyes, and a sunburned face. He wore a knickerbocker suit, old but neat, and a tweed cap. He looked a man who never willingly spent a minute of daylight indoors. He looked down at me, smiling, holding the beautiful head of his chestnut horse.

'I won't ask your name,' he said. 'And if you would rather not tell me what disastrous circumstance brought you here, weeping and alone, then of course I'll bite back my curiosity. And that, I assure you, will be a far greater sacrifice than driving you wherever you want to go.'

'Oh,' I said helplessly. 'I wonder what I ought to do.'

'Weel, ye'll no' bide here the nicht,' said the lodge-keeper's wife practically.

'I do *not* believe,' I said to his lordship, 'that I ought to go with you. But I do *not* believe that I can walk back to Edinburgh.'

'Certainly you can't,' he said at once. 'Allow me to help you up.'

He extended his free hand, which I took. He pulled me to my feet as though I were made of paper. His hand felt very strong: and it was dry.

He said, 'I think we can accept that as a kind of introduction, don't you? My name is Cricklade. I am staying at present with the Duke, who is my godfather. I hope,' he smiled, 'you will think that sufficient evidence of my respectability.'

'Hoots toots,' said the lodge-keeper's wife (whom I was beginning to like very much), laughing at the idea of Lord Cricklade having to prove that he was respectable.

'I will take you down the road to Edinburgh with the greatest pleasure,' said Lord Cricklade, 'but can I not take you up to the castle first, for the refreshment which you look as though you badly needed, and for the services of a maidservant, which, er, you also look as though you needed?'

I was tempted. I longed to see the inside of a ducal palace. The refreshment might include a glass of wine; and I was so far gone in wickedness today that the Devil's Brew, which I had never tasted, was an alluring prospect. But for once I resisted temptation. The thought of a ducal maidservant sniffing at my wretched dowdy clothes, and my untidy hair, and my tear-blotched, dust-stained face, was too awful to contemplate.

Lord Cricklade read my mind in a most unnerving way. Smiling again, he said, 'I could probably arrange the refreshment without the maidservant, if you think, as I do myself, that she might be a gorgon.'

I was tempted again; but I thought of my return and of my grandparents. Since I had to go back, the sooner I went the better. I could think of a story on the way.

I said, 'There will be people worrying at home, my lord – your lordship—'

'I think you might bring yourself to call me "Lord Cricklade". It is just as correct, and less stilted.'

'Oh! Thank you. I wasn't sure.'

'You feel you must stop the people from worrying? I dare say that is quite right, and it does you credit.'

I said goodbye to the lodge-keeper's wife, and Lord Cricklade helped me up on to the seat of the gig. I had never sat in one before, it seemed so flimsy and elegant, with two huge wheels with spokes as fine as pencils, and very little to stop one falling out.

We turned out on to the road, and the big chestnut horse started trotting smartly back towards my prison.

28

Lord Cricklade was almost miraculously kind to me. I knew quite well how curious he must feel about me – it *was* a most peculiar thing to have stumbled on, a dishevelled female, in floods of tears, lying on the ground in the avenue, who now only wanted to hurry back into Edinburgh. But he never asked me so much as my name. Instead he talked about himself, not boastfully at all, but laughing at himself, and simply in the way of conversation. He was English, and had an estate in Wiltshire. He said he lived entirely to amuse himself. He always came to Scotland in the summer for the fishing, and then the grouse-shooting, and then the deer-stalking, and then he went home for the partridge-shooting, and then the pheasant-shooting, and then the foxhunting with Lord Bathurst's hounds. He said he was too selfish to be married, and too lazy to do anything useful; but he smiled as he spoke, and it was not really his picture of himself, or my picture of him.

What struck me most about him was the easy friendliness of his manners. We might have known each other for years. I had never met anything in the least like it, in my grandparents' circle in Edinburgh. In those grim parlours, all conversation was a series of careful speeches, about professional topics or politics or religion, or illnesses, or the iniquities of servants, or nephews in India or Canada. Lord Cricklade and I *chatted*. It was something I had never done before; he made it marvellously easy; he made me laugh; he even made me forget, for a few seconds at a time, the misery that sat like a sandbag on my head.

'For a man like me,' said Lord Cricklade, 'September is an impossibly difficult month, quite the most vexing of the year. I should be at home, shooting my own partridges, and cub-hunting with Lord Bathurst to get my horses fit for November. But how can a fellow leave the grouse and the stags and the autumn salmon?'

'How will you resolve such an awful dilemma?' I asked.

'Every year I toss a coin. Last year England won. This year I believe I shall use a curious old coin I have with a head on both sides. I shall say – "Tails, Wiltshire; heads, Glendraco"—'

'*What?*'

'It's the one place where I think I might fulfil my lifelong ambition. My plan is to catch a salmon in the Draco in the morning, shoot a grouse on the low moor at noon, and stalk a stag on Ben Draco in the afternoon.'

The closed carriage with the curtained windows was trundling sedately to distant Glendraco at this moment, and with it was going all my slender hope of salvation.

I have said I was a grown-up woman, of marriageable age, mature and self-possessed. But not altogether. Because now I burst into tears again, like a young child.

Lord Cricklade pulled up his horse.

He took my hand (his was still dry) and said gently, 'I feel sure I can help you, if only with comfort, if you will only tell me how.'

'The Countess,' I sobbed, 'was my last hope.'

'Old Lady Draco?'

I nodded.

'She left Lucksie today,' he said. 'I passed her carriage on the road, just before I saw you . . . she was your last hope? Aha! You came to find her, and the bird had flown, and that explains your unhappiness?'

I nodded again.

'Why on earth,' he said cheerfully, 'did you not tell me this before? With the greatest respect, my dear, you're a goose. Now we must go back, and turn off on to the Blackhal road, and hope her funny old coachman picks the same route that I would.'

He began to turn the gig before I fully realized what he was at.

Tears flowed down my cheeks all over again (it was a terrible day for tears, that day: I did not usually cry so *very* often), but now they were tears of gratitude and wild hope.

The beautiful horse seemed just as happy going back the way he had come; he trotted on like a gleaming chestnut machine.

Lord Cricklade said, 'I do not mean to pry, and it is certainly none of my business, but can you tell me what the Dragon is your last refuge from?'

'Dragon?'

'You don't know her very well, if you don't know she is called the Dragon. It is *not* entirely a pun.'

'Is it a nickname?' I asked doubtfully.

'It is an accurate description. She is your last hope of what?'

'Escape.'

'The plot thickens. Escape from what?'

'Wet hands,' I sobbed.

'Ah,' he said comically. 'Now, of course, I fully understand everything.'

'The man they want me to marry,' I explained. 'Also he has eyes like a fish, and he watches me . . .'

'If I did not feel obliged to keep my eyes on the road,' said Lord Cricklade mildly, 'I would get great pleasure from looking at you myself.'

I glanced at him sharply. He was watching the road and his horse, his face serene. He had spoken lightly. But there was no doubt at all that he meant it. He wanted to look at me. Could the Countess have been *right*?

This seemed to me a point of such importance that I said earnestly, 'But my grandmother says that I am wrong in every way. I mean, as to eyebrows, and hair, and so forth. I take after my father, you see, which is my disaster. Nobody wants to look at me, my grandmother says. Findlay only does so because he is pathetic, and dare not raise his eyes to a pretty girl.'

'I called you a goose,' said Lord Cricklade, 'but I used too mild an expression, and must qualify it. You are a very silly goose, and your grandmother must be another. Every man in Britain would turn to look at you, and two out of three would fall in love with you.'

'Oh,' I said, extremely surprised. It was a very poor reply, I know, but I could not think of a proper answer to so very startling a speech.

He did not pursue the subject of people turning to look at me, and falling in love with me. Part of me was keenly disappointed (the wicked part), and part relieved (the modest and virtuous part). He asked me instead about my life in Edinburgh, which to him was a very gay city, with the races on Musselburgh Links, the bathing at Portobello, the fine shops of Princes Street with silks and silver and jewels, the operas by someone called Verdi at the Queen's Theatre, and the royal magnificence of Holyrood, restored to glory, quite lately, by the Queen.

I said I had never been to the races, or bathed in the sea, or worn silk or any jewels, or set foot inside a theatre, or danced at Holyrood or anywhere else.

All he said was, 'What a waste.'

He walked his horse up a hill, to rest it, and from the top we saw the crest of the next hill; and approaching that crest, at a walking pace, the closed carriage with the pair of grey horses.

'Tally-ho,' cried Lord Cricklade cheerfully. 'From a scent to a view, from a view to a death. On we go, Cinderella. We'll be up with your fairy god-dragon in a couple of minutes.'

And so we were. Lord Cricklade drove the gig past the heavy, lumbering carriage, and pulled up a little way in front of it, blocking the road. The coachman reined in his greys, looking surly until he saw who had stopped him.

He called out, grinning, 'What's to do, my lord? Wull ye hae our money or our lives?'

His lordship laughed, and helped me down from the gig. It was the fourth time I had felt the firm, dry pressure of his hand on my hand; and I began to think, in a very unmaidenly way, that I should like to feel it a great many more times. But he let go of me, the moment I was safely on the ground, and we walked back towards the carriage together. The footman had jumped down from the front of the carriage, and the groom from the back.

'I think,' said Lord Cricklade softly to me, 'that now you really are obliged to give your name.'

'Yes,' I admitted.

'And I don't see how you can forbid me to hear what you say to the Dragon.'

I stopped, suddenly aghast. What *was* I going to say? Remind her of the offer she had made to my grandparents? I did not even know what it was. Throw myself on her mercy, her charity? She was the Dragon. My behaviour today had been grossly improper, there was no denying that, even by standards much laxer than those of George Square. I could not suppose the Dragon would condone it. And I knew I looked even more of a scarecrow than when Lord Cricklade found me, after several miles of fast trotting, high on the seat of a gig.

I was about to make a ridiculous, impossible, shameless

request, to a lady they called the Dragon. I was about to be treated exactly as I deserved – stared at, sniffed at, and sent home.

'I think,' I faltered, 'I had better go back to Edinburgh after all. I am sorry to have given you and your horse so much trouble.'

'We have both enjoyed it,' said Lord Cricklade gravely. To the coachman he said, 'Hamish, this young lady has urgent business with her ladyship. It concerns a wet hand and a fishlike eye, which you'll agree is a horrible combination.'

'Yon's the lassie,' said the footman suddenly, 'stud by the lodge.'

'And now she is standing here,' said his lordship. 'Will you tell her ladyship that Miss . . . ?'

He glanced at me, smiling.

The curtain over the off-side window of the carriage was twitched back an inch by an unseen hand, and the window let down an inch. Whoever was inside could hear all that went on outside.

'Miss . . . ?' repeated Lord Cricklade, smiling more broadly, but with great kindness, and an evident curiosity that I quite forgave.

'Christina Drummond,' I said.

Immediately the curtain of the carriage window was pulled back a further inch, and an eye peeped through the gap. The eye stared at me as I stood, extremely nervous, wondering what to say to the Countess, and what she would say to me.

But it was not the Countess of Draco's clear grey eye that stared at me. It was a bright black eye, in a wrinkled chalk-white face.

Even in the little of this face that I could see, there was a reaction exactly like the Countess's, when I came forward to the window where she sat, ten days before. There was a start of astonishment, of recognition.

I thought there was also a reaction quite unlike the Countess's. I thought there was a look, at the sight of my face, of the most malevolent hatred.

I hardly had time to speculate who this might be, a white-faced and black-eyed old woman, who travelled with the Countess in her carriage, and hated the sight of my face. The invisible hand twitched the curtain across the window again; I saw only the heavy purple velvet behind the glass.

From the other side of the carriage, the footman called to me that her ladyship was yonder. I hurried round to her. The door of the carriage stood open, the footman holding it; the Countess was leaning forward in the deep velvet seat, pulling back her veil from her face.

I curtseyed. She looked at me blankly. For a terrible moment I thought she had quite forgotten me.

She said, in a terrible voice, 'What in the name of God are you doing here? You have been rushing about the public roads, in a gig of all things, alone with a gentleman? No person of refinement will ever speak to you. You look like a tinker, you act like a drab, and you interrupt my journey.'

I opened my mouth to say something, and closed it without saying anything. The Dragon was breathing fire, and I was scorched.

My escapade was over.

Lord Cricklade cleared his throat. He said mildly, 'Pray don't judge harshly, Lady Draco. They are trying to marry her to a fellow with wet hands.'

'Be silent, Cricklade!' snapped the Countess. His lordship looked distinctly abashed, which I would not have expected of him. The Dragon's fire scorched him, too.

'The only account of this disgraceful romp to which I will consent to listen is Miss Drummond's. Well, girl?'

'It is true,' I said heavily. 'His hands are very damp. And he has eyes like a fish.'

'Your worthy Strachan grandparents are intending your marriage to this person?'

'Yes. So I ran away.'

'You did quite right. Come into the carriage, child, and we shall go to Glendraco.'

The Countess smiled at Lord Cricklade: the smile I knew, that turned up the corners of her mouth like the ends of a recurved longbow.

She said, 'You have behaved very wrongly, Cricklade, and I am most grateful to you.'

He looked unexpectedly solemn. He said slowly, 'Perhaps I have behaved wrongly. I acted on an impulse which – in short, I find it difficult to blame myself.'

'Don't go falling in love with the girl. She's too young for you. Besides, I shall need her.'

He was utterly taken aback for a moment. So was I.

Then he said, still surprisingly serious, 'I did not know Miss Drummond was running away from her grandparents. I thought she simply wanted your help in preventing this marriage. Had I known what she intended, I could not have consented to help her.'

'What?' I asked, very much surprised.

'I am a Magistrate, Miss Drummond. Since I enforce the law, it is all the more my duty to keep it. Knowingly to assist a person under age to remove herself from her family or legal guardians, for whatever reason, is a crime punishable by a prison sentence.'

'You talk too much, young Cricklade,' said the Countess. 'I want to go home. You are getting as prosy as David Renfrew.'

'You cannot do this, Lady Draco.'

She looked at him with the blank expression with which she had terrified me. At last she said, 'I *cannot* do this?'

'No, ma'am. You must know that as well as I. To help Miss Drummond is legal and proper, to abduct her is a felony.'

The Countess blinked at the word 'felony'. It had an ominous ring to me, also; a leaden-toned echo of my grandfather's legal world.

'A felony,' she repeated.

I saw that she would not commit a felony – not she, Dowager Countess of Draco, a great lady, a pillar of society. Faced with the gravity of what she was doing, she would never take me away from my grandparents. She would send me back to them.

I was frightened at the thought of my punishment, but I was much more frightened at the thought of Findlay.

'His mouth is wet, too,' I said desperately. 'And he gives me lectures.'

'His mouth is wet,' echoed the Countess. 'He gives the child lectures. Would you have her lectured all her life by a man with a wet mouth?' she turned to me, frowning. 'Does he *spit*, Christina, when he lectures you?'

'N-no,' I admitted. 'Not much.'

'I expect he will when he is older. Now let us waste no more time. Come into the carriage, child, and sit down opposite Eugénie.'

Felonies did not frighten her, after all.

But before the footman could help me up, Lord Cricklade put a hand on my arm to stop me. For the first time I found his touch detestable. I shook off his hand, but he reached out again and took my arm.

'It may seem ridiculous to you, Lady Draco,' he said obstinately, 'but even you are subject to the law of the land. If you will not immediately take Miss Drummond back to her family in Edinburgh, I shall be obliged to do so.'

'By force?'

'I hope not. But, if necessary, I shall of course use such force as I must. This is not my choice, believe me, but my absolute legal obligation.'

After all, then, my escapade was ended.

'I have here a coachman,' said the Countess, 'a footman, and a groom. None is as strong as you, but the numerical advantage is overwhelming. Hamish keeps a pistol under his box, for the absurd reason that there were highwaymen in Strathearn seventy years ago. I keep a smaller pistol, presumably for the same reason, in the pocket inside the door here. I practise with it from time to time; it is, like myself, old but serviceable. I snap my fingers at your threats.'

'I shall continue,' said Lord Cricklade doggedly, 'to block the road with my gig.'

'That gimcrack toy I see in front of us? We shall smash it to matchwood. I advise you to unharness your horse before we pulverize your vehicle.'

Lord Cricklade's jaw dropped, she so very clearly meant what she said. Then he shrugged and laughed. 'You can testify,' he said, 'that I tried to do my duty as a Magistrate.' He glanced at me. 'I do have other interests besides pure sport, you see.'

'I guessed you did,' I said. 'Thank you for your crime.'

'Crime?'

'Abduction of a minor,' I explained.

He laughed again, and said he hoped to see me at Glendraco in September. He added in a low voice, 'There is one command of the Dragon's which I do not think I can obey.'

'What?'

'She ordered me not to fall in love with you. But I think she's too late.'

I felt myself blushing furiously as I climbed up into the carriage and sat down with my back to the horses.

The footman slammed the door; the groom ran from the horses' heads to his perch on the back of the carriage; we began to roll forward.

I was free.

'Christina,' said the Countess in a terrible voice, 'I may speak in a disrespectful way to a gentleman like Lord Cricklade, because I am a very old woman in a very high place, and because I have known him since he was a schoolboy. For you to do so is disgusting impertinence, and a miserable return for his kindness to you. Your grandparents, I see, have been too mild with you. That shall be put right. At Glendraco we know how to teach modesty and politeness to saucy girls.'

I was going from bad to much worse: from an Edinburgh schoolroom to a Highland prison.

'Eugénie shall have charge of you,' said the Countess grimly, 'until you are fit to be seen in public.'

Eugénie? I inspected covertly the other old face opposite to me, of which I had seen a glimpse in the carriage window. The eyes were hard and black and bright, and the face like wrinkled white paper. She wore a great cloak, in spite of the early summer heat, and fingers like misshapen claws curled out of knitted mittens.

She stared back at me, and the hatred in her face was as clear as the sun.

Some time afterwards, in the great library at Glendraco, I looked at the atlas with the help of the Reverend Lancelot Barrow, the Chaplain of the Castle, whom I was supposed to be assisting in the compilation of a new catalogue. From the map I saw that the road from Edinburgh to Glendraco was scarcely more than one hundred miles.

I have never travelled so far; and I had never travelled so slowly.

I was used to thundering short distances from Edinburgh by train, usually to stay with one or another of the vast regiment of my grandmother's cousins. (I do not say that in those houses family prayers were actually *longer* than at home in George Square: but they were certainly not much shorter. I sometimes thought there must be a competition among my grandmother's relations – among the Rutherfords, Hays, Wilsons and Jamiesons – as to who could make the longest extempore prayer for the Lord's intercession in our struggles against Satan. Quite often it was my soul that came in for special mention.) My grandparents took immense, meticulous pains in preparing for these journeys. They always travelled Second Class, not wishing to be infected with the luxurious indolence of the First, nor by the dirty and outspoken dregs in the Third. We sat in frozen silence, in a row, myself always wedged between my grandparents, lest I should be touched by a strange male hand; we all, in a row, bounced up and down with the rattling of the train; every mile was a misery, but we covered the miles extremely fast.

But there were very few miles of railway in all the Highlands, and those few had only been there a very few years; and none of them went anywhere near Glendraco. By rail it might have been a three-hour journey; the Countess's coach took three days to cover the hundred miles – of actual travelling, six more hours on that first day, six hours on the second, five on the third. With the hour they had been on the road before Lord Cricklade intercepted them, I calculated that the coach was moving for eighteen hours altogether (an easy sum, even for me) and therefore that it was travelling at an average speed of five-and-a-half miles an hour (a much more difficult sum). This leisurely progress gave me a great deal of time for looking at the scenery, and looking at the Countess and Eugénie, and looking at my knees, and thinking.

Of the scenery, that first day, I took in little and remember less. The Countess told me to open one of the curtains so that I could see out, and educate myself, and not be bored. But my brain was bubbling with doubts and terrors and questions, and a few hopes;

the whole space inside my skull was like a bowl of broth on a kitchen range. I had no mental energy, no curiosity to spare for the sheep-walks and hay-fields, the fat cattle and solid steadings, the farm women, bare-legged below their bright striped petticoats, or the small grey towns of our route.

Of the Countess's conversation I remember nothing, because there was nothing to remember; she was quite silent all the way. Most of the time her eyes were closed. In repose, her face looked old and very tired. It looked more deeply lined than when she was awake and speaking; I thought some of the lines had been etched by suffering. I do not think she slept.

Eugénie was equally silent. Often her bright black eyes were open; and when they were open they were often turned on me. When I glanced at her face, and met that unblinking stare, she did not look away at once, as people usually do when one catches them staring; she stared on, meeting my eyes, not a bit embarrassed, trying to out-face me, to force me to drop my own eyes. But I would not. I had much to be ashamed of, but I would not be out-stared by a foreign servant (I supposed she was foreign, and a servant) with a chalk-white face and a black, foreign eye full of hatred.

I read in the schoolroom once about a creature of myth called a Basilisk, which turned you to stone if you looked it in the eye. Perhaps Eugénie was trying to be a Basilisk. If so, she failed. She did not turn me to stone but, on the contrary, made me angry. It was one of the worst faults of my character (as I had been taught all my life) that when I was pushed in one direction I wanted always to go in the other. My grandparents called it perversity; I think they were probably right. Eugénie's black, malevolent eye, in trying to tame or intimidate me, made me stare back at her like a wanton, or a bold gipsy child, or an animal.

Which of the three, I wondered, did Eugénie think I was?

When Eugénie closed her eyes, then and only then did I lower mine, then only did I consent to look at my knees, pressed demurely together under the modest serge of my skirt, or at my hands, clasped demurely in my lap: to look at both hands and knees as though they were strange to me. They were, a little.

Those familiar knees, which had bent so reluctantly to prayer in my grandfather's house, had carried me all the way to Lucksie. Audacious knees, rebellious, reckless, even criminal! I had not really been altogether sure that my body would obey the wild command I gave it, there in Princes Street in the blustery morning. As to my hands – so much too thin, so lacking in the pretty dimples over my mother's plump pink knuckles – they had been grasped by Lord Cricklade no less than four times; and memory of the pressure of his fingers still made them tingle. Shameless hands!

And he said – to all intents and purposes he practically came out and said – that he had fallen in love with me.

My skull was like an iron cooking-pot simmering on a kitchen range. When you look at such a pot, with the broth preparing, you will see first one thing, then another, swim to the surface with the slow bubbles from below. My thoughts were like that. We were crawling towards Glendraco. What was it like? What would my life there be? What would become of me? Who was Eugénie? Why did she hate me? Would the Dragon be always a dragon? Why, since she disapproved of me so violently, did she take me up in her carriage? What were they saying now, in my grandfather's house in George Square? Had they told the police? Was there a search-party out? Was Findlay blamed? Were they praying for my safety? For my chastity? For my soul?

Did Lord Cricklade *mean* it?

Of all the thoughts that bubbled up to the surface of my mind, this reappeared the most frequently. I considered the question from every angle. I never tired of it. I looked forward to September.

In the late afternoon we turned off the main road, which was broad and smooth and macadamized, on to a much smaller and rougher road. The coach, and we three inside it, were jolted about in our seats, in spite of the huge springs, and the very slow pace the horses were held to.

The Countess opened her eyes. She glanced first out of the window of the coach, then at me. She said nothing, and there was no expression in her face. I wondered if she was still angry with me, and if so how long her anger would last, and what its effect would be.

I felt, rather than saw, Eugénie's Basilisk eyes also upon my face. But I did not want to embark on another staring match; I wanted to see where we were going. I kept my eyes on the country outside the window.

The road wound uphill for perhaps a mile, through rich pasture-land with a few clumps of trees. We went through an unpretentious gate in a low stone wall, and almost at once the bumping of the road gave place to the crunch of gravel. We swung in a sharp turn, and came to a halt outside a house.

This was, evidently, our stopping-place for the night. I was full of curiosity, and extremely nervous.

The house was low, of grey stone. There was an old part in the middle, and two new wings built out at either side. It looked comfortable, but not very grand. It surprised me, as I had not supposed the Dragon would stay anywhere except in a palace. On each side of the house, and in a strip of bed between the house and the gravel, there was the most startling and lurid mass of colour – banks of flowers, of all kinds and hues, as though the whole of the Princes Street Gardens had been squashed into a small space and transplanted here. The effect was cheerful but I thought it overdone – the flowers looked false, they were too big and bright and many, and put together in unpleasing combinations of red and purple, of mauve and yellow. I wondered who lived in this unalarming, unpalatial house, and surrounded themselves with such a garish and vulgar garden.

Round the corner of one of the wings, from the garden, trotted a most extraordinary old woman. She was ancient, and small and fat, with a round red face; she wore a broad-brimmed hat of felt, of a kind I had seen in drawings of the pioneers in Australia, meant I was sure for a man; untidy white hair stuck out from under it, as though she had forgotten pins, or lost them. The rest of her was clad in a kind of riding-habit, but with a very short skirt, below which were very heavy boots. The boots and the hem of the skirt were covered with mud. In her hand the strange old creature carried a trowel; both the trowel and the hand were caked with mud, too.

41

By the time she reached the coach, the groom was at our horses' heads, and the footman had the door open and the steps down.

I expected the little fat old woman to drop a curtsey to the Dragon. But she waved her trowel like a flag, or a weapon, and called out, 'Elinor, my love, are you utterly exhausted?'

The Countess of Draco was smiling with a warmth I had not seen since she asked my grandfather not to punish me. She said, 'There is nothing wrong with me, Violet, that your hospitality will not put right.'

She stood up, bending below the top of the door of the coach. The footman helped her down the steps. She accepted his help, and I thought she needed it. She and the fat old lady embraced warmly. I was entirely puzzled. They appeared to me like creatures of different species: yet they were intimate and loving friends.

I glanced at Eugénie, expecting her to go next out of the coach, with myself following humbly behind. But she made a peremptory gesture with the claw-like hands in the woolly mittens: she waved her hands at me again and again, very fast, as though I was a hen, and she was trying to shoo me down the steps.

I followed the Countess down, using the footman's arm, though not needing it.

The fat old woman took her arms from about the Countess, and turned and saw me as I reached the ground from the carriage steps.

For the third time I was aware of immediate, unmistakable astonishment. She, too, knew my face. She, too, was incapable of hiding the shock of amazed recognition.

She turned towards the Countess, looking up into her face, her eyebrows raised under the ridiculous hat; her unspoken question seemed as loud as though she had shouted it.

'This,' said the Countess expressionlessly, 'is Christina Drummond.'

'Daughter of James? What rubbish am I talkin' — granddaughter of James. Yes, of course. Amazin'. Puts me in mind of Badminton Justice.'

'Now, Violet, you *are* talking rubbish.'

'Nothin' of the sort. Justice was the great stallion hound of the old Duke of Beaufort's. You could pick his whelps out of a thousand, and their whelps too. I'm not comparin' this gel to a foxhound, Elinor, I'm simply remarkin' on the strength of the blood-line.'

The Countess smiled. 'Ah – at last I follow you. A similar idea occurred to me, when I first saw this very dirty child – although, to be fair, she was clean then. But I thought of thoroughbred horses.'

'Same thing, my love. No difference to speak of. Well, well.' The fat old lady turned her round red face towards me; she stared at me with an open curiosity which was, somehow, not in the least rude or unfriendly.

I curtseyed.

'You are paying your duty, Christina,' said the Countess, 'to her Grace, the Duchess of Bodmin.'

My incredulous surprise must – unforgivably, I know – have shown in my face. I would like to be certain that my mouth did not fall open, but I am dreadfully afraid that it did.

The Duchess laughed. She looked like a cook, and her laugh was like a cook's laugh (not my grandmother's cook in George Square, but other and merrier cooks I had met in other and merrier houses) – her laugh was loud, raucous, uninhibited, and from anybody less than a Duchess it would have sounded down-right coarse.

But the Dragon was far from laughing. I knew why, and I knew she was right. My visible astonishment that the Duchess was a Duchess was ill-bred and impertinent and ungrateful. The Queen could stare at the cat, but the cat was not allowed to look amazed at the oddity and vulgarity of the Queen. Besides, she was old.

Two menservants had meanwhile come out of the house, as stately and clean as their noble mistress was undignified and muddy. Eugénie had descended stiffly from the coach; she looked like a witch wrapped up against a hard frost. She began to give the men orders about the luggage. I tried to hear her voice – for I had not, so far, heard her utter a single word – but she spoke in a fierce, sibilant whisper which the men had to bend to hear.

Still clutching her trowel, the Duchess led the way up the shallow stone steps into the house.

She said, 'We dine early, here, Elinor. We live like peasants.'

'Not altogether like peasants,' murmured the Countess, looking at a painting in the hall of a whiskered man in a scarlet coat, riding an enormous black horse, with a pack of hounds all round him.

'I hang poor old Bodmin there to impress people,' chuckled the Duchess. 'As a matter of fact, that's the only place there's room for it, in this wee croft where I drag out my declining years. Tell me – what do you think of what you saw of my garden? Do you like it?'

'No.'

'*No?*'

'It looks like a garden in the suburbs of Manchester,' said the Countess.

'Have you ever seen the suburbs of Manchester?' asked the Duchess.

'Frequently,' said the Countess; but she could not restrain the upward twitch of the corners of her mouth.

'I like a splash of colour,' said the Duchess, 'in gardens and clothes and houses. Now I'm an impoverished widow, living on a pittance in a cottage, I can indulge my tastes. We're a small party, by the bye.'

'Good! I hoped there would be no party at all.'

'What about the girl? Shall she join us for dinner?'

'No,' said the Countess immediately. 'She has neither clothes nor anything else, to fit her for dinner in your house. Can she have some supper upstairs with Eugénie?'

'Of course, if that is what you and she would prefer.' The Duchess turned to me, her round red face full of goodwill. She said, '*Is* that what you would prefer, child?'

'Oh yes,' I said, 'thank you, your Grace, if it is quite convenient.'

'Hum.' She looked at me sharply. 'As you all like. Perhaps it is just as well if I do not have the chance to catechize you, my dear.'

The Countess followed a housekeeper upstairs to her bedroom; Eugénie had a little room next door. I was led by a house-maid to another room, far away; and somebody brought me hot water, and somebody else brought me fresh clothes to put on.

The clothes were laid across the bed in my room. I turned them over slowly, gently. They were finer and more elegant than anything I had ever worn.

'Her leddyship askit me to find what I could for ye, Miss,' said the housekeeper, knocking and coming in as I contemplated my finery. 'They'll no fit ye verra famous, ye're ower lang an' lean.'

'They're beautiful,' I said.

'Awheel, ye're no fashion-plate as ye stand – onything's mebbe an improvement.'

'Indeed it is,' I agreed.

The Countess had also got them to find me a toothbrush, a hairbrush and comb, and a nightdress.

'I joined her ladyship rather, er, suddenly,' I explained to the housekeeper, 'without preparation, or time to pack.'

'Ay,' she said. 'Puir chiel.'

I think she thought I was a slave, newly captured. I thought I was one, too.

My supper upstairs with Eugénie was even more silent than meals in my grandfather's house. There at least grace was said, before and after; with Eugénie nothing was said.

The silent, malevolent old woman looked as though she wanted to poison me; but it seemed she had no poison by her.

The food was delicious and copious; I surprised myself by eating a great deal.

By eight o'clock Eugénie and I had finished; a maid came in and took the remnants of our meal away. What now? It was a warm evening; I could not bear to go immediately to bed; I could not bear to stay in a room with Eugénie, still silent, a witch without a tongue even for curses; I could not go down unasked to the drawing-room, to join the Duchess and the Countess and the others; I did not know where there was a library, or any other room where I could sit for a time; so I decided to stroll in the garden. I did not think there could be any objection. I did not think, in fact, that I should be seen.

I stood up, and tried to smooth my skirt and bodice; but though they were so fine, they were made for a female with a fuller figure and fewer inches than mine. I said goodnight to Eugénie. She did not reply, but simply stared at me with her unnerving jet-button eyes.

I found my way downstairs, and out of a garden door. I wandered along grass paths, between flower-filled borders, the Duchess's delight; a few hard-working honey bees were still busy; I inhaled the scent which the dewy evening was drawing out of the flowers. I had never, I think, walked in a flower-garden in the cool of the evening before; the routine of my grandparents' home made such an activity impossible.

All the thoughts which had filled my mind during the day filled it still.

And of them all, the thought of Lord Cricklade most often reappeared. I did not think he was so very old. I did not think that, in all regards, I was so very young, especially in my fine if ill-fitting borrowed gown, which would have given my grandmother an attack of the vapours.

Busy with my thoughts, intoxicated by the evening scent of the flowers, bemused by the sleepy hum of the late bees, I did not look where I was walking; with the result that I found myself, to my surprise, almost walking into the side of the house. There was a large window in one of the new wings, of which the casements stood open, over which the curtains were partly drawn.

I heard voices inside. I realized that it was the drawing-room, to which they had returned after dinner. Perhaps they were drinking tea, or coffee, or liqueurs – whatever liqueurs might be.

I heard the Duchess's strong old voice talking about her son, the present Duke, and about the idiotic speeches he had been making in the House of Lords.

'Edwin's last speech,' said another voice, 'made me feel quite ill with embarrassment. But that was fifteen years ago, and he has had the wit not to open his mouth in public since.'

The voice was high, light, very precise: it made me think of chips of diamonds, or slivers of ice. I imagined the speaker thin, with hard, pale blue eyes, and a capacity for cruelty. I was glad I had not been exposed to her at dinner.

'And what about your grandson, Elinor?' asked the Duchess. 'He's active in politics, they tell me.'

'In everything you can imagine,' said the Countess, her voice as clear and arrogant as always. 'He amazes me. Who could have believed that Francis and I would have had so solemn a descendant? He carries a sense of public duty to lengths I consider excessive.'

'Does he visit the consequences on you at Glendraco?' asked the Duchess.

'Not much. He is still a sportsman, thank heavens, and is guided by that in whom he asks to Scotland. I imagine the friends he sees in London are worthy and dreary beyond bearing.'

'It's terribly infectious, this political illness,' said the Duchess. 'David Renfrew addresses even me as though I were a public meeting.'

'His godson addressed me today,' said the Countess reflectively, 'as though I were a criminal in the dock.'

The Duchess laughed incredulously. 'Which godson is that?'

'Young Henry Cricklade.'

'He?' said the hard, high, ice-and-diamond voice. 'After he had carried the Drummond child half over Scotland in a curricle?'

'Let us be fair,' said the Countess. 'It was a gig.'

'I understand,' said the stranger's voice, 'why she wanted to run away from home. I do *not* understand why you wanted her to run to Glendraco.'

'In many ways,' said the Countess, 'I am a selfish old woman. I do not like solitude. I do like Glendraco. When Francis was alive, I had his company there, a good deal more than most wives in the Highlands. He was, as *you* know, Violet, inclined to spend as much of his life as possible away from London, and bright lights, and politics, and intrigues, and so forth.'

'I know,' said the Duchess.

'By the time Francis died, our son had married, and I had his wife with me much at Glendraco. I grew very fond of her. When she herself was widowed, she spent all her time with me. I expected, naturally, to have the joy of her company until my death. *Her* death, last Christmas, was a great blow to me.'

'Because you missed her company?'

'Because I loved her. And – yes – because I missed her company. I spent the rest of the winter and all the spring alone at Glendraco, since my grandson was doing great things to improve the state of the world, which required his presence elsewhere. I was miserably lonely.'

'You wanted a companion.'

'I still do.'

'You have found one.'

'Yes. Now if you will forgive me, Violet, I think I should go to my bed. Today was quite tiring, and I believe I may have to face, tomorrow night, a party which will be less restful than this one.'

Goodnights were said.

I should not have stayed listening. I should not have started listening. Stern moralists will condemn me – but ordinary mortals, I think, will understand.

The Countess wanted company. She wanted *my* company. Why?

I was not alone in asking this question.

After the Countess had gone to bed, I heard the Duchess and the other lady settle back into their chairs.

After a pause – the comfortable silence, perhaps, of old friends – the cold-voiced stranger said, 'I understand Elinor Draco's desire for a companion, stuck out there in the screaming wilderness in a castle the size of a town.'

'Yes, Alicia?' said the Duchess, in the voice of a comfortable cook.

'But why that child? Why her?'

'Did you see her, when they arrived?'

'No. I was upstairs.'

'Of course, her face would have meant nothing to you, even if you had seen her. You are much too young to remember James Drummond. You are of an age to have met his son, this child's father, but he lived a different life from yours or mine. I never met him. That face, that Drummond face, would mean nothing to you, but to someone of my age, who remembers . . .'

'Remembers what, Violet?' said the hard, high voice of the stranger.

'The most dreadful, most horrible thing I ever heard of. I

pray to God, a thing I seldom do, that that beautiful child who came here today never learns what happened to her grandfather.'

'*What* happened?'

'Nothing would induce me to tell even you, and I only know a little of the truth.'

'Was it, then, so very dreadful?'

'Oh yes,' said the Duchess heavily, her voice quite unlike its usual cheeriness, 'oh yes.'

three

I was presented, in the morning, just before we left, to the owner of the high, hard voice, whom I had heard them call Alicia. She looked exactly as I had imagined from the voice. She was tall – taller than me, taller than the Countess; her face was pale, her jawline as sharp as a butcher's knife, her lips thin and bloodless, her eyes just such a pale and icy blue as I had pictured. Even the touch of her hand – on a blazing summer morning – was cold, and made me think of someone already dead. If the Dragon breathed flame, and scorched anyone she was angry with, this pale cold lady would breathe a bitter wind from the Pole, and freeze you to death; which I thought worse, though not much.

The lady was the Marchioness of Odiham; the Marquess was a great yachtsman, it seemed, and spent all summer aboard his schooner. I could not imagine why she did not go too; for a long cruise, in far places, on a fine yacht, seemed to me the most wonderful idea in the world. Perhaps she would have the effect of filling the sea about the boat with icebergs, and so be unpopular aboard.

She stared at me as openly as the Duchess had done (I understood why, of course, after the conversation I had heard), but no two stares could have been more different. The ice-lady's pale eyes chilled me so that I wanted to borrow Eugénie's cloak, and

even her mittens. I felt suddenly and hideously aware that my
fine new gown did not fit, but bunched baggily about the bosom
and hips where it should have fitted snugly (since I did not fill it),
and that it showed altogether too much of my sensible Edinburgh
boots. I felt that my hair was untidy, and that my hands were too
large, and that my petticoat hung below the hem of my skirt. I
felt myself blushing under this frozen, contemptuous scrutiny.
Nothing could have been more mortifying. Consequently I
became angry, which was quite wrong of me.

I said, 'Is there a smut on my nose?'

'No,' said the voice, sharp and clear as an icicle on a gutter.
'Why?'

'From the length of your ladyship's inspection, I thought
there must be.'

She gave a small, tight, thin-lipped smile; but only with her
mouth, and only for a second. There was no smile in her eyes.
She turned away to say goodbye to the Countess.

The carriage was already on the gravel sweep in front of the
house. Hamish magnificent on his box, the groom at the horses'
heads, the footman by the door. We climbed in, I last. In my
efforts to be magnificently dignified, I tripped on the step, and
fell into the carriage in a heap.

When the Countess had done waving from the window, she
sat back in her seat and looked at me.

'You have done well in twenty-four hours, Christina,' she said.
'First you were disgustingly pert to a close friend of my grandson's, who had just been extraordinarily kind to you, at great
inconvenience to himself. Then you aroused the derision of my
oldest friend, your hostess, by staring at her like a half-witted
heifer. And now you have been gratuitously insolent to one of the
most influential women in the kingdom. Are you determined to
arouse disgust in everyone with whom you come in contact?'

'No, ma'am,' I said humbly. 'But it is trying to be stared at, as
though one were a beetle.'

'To Lady Odiham,' said the Dragon, 'you are a beetle.'

Then she closed her eyes, and said no more for two hours.

Gradually the country became steeper and wilder and grander.
The comfortable farmhouses and steadings of the flat lowlands

gave way to little huddles of buildings near the road; cattle and sheep were of new kinds and colours; there were no horses, except ours, but only a few small, underfed ponies. With each slow mile, it seemed to me, the people were poorer, and the place more savage and magnificent.

And, strange as it all was to me, with each slow mile I felt more and more at home.

We turned off the road again in the late afternoon, and bumped through thick woods, along the banks of a river; here and there the declining sun found a gap in the dense foliage of the trees, and poured a patch of gold on the bracken and brambles and lush grass. The river was fast and full of rocks; often great trees grew right to the banks, so that golden water creamed about their roots. The rumble of our massive wheels, and the beat of eight great iron-shod feet, was very loud in the quiet woods. There was no one at all to be seen.

We came at last to a gaunt, blackish house, completely isolated, in the middle of a rough park. There were no bright flower-gardens here, like the Duchess's; no flowers at all, or any kind of garden, that I could see, but only rough grass, grazed by a herd of peculiar deer, growing right to the walls of the house.

'I find myself speculating,' said the Countess after a long silence, 'what enormities you will commit here, Christina.'

I could think of no answer to this; perhaps it was just as well.

The carriage crunched to a stop in front of the house; but nobody trotted cheerily round a corner to greet the Countess. A party of servants appeared, in manner like a party of soldiers under strict discipline. Their commander was an awesome, enormous man, a great deal like a medieval bishop, but really the butler; he conducted the Countess indoors. I was told to wait by the carriage with Eugénie, until I was led away too. It was a strange welcome.

Then someone did come round the corner of the house, but strolling rather than trotting, and carrying a fishing-rod instead of a trowel. He was about ten years older than myself (and so definitely younger than Lord Cricklade); he had very smooth, shiny, butter-coloured hair, and vivid blue eyes, and a dimple in his chin. He was a slight man, small-boned, hardly taller than

51

myself, but looking very wiry and active. He was wearing boots above his knees; besides his fishing-rod, he carried a wicker basket on a strap round one shoulder, and a canvas bag on a strap round the other shoulder. He looked completely contented, as though he fitted perfectly into his surroundings, and wanted nothing better than to go on exactly as he was.

He took off his straw hat, and said, 'They told me Lady Draco had arrived. Since you have clearly just arrived, and are the only lady to have done so, I am obliged to believe the evidence of my eyes, and conclude that you must be she. But I confess I would not have recognized you. May I compliment your ladyship on a spectacular rejuvenation? Was it achieved by surgery, or witchcraft, or simply a newly-discovered elixir?'

His manner was perfectly solemn when he said all this, which of course increased the absurdity. I laughed, hoping this would not be considered an enormity by the Countess.

He inspected the carriage, which was waiting with Hamish on the box while servants unloaded luggage from the roof. He said, 'Only you, dear Lady Draco, would use such a vehicle in this age. It is not quite a normal travelling coach of the old days, is it? To my eye it is more like a state coach, of which there are *very* few examples to be seen. Did your ladyship employ it for the coronation of Her Majesty? I daresay it was *built* for the coronation of George III, and has been adapted for travelling simply by placing a rack on the roof for your trunks. Your arrangements are eccentric, are not they? A groom behind, if those gaiters are anything to go by, and a footman on the box with the coachman? But I always knew that your ladyship was a law unto yourself.'

Hamish the coachman, who might have been offended, was amused; the groom, whom I expected to be amused, was offended. About Eugénie's reaction it was impossible to guess; she stared at the absurd stranger, and at me, with black unblinking eyes, muffled up as always, and said nothing

The stranger turned his attention back from the coach to myself. Once again I wished my new clothes fitted.

Still with an air of preposterous solemnity, he said, 'He must in truth be a genius, the surgeon or magician who has wrought this transformation in you, Lady Draco. I am a little young, of course, to have known you in your youth – indeed I am a little younger than my friend your grandson – but I have always heard it said that you were one of the great beauties of your day. I think, however, that science, or magic, or art, must have improved on nature. I do *not* believe that you looked in 1810 as you look today. As I say, I have heard that you were one of the great beauties of *your* day, but I have not heard that you were one of the great beauties of *any* day. Yet now, unarguably, that is what you are. Was that kind, dear Lady Draco? Was it quite fair, I wonder, not only to drop half a century, but also to cause yourself to be made into a veritable Helen of Troy? "Was this the face that launched a thousand ships, and burned the topless towers of Ilium?" Yes indeed – not a whit less. The young ladies, and their ambitious mammas, will be quite angry with you, I think, since you are so much more beautiful than any of them.'

I felt myself smiling. What he said was ridiculous, and all in friendly fun, but there is no denying that it was very pleasant to listen to.

He frowned, and said, 'But I see that another change has been wrought in you. The quick tongue, for which you are famous, has been stilled. I have heard you laugh – a sound not dissimilar to the chiming of distant silver bells across a field of newly-fallen snow –'

I burst out laughing again; I could not help it.

He lost his own gravity for a moment; the face he had kept so straight crumpled into a delighted chuckle.

Then he controlled himself again, and proceeded with deep solemnity, 'I have heard you laugh, but I have not heard you speak. Was perpetual silence the price you had to pay for your magical beauty? I challenge you – *can* you speak?'

'Have you been fishing?' I asked.

It was a very silly question; I daresay it was the silliest question anybody ever asked, but I felt I had to say something, and it was the first thing that came into my head.

'No,' said the stranger decisively. 'In spite of appearances to the contrary, I have *not*, I assure your ladyship, been fishing. I have been standing knee-deep in that river, yes, accoutred as you see me. I have been waving this rod, and with its aid endeavouring to throw this silken line out over the pools, and thereby to offer to the trout – which I know to be there – these elegantly-devised and very expensive flies. That was what I set out to do; that was my intention. What I have actually been doing is untangling my line from the branches of trees behind, unhooking my hooks from snags in the water in front, and catching the collar of my coat and the brim of my hat. I have been catching, dear Lady Draco, coats, hats, trees, and underwater branches, but not fish. I am humiliated to answer your kind enquiry in this way, but I was brought up to a strict regard for truth, and the habit has lingered. The same unfortunate instinct now obliges me to point out to your ladyship that your presence indoors appears to be requested.'

I turned, and saw that he was quite right. All the cases had been carried in. The military squad of servants had disappeared. The coach had trundled off – I had not, to my amazement, heard it go. Eugénie and a maid were waiting for me by the door, and Eugénie was gesturing impatiently.

'Thank you,' I said to my friend; for who could doubt he was my friend?

'For what?'

'Your frankness.'

He bowed low, his straw hat over his chest. I laughed again, and turned to follow Eugénie and the maid.

Eugénie had once again been placed in a little room next to the Countess's; I guessed that this was an arrangement made by all hostesses in whose houses the Countess stayed. I could not for the life of me imagine why; I would have preferred Eugénie at the other end of the house, if I had to have her with me at all.

I was in a room nearby, a much bigger and finer room than my little box at the Duchess of Bodmin's. It had a grand easy chair, and a big open fireplace, and water-colour pictures of Highland cattle, and crimson velvet curtains with great loops and swags of pelmet.

'Your bags, Miss?' said the housemaid who led me there. 'I'm tae help ye unpack, an' maid ye ony ways ye'll hae need of.'

'This is my luggage,' I said, emptying a paper bag on the bed, and revealing my new nightdress, and toothbrush, and brush and comb for my hair.

The maid laughed; she was young and pretty, and reminded me of Janet, back at home in George Square.

Home? It was the only home I had ever had, and I was still thinking of it as home. Was it not time I stopped?

I walked to the window, which was wide open, and looked at the big view spread out before me, the flattish acres of rough park, dotted with ancient trees and badged with patches of golden evening sunlight, on which were quietly grazing groups of strange foreign deer; at its edge the river, winding away among the woods beyond; the woods themselves, dense green, pines and hardwood-trees, with drifts of bracken in the glades; and far away, clear in the clear evening light, the high blue shapes of big hills.

This felt more like home. I breathed in, deeply, luxuriously, the pure air of the countryside. It felt quite strange, cool and clean, like water from a spring on a mountain-top; it was a different element from the soot-laden mist which passed for air in Edinburgh. It felt quite strange, but it felt like the air of home.

Like Janet, the maid was voluble and friendly, and full of information. The house, it seemed, was called Gaultstower. Its owner, my hostess, was Mrs Carlyle, widow of a Chancellor of the Exchequer; it was not his house, but her own, for she had been Miss Gault, and her father's heiress.

I had become so used to the high aristocracy that I was surprised, and even dismayed, to find myself under the roof of an ordinary Mrs, even an heiress and the widow of a Cabinet Minister. But Mrs Carlyle, it seemed was no ordinary Mrs; to the maid she was a very great lady, and the Gaults were more important than dukes. Certainly some of her guests were resplendent enough to satisfy even my new taste for grandeur; for besides my own Countess there was a German Prince, very nearly a king, and best of all (in the eyes of the maid), a gentleman called Lord Caerlaverock. When the maid announced this name, I had no idea how it might be spelled; had I first met it in writing, I should have had no idea how to pronounce it. Its owner, according to the maid, was a mixture of Sir Galahad and Rob Roy.

I pictured a stiff and superb grandee, with a white moustache and a courtly manner, who had commanded armies, or governed

India. I wondered if I should meet him, and thought, perhaps, I would rather not.

I looked out of the window again, and could not help smiling; for crossing the park towards the river was the most delightful man I had ever met (or possibly the second most delightful – Lord Cricklade had undoubted claims) – the slight figure, with butter-coloured hair and vivid blue eyes, who was so solemn and so funny.

'Who is that gentleman?' I asked the maid.

She came to the window. She looked out, but did not at first see my friend. She looked in every wrong direction, as people do when you want imperatively for them to look in the right direction.

She spotted him just before he disappeared in a clump of trees on the river bank.

'Why,' she said, 'yon's his lordship.'

'Lord —'

'Lord Caerlaverock.'

I was to dine upstairs again, with Eugénie, as I was not dressed for civilized company, or fit for it in any way.

Before our tray came up from the kitchens, and long before the company dined, some of Mrs Carlyle's party strolled in the cool of the evening in the park near the house.

The little housemaid returned, to maid me she said. I did not know what she could possibly do for me. I was incredulous when she suggested brushing my hair: no one had ever brushed my hair for me, though when I was small Carstairs had sometimes dragged a comb through the tangles, making me cry with pain. So, instead, the maid and I both looked out of the window, and she told me who the people were.

The Prince was not at all like a Prince: more like a sort of toy. He was a little tubby man, built somewhat on the lines of the Duchess of Bodmin, with long white whiskers, and a high voice in which he said things that made everybody laugh. Mrs Carlyle was a stately old lady, very stiff, who wore a huge hat for strolling in her park. Lord Caerlaverock I knew; with him, on his arm, somewhat apart from the rest, was a girl who might have been his sister – she was slight, like himself, and with bright corn-coloured hair.

The maid sniffed when I asked her about the girl. She was not Lord Caerlaverock's sister. She looked to me fragile, and graceful in movement; she looked very pretty, but it is difficult to judge prettiness from a distance, and from far above. Even at a distance I could see that her dress was very beautiful, blue and gold, of a filmy material that fluttered in the light evening breeze.

I remembered, in what seemed a previous life, my bitter envy of Jennie Ross the fishwife. Now I bitterly envied the golden-haired girl, in the beautiful gown, on the arm of Lord Caerlaverock.

If I had been she, no doubt, the housemaid would have sniffed at me. There are no class barriers to jealousy.

Our dinner arrived not on one tray but three, each carried by a manservant. The numbers of plates and knives and forks and spoons amazed me. Eugénie and I sat down, facing each other, at a narrow table in a sort of old schoolroom near my bedroom.

The first course was a sort of shellfish I had never seen before. I picked up, to eat it with, a small knife and fork with mother-of-pearl handles; they seemed the right size. I kept my eyes on my plate; I did not wish to look at Eugénie, or catch the eye of the footman who had stayed to wait on us. Just before I began to eat, I was startled to feel a sudden jab on the back of my left hand. It was Eugénie, stabbing my hand with a fork. I let out a cry, more of amazement than of pain. The footman hurried forward from the end of the room, but Eugénie waved him away furiously. Eugénie pointed at the knife and fork I had picked up (pointed with the claw-like, misshapen finger which curled from the woolly mitten she wore even for dinner); she made a hissing noise, and in a loud whisper said something I could not understand. She picked up two silver forks, oddly shaped, and wagged them at me. She looked angry and contemptuous.

I realized that I was being taught proper table manners. Eugénie was taking me in hand. My education had begun. Four red spots, in a straight line, still showed quite plainly on the back of my left hand.

As the long and complicated meal went on, Eugénie showed me, with sharp gestures, what implements to use. None of the knives and forks were quite like the ones I was used to in George Square. The ones with mother-of-pearl handles were for fruit. I thanked Eugénie, as politely as I could, each time; she said nothing. She did not stab me again, but she looked as though she wanted to.

Later I sat in my bedroom, in the window, looking out over the park and woods, and watching the sky turn from purple to black.

I wondered how long my education would last – how long Eugénie would be my gaoler; and whether she hated teaching me as much as I hated learning from her; and what my grandfather's end had been.

The little maid had come in long before with a lamp; I had turned it low, because it attracted strange large moths in through the open window.

There was a knock on the door; a shy, gentle knock.

I called, 'Come in.'

The door opened. There was a whisper of silk. A bright gold head caught the light of the lamp by my bedside.

A soft voice, shy and gentle as the knock on the door, said, 'Miss Drummond? Am I disturbing you?'

'Of course not! I was only looking at the sky.'

'How dark it is,' said the golden-haired girl. 'May I turn up the lamp a little?'

'Yes, but the moths will come.'

'I will see that they do not hurt themselves.'

She turned up the lamp, and I was able to look at her, and she at me. She was quite as pretty as I had thought, and her dress quite as magical. Her face was small, but with large blue eyes. Her nose was tiny and upturned, her mouth small but with a 'bee-stung' lower lip. When she smiled there were dimples in her cheeks. She was smaller than myself; her form, though on a miniature scale, was exquisite, and her hands were tiny and very white. She looked as though a strong gust of wind would blow her away; but as though no gust of wind would be so heartless as to blow at her at all.

She said shyly, 'I am Charlotte Long. Lady Draco said I might come to see you. I thought you would be lonely and bored.'

'It is very kind of you,' I said.

'I often feel dreadfully lonely myself, so I know how low-lowering it is.'

'You?' I asked incredulously. 'Why are you ever lonely?'

'My Mamma and Papa are in India, you see, but I was sent back to be educated and finished and brought out. Luckily my aunt has a house in Berkeley Square, and I live with her in the ordinary way, but it is not the same as a Mamma, is it? Lady Draco told me that your Mamma is dead?'

'Yes.'

'And your Papa?'

'He died before I was born. That is why my mother came back to Scotland, to her own parents.'

'That is very sad, it is horrid for you. I am so sorry. You have been all your life as lonely as I have been just for a few years. I feel ashamed to have been so sorry for myself, when it is so much worse for you.'

I did not want to talk about my dead parents, so to change the subject I said, 'You are staying here?'

'Yes, for a short time. Mrs Carlyle is a great friend of my aunt. But soon I shall be going to stay with my dearest friend, who lives quite near Glendraco. I shall be there all summer. We shall be neighbours, you see! That is another reason why I wanted to come and see you tonight.'

I was extraordinarily pleased. More than anything I wanted a friend, someone of my own age, who knew the world I was going into.

We sat for nearly an hour, telling each other about ourselves. We were not 'Miss Long' and 'Miss Drummond' for more than a minute, and I was not 'Christina' for many minutes after that. We talked with the greatest freedom, although Charlotte was, all the time, shy and hesitant in everything she said. I realized that she had a very slight stammer. I thought that if she got excited or angry, it would be worse; but it was impossible to imagine her angry, she was so gentle.

Her father, Colonel Long, commanded the Lennox Highlanders, then stationed at Lahore. Charlotte had spent most of her childhood in India; she spoke of the crushing heat of the plains and the cool of the hills; of wonderful ponies to ride, and glittering uniforms, and parades with lancers and elephants and horse-batteries, and of her father's regiment with its pipes and drums. She said she liked Scotland far better than London, and the country about Glendraco the best of any part of Scotland.

Her schoolfriend was Georgina Campbell, whose father was Sir Francis Campbell of Drumlaw. Georgina had had at different times a pet lamb, a pet piglet, a pet goose, and a pet owl, as well as rabbits and dogs and kittens and ponies.

'I expect you will think her quite mad,' said Charlotte. 'I used to think so myself, when I saw her taking her piglet for a walk on a lead.'

I burst out laughing. 'Did the piglet *like* being taken for a walk?'

Charlotte laughed too, a little high squeak of amusement, like a small bird with a sense of humour. 'I *think* so. Georgina insisted Doctor Ramsay liked his walks. Doctor Ramsay was the piglet's name, after a Minister or dominie or something, who Georgina said was the piglet's Papa.'

'His Papa?'

'Yes, she said the resemblance was too strong to be a co-co-incidence.'

We both laughed again. I looked forward to meeting Georgina Campbell. She sounded to me not mad at all, but very sensible.

Charlotte said, 'Lady Draco was saying at dinner, to the Prince, that you stayed last night with the Duchess of Bodmin. She is so funny. I like her very much. She was kind to me when I was first in London, frightened to death! Especially of people like Lady Odiham.'

'The Marchioness?'

'The Snow Queen, that is what she is called. How horrid for you that she was staying with the Duchess too! It would spoil everything, because she is so sharp and severe. I have known her for quite a long time now, and I still feel like a naughty little girl when she is in the same room. I suppose – I suppose it is right to be so correct, and to make rules for behaviour'—

'Does she do that?'

'Oh yes! There is just a small group of ladies, you know, who really rule Society. If one of them takes a dislike to you, you might as well go to Lahore with my Papa, and stay there! Lady Draco used to be one of the rulers, but now she is so very old. The Duchess was *never* one, I think, because she does not care much about rules. Lady Odiham is the *most* important person – it would be simply dreadful to offend her. Not only because it would be such a sti-stigma, but also because she is so cruel.'

I remembered the pale icy eye and the blade-sharp jawbone; I nodded thoughtfully. I thought that perhaps, after all, the longer I stayed out of sight with Eugénie the better, to give the Snow Queen a chance to forget my rudeness.

'Oh,' cried Charlotte suddenly, interrupting my thoughts, 'a moth *has* burned itself!'

'I don't think it's badly hurt,' I said. 'It's making a great fuss, but that is only silly fright.'

It was a big, pale moth, soft and fluffy like velvet. I caught the silly thing in my cupped hands, where it flapped in terror as though I wanted to hurt it, instead of saving it from its folly. I put it out of the window, and it flew away quite briskly.

'There,' I said, 'I expect it will go and bother someone else.'

'Georgina would have done that,' said Charlotte. 'But I don't think I could have.'

'Your hands are hardly big enough.'

'Oh! Thank you. But it's not that. I couldn't have borne to feel it flapping . . . Look! There are some tiny moths, too, going round and round the light . . .' Charlotte turned to look at me. She said, 'At Glendraco you will be like that.'

'A moth?'

'A light. Is it true that Lord Cricklade took you for twenty miles in his gig?'

'I don't think it was twenty miles. But he took me in his gig.'

'Good gracious! I would have been frightened.'

'Of the gig, or Lord Cricklade?'

'Oh, both! He is so stern, and proper, and serious. He is called the Rock of Gibraltar, you know, because he is so impervious. He never looks at girls at all, or if he does he does not notice them.'

'Oh yes,' I said, 'he does.'

I did not mean to boast, precisely, but I thought it was time I showed Charlotte that I was not completely childish, or without friends.

'Oh Kirstie,' said Charlotte, wide-eyed, 'did he fall in love with you?'

'I don't know if he really did,' I replied, with all the honesty I could, but with a certain amount of satisfaction too. 'But he certainly *said* he did.'

'Then it is true. He would never say such a thing if it were not true. He is the soul of honour, everybody knows that. Indeed, you can tell it by looking at him. It is the most romantic thing I ever heard of! But it is not fair, you know. First the Rock of Gibraltar, and now Jack.'

'Jack?'

'Your new slave,' said Charlotte. 'Jack Caerlaverock.'

'I thought,' I said, 'he was your slave.'

She smiled. 'I thought so too, but all he could talk about when we were walking in the park before dinner, was the mysterious beauty he met by Lady Draco's carriage. That was *another* reason I came to see you – I was so burning with curiosity!'

She said she did not mind at all that Lord Caerlaverock was what she called my slave; they were simply old friends, who laughed and gossiped together, without tender emotion.

'Two Lords in two days,' said Charlotte. 'It is lucky the Prince is so old.'

Soon afterwards she went to the door. As she left the room she turned, and to my astonishment kissed me.

'Goodnight, dear,' she said. Seeing the look in my face, she added, 'Have I annoyed you? Should I not have kissed you goodnight? I do not know quite why I did it – it just seemed a good thing to do.'

'It *was*, it *was*,' I said earnestly. 'It is simply that no one has ever kissed me goodnight before.'

Her eyes grew as wide as crown pieces. 'No one? Ever? Not when you were little?'

'No. My grandparents in Edinburgh don't believe in softness.'

At that she kissed me again. And as she turned to go, I saw by the glow of the lamp at my bedside that there were tears in her eyes.

I went to bed happy for the first time for days.
I went to bed happy, I think, for the first time in my life.

Next day, trundling along behind the greys, we seemed to leave behind all trees, all habitations, almost all people, even animals. We went through a long glen, with a small burn coiling along the bottom. Sometimes our road was far up on the hillside walling the glen, and then the sunshine blazed on the roof of the carriage, and in through the half-curtained window. Sometimes we were deep in the bottom of the glen, the road so close beside the burn that I could have thrown my hat into it from the carriage, and then we went along in the deep blue shadow cast by the enormous hills. I had never been in so silent and empty a place. There were no sheep or cattle or even birds on those precipitous slopes of rock-strewn grass and heather.

I learned afterwards that it was called the Dead Glen. Hundreds of years before, as the Reverend Lancelot Barrow later instructed me, a raiding party from the west had been trapped at the burnside by groups of local clansmen who came at them from three directions. All the raiders were butchered, even young boys among them, and the glen had been 'Dead' ever since, colder than any nearby place, shadowed when the sun was high, feared, haunted.

'You understand, Miss Christina,' said the Reverend Lancelot Barrow with his quick, cold smile, 'that the simple people here are still absurdly superstitious. They will not take either flocks or herds on to that ground, for fear of having to spend a night there in the open. To my mind his Lordship should let the whole parcel to a grazier from the Lowlands, who would pay a far higher rent, and be untroubled by bogeys in the darkness. My advice on the subject, needless to say, goes unheeded.'

During that conversation (or rather lecture) in the library at Glendraco, I remembered the journey up the Dead Glen, and the eerie chill of the place; I did not blame the local people, whose own ancestors had cut down the raiders with their claymores, for not wishing to face their reproachful ghosts at midnight.

Eugénie's eyes were more and more often closed, as though the long, slow journey had exhausted her. The Countess's eyes were more and more often open, as though she were revived by silence and emptiness, or by nearing home.

Sometimes she glanced at my face. I thought I saw, in those clear grey eyes, a little of the childlike quality that had captivated me in George Square. But no smile lifted the corners of her mouth; no softness smoothed the deep-etched lines on her brow.

I was still in disgrace.

The horses went very slowly to the top of a pass at the head of the Dead Glen, and were there stopped to be breathed.

The Countess, opposite me, could see forward along the way we were going; I, with my back to the horses, only backwards. Her eyes, suddenly, were wide and excited, and her lips parted; suddenly lines *were* smoothed from her brow, and the corners of her mouth *were* lifted.

I heard hoofbeats and a shout, and the blast of a shrill horn.

Further up and further went the corners of the Countess's mouth; she was smiling as broadly as an excited girl; she waved vigorously out of the window.

The hoofbeats came nearer. It sounded like a regiment of cavalry – like one of those resplendent parades that Charlotte Long had talked of. A horseman trotted up to the Countess's side of the carriage, swept off his bonnet, and bowed from the saddle.

He called something I could not understand, but took to be a Gaelic greeting. The Countess replied, a few words in the same strange language.

The horseman was a tall, grizzled man of perhaps fifty, with a deeply weatherbeaten face, clean-shaven; his clothes were a curious mixture, all tartan above, but riding boots and breeches below. He was grinning broadly; he seemed as pleased to see the Dragon as she to see him.

'Your loyal mounted escort, ma'am,' he said, 'stands ready to convey you to your hearthstone.'

'Thank you, Ardmeggar,' said the Countess. She laughed suddenly. 'We all feel much safer for your company.'

'All? Hamish too?'

I heard the coachman laugh, and say something which sounded disrespectful. Ardmeggar took no offence; it was all very merry and informal. Other cheerful gentlemen on horseback paid their respects to the Countess through the carriage window. Greetings were called from our three men to horsemen ahead; greetings were shouted back. Even Eugénie made a gesture, almost friendly, to someone I could not see. Only I was left completely out of it.

The coach started again, with two dozen horsemen as out-riders. They were variously dressed and of all ages. A few were obviously gentlemen, like the grizzled man the Countess called Ardmeggar; some were neat grooms, belted and gaitered; one or two looked like shepherds surprised to find themselves on ponies.

We were another hour on the road, and we were in the great glen of the Draco.

The glen seemed to me to be in the shape of a slow curve, like a young moon. The road went gradually downhill, near or far from the River Draco; the river, even in this dry summer, was a rushing, angry water between rocks, but here and there smoothing itself into long pools. After two miles or thereabouts, when we were well clear of the pass and the point of the crescent, the glen broadened out, so that it was far wider than the narrow, oppressive Dead Glen; there was room by the river for fat pasture-land and a few fields of growing crops; then the ground swept upwards more and more steeply, until it rose in tremendous green cliffs. Here and there the hillsides were laced with burns, silver in the afternoon sunlight, or scarred by precipitous screes.

As the road continued its slow curve down the glen. I was able to see much of it by looking back out of the window. A bare-legged boy was driving a few sheep towards a croft; an old woman hobbled along with a single rough-coated cow. Then, unexpectedly, from behind the shoulder of a hill, appeared a single horseman, cantering sharply across the pastureland towards the road. Joining the road, he tried to make his best speed in pursuit of us; I could see him spurring and whipping his horse, which seemed tired or lazy; he caught up with us rapidly, as we were going so slowly and he as fast as he could.

Others saw him. They knew who he was; they were expecting him. There was general laughter.

The weatherbeaten gentleman called Ardmeggar trotted up to the Countess's window, laughing; he reined his horse to a walk.

'Did you notice a significant absentee, when we met you?' he asked.

'Inverlarig,' replied the Countess immediately.

'Inverlarig himself was not expected,' said the horseman, 'having, I hear, a touch of the gout.'

'I am very sorry. So is his household, I imagine.'

'I should hate to be his body-servant just now,' agreed Ardmeggar. 'Anyway, in Inverlarig's place we were naturally expecting young David.'

'He mistook the day or the hour, I daresay,' said the Countess. 'David has no vices, but he appears to have no clock or calendar either.'

'Another possibility,' said Ardmeggar, 'is that he had to run an errand for his mother. At any rate, here he comes now, his unfortunate old horse whipped to a lather, his own face like a beetroot, one stirrup-leader longer than the other, and his spurs put on upside-down.'

Up cantered, as he spoke, the late-comer. He was indeed very red in the face, and appeared dishevelled and discomfited. It was evident even to me that one stirrup *did* hang considerably lower than the other, but I did not know enough about spurs to determine if his were upside-down.

He was a young man, only a few years older than myself: perhaps exactly of an age with Findlay Nicholson. He was of Findlay's height, too; but there the resemblance ended. His face was healthy and open and innocent, as well as very red, while Findlay's was unhealthy, and shut up tight, and as pallid and greasy as suet; he was lean while Findlay was pudgy; he belonged out here, under the huge sky, while Findlay was a creature of stuffy rooms in sooty streets; he looked as incapable of meanness as Lord Cricklade, as incapable of cruelty as Charlotte Long. He did not look very intelligent. He might be as absurd as they all seemed to think, but I hoped he was another near neighbour.

He reined in beside the coach in the midst of a chorus of ironical cheers. He was panting and blowing as much as his horse.

After getting his breath back, he managed to blurt out, as though it was a lesson he had just painfully learned, 'We welcome you home from your journeyings, and offer you the service of our swords.'

'Thank you, David,' said the Countess with a smile. 'But those words are usually spoken in the Gaelic.'

'I know, ma'am,' said David miserably, 'but – but I've forgotten how to pronounce the Gaelic.'

There was another burst of laughter.

'Were you not taught to apologize for lateness?' asked Ardmeggar, pretending to be severe.

'Am I late?' asked David innocently.

This time the laughter was louder than ever; the chorus included our coachman and footman and groom, and the grooms of the horsemen, and the shepherds on their ponies.

The young man blushed even redder than exertion in the sun had made him; he looked acutely miserable.

Then one man began to tease him about his spurs, and another about his stirrup-leathers, and a third about the tying of his neckcloth. (It did indeed have a curious knot, which made it resemble a white bootlace.) Every joke brought laughter. Every one made him unhappier and more self-conscious. Yet there was no ill-will in the teasing – I was sure of that. They did not in the least *dislike* poor red-faced David. They were simply insensitive, like schoolboys; if they were cruel, it was unconsciously, and without deliberate malice. Yet, consciously or not, they *were* cruel; and he hated being the centre of attention, and the butt of all the jokes.

He looked almost as though he wanted to cry. I was terrified in case he did so, for that would have opened the flood-gates of mirth among the rest; and then I might have lost my temper, and shouted at them to leave him alone; and there would be no end to my disgrace.

But I need not have worried. He was a Highland gentleman, the son of a laird; he would not disgrace himself. In any case, since he was so ridiculous, he must be used to teasing.

The road climbed a little, away from the river, on to a spur which jutted from the mountainside. At the top of the shoulder, the Countess looked out of her window with excited eyes and an excited smile. Eugénie, too, craned forward to look.

I realized that we had come in sight of the castle. Yet, since I was facing backwards, I could see only backwards; I could see only the road behind, and the unhappy red face of the young man who had joined the escort late.

The Countess glanced at me sharply. But she was still smiling. It was the first time she had smiled directly at me since I had climbed into the carriage two days before. She pulled the velvet-tasselled string which hung beside her seat, which worked some kind of signal to the coachman. The horses stopped; the groom jumped down and went to their heads; the footman came to the Countess's window.

The Countess, still smiling at me, said, 'You may like to get down here, Christina, to see your new home. From this spot you get the most famous view of it – not because it is the best view, but because it is on the road. That is why artists choose it so often. If you climb a little up the hillside, you will find the view better still, and the air also. We shall drive on a little way, and take leave of our friends. You can walk after us. Would you like that?'

'Yes, ma'am, if you please,' I said. 'Thank you for thinking of it.'

'There is a great deal I should have thought of,' said the Countess, 'before I made a decision I should not have made . . . Don't climb too far. We shall not wait long before driving home, and it is easy to twist an ankle on the steep ground.'

'Yes, ma'am,' I said submissively; but what I wanted was to run up Ben Draco, four thousand feet to the top.

The footman opened the door and hinged down the steps. I was down on the road before he could offer me his arm; I went away up the hillside, half walking and half scrambling, deliberately postponing looking at the castle until I was higher, and more alone.

I heard the Countess call, 'David! David Baillie!'

The red-faced young man called some reply.

She said, 'Will you stay behind with Miss Drummond, David, just in case she should fall and hurt herself? She is not used to steeper hills than the streets of Edinburgh.'

'With pleasure, Lady Draco.'

'But afterwards, don't ride away without saying goodbye. I am very grateful to you for joining the escort. It did not matter in the least that you were a minute late, and spurs work just as well whichever way up you wear them.'

Her voice was soft, but I could hear it well, because she spoke so clearly, and the hillside was so quiet. The other horsemen had ridden on, and the coach had not yet started. Now it did start, with footman and groom aboard again.

I scrambled another few yards up the spur of the hillside, then turned at last to look north-eastwards at the castle, the sun directly behind me.

I caught my breath. What I saw was scarcely possible. I had expected something ancient and splendid and romantic: I had not expected such truly awesome grandeur, or a setting so unbelievably beautiful.

The castle was in truth a castle, with battlements, and towers, and a high central keep. It stood on a knoll above the river, which curved round the knoll so that two sides of the castle were water. There was an enormous gateway which a portcullis must once have closed: perhaps it was there still, to repel unwelcome guests. In front of it was a moat, spanned by a chain-hung drawbridge; I wondered if there was water in the moat, and whether the drawbridge worked. About the keep, and beyond the first outer courtyard, there clustered so many towers and turrets that it seemed rather a town than a single house. A hundred yards beyond, downstream, where the river curved again, there was another seeming town, but huddled close to the ground, like a herd of animals in a rainstorm. I took this to be all the outbuildings supporting the castle – the stables and coach-houses, the dwellings of outdoor servants, steadings and storehouses, mews, kennels, dovecotes, byres, granaries.

The afternoon sun shone full on the castle, which turned glowing walls towards me. Perhaps because of the reassuring sunlight, there was nothing grim about the place; nothing alarming, large as it was, except its daunting vastness. Size apart, it looked quite welcoming: I could see that, if one were a great noble, and used to this kind of thing, one could think of it as home, and be comfortable there, and pine for it when one was away.

If. Would I be comfortable there? Could I ever feel at ease in such a place? In which of the spiked towers would I be imprisoned with Eugénie, to be hissed at, and stabbed with fish-forks?

The Countess was right about the air. I filled my lungs with it, seeming as I did so to grow in health and courage. It was almost intoxicating; I did not know if it was like wine, because I had still never tasted wine.

There was a small, sudden noise, a little above me on the hillside, a *chink* of metal on stone. I glanced to my left, uphill. I gave, I think, a little startled cry: for I had *known* that the hillside was completely empty apart from myself; I had *known* that no other person was nearer than red-faced David waiting with his horse on the road. Yet, only a dozen feet from me, stood an enormous man, who had risen from the ground, and now stared down at me. He was dressed in the most abject rags, from which emerged huge limbs, covered in black hair and caked with dirt. He carried in one hand a knife, in the other a stick like a young tree. He had long, matted black hair, and a black, matted beard. His mouth, wide open as though he were in the midst of a yawn, was full of ruined teeth. His face – his expression – was not that of a man at all, but of an animal, a dangerous, hungry beast. There seemed to be no flicker of intelligence in his small eyes, or of humanity in his great, wide-open, idiot's mouth.

I thought instantly that he was a madman and that he would kill me.

The coach was three hundred yards away. The breeze blew from the north-east, from it to me, so that my voice would never reach it, or the horsemen about it, but be whisked away up the glen.

But there was red-faced David, a hundred feet away, below me on the road.

I turned and screamed, 'Help!'

He turned, looked up, saw me and the idiot giant. He dug his spurs into the poor fat horse's flanks, and they started struggling towards me up the steep slope. I, at the same time, began to run down the hill towards the road. But I had only gone two paces when I fell; and, as I fell, I felt a shocking pain in my ankle, and the wind was knocked out of my body, and I lay completely helpless. I could hear the horse crashing up the hillside; in a moment I could hear its laboured breathing. The rider was shouting incoherently: whether threateningly to the giant or reassuringly to me I could not tell.

As soon as I could breathe I sat up, to see what was happening. The horse had nearly climbed to my level; the giant had not moved, nor his expression changed. He showed no sign of attacking me, or of running away from the horse.

Then, directly in front of the horse, another man rose from the ground. It was as though he suddenly materialized, or grew in a split second from an acorn. He looked very old. He had once, I thought, been as large as the giant, but was now bent and emaciated. He had the same matted hair and beard as the first man, but his were a dirty white. He rose up from his hole in the ground two yards in front of the horse – and the horse shied. It tossed up its head and leaped sideways, snorting in sudden alarm. The rider was leaning forward over his mount's neck, owing to the steepness of the hill, and it seemed that the horse's head hit his. When the horse jumped sideways, the rider was thrown off. He fell heavily, in a heap, and lay still. The horse stood for a moment, trembling, and then trotted down towards the road.

The old man looked without expression at the motionless, crumpled form of David Baillie.

He said, 'Young Inverlarig. Likely daid. Nae loss.' His voice was high and quavering; he chanted rather than spoke.

He seemed neither pleased nor sorry that the horseman was dead; it seemed a matter of the most total indifference to him. I myself felt suffocated with horror, near to screaming or to fainting. I had never seen sudden death before, nor any men like these two hideous, ragged savages.

The black-bearded giant answered the older one, but not in words I could understand. It was not a strange language; it was gibberish, the jabber of an imbecile. His voice too was high, an astonishing little piping from so enormous and powerful a man.

The old man turned towards me, to where I still sat helpless on the steep ground. He advanced a few paces towards me; in spite of his bent back and starved frame he moved swiftly and gracefully.

He stopped a yard away from me. He stared at my face. Into his face came, gradually, like an incoming tide on a steep beach, an expression I had seen on other faces – that I had seen three times before – a look of amazement and of recognition.

He, too, knew my features.

He, like the Countess, and Eugénie, and the fat Duchess, was old enough to have known my grandfather, and in my face saw his face.

Staring at me fixedly, he began to speak in the high, keening voice, so that what he said sounded like the incantation of the mad priest of a horrible religion. He said, 'I cursit a' o' yon blude lang syne, an' I curse ye still. Ye'll nae bide here if ye're wishfu' tae live. Begone, spawn o' Satan, cursit Drummond! Your blude spilt blude, an' it sha' spill. Ye'll nae bide here.'

Cursed Drummond? Someone of my blood had spilled blood, and my blood would spill?

He had a knife like the black-bearded man's. Help was far away; my one rescuer was likely dead.

He did not use his knife; but spat at me. I was utterly astonished, and angry. I was very frightened. But my ankle was hurting badly; I could not move.

All the astonished recognition had gone from his face; in it there was only the most beastly hatred.

He turned and strode away like a deer over the hillside, beckoning Black-beard to follow. The younger man, for all his bulk, moved with the same grace. I was young and active, yet even without a sprained ankle I could not have kept up with them for two yards on the steep, broken ground. In a few moments they had disappeared beyond another spur, and were lost to sight in the tangle of mountains.

four

The fat horse reached the road. It turned towards the castle, the coach, the other horses. I thought it would run to join them. Everybody then, seeing the riderless horse, would know an accident had happened, and someone would come galloping back.

The fat horse seemed to debate in his mind whether to follow the others. But it decided it preferred to go homewards. It turned briskly, and trotted back up the glen and away.

I could not scream to attract the attention of the Countess's escort: they were too far, and the wind was in the wrong direction. Unless I stood up, I could not be seen by them, however wildly I waved my hat.

It was a moment for tears of despair, but I was in no mood for tears, because I was so angry at being spat upon by the old man who hated me.

For the tenth time I got precariously to my feet, and tried to support myself on my injured ankle. But it simply collapsed, and so did I. I thought I might be able to do something for David Baillie, if only to close his lids over his eyes; I thought at least that I should try. So I began to crawl. I crawled over the rough ground on my hands and knees, tearing my fine new gown and making it extremely dirty, becoming very hot in spite of the sweet mountain air, falling often forward on to my face. Though I did not have to use my bad ankle when I crawled, still it was very painful, and I saw that it was quite swollen.

I reached the body at last. It was lying dreadfully still. All the blood had gone from the face, which was deathly pale. I did not have to close the eyes, which were tight shut.

I began to say a prayer for his soul, in defiance of the teaching of the Free Church, when to my horror his eyes suddenly opened.

Of course I was only horrified for half a second, because I had been so sure he was dead. Immediately I was delighted and relieved, both for his sake and, indeed, for my own.

He blinked, and in a faint voice said, 'Who are you?'

'Christina Drummond,' I said. 'How do you do?'

He stared at me, making no attempt to move, with his wide, kind, stupid eyes. All the colour that had left his face came flooding back into it, until it burned as it had when they teased him by the coach.

'Do you know my face?' I asked, for that was why other people had been staring at me.

'No,' he breathed, 'but I've dreamed of it.'

I smiled. I thought it a very pretty remark from a young man that everybody laughed at, who had just been knocked unconscious.

But from the way he was still looking at me, especially after I started smiling, I saw that it was not a good remark in the way of being a pretty compliment, but simply what he thought was true.

He sighed after a time, and said, 'What happened? Where am I?'

'You were thrown off your horse,' I said gently. 'It shied at a horrid old man who jumped up out of the ground.'

'Oh! Of course, I remember. It was old Dandie McKillop. I was surprised to see him – I thought he was in prison. I don't blame old Bess for being frightened – he's enough to frighten any horse.'

'He frightened me,' I said. 'Who is the huge man with the black beard?'

'Oh, that is poor Adam. He is Dandie's son. He has never been quite right in the head. He is quite harmless.'

'Oh,' I said, very unconvinced.

David Baillie sat up, rather tentatively, a hand to his head.

'I've a bump like a whaup's egg on my skull,' he said ruefully.

'Like a Countess's diamond,' I murmured.

'Did Bess run off?'

'Your horse? Yes, she had gone away up the road. I suppose she is going home?'

'She'll arrive with an empty saddle, and my mother will be worried to death, and my father will be in a rage—'

'Why, if you have been hurt?'

'Oh! Just because of his gout, you know. This is such an unfortunate thing to have happened – I don't want my mother to be worried or my father angry . . . They'll lend me a horse at the castle, I suppose, though they may not want to very much . . . Well, we must make a start, I suppose. My head is swimming rather, but I think I can walk down the hill—'

'I can't,' I said. 'I've sprained my ankle.'

'Then—' he began. He seemed to struggle, to know what he wanted to say, but to have the greatest difficulty in saying it. He almost choked. If his face had been red before, it was now purple. I thought it was a nice face, though not exactly handsome, or full of intelligence.

At last he burst out, as though in agony, 'If you can't walk – I'll have to carry you!'

'Are you strong enough?' I asked dubiously.

'Oh yes! I carried a large calf yesterday, two miles, because it had hurt its leg. I should think you would be lighter than the calf.'

'But the hill is very steep.'

'But I was brought up on these hills, you know. I can walk up and down them as easily as you can walk on a flat road.'

'But,' I said, 'even if you are strong enough, and clever enough not to drop me down a cliff, are you well enough, with your poor head?'

'Yes,' he said firmly, 'quite well enough. Only please don't mind if I do drop you. I'll drop you if I faint, you see, and I daresay I might faint.'

'Men don't faint!'

'They do,' he said, 'with a bump on the head like this. Now . . .' he looked at me in utter perplexity. 'How are we to go about it? How am I to pick you up?'

'I expect we'll contrive,' I said, suddenly feeling shy about it myself. Other girls, who danced waltzes, were used to feeling a man's arm about their waists, but I had never been allowed to dance so much as an eightsome reel. Now David Baillie, who was a stranger, was about to clasp my person with both arms, and hoist me clear of the ground! Of course it was necessary, but it would be a new and strange sensation.

'The first thing,' I said, trying to be firmly practical, 'is for you to stand up. Then you must give me your hands, and pull me up. You will have to keep hold of me, if you don't mind, or I shall fall down again. When we have reached that stage we can plan the next one.'

He was so excessively shy that I thought we should spend the rest of our lives on the hillside, before he picked me up and started down to the road; consequently, to hurry him along, I had to pretend not to be shy at all. In truth I was less shy with him than I would have been with any other man, because he was so ridiculous. But at least he was strong, and by and by he had one arm under my shoulder and the other under my knees, and I, shamelessly, had both arms round his neck, with my fingers joined at the back, to take some of my own weight.

'I am sorry to be so heavy,' I said.

'You're not,' he said hoarsely. 'You're as light as . . .'

'A feather?' I suggested.

'No,' he said seriously, 'heavier than a feather. You weigh about as much as the calf I was carrying yesterday. But of course I put that over my shoulder, like a sack.'

'You could carry me like that,' I said, 'if it would be safer for us both.'

But he thought I should not be carried like a calf, or a sack; and we started very slowly down the hill.

It was quite true that he was sure-footed on the steep ground, and he did not seem at all overburdened by my weight. I thought how lucky it was that I was skinny, and did not have the generous curves my grandmother would have preferred. His face remained as red as a beetroot, and his breathing was quite tortured, but that was not physical effort, but emotion.

Because it seemed, from the way he looked at me, and from his tortured breathing, that I had collected another slave.

I did not feel triumphant about it, or hard, or cynical, but simply amazed.

At the same time I was a little alarmed for my own safety, for the hillside was very steep; he looked into my eyes with a stunned expression, and I thought he would be better looking where he was going.

By the time we had got near the road, someone had realized something was wrong, and three horsemen had come back. One was Ardmeggar, who was most kind and sensible, and saw at once what had to be done. Since the road was too narrow for the coach to be turned round to come back and fetch me, Ardmeggar lifted me up on to his own horse, from which he had dismounted. I sat side-saddle, on account of decency, but on the wrong side: this was so that the foot of my good leg could go in the stirrup, while the bad one simply rested on the horse's shoulder.

'My saddle's not adapted for that style of riding, Miss Drummond,' said Ardmeggar, 'but we'll walk along quiet and you'll come to no harm. If I were you I'd forget about the reins and take hold of his mane.'

I did so, and felt much safer.

'Dandie McKillop, was it?' said Ardmeggar to David. 'I knew he was out of prison, but I hoped he'd stay away. And poor Adam? He'd be best shut up somewhere, but I suppose that would be cruelty.'

'What was the old man sent to prison for?' I asked.

'Oh, he spends most of his time there – vagrancy, petty theft, trespass, poaching. And he's drawn back here every time he gets out, as though there was a magnet in the glen – it's foolish of him, because every herd and keeper hereabouts knows him, and he can't get away with a trout or a turnip.'

'Does he spit at people often?' I asked.

Ardmeggar, walking beside me, looked up, startled. 'No, I never heard of him doing that. He's not half-witted, you know – by no means. He could be a good craftsman – I believe he was a farrier once. But something soured him and sent him on the wrong road. Now he's worse than a tinker, except that I don't think he drinks as much as they do. He could earn good wages, and be a useful member of society, could Dandie; but he's possessed of some kind of devil. You're comfortable, Miss Drummond? Secure on the pigskin? And you, David? How's the head?'

'Very well, thank you,' said David, who trudged along on the other side of the horse, sometimes with his head bowed, and sometimes staring up at me.

I found myself wishing he would stop being my slave at once, not because I disliked him but because I liked him. I did not want him to be unhappy on my account. I think this was the first generous and unselfish idea I had had for a long time, since I had been so absorbed in myself and my own problems.

The Countess had a generous idea, too. As soon as she knew what had happened, she asked Ardmeggar to send a groom, as fast as he could go, to Inverlarig, to tell David's mother and father that he was all right: for she understood at once that they would be frightened, or angry, when his horse came back without him.

So I made my entry into Glendraco in a strange and unfortunate fashion, supported by two servants, hobbling, with a torn and stained gown, and a dirty face and hands, and my hair in wild confusion, and my hat squashed; and as I went in just behind the Countess, I was brought face to face with an army of upper servants who stood in ranks to welcome their mistress home.

They did welcome her home, most formally; but what they kept stealing glances at was me, with various expressions of disapproval, derision, curiosity, pity, and sympathy.

At least I saw no look of recognition.

My first impressions of Glendraco would have been blurred and awestruck at any time; as it was, I was hardly in a condition to notice anything sensibly.

We had been, I understood, on the Glendraco estate for the last hour and more, so there was no need of lodges and gates and fences. The road curved away from the river where the river itself curved round the knoll; there was scarcely a drive – only fifty yards of road which led to a great open space in the rough grass, and at its edge the drawbridge.

I had been transferred to the coach from Ardmeggar's horse, lifted in by Ardmeggar, with the help of the Countess's footman. I apologized to the Countess for my appearance; she said drily, 'David Baillie found it passable.'

Nearing the castle was like coming up, on a beach, to the foot of enormous cliffs. Grey stone, sun-gilded, filled the sky. It seemed less and less like a house, or even a castle: more and more like a sheer-sided mountain.

Eugénie stared at me, her unblinking eyes like jet beads in her chalk-white face. It had seemed to me that she had put me out of her mind, in the flurry of the escort and of arrival: but now she was seeing me *at* Glendraco – my face, against the sun-warmed cliffs of the castle walls – and the sight re-awakened all the hatred and fury in her eyes.

I wondered, idiotically, what ancient memory she shared with Dandie McKillop.

The coach trundled over the gravel, then very slowly over the drawbridge. The wheels thundered on the wood of the bridge, echoing and reverberating. I saw that the moat was dry, but very deep, lined with cropped grass and purple clumps of willow-herb. We went through the great gates into the outer courtyard, where a swarm of people surrounded us, as though taking the coach and its occupants prisoner. It was like being at the bottom of an enormous well. The courtyard was granite-paved, the windows on to it high and small and barred. Low steps led to a prodigious door, now thrown wide open, with liveried footmen at each side.

The Countess descended from her coach, then crossed the courtyard to the great door with an elasticity in her tread that I had not seen before; I hobbled after, between a footman and a maidservant. I said that I could walk, with assistance, and did not want to be carried. It was true; but my ankle was very painful.

The great hall seemed at least as large as the courtyard, but dark and chill. I had a blurred impression of animal heads and horns, shields and spears, suits of armour, tapestries, a fireplace the size of an ordinary house, skins on the stone-flagged floor, a few immense pieces of black furniture, like thrones or heathen altars, high doors leading away in all directions, and a great flight of stone stairs leading to a landing under a window the size of a cathedral.

Drawn up in their ranks were the upper servants. They were so many that I despaired of remembering their names and faces. There were so many doors leading out of the hall that I despaired of ever being clear which led to where. It was all too big for me. I felt dwarfed, crushed, by sheer size.

But I had no wish to seem cowed or abject. They would expect me to be so, all that army of magnificent, supercilious servants; on account of my usual perversity, that was enough to make me refuse to be so. When I caught a derisive or pitying eye, I stared back with what I thought was a proper haughtiness, suitable to such a hall. But I had to make an effort to be haughty, as it was all so large and strange, and as I guessed my whole appearance was undignified in the last degree.

I was put in charge of Mrs Weir, the housekeeper. Mrs Weir resembled old Carstairs in George Square, except that she was far more sumptuously dressed. Her face was made of granite, and her eyes were as icy as Lady Odiham's. She called forward two strapping young men in aprons, who brought a small elbow chair from some nearby room. I sat on the chair, and they carried me upstairs. It was a strange mode of travel; I felt like an oriental princess, or a human sacrifice.

We went up the first huge flight of stairs, to the landing under the cathedral window. I had a chance to glimpse, through the window, an inner courtyard, beyond which rose the keep. Stairs rose from each end of the landing. We took the right-hand flight. We went along a cavernous corridor, carpeted in dark tartan, hung with pictures as large as dining-tables, and up more stairs, and along again, and up yet more stairs, narrow and winding, and along, turning often, passing innumerable windows and doors, going through arches, until I was utterly confused. When my conveyance was put down at last outside a bedroom door, I did not even know for certain what floor of the castle we were on.

At a certain point in our journey, Mrs Weir had handed me over (like one guard handing a prisoner to another guard) to a plump girl with black hair and apple cheeks, in a black dress and neat white cap, who looked at me with deep and solemn concern: and barely managed to cover up a giggle.

'Yon's Annie Simpson, Miss,' said Mrs Weir, speaking to me for the first time. 'Annie wull tend ye. Ye'll gang tae your bed, an' rest yon puir ankle, an' Morag Laurie wull strap it, in a wee time, wi' a bittock o' flannel.'

And her face was not granite at all, and her eye no harder than Charlotte Long's. Perhaps, I thought, the housekeeper of a castle must pretend to be as much of a dragon as *the* Dragon: but with Mrs Weir the pretence did not go very deep.

So it was Annie Simpson who ushered me, still carried in my

chair, into my room at Glendraco, which I got to know so well. The men put me down and left. I called my thanks, attempting a tone which was not so much haughty as tempering dignity with gratitude; but I found I had to clear my throat, and I made a noise, in the end, like Georgina Campbell's tame piglet. One of the men grinned as he left; the other went out as solemn as an Elder on the Sabbath.

I looked round the room. My heart rose. The declining sun poured in, filling it with golden welcome. Everything about the room was magnificent, beautiful by my standards, comfortable and comforting by any standards: and the best thing in it was Annie Simpson.

She had been struggling with her mirth, poor Annie, and was struggling still: her fine bosom heaved under the tight black bodice with her efforts to contain her laughter, and she blinked her eyes, and clamped shut her broad, friendly mouth, and the sight was so comical that, in spite of my confusion and the pain in my ankle – in spite of the terrifying size and splendour of Glendraco – I burst out laughing. This, of course, was too much for her, and she began to laugh so helplessly that she had to sit down on the bed.

At last I managed to say, 'I know I look a tinker, Annie, but am I so *very* funny?'

Wiping her eyes, Annie brought me a hand-mirror from the dressing-table. I looked at myself aghast. To Lady Odiham I said (with unforgivable and unforgiven pertness), 'Have I a smut on my nose?' Now there was no smut, but a large smear of earth, or mud. Another smear on my forehead made one of my eyebrows appear three times as heavy as the other, and gave it the arch my grandmother wished it had naturally: so that I had a startled and astonished look, but only on one side. I looked like a strolling player, a tumbler entertaining passers-by in an Edinburgh street, in comical make-up, for pennies collected in a tambourine.

And I had tried to impress, with my haughty dignity, the servants assembled in the great hall.

It seemed that when I attempted to be dignified, I made myself most ridiculous. I thought perhaps I would abandon the

attempt, at least for the time being, and be childish and undignified. And I was, dreadfully, because for no reason at all I
suddenly burst into tears, and sobbed on Annie's ample bosom.

When my howls had subsided to snuffles, Annie said cheerfully, 'When I fairst cam frae the village, I passit a' nicht greetin'.
An' I hadnae wrenchit a fut. Yon's nae shame. It's what they ca'
pullin' the bung frae the keg.'

That seemed to be a good description. I had pulled the bung
from the keg, and spilled out gallons of salt water; so that my
face was now blotched with tears as well as stained with earth.

Annie fetched copious hot water, and helped me to undress.
Between us, we scrubbed me quite clean. I let her brush my hair
– like the little maid at Gaultstower, she thought she should do
so, and she had a much stronger character than that girl. She
exclaimed at the colour of my hair – she had never seen the like,
she said, on a human head, but it put her in mind of an Irish
thoroughbred horse of his lordship's. When my hair was down
my back, and brushed until it squeaked, Annie helped me to bed.

Morag Laurie came, as promised, a little bustling woman with
a face like a russet apple in the spring. Annie said she was the resi-
dent nurse of the castle, in constant demand for minor injuries,
such as burns in the kitchen, and scalds, and cuts, and bruises.

'Och, I'll set a bustit laig, or stitch a slash frae a goose-neck,'
said Morag Laurie: and I believed her. I much preferred being
treated by her than by Doctor Nicholson, who believed that
suffering was good for the soul, and especially for mine. Morag
clucked over my swollen ankle, prodded it gently, bathed it, put
on an enormous cold compress, and then swathed it all about
with miles of soft bandages. The result was the size of one of my
pillows. I thought I must look like a man with gout, like David's
angry father at Inverlarig. I thought that even the dressings on
injuries were much bigger at Glendraco than anywhere else.

In the early evening, as I sat up in bed with more to think about
than ever, I heard a monstrous squeaking in the corridor outside
my door, as though a clutch of baby starlings was trying to get
out of a paper bag, or a nest of mice was complaining of violent
hunger.

My door opened, and Annie backed into the room. She was

followed by a young footman pushing the most extraordinary contraption I had ever seen. It was like a small table with castors at the feet, but instead of a normal table-top it had a great brass tray with a high rim, and instead of castors it had wheels half-a-foot across. Below the top tray there were others, like shelves, which could be removed. On it was my supper, with little flames on spirit-lamps below silver chafing-dishes. The squeaking was made by its wheels, which urgently needed butter or goose-fat to make them turn quietly.

It was the invention, I was told, of the late Earl, the Countess's son, who called it the *porte-dîner*. He invented it because he was often in his bed, being ill or imagining himself so, and his meals arrived cold from the kitchens. Dishes kept hot by lamps could not be carried, even by the Glendraco servants, on ordinary trays; and his lordship greatly disliked cold food. Also, he was concerned for his servants, and preferred to think of them pushing a wagon rather than carrying heavy trays. It was one of very many inventions for which the late Earl was responsible, and which he caused to be made by the estate craftsmen; it was the only one still in use.

I said, 'But how does this great wagon come up from the kitchens?'

'Och,' said the footman, 'twa-three o' us carry it.'

So I saw that even the most useful inventions have drawbacks.

Among the dozens of things on the *porte-dîner* was a slender glass jug with a glass stopper cut into facets like a diamond. In it was a dark red liquid, which I took to be blackcurrant-juice. I imagined the juice was to be poured over some later course, a dessert of fruit or a pastry. To my surprise, a glass was filled with it and placed in my hand.

'Her leddyship,' said Annie, 'said ye were tae take a sup, Miss Kirstie.'

'Of blackcurrant juice?'

'O' gude red wine.'

So, for the first time in my life, I had wine to my dinner.

Much later I lay back on my pillows, comfortable in my comfortable bed, my ankle feeling quite well because I had put no weight on it for hours. Annie had tucked me up, and opened the curtains of the windows, and taken away the lamp. A half-moon filled the room with silver, casting deep shadows in which there were no bogeys like the ghosts of the Dead Glen.

I was half asleep when the door opened softly. Candlelight flickered in the corridor. A voice murmured, 'Wait here for me, Rutherford.'

A figure came softly forward into the moonlight; I saw a cloud of white hair and, in the silver light, a smiling mouth whose corners were turned up like the ends of a recurved long-bow.

The Countess came up to my bedside, and put a hand on mine where it lay above the covers.

She said, 'Goodnight, Christina. I have made a terrible mistake, but I believe in abiding by my mistakes. I have not properly welcomed you to Glendraco. I do so now. Tell me, Kirstie, did you enjoy your wine?'

'I expect I shall grow to like it,' I said.

'Yes.' She laughed softly. 'I expect you will. Dear God, what have I done? But I have done it. It is done. I cannot see where things will end. They have begun most oddly. Goodnight, dear child.'

She bent and kissed me on the forehead.

I met my new world in two stages. First it came to me, as I spent three days in bed, on Morag Laurie's orders. Then I went out to it.

The first morning, after my breakfast had been taken away, Eugénie came into my room. She was apparently still feeling the cold, for she wore a great fringed shawl over her shoulders instead of the cloak, and her fingers still curled like talons out of her woolly mittens. She scarcely looked at me, but sat in a chair near the window. With her came a little fussy woman, dressed as grandly as the Countess herself, with eyes as hard and black as Eugénie's. She and Eugénie talked to each other, extremely fast, in French. I could not follow a word. Eugénie hissed and whispered, as usual; the newcomer croaked like a magpie, very harsh and hoarse and hectoring. In the train of the magpie-woman came a much younger one, who said nothing at all, but carried swatches of silks, and a large carpet-bag, and had a tape-measure round her neck.

Annie helped me out of bed. I stood in my nightdress and was measured, every bit of me: my height and waist and hips and bosom and legs and arms and neck and shoulders. The magpie-woman croaked figures (I supposed they were figures) to her assistant, who wrote them down in a book.

When she had finished measuring she stood back and looked at me, very slowly, up and down. I was glad that my face was now quite clean, and that Annie had brushed my hair, which was over my shoulders and down my back.

She said harshly, *'Très belle, comme m'a dit miladi. Forme superbe, couleur épatant. C'serait grand plaisir d'habiller une telle mademoiselle.'*

Even my sketchy knowledge of French enabled me to understand the gist of this judgement. I did not know what *épatant* meant, but I thought it not positively insulting, in spite of what my grandmother had always said about my colouring. The whole remark was, to say the least, encouraging. The assistant, staring at me solemnly, nodded, as though she agreed. Eugénie continued to look fixedly out of the window; it seemed to disgust her that I was described as *très belle*.

Some time later there was a knock at my door as timid as Charlotte Long's. In came an old lady – not so very old, perhaps sixty – with an old-fashioned lace cap framing a perfectly round face like the dial of a clock. She was small and plump, and dressed in black, and hung about with little chains and lockets and bangles, and stuck about with jet brooches, as though she had put on every ornament she had, without considering the total effect, or thinking where each should go. Her eyes were wide and blue, and not much cleverer than David Baillie's, and her face was as open and kindly as his.

She struck me as another ridiculous person, whom it would be impossible to take seriously, and impossible not to like. Indeed she gave off a friendliness as warm as the midday sunshine, and I found myself smiling before she had opened her mouth.

She began to speak almost at once, breathlessly, as though she was frightened to speak, but obliged to by an inner force. 'Oh my dear!' she said in a rush, 'may I come in? Gracious me, the colour of your hair is *all* that I had been led to expect! I thought dear Elinor, that is Lady Draco, was exaggerating, forgetting that she seldom, if ever does, but that if anyone exaggerates it is I, I'm afraid ... What a nice room! Do you like it? No direct sun, of course, at this hour, since you have a western aspect, but I imagine it is quite overpoweringly bright in the middle of the afternoon. Not everyone likes direct sunlight, of course, and it can fade carpets and curtains quite dreadfully, as I know to my cost ... Dear Elinor, that is Lady Draco, encouraged me to suppose that you might not find a visit unwelcome, so I made bold to climb *all* those stairs and come knocking at your door. I expect you are wondering who I am. I am nobody! Nobody! A poor old widow, given haven under this glorious roof. Like yourself, dear, though of course you are not a widow, are you? Unless there are things I have not been told ... You are wondering who I am, and why I talk so much. As to that, I don't know *why* I do, but I always did! My late husband was a retiring, academic soul – he was Professor Forbes, Professor Pericles Forbes, of Aberdeen University, a *great* man, perhaps you have heard of him? Or perhaps you are *not* a student of oriental languages? To tell you the awful truth, I never was interested in them myself! Not the smallest bit! I never was even clear what all those languages were called, nor in what lands they were spoken. The Professor used to read me his articles, before they were published, and his lectures, before he gave them, and in order to stay awake I had to prick myself with a hat-pin! I have never been certain, in my own mind, whether this shows me to have been a very *good* wife, or a very *bad* one ...'

The breathless voice faltered to a halt. The wide blue eyes looked at me in perplexity, as though in despair of finding the answer to this difficult question.

I burst out laughing; I could not help it. She laughed too, not offended at all, but in the greatest good humour.

I said, 'I think you were a very good wife, Mrs Forbes, if you pricked yourself with a pin in order not to hurt the Professor's feelings.'

'Oh, thank you for saying so! Bless you for saying so! I have often and often tried to tell myself the same thing, but always and always the *sneaking* suspicion returns, that if I had *truly* been a good wife I would have been interested in oriental languages. And then the pin would have been unnecessary ... I am, you know, what they call a poor relation. I am an extreme case, you know, because I am *very poor indeed*, and a *very distant relation*. I do not suppose that anybody but dear Elinor, that is Lady Draco, would have acknowledged the relationship. I believe that we are seventh cousins, twice removed! So she offered me a home here, when the Professor passed on six years ago. I have been accepting her charity ever since! I know that my pride should make me reluctant to accept *so* much charity for *so* long, but really, you know, I feel I have no pride at all! Not a scrap! It is a luxury I cannot afford! They say that it is more blessed to give than to receive, but I must admit to you, dear, that here at Glendraco I find it *exceedingly* blessed to receive ...'

'I hope I shall find that, too,' I said.

'Well, dear,' said Mrs Forbes, clasping her fat little hands together, 'I don't know why you should listen to me – nobody *else* here does so, and the Professor *never* did so, quite rightly, because *very* little that I say is either sensible or interesting – but if you will be guided by me, you will take what dear Elinor, that is Lady Draco, gives you, in the spirit in which it is given, which is a spirit, I suppose, of affection—'

'Is it?' I asked, half aloud. For I had not at all fathomed what the Countess felt about me. Sometimes she seemed as affectionate as Charlotte Long, and sometimes as hostile as Eugénie.

Mrs Forbes did not notice my interruption. She swept on breathlessly, 'I do not, to be honest, know *why* she has brought you here, although I am *very* glad she did so, for we are often lonely, and quite dull. But ... Where was I? I often lose the thread of what I am saying ... Our great excitement this morning is the news that his lordship is coming home soon. Have you met him?'

'No.'

'I wonder what you will think of him? And he of you? He has always been most kind and considerate to me. He calls me "Cousin Amy", and I call him "Cousin Neil", and it is true that we are cousins, though somewhat remote. And at the same time we are to welcome Lady Arabella Paston and her daughter. Dear Angelica! I have heard her described as the most beautiful young lady in three kingdoms, and I do believe it is very likely quite true. And so kind! And so accomplished! Her renderings on the pianoforte give unspeakable delight! She could, I have often heard it said, make a career as a professional in the concert-halls, if such a thing were possible to someone like herself. And her paintings! There is no gallery in London itself that would not be proud to hang them on its walls! But soon you shall judge for yourself . . . Gracious me, can it really be noon? I have been so interested in all that you have been telling me, dear, that time has quite raced by! How dreadful! There is an old woman that I must visit in the village; she says her end is near, but I think, myself, that she simply likes the broth and Madeira wine I take her . . . But I do not feel morally able to criticize her for enjoying such good things at dear Elinor's expense – I mean Lady Draco's – since I have been doing the same thing myself for six years . . . So I am afraid I must leave you, dear, but I have *so much* enjoyed our talk, and hope it is the first of many.'

Mrs Forbes beamed at me with the warmest goodwill, and bustled away on her errand of mercy.

The old woman in the village might enjoy her broth and Madeira wine, but it struck me she paid quite heavily for it, unless she found it restful to listen. Yet there was something very nice about Mrs Forbes, something I could not help liking very much. Above all she laughed at herself, and had no illusions. I hoped I should be as wise.

I wondered about the Lady Arabella Paston and her daughter Angelica, the most beautiful girl in three kingdoms, kind, amazingly accomplished. I could not bring myself to believe that I was beautiful, although people had taken to telling me so, owing to having been brought up to believe the opposite. I thought I was quite kind, though perhaps not kind enough to people like Findlay Nicholson. But I was certainly not accomplished. I could do nothing! Perhaps Eugénie would give me an intensive course in embroidery, or the harp; or Mrs Forbes could teach me oriental languages.

All I knew about the Earl was what his grandmother said to

the Duchess of Bodmin: he was very serious, and high-minded, and involved with politics and the condition of the world. I wondered, idly, about the Earl and the beautiful and accomplished Angelica Paston. To have acquired such accomplishments she must be serious, too, and have great application, of which I had so little. She belonged to his world, since her mother was called Lady Arabella. Perhaps they were in love with each other. It did not affect me.

I wanted to see Lord Cricklade again, and although I knew it was unmaidenly I wanted to feel the pressure of his hand on mine. I wanted to see Lord Caerlaverock, who was so solemn and so very comical. I wanted to see the ridiculous David Baillie.

Annie Simpson giggled when I asked her about Mrs Forbes. Indeed, no other answer was necessary. It seemed she was a great friend of Lady Arabella Paston. Miss Angelica, said Annie, was indeed beautiful, and kind, and accomplished.

'But she's no the lass for laughin', Miss Kirstie,' said Annie. 'She'll hae ay the face for the Sabbath. No sae *dour*, ye ken, but no laughin' like yersel'.'

The newcomers all sounded a dull lot to me.

That was all the excitement of my first day at Glendraco, except that I again had a glass of wine to my dinner, which again arrived, piping hot, on the late Earl's *porte-dîner*.

Next morning there came a note for me from David Baillie, delivered by himself, so that it seemed that he and his horse had both recovered. He was not, of course, permitted up to my room; only his letter was. It was written in a very round, very childish, very careful hand; one could almost picture poor David sucking his pen, and then with great deliberation forming his letters, out of pot-hooks and hangers, as he had been taught.

Inverlarig, 21 June

Dear Miss Drummond,
I take up my pen, to inquire, after your health. Hoping your injury, is slight, and you are quite recovered. Hoping, I may have the honour, of meeting you again, shortly.
I am, your obedient servant,
   David Baillie, yr of Inverlarig

There were writing things on a table in my room; Annie brought them to me. At the best of times, I found writing letters as difficult as David Baillie did, in spite of my superior Edinburgh education; and this was not the best of times, as the nib scratched, and I found it awkward writing on my lap in bed. But at last I produced this masterpiece:

Glendraco, 22 June

Dear Mr Baillie,

I thank you for your kind letter. My injury is indeed slight, and soon I shall be quite recovered. From your riding here, it seems your head is better, for which I am very glad. I hope your horse is none the worse from going home by herself. I hope I am to have the pleasure of meeting you again, when I am allowed to walk about.

Your obedient servant,

   Christina Drummond

I was not sure about that last sentence, saying that I hoped to meet him again, in case it had a forward and saucy sound; but I thought I could not be less polite than he, especially as he had hurt himself in coming to my rescue.

I was ashamed of the way my letter was written. My handwriting was always extremely bad, and writing on my lap made it worse, and the nib made splutters and splatters, and almost tore holes in the paper. Professor Pericles Forbes would have been greatly shocked, but I thought David Baillie might not mind.

Another visitor came to see me at the end of the morning, for whom I was wrapped up in a shawl for modesty: for it was a gentleman, the Reverend Lancelot Barrow, the castle Chaplain.

He was about thirty, tall and thin but soft-looking, with a long, pale, clean-shaven face, and a black suit, and bands. He had enormously long pale hands, with large knuckles and big, yellowish fingernails. He looked as though he scrubbed himself perfectly clean several times a day; I do not mean that I like dirt, but it is possible to look *too* clean, or at least too thoroughly scrubbed, and that is how the Reverend Lancelot Barrow looked. He had a quick, cold smile, which came and went occasionally as he talked.

He said, 'I greatly regret, as we all must, that your arrival here should have been attended by this mischance, Miss Drummond. The hillsides here are dangerously steep and rough – deplorably so. I never venture up them myself, preferring the gentler gradients on which the Lord must, from their design, have intended us to place our feet. Besides, I would scarcely find time from my duties here to run up and down the mountains like the goat of Scripture. Of these duties to which I advert, the most onerous at the present time is the task of re-cataloguing the library. Mrs Forbes has been kind enough to give me some assistance, but' – here came the quick, cold smile – 'her participation has not had the effect of accelerating the compilation of the catalogue. Her ladyship has been gracious enough to suggest that you may be able to spare a few hours a week to assisting me, when you are quite recovered. Another of my duties is, of course, the pastoral obligation of visiting the sick – those, that is to say, who are members of my own flock. I would not be welcome at the crofts of the Kirk people – what in England we might term the chapel folk – nor at the homes of the Roman Catholics, of which there are, I regret to say, several about here, audaciously proclaiming their allegiance to the Vatican.'

'You do not visit the Kirk people, nor the Romans, Mr Barrow,' I said puzzled. 'Then who *do* you visit?'

He looked equally puzzled. 'We are, of course, Episcopalians at the Castle,' he said, 'like almost all the leading families of Scotland since the light from Canterbury has broken through. I take it . . . I cannot doubt, that as an inmate of this place, you yourself . . . ?'

'I was brought up in the United Free Kirk,' I said. 'But I trust I am not bigoted.'

'Oh dear,' he said, with a stricken air, 'oh dear, oh dear.'

And soon afterwards he left, his long pale hands fluttering like butter-paddles.

The Countess came to see me. Her manner was as distant and severe as, the previous night, it had been warm and affectionate.

She said, 'You have not, I think, written to your grandparents in Edinburgh, Christina?'

'No, ma'am, not yet.'

'Did it not occur to you how desperately they would be worrying about you?'

91

My heart jumped with horror at myself. I had *not* thought of that. I had thought of them, to be sure, by way of contrast with the new world I was meeting, but I had *not* thought of their feelings. I had gone for a walk in the Princes Street Gardens with Findlay Nicholson – and simply disappeared. They must be beside themselves with worry.

'Your selfishness and thoughtlessness are shocking, Christina,' said the Countess.

'Yes, ma'am,' I said, my eyes downcast, feeling truly awful about it. And I had told myself comfortably, while thinking of Angelica Paston, that even if I were not accomplished, I was at least tolerably kind!

'Fortunately,' said the Countess, 'others have repaired your unforgivable omission. I wrote to Mr Strachan myself, from the Duchess of Bodmin's house, the moment we arrived there, and she was kind enough to send a man on horseback with my letter, and not wait for the post. They received it the evening of your escapade.'

'Oh,' I said. 'I am glad of that.'

'I received this morning a reply, also sent by hand, from which it emerges that Lord Cricklade had already, hours before my letter reached George Square, been there himself in his gig to tell your grandparents that you were safe.'

'That was kind of Lord Cricklade.'

'Yes, it was. You had told him, I suppose, where you lived. It is typical of Cricklade that he should have driven many extra miles, to allay the anxieties of people whom he had never met or heard of, and of whom you had probably drawn for him a very unsympathetic picture.'

'Yes, ma'am, I think that is typical of him.'

'Behaviour in some contrast to your own, I think you will agree?'

'Yes, ma'am, I do agree. I am ashamed of myself.'

'I cannot show you your grandfather's letter, which is long and outspoken, and I would not if I could. It is for my eyes only. I do not think you appreciate the deep sincerity of his beliefs, or the courage with which they both refused a request from me.'

'I have never doubted their sincerity or their courage, ma'am,' I said.

'But you do not, perhaps, hold those qualities in high esteem? No higher than simple thoughtfulness, a regard for the feelings of others? You have shown how little you value *that*.'

'There is no need to say it again and again,' I cried suddenly.

'What?' she said in a terrible voice.

'When you came to George Square,' I said, 'you asked my grandfather not to repeat himself, because it was fatiguing and pointless —'

'Be silent! How dare you talk to me like that?'

The Dragon was breathing fire. I gulped and dropped my eyes. My temper had got me into trouble again.

'Your grandfather,' said the Dragon, in a voice like an iron bell, 'reminds me that he can at any moment take legal action obliging me to return you to his roof.'

'Yes, ma'am.'

'In which event, no doubt, your planned marriage to the person you described to me will take place.'

'Yes . . . I—'

'Be silent! You shall speak when I require you to do so. Otherwise hold your tongue. Your grandfather is not immediately proposing legal action, for reasons which do not concern you. Nor am I immediately proposing to return you to George Square, though many considerations urge me to do so. I shall do so, without a second's hesitation, if and when I think fit.'

'Return me to Findlay Nicholson,' I faltered. 'You are holding this threat over my head.'

'Yes,' said the Countess. 'This is exactly what I am doing.'

The first of my new clothes arrived in my room – some things which Madame Massenet and her assistant had made for me very quickly, so that I had something to wear. I held them up against myself in front of the full-length glass (a thing which would have been cast out from George Square, as an inducement to vanity) and nearly wept with delight. Although they had been made in forty-eight hours, out of stuffs which Madame Massenet had to hand in her workroom, they were the right size and shape, and they were beautiful, and I longed to wear them all, and be seen by the greatest possible number of people. I forgot the discomfort of my ankle as Annie handed me the clothes, for me to hold up. Afterwards Annie crooned over them as she hung them up, or laid them, carefully folded, among lavender-bags in drawers.

I could now cross the room without help, and almost without pain, although my ankle was still strapped up tight. Morag Laurie said I might go downstairs, and soon out of doors, provided that I walked with a stick and did not try to do too much.

Between us, Annie and I chose a grey silk afternoon dress for my first appearance (after my dreadful *first* appearance) downstairs in the Castle. For the first time in my life I realized the joy of wearing perfectly-fitting, well-made, fashionable clothes. I had grown no plumper since leaving Edinburgh; yet Carstairs could hardly have confused me with a 'scrawny boy'. Annie did my hair, and I started, tentatively, out of the room with the stick Morag had brought me.

I opened the door – and gave a start: for there stood Eugénie. With her usual sharp, repeated getures, and her usual furious hissing, she drove me back into the room, and ordered me to change my gown. She picked a different one, green, simpler. Annie looked rebellious, but she helped me to change. Only then did Eugénie give me permission to sally forth.

So I renewed acquaintance with Mrs Forbes and the Reverend Lancelot Barrow, and with Mrs Weir the housekeeper; and I met Patterson the butler, who had long white Dundreary whiskers, and a mournful air; and I saw the great drawing-room, and the amber room, and the Chinese room, and the Raeburn room, which was full of portraits, and the gallery, and the dining-room, which seemed to me as large as the Edinburgh Academy football fields, and the blue room, and the Italian room, and a great many other rooms. Everywhere there was bustle, with housemaids taking dust-sheets off brocaded chairs and footmen carrying them away: and I understood that the castle was half shut up when the Earl was away, but restored to grandeur the moment he was expected home.

I remembered that, when I first went into the Great Hall, I thought I would get lost. I was right: I did get lost, again and again; but cheerful servants put me right, and I saw a great deal, though I was in utter confusion about what I had seen.

Mrs Forbes was ecstatic, for a long time, about my green dress; Mr Barrow was solicitous, for a short time, about my ankle.

I did not see the Countess.

Next day, much stronger, I ventured into the outer courtyard, and across the drawbridge, and along the road to the steadings and stables. The Reverend Lancelot Barrow caught me up as I went, and offered to show me round.

'Parts of these buildings,' he instructed me, somewhat in the manner of Findlay Nicholson, 'have grown up from the ruins of an older castle, which was destroyed in the thirteenth century. Observe, Miss Drummond, that wall, which is not less than nine feet thick.'

I observed dutifully. It was indeed a thick wall for a cow-house. I could see that it was the remnant of a very ancient and strong castle.

'Whose fortress was it when it was destroyed?' I asked.

'History does not relate – at least, not reliably, as far as my own researches have been able to determine. You must remember, Miss Drummond, that this region was inhabited by uncouth savages, even more so than now.' His quick, cold smile came and went. 'Even the chiefs were illiterate, and I suspect most of their priests also. Written record is obscure and unreliable, since historical traditions relied on the recitations of bards.'

'Bards,' I said, 'would be a more pleasant way of learning history than reading some of the books I was obliged to study.'

He smiled even more briefly than before, but whether from agreement or contempt it was impossible to say.

We had walked (myself limping somewhat, and with my stick) among barns and stores and byres and all kinds of massive old stone buildings. Everywhere there was a comfortable smell of animals; everything was very tidy. The busy people greeted Mr Barrow with varying degrees of respect; they stared at me unabashed. None was very old. I saw no recognition.

We came at length to the stables, a big cobbled yard reached through an arch with tower and clock and weathercock above. There were a great many horses, of all sizes and colours, either tied up in stalls or looking out over the open half-doors of loose-boxes.

A small green-painted door opened in a massive wall, and I glimpsed, in the room beyond, dozens of saddles perched on wooden brackets. Out of the door came an old, gnarled man, who looked like an elderly thorn-tree, twisted by the wind but still strong and vigorous. He turned to lock the door he had come through, then started across the stable-yard with a rolling, bow-legged gait, as though his legs had been shaped by saddles, and could no longer straighten.

'That,' said the Reverend Lancelot Barrow, 'is Geordie Buchan, who was his late lordship's head groom, but is now retired.' Raising his voice, Mr Barrow called, 'Can you not stay away from the scenes of your labours, Geordie?'

The old man looked up and snorted, his face like ancient wood. 'Och,' he said, 'the bairns leave the tack like a tinker's rubbish. We'll no hae his lordship hame tae siccan disgracefu' confushon.'

He glanced then from Mr Barrow to me: and for the fifth time I saw the look of amazement, of startled, incredulous, unmistakable recognition.

The Countess had been made thoughtful. Eugénie had been filled with hatred. The Duchess of Bodmin had been saddened. Dandie McKillop had been angry and threatening. Geordie Buchan reacted in a new way. A grin of the purest joy grew and grew on his face, like the opening of a Japanese paper flower in a bowl of water. It seemed impossible that a smile could grow so broad without cracking his face in half. He was, I reflected, old enough to have known my grandfather.

'This is Miss Drummond, who has come to stay at the castle,' said Mr Barrow.

'Ay,' said the old man. 'I believe ye.'

'Perhaps she will like to try a quiet pony, one of these days, and go for a brief ride on a leading-rein.'

'Ay,' the old man chuckled. 'A quiet pony, is't, an' a leadin'-rein? Ay, verra like.' He laughed again. To me he said, 'Ye'll be weel accustomit tae ridin', Miss?'

'No,' I said yearningly. 'Not yet.'

"Twull be my honour to schule ye.'

'Thank you very much,' I said. 'As soon as my ankle is well, and her ladyship permits . . .'

Geordie Buchan laughed again, a deep rich gurgle like a waterfall of black treacle; he looked like a gnome who had just been given the crown jewels.

More of my new clothes arrived in my room, to be held up by me and crooned over by Annie. They included, as though by magic, a riding habit. The Countess had given her permission, without looking up from the letter she was writing. I walked to the stables, trying not to swagger in my unfamiliar riding-boots and habit, or to slash at everything with my little plaited whip.

I had my first ride on a small, elderly, ash-coloured pony called Solomon, as fat as a grouse, who walked round and round, sedately, stopping and starting when Geordie whistled at him. I found the side-saddle comfortable and secure, and concentrated on sitting properly, and holding the two reins so as to control Solomon without hurting his mouth, as Geordie taught me. Geordie was very severe with me, and shouted at me much more loudly than he shouted at Solomon; but every so often he seemed to forget the lesson entirely, and stop and stare at me: and when he did so his grin threatened to split his old face in two.

At last I was down on the ground again, and Solomon was led away.

I said, 'Geordie, do you know my face? Have you seen it before?'

He looked down at his boots, and shook his head.

'You seemed to recognize me,' I prompted him.

'Ye're ower bonny, Miss,' he said. 'Yon's a' the cause o' my starin'.'

I could get no more out of him; we arranged another lesson tomorrow.

I walked back the short way to the castle, and arrived at the drawbridge at the same time as a closed carriage, which was followed by a man on a tall bay horse.

Through the window of the carriage I saw two ladies in magnificent hats, one a girl of about twenty, one a woman of about forty-five. Guessing immediately who they might be, I was keenly interested, but the carriage was gone into the courtyard before I had time to do more than glimpse them.

The gentleman stopped his horse and looked down at me. He was very neatly and severely dressed in a black coat and black top hat and drab breeches; his black boots were so shiny that they looked as though they had been dipped in ink which was still wet; his spurs, I was sure, were worn the right way up. He was tall and slim, but his shoulders were broad. I supposed him to be about thirty, but his black coat and his gravity made him seem more. His face was pale, as though he had been indoors all the summer: and it was that pale face that made me gasp for a moment, as the family resemblance was so striking. He had a high-bridged beak of a nose, like an eagle or the prow of a Viking ship. His eyebrows were heavy and as black as his boots; they looked as though they were only used for frowning. Yet his eyes were clear and grey and direct, and his mouth had a sensuous curve. That mouth might turn up at the corners when he smiled, like the ends of a recurved longbow, but there was no way of knowing, as he showed no signs of smiling. Indeed he looked incapable of smiling or of laughter. He looked exactly as his grandmother had described him – a high-minded bore, a worthy, dreary, humourless, conscientious stick. I preferred Geordie Buchan.

The Earl looked down at me without expression. He raised his hat a bare inch with his whip hand, and replaced it on his smooth dark hair.

He said, in a voice as cold as the granite of his castle, 'It is customary to wear hats of that style exactly level on the head.'

I blushed. My hand flew to my hat. Perhaps it was a little aslant.

The Earl walked his horse sedately away over the drawbridge.

five

My hat was exceedingly proper. I thought it was exceedingly smart. It was brand-new. I imagined it was expensive. In form it was a sort of cut-down version of the Earl's own tall hat – a low-crowned 'topper' with a bandeau tied round it. Eugénie had inspected me, and passed it. Mrs Forbes had exclaimed at it. The Reverend Lancelot Barrow had bowed towards it, gently flapping his long white hands as though to dry them after yet another scrub. Geordie Buchan had looked at it – at all of me – with undisguised delight. I thought I had grounds for believing that there was nothing wrong with my hat, nor with the way I wore it. I thought the Earl was insufferably pompous and rude.

I was tempted to tilt my hat rakishly over one ear, and so swagger into the courtyard. That would, most clearly, show the Earl what I thought of him. But it was just the sort of thing which most enraged the Countess, and I thought, perhaps, as a punishment, she might forbid me to ride. I was torn, I wanted very badly to defy this odious Earl, but I wanted still more passionately to ride – to learn properly, to be put up on a full-sized, high-mettled, thoroughbred horse, and canter, and gallop up the glen on the springy turf, and jump . . .

So I settled my hat perfectly level on my head, and walked demurely into the courtyard.

I was angry! What sort of man, I asked myself, addressed a perfectly strange young lady, at his own door, in such arrogant and insulting terms? The Earl might be a nobleman, but he was not a gentleman. He had less feeling than a fish, less courtesy than a toad. He was as cold as Lady Odiham, as offensive as Dandie McKillop, as disapproving as Eugénie. What if he had spoken with that indifferent cruelty to a shy, sensitive, vulnerable girl like Charlotte Long? She would have been acutely miserable, made almost ill with embarrassment. As it was me, it did not matter, because I was a different sort of person. It simply made me angry!

*

My anger persisted until I was told that I was expected to join the party for dinner. It was only a little party, of the household and a few near neighbours assembled to welcome his lordship home – sixteen in all. I was to be in the drawing-room not later than half-past six.

'It is in order to make up the numbers, dear,' explained Mrs Forbes, who brought the message. 'Dear Georgina Campbell was expected, with her Mamma and Papa, but her greatest friend has just arrived at Drumlaw, exhausted from her journey, and Georgina feels she must stay to bear her guest company. Lady Campbell has sent over a note, by the hand of a groom, explaining *everything*. The unfortunate part is, that it has made the table a lady short, you see. It would oblige two gentlemen to sit together, which I daresay they would not mind, but it presents an odd appearance. So dear Elinor, that is Lady Draco, asked my cousin Neil if you should not be asked to make up the numbers.'

'What did his lordship say?' I asked.

'He said, dear, "I hope she knows which fork to use." And for your sake, I hope you do! He can be so very crushing. I myself am *never* certain which fork to use, although, dear knows, I have been using forks of all varieties for more years than I care to think of ... I watch the others, you know, and select the fork that seems generally chosen ... The late Professor, for his part, was quite unconcerned by such things! He did not care a rap which fork he used! He said that the function of the fork was simply to carry the food to the mouth, and the idea of *correctness*, as between one fork and another, was perfect nonsense! I do not know if I quite agree with him, though of course I pretended to at the time. It seems to open the doors to *anarchy*, does it not, if *all standards* are allowed to lapse? But dear cousin Neil, that is Lord Draco, to my mind, insists almost *too rigidly* on such things. It is as though he were a much older man, fallen into disciplined habits of thought, something I myself have never *even attempted* ... It goes, I fancy, with his concern for the poor factory workers, but *how* it goes I do not really see ...'

We took a great deal of trouble, Annie and I, to get me looking presentable. Eugénie appeared at my door, like a black crow; she nodded curtly when Annie showed her the dress we had chosen.

She wagged a talon at my hair, and hissed. Annie nodded reassuringly; my hair was in good hands.

I contemplated myself in the full-length glass, when I was dressed and ready, with a curious sensation. Below the neck I was a complete stranger: a fashionable young lady, in a very tight bodice, with bare shoulders and arms (far more of me was on public display than ever before in my life: it was terrible to think what effect it might have had on Findlay Nicholson). And above the neck? My face? It was the same face I had grown used to, and which seemed to have such different effects on people.

At least it had no effect on the Earl. He only noticed if my hat was aslant, and wondered if my table manners were worthy of his company.

At twenty-five minutes past six, Annie gave the ends of my hair a final twirl, and smiled encouragingly. At half-past six I stood nervously outside the drawing-room door, listening to a chorus of voices inside, and devoutly wishing I was back in my bed, having dinner by myself off the *porte-diner*.

I gulped, and went in.

The Countess was seated, very upright in an upright chair, wearing the diamonds which were as big as the lump on David Baillie's head. On a foot-stool at her feet sat a tall girl with light brown ringlets, with a face which was almost too sculpturally perfect to be made of flesh and blood. In an easy chair nearby sat a lady with a soldierly figure and a strong, soldierly face; she was talking in a soldierly voice to the Earl, who stood with his hands behind his back looking gravely down at her. Somewhere near the soldier-lady, like a tame but nervous bird, fluttered Mrs Forbes. Even further in the background, the Reverend Lancelot Barrow flapped his long white hands and cleared his throat, as though he wanted it to be clear that he was taking part in the party.

I was presented to Lady Arabella Paston, Miss Angelica Paston, and the Earl of Draco.

Lady Arabella noticed my curtsey with the minutest inclination of the head. She turned immediately back to the Earl, and continued her interrupted speech. I was dismissed. I was put in my place. I was of no account. I was not worth a word.

Miss Angelica Paston rose from her stool, like a remote god-

101

dess rising from mist or waves. Her gown and figure were superb; her neck was amazingly long and slim, and her shoulders like alabaster. She was a girl one could stare and stare at, in sheer admiration, in astonishment that a living creature could be so perfectly beautiful. In a low, serious voice she said, 'How do you do, Miss Drummond?' as though she were a doctor asking the question of a patient.

The Earl of Draco looked me up and down: not as Findlay Nicholson did; not quite as Eugénie did; more, perhaps, as my grandmother had done so often in George Square. He was examining me for faults, for an untied lace or a missing button, like a strict officer inspecting a recruit on parade. His face was severe, attentive; he wore a slight frown, not of open disapproval, but of serious concentration.

I wanted to stick out my tongue at him.

Without any word or gesture of greeting he turned back to Lady Arabella.

At no point in the evening that followed did I see the Earl smile, or Lady Arabella smile, or Angelica smile. They were the most unsmiling people I ever heard of. Even my grandfather, in the course of an evening, would suffer a sort of distortion of the face which was his smile; even old Carstairs: but not those three.

The next arrivals made up for them: Mr and Mrs Barstow of Ardmeggar. After paying his respects to the ladies, and welcoming the Earl home, Ardmeggar strode across the room, holding out his hand and shaking mine heartily. His kind, weatherbeaten face was crinkled into a smile of the greatest warmth. He was delighted that my ankle was recovered; he was delighted that I had started riding-lessons with Geordie Buchan: he was delighted with my gown.

'You're a different sight from the other day, my dear,' he said to me. 'Not that you didn't look charming sitting on my old horse.'

'But my face was dirty,' I said.

'Well, yes, now you mention it, your face was a *little* dirty.'

'In a comical way, like a clown?'

'A *little* like a clown. Yes, the thought did occur to me at the time – you were a *little* like a clown.'

Mrs Barstow came up at this moment, a big red lady with a face almost as weatherbeaten as his.

She said, 'When my husband came home the other evening, he talked for ninety minutes, without drawing breath, about a divine creature with, er, signs of recent contact with the hillside, sitting astride his horse —'

'Side-saddle!' said Ardmeggar.

'Archie! Shame on you! You're spoiling my story.'

'You're improving mine.'

They both laughed, and so did I.

Mrs Barstow went on, 'My husband, as I say, made himself quite a bore on the subject of this wondrous Gipsy he put up on his horse. What I wonder at now is, having seen you, why did he stop after only ninety minutes? In fact, I wonder that he came home at all. If I'd been a man, I'd have stayed wherever you were.'

My heart went out to the Barstows of Ardmeggar. They could have hobnobbed with the great aristocrats in the room, with whom they were evidently on close terms; they could have contemplated the sculptural, unreal beauty of Angelica Paston; but they devoted themselves to me, and made me feel happy and confident.

It was another lesson in the meaning of kindness.

Patterson, the mournful butler, mournfully announced General and Mrs Drummond. I gave a start at hearing my own name; but there are a great many Drummonds in Scotland. I felt no kin, certainly, to the scarlet, bustling pop-eyed little man who came into the drawing-room. He felt no kin to me, either. The people he wanted to talk to were the Earl, the Countess, and Lady Arabella. Mrs Drummond was a little taller than the General: a grey lady, with a defeated face; she looked as though she had been defeated by the General in a long series of decisive battles, and was now a prisoner of war, having lost all hope. Where he went in the room she followed; when he talked she listened; if she opened her mouth it was to agree.

Ardmeggar, the friendliest of men, was a little short in his greeting to the General. His wife thought so too, and glanced at him with eyebrows raised.

'He's let five farms to one grazier from Kincardine,' said Ardmeggar quietly. 'That's five families evicted who have been tenants of the estate for generations. And he only bought the place fifteen years ago.'

'He needs the rents,' said Mrs Barstow. 'The Highlanders don't pay the rents he needs.'

'No. Their farms are too small, and they won't change their ignorant old ways. All of us know that. It's good business to have one steading instead of five, and one rich tenant with money to invest in stock, instead of five on the edge of starvation.'

'Well, then—'

'Well, then. If I start behaving like that, to people who've been our tenants since the 'forty-five, much as we *would* like the rent, then kindly push me into the Draco and hold my head under the water . . . I'm sorry, my dear,' he turned to me, 'that's of no interest to you. D'you realize how honoured you are, to be taught your horsemanship by the great Geordie Buchan? If there was a riding-school up here, he'd be its chief instructor. If there was a pack of foxhounds, he'd be its huntsman.'

I began to reply that I loved both Geordie and the old pony Solomon, when Patterson, with his tragic air, announced Baillie of Inverlarig and Mr David Baillie.

'Madame not with them?' murmured Ardmeggar.

'Thrown into a fit of melancholia,' said his wife, 'by David's horse coming home by itself, the day this child arrived.'

'Oh dear,' I said, 'that is my fault.'

'No, it is not,' said Mrs Barstow briskly. 'It is tight-lacing and self-pity.'

It was unfortunate that I should have burst out laughing at just the moment that I was presented to Baillie of Inverlarig. He looked scarcely more intelligent than his son, but he had a stronger character. He bowed to me, and made a correct remark, but stared at me with a hostility that he did not attempt to conceal.

David stared at me, too; his eyes were wide and his mouth had fallen open. In hurrying across the room towards me, he knocked over a little table on which stood a lacquered box. The box burst open when it struck the floor, and embroidery things were strewn about the carpet.

No great damage was done; the mess was cleared up in an instant; but poor David was thrown into extremities of embarrassment, and was hardly able to bring out his stammered apologies.

I could not help noticing the different reactions to this unimportant disaster.

Ardmeggar said cheerily, 'Hold hard, old fellow!' and stooped at once to help pick up the scissors and thimbles and skeins of thread.

Mrs Barstow smiled kindly at David, then turned to talk to me about Solomon.

General Drummond glared contemptuously at David, snorted audibly, and turned back to Lady Arabella.

Mrs Drummond looked as though she would like to have snorted too, but did not know how.

Mrs Forbes twittered incoherently and fluttered to the scene of the accident; for they were her embroidery things.

The Reverend Lancelot Barrow flapped his hands; he started forward to help, then thought better of it and withdrew, as though recognizing a Christian obligation to help the unfortunate, but dreading to thrust himself into the limelight.

Miss Angelica Paston, without moving from her stool, stared at the scene with solemn concern; it appeared to sadden her, and to give grounds for grave moral reflections about the folly of mankind.

Lady Arabella glanced briefly across the room, then turned back to the Earl and their conversation.

The Earl did not even glance. For him the episode had not happened.

Baillie of Inverlarig was the only one who was really angry. Perhaps his gout hurt him.

The Countess called out, 'It does not matter the least bit, David. No harm has been done. I myself knocked over that table twice yesterday, with exactly the same result, so I know the box can take a few knocks. Come over here and tell me how your poor head feels today.'

Patterson announced Sir Francis and Lady Campbell of Drumlaw. I looked with interest at the parents of the animal-loving Georgina Campbell, friend of my friend. Sir Francis was a fine upstanding man, grown a little fat, with a heavy beard; he had the air of an ancient savage chief who enjoyed life, and wanted everybody else to enjoy it too. Lady Campbell was a little sprightly woman with quick gestures and a high, rapid voice. If the Countess was an eagle, and Mrs Forbes was a pet canary, then Lady Campbell was a robin. She flew about, greeting everybody with amiable chirrupings; Sir Francis strode about, booming affably, on the same errand. It chanced that they came together beside myself.

'I am so *very* pleased to meet you, my dear,' said Lady Campbell. 'Charlotte Long arrived with us today, and has been full of your praises. You had such a long talk, she says, at Gaultstower, and it was much the nicest thing that happened to her while she was there! We do hope Lady Draco can spare you to come over to us often. Georgina is agog to meet you, and Charlotte wants to see you again as soon as possible.'

'Has Georgina still got her pet piglet?' I asked.

Sir Francis laughed, a merry noise which rattled the great windows and threatened to upset the little table all over again. 'Children grow up, thank Heavens,' he said. 'The best butler we ever had gave notice when Georgina's pet owl bit him on the thumb.'

'Had he been teasing it?' I asked.

'I *think*,' said Lady Campbell, 'the owl was teasing him.'

In response to a stream of the most friendly questions, I told them that I did not yet ride, but was learning; that I had never been fishing, but hoped to; that I had never climbed a hill, but only fallen down one.

Two things I noticed while I was talking to the Campbells. One was that the other truly cheery and kind people present, the Barstows of Ardmeggar, seemed on oddly distant terms with the Campbells. Ardmeggar was too direct a person to conceal his feelings; his dislike of Sir Francis was unmistakable. I thought it most strange, as I liked them both so much. The other curious thing was that, while I was talking of the things I hoped to do, I found Angelica Paston's eye upon me; she was looking at me intently, and listening to all that I said. I suppose she deplored all the active and brainless things I so much longed for, the empty hillside, the wind on my face, the surge of power of a fine horse: preferring her studies and music and painting. What surprised me was that she was interested in me at all.

Patterson came to murmur something to the Countess. She thanked him, and said to the room at large, 'I am afraid the numbers will be wrong after all. Billy Mainwaring was supposed to arrive here this afternoon, but he has still not come. We will not wait any longer. Shall we go in!'

There was a spare female; it was me. I sat between Mrs Forbes and David Baillie. I hardly spoke at all, throughout the enormous and complicated meal, since David had lost the power of speech, and Mrs Forbes had lost the power of stopping herself from speaking. It was restful, but not amusing. As to the problem of forks, I adopted Mrs Forbes's notion, and tried to remember also what Eugénie had taught me; by being watchful and careful I did nothing to arouse the Earl's contempt.

'How miserable for you, dear,' said Mrs Forbes, 'to be sat next to me, though to be sure your loss is my gain. Wine? Oh no indeed, I thank you, it goes straight to my head, and I talk more nonsense even than usual, if you can believe such a thing possible ... Was I not right about dear Angelica? Have you ever seen so perfect a face? And see how her head is set upon her neck, and her neck on her shoulders! I do not believe the sculptors of ancient Greece ever achieved such perfection in their marbles. Of course her father was an outstandingly handsome man, George Paston, most eminent, at one time Senior Steward of the Jockey club, not a Scotchman, you know, but a Lincolnshire family. He was most tragically killed in the hunting field, with the Duke of Rutland's hounds at Belvoir, oh, quite a dozen years ago. I forget how many winners of the Derby he owned. Perhaps none! I am sadly ignorant about turf matters, as, indeed, about everything else! Are you fond of racing, dear? I have never been to the races! Not once! I would be frightened of the pickpockets, and cutpurses, and bravos ...'

David Baillie, meanwhile, alternated between struggling with his knife and fork, and staring at me. I saw his father scowling at him. For a man who suffered from gout, Inverlarig drank a great deal of wine.

Mrs Forbes returned to the subject of my misfortune in sitting next to herself. 'It is all Sir Hannibal Mainwaring's fault, of course. He was expected this afternoon, to stay for a week or two. And he has not come! And there has been no word! We all hope that nothing dreadful has occurred, as he is a great favourite here. Only look at dear Angelica's face when she turns her head to listen! She is worthy of the brush of a Winterhalter. Her cousin you know, is the Earl of Benmore, quite a young man. I do not think he is *quite* as generous to his aunt and cousin as he should be. Life is difficult for widows, as I have reason to know. But I have heard dear Lady Arabella say that his expenses are dreadfully heavy. He is another racing man, you know, like her late husband, and it is so difficult, Lady Arabella says, to get racehorses to pay . . .'

I glanced at Lady Arabella, sitting opposite. She was superbly dressed and bejewelled; if she was kept short of money by her noble nephew, she showed no signs of it. I caught her eye, since, to my surprise, she was looking at me. General Drummond was sitting next to her, talking rapidly in a low voice. He too looked in my direction as he spoke. They both looked away from my eyes. They were talking about me; there was no possible doubt of it. They disliked and despised me; there was no doubt of that either.

After dinner, Angelica played the piano. Even I could appreciate that she played very well indeed, with a virtuosity far out of sight of my own incompetent strummings of the metrical psalms. The Earl stood by her, turning the pages of her music, as solemn as a post.

Strangely enough, although Angelica's playing of the difficult music was brilliant, the effect was dull. It was like a mechanical piano, playing the notes with wonderful accuracy, but without feeling. But we all sat listening in the most utter and reverential silence. All eyes were fixed on the beautiful pianist, except David Baillie's, which were fixed on me. It was a little embarrassing, because it was so very obvious. To avoid his eye, I let mine wander round the room, while sitting as quiet and attentive as the rest. I looked at the Countess. She was looking at Angelica, of course; she wore the slightest of smiles, which barely lifted the corners of her mouth. She glanced at me. The corners of her mouth went suddenly up, and into her clear grey eyes came a gleam of the purest mischief.

It was a look of complicity. It was fellow-feeling. She wanted to laugh. Angelica's playing bored her! The Earl's solemnity bored her! Once again I was seeing, as I had seen in the parlour at George Square, into the heart of another rebel.

I fought to keep a perfectly straight face, but I knew she could see the laughter I was concealing.

Mrs Forbes and the Reverend Lancelot Barrow led the applause.

Afterwards, Angelica and the Earl had a long conversation, in low voices, in a corner, their faces just as serious as before.

And then at last Sir Hannibal Mainwaring did arrive, in day clothes and riding boots. Almost everybody called him 'Billy', including Mrs Forbes, although both Pastons called him 'Sir Hannibal', and the Earl called him 'Mainwaring'.

He was a year or two younger than the Earl; in person he resembled a male version of Mrs Forbes, being small and plump and round-faced; he had the happiest air of anybody I ever saw.

'I am very sorry to be so late, Lady Draco,' he said, 'but when you hear my story you will pity rather than censure. To understand all is to forgive all. It is a tale that would wring tears from a stone. I was arrested and put in prison!'

'For talking too much, Billy?' asked the Countess, smiling broadly.

'For not talking enough! I was confused with a notorious brigand! I was pausing in a, ah, well, a kind of tavern, near Callander, entirely with the object of baiting my horse, when I felt on my shoulder a heavy hand, and a zealous officer of the constabulary proclaimed that I was an impudent malefactor called ... I can hardly bring myself to say the words ... called Fat Menteith.'

There was a burst of laughter, in which the Earl, and Lady Arabella, and Angelica all forbore to join.

'Do I *look*,' cried Sir Hannibal pathetically, 'like an impudent malefactor called Fat Menteith?'

The Countess looked at him gravely. 'Yes,' she said.

Sir Hannibal coming into the room was like the sun coming

into a room. Everything brightened. The party had become somewhat muted: perhaps drowsy: distinctly insipid. The Countess looked very tired; Mrs Forbes was pouring a twittering saga at Lady Arabella; the Earl was off in a corner in sombre colloquy with Angelica; Mrs Drummond, her eyes on her husband, was desperately making conversation with the Reverend Lancelot Barrow; there were areas of silence; I had been wondering if I could excuse myself, on the grounds that my ankle was paining me, which was true. Now all at once there was laughter and gaiety. I could see that Sir Hannibal was a favourite; I could see why. He had the friendly directness of Lord Cricklade and Barstow of Ardmeggar, and the drollery of Lord Caerlaverock; and he laughed at himself like Mrs Forbes. He was no beauty but he was a dear.

I scarcely spoke to him, as he was surrounded by old friends; but he smiled at me across the room, and called out that he hoped I would come fishing with him. I said I would be pleased to, and it was true.

Lady Arabella glanced fleetingly at us both. Angelica looked at me with serious wonderment. The Earl did not notice the exchange. David Baillie turned scarlet, and looked desperately jealous. General Drummond snorted. The Reverend Lancelot Barrow flapped his hands, as though imitating long white fish, new-caught, thumping about in the bottom of a boat. Mrs Forbes began to tell an inconsequential story of a fishing expedition once embarked upon by the late Professor.

Mrs Barstow said, 'You'll have an amusing time on the river with Billy, dear – do go if you can.'

Then Inverlarig said he must get back to his wife, and Lady Campbell said they must get back to Georgina and Charlotte, and the party was at an end.

'Remember, dear,' Lady Campbell chirruped to me, 'we are counting on seeing a great deal of you. You will be doing us nothing but a favour, if you come, to keep those two girls amused.'

'As a substitute for the piglet,' I said.

Sir Francis thought this the best and funniest remark he had ever heard, and I was more than ever frightened for the windows.

'G-goodbye,' said David Baillie in a strangled voice, once more as red as a beetroot, under his father's baleful eye.

'Courage, Kirstie,' whispered Mrs Barstow.

'She's got it,' said Ardmeggar.

It seemed to me that I needed it; but that I had good friends on my side.

During the next few days I explored, both inside the castle and out. There was much of the castle I did not see – much that almost nobody ever saw – but at least I no longer got lost between the Chinese room and the Countess's boudoir, or between the drawing-room and my own bedroom. I commenced my duties as the Reverend Lancelot Barrow's assistant in compiling the new catalogue for the library. I went daily, and sometimes twice daily, to Geordie Buchan for riding lessons. I sat with the Countess a little, and Mrs Forbes a little, and by myself in my bedroom a lot.

I saw little of the other members of the household. Sir Hannibal was constantly off to the river; he came back, dripping and beaming, in the evening, with both trout and salmon. He did not repeat his invitation to me; I was puzzled and saddened by this, as it seemed unlike him to say something he did not mean, or break what was almost a promise. Angelica Paston was often out with her easel, though never venturing far from the castle or from the phaeton in which Hamish or the Earl took her out. The Earl was often with her, though often in his office, interviewing factors and tenants (so the Reverend Lancelot Barrow told me), or inspecting the accounts, or making other arrangements about his estates. He did not care for fishing, it seemed, and there was no other form of sport in midsummer.

Mrs Forbes was much with the Countess, more with Lady Arabella. I could not imagine what those two had to say to each other, or what they had in common, as they seemed so very different; but they spent hours in murmuring conversation.

I was surprised also to see Mrs Forbes in deep conversation with Eugénie. It appeared that she understood Eugénie's hissing, which I had not yet learned to do.

After ten days Geordie Buchan introduced me to a taller and

younger pony than Solomon. He was a dun Connemara, called Malachi, and he pawed the ground and blew gently into my face when I patted him. Another groom, a gloomy man called Wattie Dewar, said it was madness to put me up on Malachi when I had been riding for only ten days.

But Geordie grinned, and stood firm. 'Miss Kirstie is what they ca' a natural equestrienne,' he said, making the long word twice as long as he rolled it out with relish. 'She'll hae a seat like a stane an' hands like an angel. It's in the blude, I'm thinkin'.'

'Her leddyship wull be unco' fashed when the lassie kills hersel',' said Wattie in a graveyard voice.

'Hoot toots,' said Geordie cheerfully, and helped me into the saddle.

I walked Malachi round, to get the feel of his mouth, and to get him used to me; he broke into a sharp, invigorating trot the moment I touched him – touched him no harder than I would have patted a baby's hand – on the quarters with my whip. I shouted happily to Wattie. Malachi thought I was calling to him. He broke smoothly into a canter which bore me up and down like the waves of the sea. I had not cantered before; I loved it; I sat snug down in the saddle, moving with Malachi, keeping the snaffle-rein tight but not the curb-rein, as Geordie had taught me, and steering the glorious pony in circles and figures-of-eight. Round and round bouncily we went, with Geordie grinning like a gargoyle in the middle of the paddock.

I do not know what it was that made Malachi buck. Geordie afterwards said that perhaps he was stung by a wasp. If that was it, I do not at all blame Malachi. He began to jump high walls which were not there, and kick out furiously behind at enemies that were not there either, while still performing a sort of prancing canter; I tried to sit very firmly down in the saddle, and I took hold of the mane so as not to jab his mouth, but in the end he bucked me off. I landed on all fours, with my hat on my nose, undamaged except in dignity, but startled and annoyed.

Geordie caught Malachi and led him back to me.

'Ye did verra weel to bide as lang as ye did,' he said. 'Up wi' ye the noo.'

I was to get on again? Now at once? My heart sank a moment:

but Malachi seemed quiet, and Geordie said that from his point of view, as well as mine, I must without fail mount at once, unless I had broken my head.

I rode round a few more times, walking and trotting, without mishap. I had the feeling Malachi was ashamed of himself, and determined to be on his best behaviour.

Wattie Dewar's face wore a look of funereal gloom; but Geordie said, 'Ye'll nae lairn tae ride wi'oot a fa'.' So I regarded it as simply part of my equestrian education.

I walked back to the castle with my hat at a deliberate slant. But I straightened it before I crossed the drawbridge.

The library was as large as an Edinburgh kirk, and quite as solemn in atmosphere. Although there was no one else by, the Reverend Lancelot Barrow and I always talked in hushed tones, as though the ghosts of antique scholars would otherwise be distracted.

Most of the books had been collected in the eighteenth century. They were very dusty. A great number were French and Italian, procured by people on the Grand Tour. Shelves and shelves of these foreign books had uniform, resplendent leather bindings, heavily tooled with gold, with a great golden coat of arms on the front. The Reverend Lancelot Barrow told me (in a respectful murmur) that all these uniform bindings had been done for a private library, by some rich and learned eighteenth-century collector. In the middle of the shield of the golden arms a leopard pranced, with a flower in its mouth, which I thought charming. Inside all the books, book-plates were pasted, with a different coat of arms; this one involved chevrons and half-moons, with unicorns each side, and an Earl's coronet above. These were the arms of the Stewarts of Glendraco, Earls of Draco. I preferred the prancing leopard with the flower in its mouth.

The higher shelves were reached by a beautiful little spiral staircase, of polished wood, which could be trundled from shelf to shelf on castors. The late Earl had invented a different kind of ladder, which was easier to move about; but his chaplain fell off it and broke his leg, so the old spiral staircase was brought out again and polished up. The Reverend Lancelot Barrow had no head for heights, so it was horrid for him to stand at the top of the spiral staircase to see the books on the upper shelves; I accordingly did this, while he stood below and wrote down the names. Every book had to be taken out, and its title-page examined, which made me extremely dirty. This was, perhaps, another reason why the Reverend Lancelot Barrow preferred me to do it.

We talked freely while we worked; or rather, he talked, and I often listened. Like Mrs Forbes, he was a distant relation of the Earl, but even more widely separated from him in fortune. His father had been a clergyman also, very poor, with a large family all of girls except this one son. The late Earl had been appealed to, and had paid for the son's education at Westminster and Cambridge, and then used influence to place him in a curacy. The old Countess had brought him to Glendraco. He was immeasurably grateful – he often said so – but pained that his opinion was not more often sought, as he was a man of wide reading and information, and would, he said, have repaid a little of the charity of Glendraco by good advice in the running of the estates. When he was lecturing me, on any of the thousand topics he knew all about, he seemed much older than his thirty years; when he unconsciously revealed his helplessness, and his resentment, he seemed much younger. I grew to respect him in some ways, and to feel sorry for him in others; but he was difficult to *like* very much, if only because he was so excessively clean.

During the afternoon after my fall, I was on top of the spiral library steps, as usual, with Mr Barrow, at the foot, noting the names in a ledger. I was struggling to hold a heavy and awkward volume of engravings of mythical animals, and struggling also to pronounce a long Italian title. Preoccupied by these struggles, I did not hear or see anyone come in. I was startled to hear a voice below me, speaking not in Mr Barrow's hushed tones, but firmly and loudly.

The Earl said, 'This is most useful work, Barrow. An accurate catalogue is long overdue.'

'It is a considerable labour, my lord,' said Mr Barrow. 'Quite Herculean.' He added handsomely, 'I am very greatly aided by Miss Drummond.'

'I am grateful to Miss Drummond,' said the Earl. 'I hope she will be careful not to fall off the steps.'

He glanced up at me as he spoke. On account of the dirtiness of the books, I was wearing an old dress that Annie Simpson had found for me, and I had a piece of stuff bound round my head, like a fishwife, to keep the dust out of my hair; my sleeves were rolled up, my hands and arms were black, and there was doubtless quite a lot of dirt on my face. I looked like a scullery-maid in the midst of cleaning a boiler. If any other man as handsome as himself (in spite of his dreary solemnity he was undoubtedly very handsome, since he was the image of his grandmother) – if any other man had been looking at me, I should have regretted exceedingly the way I looked. Since it was he, I did not care. If I disgusted him, it was no more than his humourless arrogance disgusted me.

He hoped, did he, that I would be careful not to fall off the steps? From his expression, I did not think he minded whether I fell off the steps or not.

He looked away from me at once, and began discussing with Mr Barrow the merit of moving some of the larger books to the lower shelves.

I waited patiently, clutching the large awkward book of mythical beasts.

The Earl looked up at me again. He said, 'Speaking of falls, Miss Drummond, I understand that the dun pony threw you this morning.'

'Malachi? Yes, Geordie thought he was stung by a wasp.'

'He is too strong for a rider of your inexperience. You are not to ride him again.'

'But, sir—'

'Since you are making free use of animals in my stable, you must allow me the privilege of deciding which ones you ride. You are probably not aware that a curb bit in the hands of a beginner can do permanent damage to a horse's mouth.'

'I see, sir, that you are thinking of the pony.'

'In part, certainly. The owner of any animal has an obligation to it. There is another aspect. Since my grandmother, for reasons of her own, introduced you into my house, I am in a measure responsible for your safety. As long as you are riding my horses, you will ride the grey pony Solomon. You will not damage him, nor he you.'

He turned and left the library, his face as grave as ever.

My first feeling was fury, my second helplessness.

Wattie Dewar had informed on us – on Malachi and Geordie and me.

As long as I rode the Earl's horses, it must be fat old Solomon I rode. Then, to be sure, I must ride someone else's horses. I *did* have friends. They *might* help me. With this thought I still felt furious but not quite so helpless.

'I did not know that you had had a fall, Miss Drummond,' said the Reverend Lancelot Barrow in a shocked voice. 'You must on no account have a serious accident, as long as I require your assistance with this catalogue.'

But for days, in spite of my fine idea, I saw none of the people I thought were my friends – not the Barstows of Ardmeggar nor the Campbells of Drumlaw, nor David Baillie of Inverlarig: any of whom, I thought, might lend me a horse to ride. So I rode Solomon, and Geordie Buchan was as cross as I was. Geordie was very outspoken to Wattie Dewar, using words I had never heard before, even from the Edinburgh fishwives; but Wattie kept an air of gloomy self-satisfaction, as though he had done an unpleasant but necessary duty.

He and my grandfather, I thought, would have got on well together.

Geordie climbed up on to a big Welsh cob, and we went for long rides up the glen towards its head, and down the glen, past the village of Balinburn; we rode for hours, yet never crossed the march of the estate. Since I was compelled to ride Solomon, Geordie addressed himself to perfecting my hands and seat: for, he said, if they were truly right, I could ride a thoroughbred over the Melton oxers.

We passed, one day, the phaeton in which Angelica Paston went out with her paints and easel. It stood at the bend in the road from which, the Countess had told me, the castle was most often painted. It was being painted from there again; Miss

116

Paston's easel was set up by the roadside. She sat on a folding stool, wearing a very large hat, intent on her work; no sunbeam was ever allowed to reach her face, which remained as pale and perfectly beautiful as marble. The Earl sat on the ground nearby with a book. He was reading it aloud to her as she painted. I wondered idly what the book was; I had the feeling that, if they both enjoyed it, I should find it hard work.

They both looked up as Geordie and I rode by. I made sure that my back was very straight, and everything just as it should be: and although Solomon wanted to stop to talk to the coach-horse, I would not let him, but drove him on.

Miss Paston gave me a long, inscrutable look; and I wondered once again what it was about me that made her stare so. The Earl also looked at me intently, searching for faults. When we were fifty yards beyond them, I glanced back. The Earl had returned to his book but Angelica Paston was still looking at me.

Further on, we saw ahead of us a little pony-phaeton, a vehicle like a sewing-basket on four small wheels, pulled by a fat Shetland pony (whom Solomon detested) called Rob Roy. Someone in a black shawl was sitting in the phaeton, and a man was standing on the roadside beside it. Faces turned towards us. The man immediately disappeared, as though he had jumped down a well at the edge of the road.

We left the road, to follow a green track down to the river, but I had seen, to my great astonishment, who the driver of the pony-phaeton was.

'Does Eugénie often drive herself?' I asked Geordie.

'The French leddy? No – she's ower auld an' rheumaticky. But she'll hae been a grand whip langsyne, an' wad dreeve the bairns in yon fish-bass tae Ardmeggar and sichlike. Did ye ken the mon, Miss Kirstie? I cudnae see sae far wi' these auld ees.'

'Yes,' I said. 'It was Dandie McKillop.'

'Ma Goad. Yon's a gey strange coople tae be fettlin' at the roadside.'

So I thought too – a very strange couple. And Dandie McKillop had run away, not wishful to be seen talking to Eugénie.

I felt a cold finger of alarm in the small of my back.

*

At dinner the Countess announced a picnic party. We were to go, on horseback or in carriages, to Meiklejohn's Leap, where a little river called the Crombie Burn curled below a startling cliff. It was another place often painted, which should suit Angelica Paston. There was famous trout-fishing in the burn, which should suit Sir Hannibal Mainwaring. It was on a remote part of the estate, which the Earl had not recently visited, so that going there suited him. It was a delightful ride, which suited me. It was not at all far from Drumlaw House, which suited Lady Campbell and Georgina and Charlotte Long, who were bidden to join us. A note had also gone to David Baillie, asking him too, but no reply had come back; it was not certain if his father's gout and his mother's melancholia would allow him to come to the picnic.

Mrs Forbes was in high excitement; she told everyone who would listen long stories of picnics of the past, in which they had got caught in torrential rain, or she forgot the food, or they got benighted and lost on the way home. What was so nice about her stories, was that the great joke was always some ridiculous mistake made by herself. What was not so good about them was that they went on too long.

The morning of the picnic was brilliantly fair. A wagonette was driven into the courtyard, and loaded with table tops, and trestles, and small chairs, and linen, and hampers of provisions, and bottles of wine in tubs of ice: above all of which perched two parlourmaids and two footmen. At this stage Lady Arabella declared that she would not come, as she feared a headache from the sun. Angelica immediately said that she would stay at home with her mother. A look passed between Lady Arabella and Mrs Forbes. Mrs Forbes said that Angelica must on no account stay behind: she, Mrs Forbes, would stay and keep Lady Arabella company.

'I wish for you to go, Angelica,' said Lady Arabella.

'Indeed, dear, you should,' twittered Mrs Forbes, 'for just think! If you don't go, we shall never have the joy of seeing your painting of the gentleman's leap – I forget his name – was it Carmichael? There was a Doctor Carmichael at Aberdeen, an associate of the late Professor's, a man of the greatest piety. I cannot picture him *leaping*. I do not think that the place you talk of can be named after him . . .'

Sir Hannibal Mainwaring set off alone in a dog-cart, on account of taking his fishing-rod, and wading-boots, and creel, and tackle. The Earl set off on horseback, leaving early because he was making a detour to visit a tenant farmer. The Countess and Angelica went off in a carriage and pair, with Hamish in front driving, and Wattie Dewar behind. Geordie Buchan, on his cob, led Solomon to the courtyard; we passed the carriage almost at once, and presently caught up with the dog-cart.

I trotted along beside Sir Hannibal, who gave as usual the impression of being in the seventh heaven of happiness. Geordie's cob bucketed along some way behind.

Sir Hannibal said, 'Now at last, Miss Christina, I think we may plan your fishing lesson.'

'Well, I had been hoping for it,' I said, 'but I had lost hope.'

'I'm very sorry,' he said. 'I am truly. It was not of my doing. Did you think I'd forgotten?'

'Of course I did. Or else that you had changed your mind.'

'No! How could you suppose that? The fact of the matter is . . . I'm sure I shouldn't be telling you this, but I feel I must clear my name of the dreadful suspicions you have been harbouring. *Forget*? Change my *mind*? Oh no, no no no. The fact of the matter is, I was acting on orders from my host.'

'From Lord Draco?'

'The same. He said he wished me, most particularly, *not* to take you fishing. As his guest, I could hardly seek you out the next minute, and ask you to come fishing, could I?'

'No,' I admitted. 'But why did he . . . ?'

'He mentioned something unspeakable called a library catalogue. Personally, I have never even *seen* a library catalogue. I never *want* to see one. Since one of the wretched things has kept you away from the river-bank, I declare a lifelong *hatred* of library catalogues. All of them, indifferently. They are my enemy. I give them fair warning. Any library catalogue that has the temerity to cross my path, I shall . . . I shall . . .'

'Burn?'

'Too good for it.'

'I don't think,' I said, puzzled, 'the library catalogue can be the real reason—'

'Of course it isn't,' said Sir Hannibal.

'Well, then—?'

He reined in his horse to walk. He looked round conspiratorially, and even peeped under the high seat of the dog-cart, to make sure there was no eavesdropper lurking there.

There was nobody within earshot. Except for Geordie Buchan, thirty yards behind, there was nobody even in sight.

'He's jealous,' said Sir Hannibal dramatically.

'Oh no,' I said immediately. 'He's not interested in me at all.'

'If not, why not? Who could fail to be?'

He smiled at me with such affectionate warmth that I nearly fell off Solomon.

'Well,' I said at last, getting a grip of myself and of my pony, 'he can fail to be. He only looks at me to see if my hat is on straight.'

'It is perfectly straight, dear Miss Christina.'

'Thank you, Sir Hannibal.'

'I wish you would call me Billy.'

'I could not possibly.'

'Everybody does.'

'Everybody is not in my awkward position.'

'I understand. Then, to avoid fuss, call me Billy in private.'

'N-no. I think that would be a little – deceitful, as well as improper.'

'Oh dear. I hoped we should become close friends very quickly, but I see we must go on by gradual stages. I do think it is a pity, if you like someone very much immediately, not to be great friends immediately.'

I agreed with him completely, but I did not think I should say so. Instead, to change the subject, I said, 'Lord Draco is interested not in me, but in Angelica Paston.'

'Why?'

'She is so very beautiful, and accomplished.'

'Yes,' he acknowledged. 'And she is also, in my opinion . . .' He looked round again, his face solemn and watchful. Assured that there was still no eavesdropper, he said, 'Angelica Paston is a bore.'

I laughed with delight. I could not help it. It was ill-natured, and uncharitable; she had done me no harm; she was perfectly polite to me, the few times she spoke to me; but I was enchanted that Sir Hannibal said she was a bore.

We came down on to the Crombie Burn, half a mile downstream from Meiklejohn's Leap, which was hidden beyond a bluff.

'This is where we start fishing,' said Sir Hannibal. 'And we move gently upstream towards our luncheon. By that manoeuvre, you see, the trout don't glimpse us. The sight even of you will startle a shy fish, though if they had any sense they would be forming crowds to look at you.'

I jumped off Solomon (I needed no help), and with the reins looped over my arm helped Sir Hannibal to unload the dog-cart. Geordie Buchan, riding up, agreed wistfully that it was a grand place for trout. He put a rope halter on Solomon, over the bridge, and tied him to the back of the dog-cart. Then he started up the path towards the rendezvous, leading the harness-horse and his cob one in each hand. He looked back over his shoulder longingly; he wanted to come fishing too.

Sir Hannibal put up his rod, and began to teach me how to cast a fly. At first I found it impossibly difficult; the line landed in loops about my head, or the hooks caught in the heather behind. Then suddenly I got the knack, and was hugely pleased with myself.

'No one,' said Sir Hannibal, 'has ever picked it up so quick. Kirstie, you're a marvel.'

'Should you call me that?' I asked dubiously.

'No. Do you mind?'

'No,' I admitted; and we both laughed.

We worked our way up the bank of the burn, which was a succession of dark-red, peaty pools, punctuated by furious little rapids and waterfalls. It was utterly quiet except for the gurgle of water and the cry of birds. There was no sign of the rest of the party. Geordie by now was far away, at the place of the picnic, helping to unload the wagonette and set up the tables.

We rounded the bluff, and came in sight of Meiklejohn's Leap. It was most grand and impressive – a very steep slope, not far out of the vertical, of fissured and broken rocks, falling almost into the burn. Near its foot there was a patch of smooth sward near the burn, on which the picnic was being made ready. The horses were all tethered some way off.

I continued to cast my flies assiduously where Sir Hannibal told me to. To my intense excitement, I felt several times a nip, or snatch, but was too slow pulling my line tight; Sir Hannibal said it was the most difficult trick in this sort of fishing, and that I would only learn it by trying.

I liked him more and more with each yard we walked. He was right, I thought – why should not people who liked each other very much immediately be great friends immediately? He *was* plump and pink and small and undistinguished looking: but one less and less noticed that, and more and more felt the happiness and sweetness of his nature.

We worked our way almost to the sward of the picnic. A large pool swept smooth from broad rapids to a narrow waterfall. I cast my flies to its head, and was relieved to see them fall not far from where I meant.

'Beautiful,' said Sir Hannibal. 'You might have been doing it for years.'

As my flies came rapidly downstream towards me, I felt a violent tug. I tightened, more by instinct than judgement, and a silver fish leaped from the water, and crashed back in a shower of spray, on the end of my line! I felt it rush madly about the pool, bending the frail rod almost double.

'Billy!' I screamed.

He was dancing on the bank beside me, trying to tell me what to do.

Something, even in the midst of my excitement, made me glance up. The Earl stood there, not five yards away, holding his horse.

Presently Sir Hannibal netted out my fish, which he said was a monster, a record for the burn. I felt most joyful and triumphant; my glee was not dampened even by the chilly fixed eye of the Earl.

'There, Draco!' cried Sir Hannibal, holding up the fish and grinning all over his face. 'What do you think of that?'

'I think,' said the Earl, in a tone of cold fury, turning from Sir Hannibal to me, 'that you will refrain from addressing my friends as though they were your social equals.'

SIX

Sir Hannibal's jaw dropped. I felt myself blushing furiously.

The Earl turned and led his horse away.

Sir Hannibal and I looked at each other. I could feel my cheeks burning; I was near tears of pure rage.

'I apologize,' said Sir Hannibal quietly.

'*You*? What have *you*—?'

'I apologise for the shocking manners of my social equal. Draco should be horsewhipped for talking to you like that. And now I don't know what to do. I do not want to continue under Draco's roof, as I do not think it right to accept hospitality from someone one has come to dislike. But I do not want to go away, either.'

'Why?'

'I don't want to leave you.'

'Oh,' I said. 'I hope you don't go.'

'Do you mean that, Kirstie?'

'Yes! Yes, I do mean it! Please stay, if you can bear to.'

He gave a lop-sided smile.

A merciful diversion arrived, a carriage containing Lady Campbell, and Charlotte Long, and a girl I did not know, who was obviously Georgina.

I had a happy reunion with Charlotte; we embraced each other; she exclaimed at my riding-habit, and I pointed ruefully at little Solomon tethered some way off.

'But he is sweet,' said Charlotte.

'Yes,' I said, 'he is very sweet, but he is also very old, and fat, and small, and slow—'

'All those would be good points to me,' said Charlotte. 'But here is Georgina, my dearest friend, that I told you about!'

Georgina took after her mother; she was like a little cheerful bird, with quick movements, a quick voice, a quick smile; she had a most infectious laugh, which started high and went down the scale, and ended in a gurgle, like the song of a chaffinch. Like her parents, she was instantly likeable. Her hair was dark and she had a high colouring, so that she was in amusing contrast to Charlotte, who was so fair.

'I was very sorry to hear,' I said to her, 'that you no longer have a pet piglet.'

'I miss him dreadfully,' said Georgina. 'But, you see, the point I had not taken into account, is that piglets grow up into pigs! And he grew into the largest boar-pig you ever saw in your life! He was as big as a cow! And, you know, that is not the same thing at all as a piglet the size of a puppy, with freckles on his nose.'

'Did he really have freckles?'

'The most adorable freckles,' confirmed Charlotte, 'as though his nursemaid had let him out into the sun. And *what* is it like at Glendraco, Kirstie? Is it terrifying? Do you like Draco, who frightens me into fits? And have many more lords fallen in love with you?'

We sat down in a little circle on the grass – Georgina as lively as a sparrow, Charlotte so gentle and pretty; and myself. And in Georgina's high spirits and ridiculous stories about her various pets, and in Charlotte's pleasure at seeing me again, I gradually recovered from the sick anger I felt at the way the Earl had spoken to me.

Sir Hannibal now was deep in talk with the Earl, which surprised me a good deal, after what had just happened. They were walking slowly up and down the bank of the burn. Sir Hannibal looked to me more serious than usual, the Earl exactly as serious as usual. Sir Hannibal glanced at me as he spoke. The Earl, solemn as an owl, glanced at me as he listened. Once more I knew I was being talked about.

'Is Billy Mainwaring in love with you, Kirstie?' asked Charlotte, smiling mischievously.

'Oh no,' I said. 'He is only my fishing tutor. I do not sink as low as baronets.'

'Be careful what you say to a baronet's daughter,' said Georgina, laughing.

'Billy would not be sinking so very low,' said Charlotte. 'He is amazingly rich.'

'Indecently rich, Papa says,' said Georgina. 'It is a pity he is not better looking, because he is so gay and amusing, as well as rich.'

'He is not *evil* looking,' said Charlotte.

'He is nice looking,' I said, 'I mean, in the way of looking nice.'

'But still,' said Georgina, 'It would be better if he was tall and more dignified and more striking and not so fat and with a more classic face—'

'More like Lord Draco,' said Charlotte.

'Yes,' agreed Georgina. 'Much more like Draco.'

'I infinitely prefer Sir Hannibal's looks to Lord Draco's,' I said.

'That is lucky,' laughed Georgina. 'We shall not be after the same objectives.'

'I am not after anybody,' I said.

But then I remembered Lord Cricklade, who was never so very far from my thoughts; and I thought that perhaps I had lied.

My head spun with memories of that glorious drive in the gig; I saw his kind face, and his cheerful voice, and felt the strong dry pressure of his hand on mine. The contrast between him and the Earl of Draco was so very dramatic. I missed Lord Cricklade the more, because he was so different from Draco, and I hated Lord Draco the more, because he was so very different from Cricklade. I found myself longing for Cricklade, with an emotion like home-sickness; and my longing was so keen that I felt most unwelcome tears pricking at my eyelids.

'What is it, Kirstie?' asked Charlotte softly.

'The smoke from the fire,' I said.

Someone had indeed lit a small fire of rowan-branches in a circle of stones fetched from the burn; Geordie Buchan was tending it; I suppose the servants were boiling a kettle for tea.

'Is poor little David Baillie coming today?' Georgina asked me.

'It depends on gout and melancholia,' I said.

'He has gout?' said Charlotte, startled. 'At his age?'

'No,' said Georgina, 'but he has melancholia. Your horrible fascinating friend has bewitched him.'

'That,' said Charlotte, 'is sinking even lower than baronets.'

'It is very disagreeable,' I said. 'I am sorry for him, but he stares, with his mouth open . . .'

'I expect that is why his father forbade him to come,' said Georgina. 'Inverlarig is very cross with you, Kirstie.'

'I didn't think he liked me very much,' I said, 'but I thought that was just his gout.'

'Oh no, gout only makes it worse. He has mismanaged his affairs dreadfully, Papa says, so he insists that David must marry money. Have you any money, Kirstie?'

'About sevenpence,' I said.

'That would *not* be enough to save the Inverlarig estate.'

'I can't see poor David marrying an heiress,' said Charlotte. 'But I don't see how he is going to get through life if he doesn't. You should not encourage him, Kirstie.'

'I *don't* encourage him.'

'You wrote to him,' said Georgina accusingly, 'saying you hoped to see him again soon. He carries your letter against his heart. But he took it out and showed it to me, because we are supposed to be childhood friends.'

'But,' I began to protest, 'I had to send him a polite reply . . .'

They both laughed, Charlotte with her little high squeak, and Georgina going down the scale and ending in her infectious gurgle.

The other carriage arrived, at last, with the Countess and Angelica. Hamish and Wattie Dewar were both very red in the face, but Angelica was as palely perfect as ever.

Luncheon was ready almost immediately – not much different from a meal in the dining-room at Glendraco, in the way of silver and glass and linen and wine and hovering servants. I thought a picnic might be eating the leg of a cold chicken, in one's fingers, sitting on the ground on a hill-top; but that would not have suited the dignity of the Earl of Draco. It was all cold food, of course, and chilled white wine, but it was as formal and elaborate as a banquet.

Suddenly, from the little fire, a single hot silver dish was brought to the table by a footman. I wondered what it might be: something special, perhaps, for the Countess. But it was set in front of me. On it was my trout, fried in oatmeal! There was applause! They clapped! And Sir Hannibal solemnly proposed a toast to my first trout. I laughed, and felt myself blushing at being the centre of so much attention. The Countess gave me one of her warmest and widest smiles, which came so seldom, and which I valued so much. Sir Hannibal raised his glass to me again, with that affectionate look which had touched me before. Lady Campbell chirruped excitedly, and Georgina and Charlotte made a birdlike clamour of astonishment, for none of them had heard about my triumph. The Earl glanced at me gravely, and Angelica gave me one of those long, intent looks which I found so puzzling and unnerving.

I guessed it was all Geordie Buchan's idea. Much later, when luncheon was finished, I went over to where he sat among the horses, to thank him.

We chatted for a short time. I was right: it was his idea, and he had cooked the fish. He had even brought oatmeal in a saddle-bag, as he knew Sir Hannibal would be fishing.

'But I didna think, Miss Kirstie,' he said, 'tae be cukin' yon troot for ye.'

His dear old face almost split in two with his grin.

Angelica had set up her easel, and the Earl was with her. But as I started strolling back from Geordie to the others, he left Angelica and strode across the heather to intercept me.

He stopped, and we stood face to face.

He said gravely, 'You had business with Geordie Buchan, Miss Drummond?'

'Yes,' I said. 'I went to thank him for his kind idea about the trout.'

'That was well thought of.'

I thought there was, in his tone, a note of patronizing approval which infuriated me.

I said hotly, 'I was taught to be polite to servants, and to those less fortunate, though I know that lesson is not taught in castles.'

'You are wrong, Miss Drummond. It is taught, but sometimes in the heat of the moment forgotten. I have been persuaded that I was needlessly brusque to you. I continue to deplore the familiarity with which you addressed Sir Hannibal, but I regret the terms in which I said so.'

He made a very small, stiff, inclination of his body from the waist, as though he knew he should bow, but could not induce his backbone to bend. Then he turned and went back to Angelica.

He had apologized.

It was not the most gracious apology ever made, but he had used the word 'regret'.

'Good gracious, Kirstie,' said Georgina a moment later, 'what was that about?'

'We were discussing education,' I said.

Georgina looked at me with a little frown, which came and went as quickly as her smile. It came again, that rapid puckering of her brow, as she turned to look at Angelica.

'The most beautiful girl in three kingdoms,' she said.

'I have heard that said about her, too,' said Charlotte. 'I heard it in London, and in Edinburgh. I daresay it is true.'

'I wish she would fall in the river and drown,' said Georgina. 'Then perhaps Draco would learn to laugh again.'

'Did he ever know how to?' I asked.

'Oh yes. He knew. Now he has lost the knack. She has put starch on his face, you know, so it is like a man's evening shirt. It cannot be bent, or go into creases. I shall call her "the Laundress". If I were to tell you what I truly feel about Angelica Paston—'

But I did not hear what she truly felt, because at that moment Lady Campbell came fluttering up to say they must be going home.

'Visitors,' she said. 'And they have probably arrived by now. So Frank will be compelled to sit and talk to them. And he has so much to do at this time of the year, getting in the hay, such as it is . . .'

'It may be a great bore for Sir Francis,' I said, 'but it will be very nice for the visitors.'

'Oh! Thank you! Can I tell him you said so? He will be so

pleased, after the way you made him laugh the other evening. Now we shall make a plan, and persuade Elinor Draco to lend you to us, dear, for as long as you can bear it.'

'Oh, do come and stay with us, Kirstie,' cried Georgina. 'Come for weeks! There will be ponies to ride, and us to talk to, and we will find some Dukes to come and fall in love with you. Just for your collection, you know.'

'Yes, do come,' echoed Charlotte with earnestness.

They seemed to mean it: so, when their carriage moved off, I waved until my arm ached.

'Careful, Kirstie,' said Sir Hannibal. 'That's your fishing arm you're trying to break off at the shoulder. Come and catch another Leviathan for dinner.'

I thought the Countess might want me to keep her company, but she said she would be restful alone. She gave me permission to go: 'Because, Billy Mainwaring,' she said, looking at him with great directness, 'I trust you to behave both sensibly and properly.'

'Oh dear,' said Sir Hannibal, as soon as we had walked upstream out of earshot. 'Now I am obliged to behave sensibly and properly, as a point of honour. And I had quite set my heart on behaving foolishly and improperly.'

I felt the smile forming itself on my face, although I knew it should not be there. I said, 'Why?' stupidly; but I was not used to such speeches.

'I'll tell you why,' said Sir Hannibal, 'when I know you better, and can speak freely to you. Possibly tomorrow, or the day after. And then I devoutly hope, and fully intend, to behave *most* improperly, whatever the Dragon says.'

'Oh,' I said, in a high voice like a little girl. I added awkwardly, 'Don't you think we ought to try to catch a fish?'

The memory of Lord Cricklade might make my head swim, but he was far away, and Sir Hannibal was very near and he was so very endearing, and made me feel as happy as he looked.

I wondered if it was possible to be in love with two men. Remembering Lord Caerlaverock, I wondered it it was even possible to be in love with three.

I insisted that Sir Billy took the rod, to show me how; he insisted that I took it, to show him how; we had a violent argument about it, most friendly, and ended by fishing turn about, on alternate pools. We were soon out of sight of the others, immediately below the fractured, nearly-vertical stone face of Meiklejohn's Leap.

I felt confused, and embarrassed, and excited, and very guilty: because I wanted Billy to make love to me. What was exciting was, that I knew he wanted to do it, too. The face of Lord Cricklade reproached me from the outside edge of my mind: but Billy was close beside me on the burnside, and he was a darling. Tomorrow, or the day after, he was going to behave improperly: and in a most shocking way, I looked forward to that hungrily. I giggled, inwardly and guiltily, when I thought of my grandparents in George Square. I was getting enmeshed in a life which was quite as dreadful as they feared!

I caught one fish, a tiny one, beautifully speckled, which Billy unhooked and put back. It swam away happily. He caught two, of proper size. We were very absorbed. The burn, laughing between its rocks, or sweeping in smooth brown pools, was the most delightful third member of our party.

Billy cast his flies to the head of a fresh pool, with that absolute concentration which I already recognized as the mark of a fisherman. I watched his skill with admiration, and tried to learn by watching, when I heard a curious whine from far above. I looked up at the crannied and fissured face of the wall of rock. The sound came again; a whimper, a sort of sob. It was not the cry of any bird.

Billy heard it, too. He looked up, with a puzzled face.

'I can't see from here,' he said. 'I'll cross the burn, and go up a little on the other side.'

I nodded. He handed me the rod, and with surprising agility crossed the burn by the rocks at the tail of the pool. He climbed a short way up the gentle slope opposite, and then took a small spy-glass from the inside pocket of his fishing coat.

'Got it,' he called. 'It's . . . a hare? No. Too small to be a deer calf. Wrong colour for a lamb. I believe it's a dog.' He stared through his spy-glass, then called again, 'Yes, definitely a dog, on a ledge about fifty feet above you. I think it's hurt.'

I looked up the face of the cliff from where I stood. It did not look difficult to climb. I had no doubt that Billy would go up and rescue the dog. He had no doubt, either. As he came down to the burn he called, 'I marked exactly where it is, and there's an easy route to the place. I hope he doesn't bite me when I get to him.'

'How ever did he get there?' I asked.

'I suppose he fell from the top. A young sheepdog, perhaps. But it is odd. I wonder how he *did* get there?'

Billy started across the burn again, by the rocks which made natural stepping-stones: but one of them rolled under his weight. He struggled to keep his balance, but fell heavily, with a great splash. He pulled himself to the bank, laughing ruefully, soaked to the skin.

'Curse my clumsy stupidity,' he said.

'It's only water,' I said, anxious about the dog.

'Unfortunately it's not only water. I've sprained my ankle, as I understand you did recently. I don't think I can walk, and I'm very sure I can't climb.'

'Well, then,' I said, 'if you wait here and tell me exactly how to go, I'll get the dog.'

'Kirstie, you can't! I forbid you to climb that cliff!'

'You're talking like Lord Draco,' I said.

'We'll run and fetch Draco.'

'You will?'

'You must.'

'By the time he gets here the dog may have fallen off the ledge. Think how thirsty it must be, if it's hurt. I must go now, don't you see?'

He began to say, 'It is absolutely out of the question—' but I was already scrambling up among the tumbled rocks.

'*Force majeure*,' he called. 'I can't follow you, and I can't go for help.'

'Then guide me,' I called back.

He told me to go along a ledge to my right, then scramble up a sort of chimney in the rock-face. I cannot pretend it was a difficult climb, even for a mountaineer of my experience, which was limited to flights of stairs. Soon the burn was far below me, and of Billy I could only see an anxious upturned face. I came to a flat rock, and paused to get my breath, and waved. I would have been enjoying myself immensely, but for the thought of the poor dog above, which from time to time whined or yelped.

Suddenly there was a cry in a female voice, 'Neil! Look!'

I looked down. Far below, some distance downstream from Billy, the Earl and Angelica stood. He was carrying the easel and folding stool. They had come to find a new prospect for her to paint; but instead they found me perched half way up the cliff like a goat.

Exhilarated by being so high, I waved to them too.

The Earl's voice came roaring up from below, 'Christina! Come down at once!'

There was a parade-ground rasp in his voice. I was sure that if I disobeyed he would be very angry indeed. He might turn me out of Glendraco, which he could do at any moment he chose. Then I was back to George Square, and back to Findlay.

I wondered why, when he gave his furious command, he used my Christian name for the first time. I supposed it was better for shouting.

I had a moment of the most awful indecision, thinking of being sent back to Edinburgh. Then, quite close above, came the whimper of the dog. It sounded like a young puppy. It sounded terrified, hurt and in despair.

I climbed on. The Earl bellowed again. But the wind was brisker on the cliff-face, and gusted away his words. In a moment I heaved myself over the lip of a broad ledge, where a stunted blueberry bush grew in a cranny in a rock: and I came face to face with the dog.

It was a black and white collie, very young. It wore a sort of harness, made of rope, like a pony's halter. It shrank back from me, when I crawled towards it, and bared its teeth. It was very thin, and its ribs showed through a ragged coat. I thought it had been underfed and ill-treated, and had reason to be suspicious of humans.

Very patiently I set myself to make friends with him, so that I could carry him to the ground. I spoke to him softly; I was talking nonsense, but I hoped he would understand the friendliness of my voice. After a time he trembled less, and did not bare his teeth. After a longer time, he allowed me to stroke him, and very gently pull his silky ears. But when I touched his left foreleg, he tried to bite me, and I pulled my hand away in the nick of time. The leg hurt him, which would make it much more difficult for me when I climbed down. I did not want to be covered with dog-bites, and catch the dumb-madness, apart from the chance of dropping him, or falling down the cliff myself.

Very patiently I went on making friends with the puppy, and getting him to trust me, and by and by I was able to lift him on to my lap. I went on stroking him, and talking to him, telling him that everything would be all right, and he would get bread-and-milk and bones, and be cared for always.

Suddenly there was a hoarse cry from below, and a scream which must have been Angelica's. At the same moment I heard a pattering noise above, like heavy drops of rain on a glass skylight, and a few pebbles showered down about me. Then the pattering grew into a rumble. A stone the size of my head plummeted down, six feet away from me, glancing off the rocks, and crashing and bouncing down the cliff. The word 'avalanche' came into my head, a terrifying word, carrying with it pictures of a whole mountainside descending in fury like a cataract. I flung myself, clutching the puppy to my breast, to the innermost corner of the ledge, where the rock above overhung a little. I tried to flatten myself against the cliff-face. Idiotically I thought that if I were killed, which seemed certain, the puppy would be killed too, so it would all be a waste, including Billy's sprained ankle. Rocks thundered down the cliff-face. It seemed to me that I felt the wind of their passing, so close did they fly by me. Dust swirled round. I prayed, in gasps, for the puppy. I did not know why then, and I do not know now, but I know that I prayed for the safety of the puppy I was holding tight to my breast. Suddenly there was quiet, except for the pattering of a few pebbles which followed the big rocks as scattered raindrops follow a cloudburst. They, too, stopped. A great silence fell, and the clouds of dust blew away on the sweet hill wind.

I was alive.

The puppy twisted in my arms, and licked the back of my hand. It was as though he knew we had both been through the Valley of the Shadow of Death.

'You and I,' I said to him, 'must look after each other now.'

His plumy tail twitched, and he licked my hand again.

Coming down was much more difficult, because I could not see where I was going, and had to use one arm all the time to hold the dog. The rope harness round his chest and neck was a help; I had never seen such a thing on a dog before, but I was glad of it, since I could be sure of not dropping my burden.

People were shouting from below. I could not make out what they said, and did not try to. I had too much on my mind. At least, I thought, they had not all been killed by the rock-fall.

I saw that my hands were bleeding from the rocks, and my habit was torn in a dozen places. I had lost my hat. These things seemed very unimportant.

The puppy was frightened, but trusting. He whimpered, but never yelped or snapped, although sometimes I must have hurt his injured leg.

And suddenly, long before I expected it, I was safe on the ground.

I looked round, dazed with happiness, and saw Billy hobbling towards me, using his landing-net as a stick.

'By God,' he said hoarsely, 'what a girl you are.'

I saw that there were tears on his cheeks.

The Earl strode up. His face was as white as chalk, as white as Eugénie's, and his hands were trembling. He looked beside himself with anger.

He said, pointing at my puppy, 'Is that cur the cause of this folly?'

'Yes,' I said.

And suddenly, to my own intense surprise, I burst out laughing with relief, with joy at being alive when I thought I was dead, with joy at having saved the poor little dog.

At that point Angelica swayed, put her hand to her head, and collapsed to the ground in a faint.

'Of course she wants to keep it,' said the Countess. 'Are you thinking of drowning it, after the trouble she took?'

'It may carry all kinds of distemper into the kennels,' said the Earl. 'I have the pointers and setters to consider, the terriers, retrievers, greyhounds, the sheepdogs and cattle-dogs—'

'And Kirstie has that puppy to consider. What are you calling him, dear?'

'Rockfall,' I said.

'He looks nearly as disreputable as you do. Rockfall! Come here, sir!'

'I'm sure he would if he could, ma'am, but he has hurt his leg.'

'Geordie Buchan's the man to see to that.'

And so he was. While I stroked Rockfall, and told him to be brave, Geordie very gently felt the injured leg, and understood what was wrong by means of the tips of his fingers. Presently the leg was bound up in a bandage, of which Rockfall seemed to be proud; he even walked a few steps to follow me, wagging his tail and panting.

As to the other victims: it seemed that Angelica had recovered within seconds, and had walked back slowly on the Earl's arm. Billy had also managed most of the journey on his own, putting his weight on his landing-net. He gave the Countess an account of my adventure, while Geordie and I were tending to Rockfall; I never knew what he said to her, but I imagined it was a different account from the Earl's.

I had washed my raw and bleeding hands in the burn, and although they were tender I thought I could ride Solomon home. I wanted to do so, so as not to seem weak and pathetic. I did not know if this plan would have been allowed by the Countess, or by Geordie Buchan: it was definitely not allowed by Rockfall. The idea of being parted from me was odious to him. He squirmed along the ground, in the manner of collies, his plumy tail waving madly, fixing me with irresistible eyes, and making little high heart-breaking cries. So the idea of being parted from him was odious to me. I could not carry him home across Solomon's withers, on account of his injured leg; so I was obliged to go in the carriage, and hold the shameless dog on my lap.

Angelica looked at me more oddly than ever before, all during the drive home, as though I were a creature of another species.

Unusually, Eugénie was waiting in the outer courtyard when Hamish drove us in over the drawbridge. She looked at the carriage, with an almost avid expression on her face. When she saw me opposite the Countess, a look of blank disbelief crossed her

135

face, which was as white as the face of the Earl at the cliff-foot.

I thought: she expected me to be dead.

Who could I talk to about it, about my terrible suspicions?

A letter to my grandparents would haul me straight back to Edinburgh.

Annie Simpson knew nothing of my grandfather, of Dandie McKillop, of the spilling of blood. Good and loving soul as she was, her advice would not be much use to me.

Geordie Buchan knew no ill of Eugénie, whom he rather admired for her skill with the ribbons in the pony-phaeton. I had asked him about Dandie McKillop a fortnight before, and he had answered indifferently. He knew about animals; he was no help with people.

Billy Mainwaring wished me well, no doubt of that, and for all his assumed foolishness he was a worldly and well-informed man. But he knew nothing of all that touched on this story. And he told me that a rock-fall could often start, entirely by itself, from the action of a hot sun on a split rock, the swelling of a root, a dozen causes. He was a down-to-earth man, a practical active man; he would not be inclined to believe ideas as wild as mine.

The Countess would not believe ill of Eugénie, who had been with her for more than fifty years.

The Reverend Lancelot Barrow thought I was an ignorant and silly girl.

Mrs Forbes's advice was something it would be wise not to seek, and the greatest folly to follow.

I did not think I could voice what I thought to the Barstows of Ardmeggar, or the Campbells of Drumlaw, or Charlotte, or David Baillie. It was none of their affair, and they would think I was overcome by hysterical imagination.

There was no one I could talk to.

And what, after all, would I have said? I thought Eugénie looked at me with hatred. But for all I knew she looked so at every stranger, at every young girl, at everybody who might be close to the Countess, at everybody who might give her extra work. For all I knew, it might be her usual expression. I thought Dandie McKillop threatened my life, and spat at me. But I had just fallen down a steep hill, and sprained my ankle, and been stupidly terrified by the harmless idiot Adam. Could reliance be placed on what I thought Dandie meant? I thought I had seen Eugénie and Dandie conferring in secret by the road side, and Dandie running away when he thought he might be spotted. But he was far away; Geordie Buchan had not recognized him. Even if it were he, Eugénie might have been asking the way, or Dandie asking for the price of a dram. Eugénie was surprised to see me alive? She might simply have been surprised to see me in the carriage, when she knew I had gone off on horseback.

And the puppy? It could have been lowered, by a string through its harness, in order to get Billy away from me, so that a falling rock meant for me would hit me only. Or it could have fallen, by purest accident. Or it could have been thrown over the cliff, by some brute with a dog too many. In spite of the oddity of the harness, anybody in the world would think these the more likely explanations.

The fall of rock? Billy had accounted for that. Anybody in the world would believe his account.

Eugénie's manner to me, in the days that followed, was exactly as it had always been. I stared at her, when she was not looking, trying to read in that wrinkled and bloodless face what was going on in her mind. Often she seemed to become aware of my inspection; she turned to face me, to stare me down, her eye as bright and black and malevolent as ever.

There were shadows across my life. There were people who hated me; people who disliked and despised me; people who disapproved of me, and resented my being at Glendraco. There was my own unappeased curiosity about myself, and the never-to-be-mentioned horror and disgrace of my grandfather. But it was impossible to be frightened all the time, in glorious weather, in the breathtaking beauty of the glen. I could not ride old Solomon with my chin always on my shoulder, looking for Dandie McKillop, or spend my days and nights worrying about Eugénie, or Lady Arabella, or General Drummond, or the Earl. The wind on the hillsides was like strong chilled wine; I was getting used to wine (although I did not much like the taste), but after my childhood in the dust and soot and poisonous fog of the city, I never quite got used to the intoxicating hillside air. It blew the doubts and fears out of my mind, while the jovial sun scorched away the shadows which followed behind me.

Wherever I went out of doors, Rockfall followed. He put on flesh, and his energy seemed to be limitless. After two days, Geordie Buchan and I gave him a bath; he almost forgot his love for us both in the horrid experience of soap and water.

The Earl, it seemed, countermanded his order that I was not to be asked to go fishing. But it was a hollow concession. Billy's sprained ankle kept him from the river-bank, the only place where he and I might have been alone together. So he did not behave 'foolishly and improperly' towards me, as he had threatened he would, which filled me with a mixture of disappointment and relief.

I was sent off to Drumlaw for a few days, taking Annie Simpson, but leaving Rockfall with Geordie Buchan. Sir Francis and Lady Campbell were kindness itself, and I spent happy hours with Georgina and Charlotte. They had heard a garbled version of my adventure on Meiklejohn's Leap, and talked of it constantly. We had no secrets from each other.

When I came back to Glendraco, the castle was filling up with guests. Some had come all the way from London, where the 'season' had ended, many from various parts of Scotland. The fishing in the Draco was very fine at this date, and the grouse-shooting was only three weeks off, but the immediate excitement was the fair and games at Lochgrannomhead, of which the Earl was Chieftain.

Most of the new arrivals I had never heard of; I was presented to them all, of course, and got to know some a little; but they were rich-plumaged birds of passage, who flew into Glendraco, and chattered and preened for a short time, and flew away again. The most exquisite exotic bird of all was a willowy young man called the Honourable Rollo Craker, who fell desperately in love with me. I was shameless enough to admit to myself that it was agreeable, having such a very fashionable swell for my new slave; but it meant no more to me than having poor David Baillie as my slave. Mr Craker was treated with tolerant amusement by nearly everybody, including me. I found that there was no vice in him, but no strength either; he was like a man made of expensive cotton-wool or of custard. He made as little secret of his devotion as Rockfall did, and followed me about like Rockfall; but Rockfall had more character, and was better company.

Among all the glittering strangers who came and went there were others who were not quite strangers; in fact, Glendraco seemed to have sucked in almost everybody with whom I had come in contact since I first climbed into the Countess's travelling carriage.

The fat old Duchess of Bodmin was there, red-faced, untidy, outspoken, and going out of her way to be friendly to me. She brought with her the Marchioness of Odiham, whose husband was off the coast of Norway in his schooner. I kept myself well away from the Snow Queen, and hoped she did not notice me in the crowd. Mrs Carlyle of Gaultstower came, in whose house I had stayed but whom I had scarcely met; I was surprised that it was her husband who had been a cabinet minister, as she seemed quite capable of being one herself. With her came Prince Rupert von Altstein, whom I had seen from far above, who made nearly everybody laugh: not me, because his stories were about people I had never heard of; not the Earl, or Lady Arabella, or Angelica, because nothing made them laugh.

And then, to my great joy, Lord Caerlaverock arrived, slight and very fair and mock-solemn; he and Billy Mainwaring and the Prince made a trio of jesters, at whom the Duchess of Bodmin laughed like a cook on her annual holiday.

'I feel, dear,' said Mrs Forbes confidentially to me, 'as if we were at the court of the Emperor of Russia, or some such. A veritable *constellation* of all that is most splendid! And such admiration as Angelica commands! All the gentlemen hanging round her! And yet she has no eyes for any of them.'

Mrs Forbes was both quite right and quite wrong. Angelica had no eyes for anybody but the Earl; but accuracy obliges me to say that some of the gentlemen were hanging round me rather than her. It was astonishing, because she was so very beautiful; perhaps they were so well used to highborn and accomplished young ladies, that an ignorant nobody came as an amusing change. The result of them seeking out my company was that I was never alone with any of them – with Rollo Craker, or Lord Caerlaverock, or Billy Mainwaring.

Nearly all the ladies spent nearly all their time talking to each other: just that, no more. Sometimes they went for little walks in the park, or little rides in a phaeton, but often, on the most perfect days, they sat in pairs or groups, dressed up as though for a presentation at Court, continuously chattering in one great dark room or another. They seemed to me no different from the nursemaids in the Princes Street Gardens, or the girls who worked in the Edinburgh shops, eternally gossiping. They may have been a veritable constellation of all that was most splendid, but I thought they had a very dull time.

One late afternoon I was on my hands and knees by a wall-cupboard, looking for an old scrap-book which the Countess wanted to show someone. I was almost hidden by a sofa, and the trio of ladies who approached across the room did not see me.

'I do not know the details,' Lady Arabella was saying, 'since it all took place just before I was born. But Amy Forbes tells me that, from things old Eugénie has let drop, it was an appalling scandal at the time.'

'I have received the same impression,' said Lady Odiham's glacial voice. 'Violet Bodmin will not talk of it.'

'I thought there was nothing Violet would not talk of,' said Mrs Carlyle.

'So did I.'

'The child has inherited a very wild, mad, unattractive streak,' said Lady Arabella. 'Nobody can understand why Elinor brought her here, or why she keeps her here. Neil is thrown into a passion of rage by some of her follies, becoming outspoken to a degree quite unlike him. I myself detest this hoydenish, errand-boy spirit, but Elinor is ridiculously indulgent.'

'Some of the gentlemen,' said Mrs Carlyle drily, 'are not merely indulgent, they are bursting with admiring approval.'

'Of course,' snorted Lady Arabella, 'any saucy girl can get herself noticed if she flirts, and shows off, and leads them on. I would box Angelica's ears if she behaved like that. It has been noticed and deplored in the county, too, at least among people who have moved in the world, and not lived entirely among rocks and peat-hags. General Drummond bought a place near here when he retired, and he told me he was aghast when he found that she was installed here.'

'Is the General a connection?' asked Lady Odiham.

'Yes, to his shame. I understand the relationship is not close. He told me there is bad blood in her branch, which comes out without fail in every generation.'

'We gather it came out in the grandfather,' said Mrs Carlyle, 'although none of us know quite how. What of the father?'

'A nobody,' said Lady Arabella. 'After the disaster, he was brought up quietly and obscurely in Edinburgh, by his mother. She showed a proper feeling, I think, to hide herself from the world. He married another little nobody, a Miss Strachan, daughter of an advocate or something of the kind—'

'My husband,' said Mrs Carlyle, 'was an advocate, or something of the kind.'

If this was a reproof, Lady Arabella did not notice it. She went straight on, 'They emigrated to Canada, and he died there soon after arriving.'

'That,' said Lady Odiham, 'shows bad luck rather than bad blood.'

'I daresay he was dissipated, and had undermined his health.'

Something snapped inside me. I lost my temper (which had brought me so many punishments as a child) and scrambled to me feet, my cheeks burning.

'You "daresay" my father was dissipated, Lady Arabella,' I cried. 'But how dare you say so? You know nothing about him, except second-hand back-stairs gossip from a malicious old servant.'

Lady Arabella looked at me with an expression of absolute fury. Nobody, perhaps, had ever spoken to her like that before: certainly no obscure and penniless orphan had spoken like that to the daughter of an Earl and the widow of a Senior Steward of the Jockey Club. I had never seen such fury on any face – not on the Earl's, when I had climbed down Meiklejohn's Leap with Rockfall; not Dandie McKillop's when he spat in my face on the hillside; not Eugénie's. She turned and stalked away, too furious to speak, much more soldierly in her bearing than my reluctant connection the General.

'You crouched in a corner, listening to a private conversation,' said Lady Odiham, her eyes as hard and her voice as cold as diamonds frozen at the pole. 'That was ill done.'

'You spoke scandalously of the dead, who cannot defend themselves,' I said hotly, still too full of indignation to be prudent, 'and of the living, who cannot defend themselves either. Was that well done?'

Lady Odiham smiled – a quicker and colder smile by far than any of the Reverend Lancelot Barrow's – a smile that would have made a ptarmigan shiver. Then she too turned, and followed Lady Arabella out of the drawing-room.

Mrs Carlyle looked at me with a magisterial frown. I wondered what awesome denunciation would come from those formidable lips. She said, 'I do not think child, you have learned to make allowances. Lady Arabella's situation is tragic and difficult. It is true that you climbed a cliff to rescue a pup?'

'Yes, ma'am,' I said, my anger evaporating in astonishment.

'Have you kept the dog?'

'Of course!'

'Of course. I doubt if I have ever asked a more foolish question. May I please meet this animal?'

'Why, yes, ma'am,' I said, more surprised with every word she spoke. 'When I have taken this book to Lady Draco—'

'She wanted to show it to me. I can postpone looking at it. I desire to make the acquaintance of your dog.'

So we went out to the kennels, and Rockfall hurled himself at me with his usual exuberance. He was putting on so much weight and muscle that he nearly bowled me over. We had one of our passionate reunions, which took place eight or ten times a day, sometimes after a parting of two minutes.

Mrs Carlyle watched, laughing; she chatted to Geordie Buchan, who appeared from nowhere, as he usually did.

Afterwards Mrs Carlyle said to me, 'Clever men have divided up mankind in all sorts of ways, but after a long and very full life I have come to the conclusion that there are just two sorts of people in the world. There are people, child, to whom other living creatures will run with their hearts full of generous love.

142

We have just seen that happen. You are such a person. Your patroness Lady Draco is such a person. I have tried to be such a person. I think that excellent old groom is such a person, because I have seen the way he talks to horses, and the way horses talk to him, and I have seen the way he talks to you, and the way you talk to him. To be the object of the sort of love your dog has just shown for you, whether it is the love of an animal or of a human creature, one must give it too. Only the loving are loved, that is what you must understand. I think you have a heart of that kind. I hope I have. We are the lucky ones. There can be great happiness in our lives, as there has been in mine. But there are others, different, poorer. There are people to whom your dog would *never* have run like that, with love pouring out of his eyes, and almost wagging the tail off his back with excitement. Imagine being such a person! Imagine the deprivation, the poverty of such a life! Imagine the bitter envy such people feel for those of us to whom the fairies, at our birth, gave the gift of love.'

'But,' I said, listening with the greatest attention, but not altogether understanding, 'but do the – loveless, the impoverished – do they know what they are missing?'

'Oh yes,' said Mrs Carlyle. 'They may not know they know, but in their hearts they know very well what they're missing.'

'It is like a – a person born without eyes?'

'It is worse. A blind man can love and be loved, but what good are eyes, if they never see love on a loved one's face?'

'I think I understand,' I said, 'about making allowances.'

'Good! You can afford to be generous. But I think I should warn you, Kirstie,' said the extraordinary woman, 'against making too many allowances. The Good Lord forgives the unforgivable, but it would be presumptuous in us to try to imitate Him too closely. To understand all is to forgive all, as that delightful young Billy Mainwaring often says – but you must *not* condone cruelty or treachery. Come now, Rockfall wants exercise and so do I. I am a garrulous old woman – I am getting as bad as poor Amy Forbes.'

We went for a walk, in great contentment, with Rockfall prancing round us; Mrs Carlyle told me about Paris and Vienna, and made me laugh as much as Lord Caerlaverock did.

*

The agricultural show was combined with the Highland games at Lochgrannomhead, and the party went from Glendraco in a fleet of carriages. Everyone who could had dressed up in all manner of tartans and plaids; Lady Arabella did not come. Our road took us down the Draco glen to the meeting of the river with the Grannom, then up the Grannom glen to the loch and the small town which had grown there.

All the lairds and many of the farmers of a wide area had sent beasts or birds to the show. There were Highland cattle, very strange and shaggy, with huge heads and monstrous horns; there were black-faced sheep, which the Highlanders hated, because sheep pushed them out of their little farms; there were pigs, and cinnamon turkeys, and white Dorking hens, and fat geese; there were judges, and prizes, and applause, and merriment from a tent where whisky was being sold by a Lochgrannomhead inn-keeper. The games were tossing the caber, and throwing the hammer, and tug-of-war, and wrestling, and dancing, and piping. Everything seemed to me as deliberately Scottish as it could possibly be, especially the English visitors.

All the neighbours I had met were there, as well as many other local people – the Barstows of Ardmeggar, the Campbells of Drumlaw, the Baillies of Inverlarig, the Drummonds. Those that were friendly were very friendly; those that were hostile were horrid; I thought of Mrs Carlyle's division of the human race.

'Well, dear,' said Mrs Barstow of Ardmeggar to me, as we dutifully inspected a very large fancy pigeon in a very small cage, 'you are a social benefactor hereabouts, you know.'

'Am I?' I said, unaware of being any such thing.

'You have given us all something to talk about, for a change. Nobody has talked about anything else for a fortnight. They tell me the dog is amiable, but *not* of the purest pedigree.'

'Oh.' Light broke into my puzzlement, but made me more puzzled. 'People are – can they all be? – talking about that little scramble among the stones—'

'Ha! I know Meiklejohn's Leap. So do many people here. Look about you, Kirstie. Do you see your neighbours gawping at those miserable pigs and chickens! No! Or at those butcher-boys pulling on a rope? No – not even their sisters and sweet-hearts! Of course not – they're all looking at you!'

'Oh,' I said, a little aghast, realizing that there *were* a lot of eyes turned in my direction. 'I shouldn't have come, perhaps . . .'

'That would have been a great shame,' said Ardmeggar, 'as you look handsomer each time I see you.'

'*Not* a dirty face this time, sir?'

'Not a *very* dirty face.'

Georgina and Charlotte came up and took me away.

'It is too bad of you, Kirstie,' said Georgina. 'I took endless and untold trouble with my appearance today, but every gentleman I meet wants only to be introduced to *you.*'

'I have found myself a celebrity, for the first time in my life,' said Charlotte, 'simply because I am your friend.'

Indeed I was introduced to a prodigious number of people, by whom I was very confused; they all asked me about Rockfall and the rock-fall, and climbing up and climbing down. I began to feel distinctly conceited.

Then, to put me right, I heard General Drummond saying extremely loudly, 'The purest criminal folly. I am irritated past all bearing, hearing this stupid praise of the wretch. Someone might have had to climb up after her, and risked a serious acci-dent. Think of the loss to the country if Draco had been injured or killed! I am not surprised he was angry. It is just the sort of madcap lunacy one would expect of that branch.'

'From what I hear,' said old Mr Baillie of Inverlarig, 'it has all been blown up out of all proportion. The chit walked up among a few rocks, and dislodged a few pebbles. I cannot imagine why everybody is making such a fuss.'

'I am confused, gentlemen,' said Prince Rupert von Altstein, in his high voice, pulling his long white whiskers. 'Are you criti-cal of the *schöne* Fräulein Christina because she did something that was too dangerous, or not dangerous enough? I think you should agree what she has done wrong, before you complain about it.'

At that moment, full of gratitude to the Prince, in the midst of the crowd, I found myself face to face with Billy Mainwaring.

'What a charming coincidence!' he said. 'I have been pushing through the mob this way and that for an hour, entirely to have a chance meeting with you.'

'I like the Prince,' I said.

'So do I, but you will kindly not discuss him now. We are never so alone as in the midst of strangers, they say; unfortunately this crowd are not all strangers. Kirstie, I have something very particular to say to you, in private.'

'Now?' I asked nervously: for I felt I was being rushed into a strange country, with problems and hazards I knew nothing about.

'Now, this instant. I've waited till I've gone nearly mad, but those other fellows have been clinging to you like miserable leeches. Tell me – do you like Rollo Craker?'

'Well, yes,' I said, 'except there is nothing inside him except custard.'

'Do you like Jack Caerlaverock?'

'Yes, I do,' I admitted. 'He makes me laugh.'

Billy groaned.

'You make me laugh, too,' I added quickly.

'Oh! Do I? It is not just politeness? Come with me – quick.'

Seizing my wrist, he pulled me behind a row of parked carriages, where we seemed to be out of sight of anyone.

'Oh Lord,' he said. 'Now that I have the chance to speak – I can't speak! The words won't come – my heart's too full—'

Suddenly he stretched out a hand, as though involuntarily, and touched my cheek. And suddenly I took his hand in mine, as though involuntarily, and pressed it to my cheek. I felt a wave of tenderness towards him; I felt real and strong affection. He was one of those Mrs Carlyle had talked of – he was loving and lovable.

I do not know just how it happened: but before I was aware that we had even moved, his arms were about me and mine were round his neck. And then I felt what I had never felt before, the gentle pressure of a man's lips on mine. I liked it very much, because the lips were Billy's. But when I closed my eyes, it was not his face I saw.

seven

'Kirstie, my very dearest,' said Billy, 'I think you are soon to be eighteen.'

'Yes, quite soon.'

'Then I may address you seriously.'

'Oh,' I said stupidly. 'Was kissing me not serious?'

'Yes,' said he, 'deeply serious. I suppose that is why I want to dance, and sing, and shout, and laugh like a maniac. Maddening girl, you know what I mean!'

I knew what he meant, and my mind was in a turmoil.

Billy was honourable, kind, considerate, amusing, the best of company. Men liked him. I had seen children run to him from the farmhouses. Rockfall adored him, which was a great point. Old people, like Mrs Carlyle and the Duchess of Bodmin, esteemed and trusted him. I could go further and fare worse; I could go to the ends of the earth, and not fare half so well. The touch of his hand was reassuring, and the pressure of his lips comforting.

But it was not his face that I had seen, when I closed my eyes, when he kissed me.

We came out from behind the carriages, and were caught in the midst of the crowd. And there was Lord Caerlaverock standing looking at us, with Charlotte Long on his arm. I thought again that they could have been brother and sister, both so slight, and with such flaxen hair and cornflower eyes. He was looking at us; she glanced from us to him. His face was hostile. For the first time since I had met him, I saw coldness and anger in his eyes; his jaw was set, and his mouth a thin line. I could not read Charlotte's expression.

Billy, I think, saw neither of them. If he saw them, he took no notice of them. His eyes were fast on my face. Anybody but a ninny could have read *his* expression, and neither Charlotte nor Caerlaverock were ninnies.

Next day a letter came for me, only the fourth I had received since coming to Glendraco.

My dear Christina:

I write in anticipation of the approaching anniversary of your birth, an event which, in the eyes of many, signalizes the transition from childhood to the Adult State. Since circumstances deprive me of the opportunity to say to you in person those things which, were you under my roof, I should feel myself obliged to say, I take this opportunity to express myself in writing. I must strictly abjure you to read what follows with Attention, and above all to recognize that the Precepts therein contained do not emanate from my own imperfect Intellect, but are the Teachings of the Church of which you have the Blessed Fortune to be a Member.

What followed was a homily, or sermon, running to eleven pages of my grandfather's cramped legal handwriting, very black and neat, every 'I' meticulously dotted, every 'T' firmly crossed. I read it all with the Attention he required of me, but it was not really necessary, as I had heard it all a thousand times before. I was to be Modest, Prudent, Thrifty, Obedient, Diligent, Silent, Sober (very Sober). I was to avoid Display, Folly, Extravagance, Wilfulness, Idleness, Drawing Attention to Myself, and Self-Indulgence.

It seemed to me that the only one of these Commandments I had kept was that of Thrift; and the only one of the sins I had not committed was Extravagance. If I had ever had a penny to spend, no doubt I would have been extravagant too.

My grandfather proceeded:

We have been vouchsafed regular Communications from the Countess of Draco, whose reports on your Conduct have been Satisfactory. We have been disturbed, however, at the intelligence that you have been riding. Your Grandmother deems this Activity to be at once Unladylike and Perilous, and desires me to instruct you . . .

I did not read the next bit. I did not want to disobey my grand-parents, and I could not disobey a command I had not seen.

My grandfather proceeded, after the bit I skipped:

Doctor Findlay Nicholson asks, in a spirit of Christian Forgiveness which would be remarkable in a less Estimable Person, to be remembered to you kindly. He requests me to state that his Emotions remain unaltered, and waits with Patience and Fortitude for your return. Your grandmother also sends her Affectionate Rememberance. You are mentioned weekly in our Family Prayers, and you may believe that our servants continue to implore the Divine Protection on your Behalf as warmly as we ourselves do.

I remain, Christina, your concerned Grandfather,
S. Strachan

In the Countess's boudoir I said, 'It is kind of you, ma'am, to tell my grandparents that my conduct is satisfactory. Because I'm afraid it has not been.'

'There has seemed to me to be no need,' said the Countess frostily, 'to distress the Strachans with accounts of some of your – indiscretions.'

'I do not *mean* to commit indiscretions, ma'am,' I said earnestly. 'They seem to jump out at me from corners.'

'As you jumped out at Lady Arabella from a corner.'

'Er, yes, rather like that . . . From this letter, it does not seem to me that my grandfather much wants me home again.'

'You do not read between the lines, then. They do want you back. But I have told them that the country air suits you, and that you are usefully employed helping Mr Barrow in the library. I have said that you are earning your keep.'

'I doubt if Mr Barrow would agree.'

'I see no reason to impose Mr Barrow's views on your grandfather. I have, however, told him that you would not go back, I thought, unless you were forced. And if you were forced, you would not stay. And if you went, you might be under some very different protection from mine.'

'Oh . . . I am not yet that sort of female, ma'am.'

'I know you're not. But you would be, faced with the alternative of the person with wet hands and a wet mouth.'

Up went the corners of her own beautiful mouth (whose softness was so much at odds with the piratical nose) like the ends of a recurved longbow; with one of her broadest smiles she said, 'I think you had better stay here for the time being, Kirstie.'

'I hope I may, ma'am, but . . .'

It was in my mind, at that moment, to pour out my story, my sick suspicions, my recurring terror. I thought she was in a mood to listen to me; I thought there might never be a better time.

Then I saw that Eugénie had come softly into the room, carrying a long milky glass of the medicine the Countess took. Shawled, mittened, taloned, chalk-faced, jet-eyed, she stared at me with a threat that was almost spoken.

My word against Eugénie's – the word of an hysterical girl, with a history of wildness and rumour of dissipation in her family – my word against that of an old and trusted confidante, an intimate of fifty years?

The worst would be believed of me, because of what was believed of my father and grandfather. I risked being sent back to 'the person with wet hands and a wet mouth', whose 'Emotions remained unaltered', and who was 'waiting with Patience and Fortitude for my return'.

Thirty falls of rock on Meiklejohn's Leap were better than that.

The Countess never mentioned my birthday. I thought she did not know of it. Billy knew I was nearly eighteen, but he did not know the date. I thought it was rather a pity to pass an eighteenth birthday with no notice taken of it at all: but I could not mention it without seeming to be asking for presents.

I thought I should get, perhaps, a handkerchief from my grandmother, which would be useful, and could be sent cheaply through the post. It would be something; it would have to be enough.

Most of the house-party now dispersed, over a day or two.

The Duchess of Bodmin left, which I was sorry for. She said she had to get back to her garden, which would be despoiled and desecrated by the gardeners if she left them unwatched any longer.

She said to me, 'I never dreamed you would become so much a part of Glendraco so quickly, my dear. I thought you would be a little mouse, peeping out for a piece of cheese only when nobody was looking. Instead you are a sort of comet, blazing from room to room. And a sort of magnet, pulling men after you like iron filings. I never had the least gift in that direction, you know, and yet I married my Duke ... I wonder what will become of you? You might be a queen or a fishwife ... It has given me so much pleasure to see you here, with your head high. I expect you are aware that you arouse a certain amount of disapproval, and resentment. I did myself. A lot of people thought I was a very unsuitable Duchess, owing to the way I looked, and the way I laughed. I learned not to mind. Do you know the trick of that? It is well worth learning. If you know why people dislike you, you don't mind, because the reason is something sad in themselves, not something bad in you ... Of course, the more I thought about it, the less surprised I was to find you here with your head high. I should have expected it, because I knew ...'

'My grandfather, your Grace?'

'I met him, I believe, yes.'

She would say no more, but kissed me when I curtseyed.

The Duchess took Lady Odiham, which I was glad of. I had not spoken to the Snow Queen since my outburst in the drawing room.

Prince Rupert von Altstein left, which I was sorry for. He kissed my hand, which was as new a sensation to me as being kissed on the lips by Billy. He said it was very improper to kiss the hand of an unmarried girl, but he was old and foreign and expected to be forgiven.

'I forgive your Highness,' I said.

'But I shall never forgive you, little one, for not being young when I was young.'

The Honourable Rollo Craker left, which I was glad of. The novelty of being pursued by a gentleman of such elegance and fashion palled more quickly than I ever would have expected. It became irritating to be pursued by a man made of custard.

'Think kindly of me, Miss Kirstie,' he said mournfully, tugging at his long straw-coloured moustache, and bending like a reed this way and that.

I said I would; and I tried to, and sometimes succeeded.

Mrs Carlyle left, which I was sorry for.

She had astonished me before; now she astonished me again. She said, 'I am a garrulous and interfering old woman, Kirstie, and I very seldom mind my own business. For thirty years I was a power in politics, and I got the habit of meddling. I am going to give you some advice, whether you like it or not. You must join your life to somebody like yourself. I do not mean somebody with that glorious hair and face and figure of yours; he can look like a pudding, or a crow, or a gnome, that is not important. I do not mean somebody who can run and ride as you do; that would be convenient, but it is not really important either. I mean somebody with your capacity for love. Choose a *warm* man, Kirstie. Whatever you do, keep away from cold people. The world is full of them, and some are attractive. But they'll never understand you. They'll only hurt you. Will you be guided by me?'

'Yes, ma'am, I expect I will.'

'Then marry Billy Mainwaring. *He* understands you. He is incapable of hurting anybody. Perhaps I shouldn't know how he feels, but I do. Perhaps I shouldn't tell you, but I'm doing it. I cannot imagine a man more certain to make you happy. I cannot, incidentally, imagine a girl more certain to make him happy. That weighs with me, you know, as I am very fond of him.'

Lady Arabella and her daughter did not leave; nor Lord Caer-laverock; nor, for the moment, Billy Mainwaring.

I woke early on my eighteenth birthday, and stared from my window at the mist which lay far below me over the river. The early sun gave promise of another brilliant day: although Geordie Buchan had said that he knew, from the creaking of his joints, that foul weather was coming.

Some knitted stockings from Skye had arrived in the post from my grandmother. It was something. It would have to be enough.

Billy Mainwaring was leaving in the afternoon. He had been appointed Trustee of an estate of which the owner was a young schoolboy, an orphan, and he had to go there and sort out a tangle with a tenant. He had to do this duty, but he did not want to leave. I did not want him to leave. It was miserable that his departure was the one event of my birthday.

Annie came in, cheerful as always. I had almost told her about my birthday, simply from bursting to tell *somebody*, but I

guessed it would be all over the castle if I did. That would have been a sly way of getting it known, and so getting my presents; I would have despised such a trick – but I was very tempted.

Annie said that another picnic had been planned, and I was to ride to the place.

Geordie Buchan was in a very queer mood. I wanted to start early, but he dragged his feet, and complained of his joints, and found mysterious things wrong with Solomon's shoes, and kept me waiting by the stables until almost noon.

'Geordie, we'll be late!' I complained.

'Ay,' he said crossly, as though it were my fault.

Never had he had less to say, or turned such a dour face to me.

Then he made me walk Solomon most of the way, because he said he was fretted about one of the old pony's tendons. I had felt Solomon's legs, as Geordie himself had most strictly taught me to do, and I was sure there was nothing wrong; he had legs like iron bars. It was all very puzzling.

And then we went by a most curious roundabout route. I knew the glen well by now, and the shortest way to every part of it, from the head of the Dead Glen to the mouth of the Draco. On that day Geordie led me up the twisting glen of the Allt Slanaidh, and across a spur by a sheep-track, and down another little glen called Chireachan, returning almost to the road and the Draco. It was a beautiful ride, but as we were late already, it seemed a silly way to go.

We came down beside the Allt Chireachan, and passed a little deserted farmhouse with a ruined steading. A great number of horses were tied up there, as though the fiery cross had gathered the clansmen for miles around.

'What is this?' I asked Geordie. 'Is there a Chireachan fair?'

'Ay, Miss Kirstie,' he replied, and at last gave me the ear-to-ear grin I had waited all morning to see.

We rounded a spur, and it was indeed as though an army had assembled – an army which was preparing to feast after victory, an army which set up a shout of welcome which nearly made placid old Solomon bolt away up the glen.

It was my birthday party.

There had been a conspiracy throughout the castle, throughout the steading and stables, to keep it a secret from me. The Countess must have known when my birthday was – must have known for some time, to arrange such a function. Yet not by so much as the twitch of an eyelid had she referred to the matter in my presence. Annie had known, Geordie Buchan, Billy Mainwaring, Jack Caerlaverock, Mrs Forbes had known, the Reverend Lancelot Barrow, the Earl, Eugénie. Mrs Weir the housekeeper had known, Patterson the mournful butler, Wattie Dewar, the maids and footmen, the grooms and kennelmen, the farmworkers and dairymaids. The neighbouring lairds had known, for here in the crowd were the beaming faces of the Barstows of Ardmeggar, the Campbells of Drumlaw, and David Baillie of Inverlarig.

I understood now Geordie Buchan's ill-tempered foot-dragging, and the route which he made us take. He was making sure I did not reach the place of the picnic until all was ready, and that I did not see the others on the road.

It was too much for me. I accepted the welcome and the greeting in the most absurd way – I burst into tears.

The Countess embraced me. 'You never said a word, Kirstie,' she said softly. 'If your grandfather had not written to me, the day would have passed like another.'

'Well,' I said, 'that was what I meant.'

'Do you not like your party, child?'

'Oh yes! Yes, I do!' I said, and began weeping again, like a baby, to my great embarrassment.

The picnic luncheon that followed is one of the most blurred of all my memories. Not because of wine, although I suppose I drank a little, or because of tears, for I did not gush any more of them, but simply because nothing in my life before had prepared me for being the centre of so many people, of so much goodwill.

I was dimly aware that Annie Simpson was there, and Mrs Weir, and mournful Patterson, although none of them would normally have been in attendance on a picnic. I did not understand at the time, but realized later, that this was forethought on the part of the Countess, who knew that their being present would give pleasure to me and to them. Annie's pleasure was extreme, and obvious, and touched me very much. Mrs Weir had always been my friend, hiding so very unsuccessfully her kindness and warmth under a mask as grim and granite as that of old Carstairs in George Square. And Patterson was amazing! This dismal, tragic, whiskered prophet of doom was beaming as broadly as anybody, and looking near dancing and scampering when he wished me, 'Mony happy retairns o' the day.'

After luncheon was at last finished, I was given my presents. Of course, I disgraced myself with baby tears again, when the Countess spread in front of me a set of silver-backed things for my dressing-table. They were not properly a set, for a silver mirror was unlike the brushes, the silver-lidded pots, and the inlaid shoehorn – it was older, heavier, more ornate. I looked at myself in the heart-shaped glass, at the face with high cheekbones and straight dark eyebrows, extremely pink now owing to sun and excitement: the face which seemed to affect so many people in such strangely different ways. Then I turned the glass over, and saw on the back an engraved design: a coat of arms: and on the shield a dancing leopard with a rose in its mouth.

'Oh,' I said, 'this is the leopard on the old books.'

'I daresay,' said the Countess, 'it was bought at the same time as the books.'

I nodded, wondering what family had so delightful a beast on its shield, and had been obliged to sell its library, and pretty pieces of antique silver.

The Barstows gave me a beautiful shawl, the Campbells a brooch of silver and cairngorms, David Baillie, from his family, a silver salver for which, in my life, I could think of no possible use, Georgina a locket, Charlotte a set of inlaid tortoiseshell combs, Angelica Paston a prayer-book bound in white leather, Billy Mainwaring a fishing-rod, Lord Caerlaverock a whip with a silver and ivory crook, Mrs Forbes a pair of gloves, the Reverend Lancelot Barrow another prayer-book (they had not consulted closely, it seemed); and there were presents left behind by the Duchess of Bodmin and Mrs Carlyle, which I thought particularly kind, as they could not stay for the party; and there were presents subscribed by the farmers and servants.

All this took a very long time, and I was almost exhausted by smiling and exclaiming and thanking everybody. And then there was a curious pause, and I saw that eyes were turned towards the

Earl. He had not given me anything. I was glad. I did not want anything from someone who so much disliked and despised me. But other people found it odd, that I could see; dear Mr Barstow of Ardmeggar, who was incapable of hiding his feelings, was staring at the Earl with his eyebrows raised so high that they almost disappeared into his iron-grey hair.

The Earl sat as grave as a judge, attending solemnly to everything that was going on, but not seeming, though he was its host, to be a member of the party at all.

The Earl turned in his chair; he looked towards the spur of ground that hid the tumbledown steading where the horses had been tied up. Over the spur came Geordie Buchan, leading a horse. It was not one I had seen before – not one in the Glendraco stables. Instantly I yearned for it. It was all that dear old Solomon was not – young, prancing, a bright chestnut, almost thoroughbred, not a big horse but not a pony; he came dancing along beside Geordie Buchan with an air of friendly arrogance; he looked with interest at all the people, and pricked his ears at the chatter. He was bridled, and carried a side-saddle which looked quite new.

I looked round, puzzled. No other woman there was wearing a riding habit. And then, with a wild surmise, I glanced towards the Earl.

'He is called Falcon, Miss Drummond,' he said gravely. (He had not called me Christina since he shouted with fury at Meiklejohn's Leap.) 'But you may change the name if you wish.'

'He is . . . mine?'

'Yes. I do not want a novice riding my horses, and you have been asking too much of the old pony. You can spoil the mouth of your own animal.'

So he did all he could to spoil my pleasure in the gift, and stifle the gratitude I would have felt.

Rather dolefully I went to make friends with Falcon. I found he was glorious and proud and friendly, anxious to show off, interested in everything. He flapped his ears at me, and whistled softly through his nostrils. I stroked the smooth and brilliant chestnut of his neck, and marvelled at the muscles of his shoulders.

I saw that Billy Mainwaring had joined Geordie and me by the horse. He smiled. Without a word he helped me to Falcon's back. I felt very far from the ground, excited, elated. We walked and then trotted round. Falcon's muscles rippled in the sunlight under his glossy skin; I felt a sense of his power, yet he was so responsive and obedient that, even though I was still very inexperienced, I was not at all alarmed.

Soon I was well used to Falcon, and longing to go far and fast. Then I saw that Billy Mainwaring had mounted his own horse, and had large saddlebags.

'Will you see me a little on my way, Kirstie?'

'Are you going now?' I asked blankly.

'Yes. I must. I should have gone this morning. Lady Draco has told me I may have your company and Falcon's for a mile or two. Geordie will come along behind, so that you will have an escort after I have gone.'

I looked back towards all the people. The Countess waved and smiled. She was giving permission for the ride, and, perhaps, for more than that: for she knew how Billy felt: and I was eighteen years old.

We did not talk much as we rode up towards the head of the glen. High and high to the east, beyond the river, rose the green cliff of Ben Draco, all bathed in the afternoon sunshine; the other big hills, on both sides of the glen, seemed the obedient courtiers of their monarch. Stags were already being stalked on the highest ground; the men came back in the evening purple with sun and exhaustion, with a dead beast over the saddle of a shooting-pony. From the grass verge of the road, as we trotted silently along, we could hear, too, the tock-tock-tock of the grouse in the heather; in a few days the Earl and his friends would be out after them with their dogs and guns.

'I'll come back in time for those,' said Billy, indicating with his chin a small pack of grouse which skimmed round the shoulder of a hill above us.

'Just for them?' I asked. I realized it was a flirtatious question; but I felt flirtatious; it was my birthday; I was riding my beautiful new horse; anything was allowed me today.

Billy smiled, but did not answer. His smile was enough answer.

A few minutes later, a mile or two on, Billy said, 'I must soon start to use my whip and spurs, Kirstie. I've a long way to go, and I'll be caught in the storm as it is.'

'Storm? But there had never been such a glorious afternoon!'

'Not for much longer, my dear. See the plumes of cloud on the tops there? The wind has changed. See the clouds massing at the head of the glen, and feel the difference in the air?'

I had not noticed these signs, and I was not wise enough to read them. I believed Billy, of course, but I was sure the storm was still a long way off.

It was then, looking round at the gathering clouds, that I glimpsed another horseman, behind Geordie Buchan and far above, keeping pace with us. I could not see who it was: he was far too far away, and only occasionally in sight. It seemed to me that he did not want to be seen. The name Dandie McKillop jumped into my head: but it was doubtful if he was a horseman, and certain that he had no horse unless he had just stolen it.

I was going to point the horseman out to Billy, because there was something odd and worrying about him; but just before I spoke, Billy himself said, answering my silly question of half-an-hour before, 'No, I am not coming back for the birds, or the beasts, or even the fish. I am coming back to . . . Oh Lord, what word should I use? To woo you? To pay court to you? Those words sound so ridiculous, from a little fat man.'

In a funny high voice, which I could not quite control, I said, 'I don't think those words are ridiculous.'

'Not ridiculous even from me?'

'From you least of all.'

'I am not quite in a class with David Baillie?'

'Not quite.'

'Poor fellow. He was looking at you during luncheon, Kirstie, with a face like a child pressing his nose against a shop-window, and staring at the unattainable treasures inside.'

'Yes, I saw him looking so. I am sorry about it, I truly am.'

'I know you are, because you are a person of kindness and goodness. You are a lovable person. Rockfall loved you within seconds, and so did Falcon, and so did I.'

I remembered Mrs Carlyle's words, about the two sorts of

people in the world. Billy was, more than anyone I had known, the sort of person she approved of. But was I? Were they both right about me? I was not at all sure. Sometimes I seemed to myself horribly hard and selfish; sometimes I seemed to myself quite as dreadful in character as I had been taught, throughout my childhood, by Carstairs and my grandparents, in George Square.

'All the same,' said Billy, smiling a little bitterly, 'I don't see how I can avoid looking a little like David Baillie. I feel exactly as he does, and my face is the same unfortunate shape. Will you promise to tell me, Kirstie, if my sheep's eyes become intolerable?'

I remembered those other words of Mrs Carlyle, about Billy, about Billy and myself. I smiled, but I did not answer, because at that moment, for the first time, Falcon stretched himself into a beautiful easy canter, and I gave myself up to exulting in his speed and grace.

We went on, postponing our leavetaking, forgetful of the approaching storm. We came to a steep, high bank, at the bottom of which raced a burn called the Allt Monaidh. Falcon scrambled delicately down the bank, following Billy's sensible big horse; holding a tight double-handful of his flaxen mane I was quite secure in the saddle. At the edge of the water Falcon jibbed; nothing would induce him into it. I tried wheedling, and severity, but he hated the look of the rapid peaty water. Then Billy took his bridle below my hand, and led him across from the back of his own horse. Falcon followed him, quite docile, not only feeling Billy's strength but also, I was sure, trusting him. Once in the water, Falcon enjoyed it, and I believed splashed me on purpose. We scrambled up the high bank on the other side, and I was safe with another firm double-handful of Falcon's mane. The only disaster was that I dropped my new whip, my present from Lord Caerlaverock: but Geordie Buchan, just behind us, jumped down and picked it up.

A little beyond the burn, we came to a belt of young pine-trees. The pine-needles blanketed the sounds of the horses' hooves, and the sun splashed the ground with patches of gold. Billy stopped and dismounted. He caught his reins on his arm, and helped me down. He gave Falcon and his own horse into Geordie

Buchan's care. Geordie nodded. A look of understanding passed between him and Billy. Geordie led the horses away through the trees; he was within earshot, but invisible to us.

'Now it is goodbye,' said Billy huskily.

'Only for a few days,' I said, in a breathless squeak.

We would both, to a stranger eavesdropping among the trees, have sounded quite idiotic.

It was the quietest place in the world. The trees muffled the rush and gurgle of the river. There were no birds among the pine-trees. The wind had dropped, and the trees themselves stood as motionless as statues.

Billy gave a sort of groan, and took a step towards me, and put his arms about me.

He had kissed me behind the carriages at Lochgrannomhead – but very gently, and for a fleeting second. Now he kissed me with a passion which was almost savage; I felt myself swimming like a cork on the rapids of a violent river, helpless, whirling. A great tenderness welled up in my breast, a great happiness to be imprisoned in his arms. I forgot everything else – the world, Falcon, Geordie, the half-seen horseman on the hillside, the dark shadows and formless terrors, and above all – my Puritan upbringing. All modesty dropped from me like an unwanted shawl! I returned Billy's kiss; I strained my arms round his dear neck, and pressed my body against his. The tenderness and happiness that filled me swirled in new and hot clouds within me; I felt a desire and excitement which almost frightened me.

'Oh Kirstie, I love you so very much,' whispered Billy into my cheek.

'I love you too,' I said.

It was true. I knew it was true. I knew I would love him always, because he was a darling.

But in the midst of the storm of passion in my heart, another voice was calling my name; and in the midst of the spinning fires in my head, there was another face.

I do not know how long we were in that silent wood. We both forgot time. We were brought back to reality by a strange shrill noise from among the trees: it was Geordie Buchan, tactfully clearing his throat, with a sound like a hoodie crow in the spring.

Billy called to Geordie; Geordie came towards us with the horses; he said that the storm had come up very fast, and was almost on us. Looking about me (for the first time for I do not know how long) I saw that the world had changed. The sky had darkened. The air was cold. The young trees were bending to winds which gusted from the cleft at the head of the glen.

It seemed impossible that we had not noticed these things; it seemed impossible that so great a change should have taken place so quickly. But Billy said that storms sometimes came up without warning in these big hills, and Glendraco was famous for torrential rain and violent wind.

Even as he spoke, shouting above the thrashing of the trees in the wind, the rain began: not descending vertically from the sky, like the well-ordered rain of a city, but thrown in stinging horizontal sheets by the gusts, this way and that, as the winds hurled themselves about in the mountains.

Billy said that he must go on at once – the storm would not last long, he had far to go, he was far behind his time, his horse would be better moving and keeping warm than standing still and getting chilled and stiff. Geordie advised him to wait until the worst of the violence had spent itself; I begged him to wait; but he laughed ruefully and mounted his shivering horse.

'You've made me late,' he called to me over the noise of the storm. 'Even you mustn't make me later.'

He turned his horse and trotted away.

'Will he be all right?' I cried to Geordie.

'Och, ay, Sirr Hennibal kens the road fine. You an' me, Miss Kirstie, maun find a mickle o' dry in the wee croft.'

'Is there a croft near?'

'Ay, Dugald Crombie an' his wumman. They'll be auld bodies, an' guid bodies, an' they'll hae a shelter o' sorts for yon puir beasties.'

We waited for a little, keeping ourselves and the horses as much as possible out of the worst of the rain. Then the stinging rain and battering wind moderated a little, and we set off out of the wood, and up the side of the burn. The burn, above where we had forded it, ran between banks twenty feet high, almost cliffs; an active man on foot could have climbed down the right-hand bank, jumped across the burn on the rocks, and climbed up the far bank: I was in no doubt that I myself could have done it: but for a horse without wings the burn was impossible to cross, except where we had crossed it. The heavy rain had filled it quickly; Geordie shouted to me that, as rainwater drained off huge areas of hillside, the burn would soon be in full spate.

We walked up the burnside, leading our horses, as Geordie said we only had a quarter of a mile to go. I was glad to stride along, partly sheltered by Falcon. When we had covered only a hundred yards, it seemed that the heavens had played a monstrous trick on us, for the wind hurled itself in a new direction, full in our faces, and with it carried a wall of ice-cold water. Mounted, I would have been soaked to the skin in six seconds; on foot, I was soaked to the skin in ten!

It was miserable, horrid, unendurable – and suddenly I found that I was enjoying myself. Wet clothes and wet hair could be dried. Rain could do me no great harm, nor Falcon. Though the rain felt cold, it was not really so very cold, since it fell from a sky of early August. Though my habit skirt clung soddenly to my legs, and my boots felt as though they were turning to pulp, and I was blinded by the rain gusting down the steep glen of Allt Monaidh, and my cheeks were stung and chilled by it, yet I laughed out loud: for this was the wild free life I had dreamed of and hungered for, looking out over the Edinburgh rooftops, neglecting the Old Testament chapters I was to learn, and the worsted stocking I was to darn . . . Geordie Buchan turned, astonished to hear laughter amidst such odious conditions. I daresay he put it down to something said, or done, during my farewell conversation with Billy: and, indeed, there was another thought to make me happy and excited.

As we neared the croft, I understood why we had not seen it earlier. It stood in a dip in the ground, and was itself so low to the ground that it was more like a big molehill than a habitation for people and animals.

The clouds that swirled about us were now blown into shreds by a brisk, steadier wind, in the little steep glen and in the great glen below: and suddenly streaks of blue appeared in the sky, between long ribbons of hurrying, tattered clouds.

'Geordie!' I cried, 'the storm has blown away!'

'Ay,' he said grumpily. 'An' it wull blaw back, forbye, an' pu' the nebs frae oor faces.'

I remembered that Geordie was old, and was quite as wet as I was: he might get dreadful rheumatics, while the worst that could happen to me was a cold in the head.

The croft itself had very low walls, partly of stone and partly of clay. The low-pitched roof was of turf, which made it look all the more like a lump in the ground, rather than a house. There was no chimney, but a hole in the roof from which a trickle of smoke came, whisked away by the wind. The shorter side of the building was not as long as two tall men, the longer side no longer than three men. There were no windows. On one side there was a small barn, built of mud up against the side of the croft, and on the other side a still smaller byre, in which there was one cow and one calf. The doorway into the croft was also the opening into the byre. By the barn there was a fair stack of peat, cut into blocks like large bricks; we ought to be able to get warm with so much fuel by, I thought, except that the peat was so wet I did not see how it could ever burn. There was a patch of ground nearby in which potatoes were growing, and a larger patch with a crop of oats, now all battered to the ground by the rain; a few sheep were huddled miserably in a pen. That seemed to be all that these crofters had.

Geordie Buchan called out, 'Dugald Crombie!'

An old woman came to the doorway of the croft (in which there hung no door); she had a shawl about her head and shoulders, and a tattered petticoat kilted up to show her bare old legs and feet. Her face seemed to have been marked by a lifetime of hunger and hopelessness; she made all her movements slowly, as though she found her skinny limbs too heavy to move quick. Yet her eye was blue and bright, and as soon as she saw Geordie Buchan she smiled a welcome and called a greeting.

Then she saw me.

It was as when the Countess saw me, Eugénie, the Duchess of Bodmin, Dandie McKillop, Geordie Buchan. The astonishment in her face was as sharp, the recognition as unmistakable. She said something to Geordie Buchan, rapidly, in a low voice, and he replied.

He led Falcon into the little byre, which was almost too low for his head; his own horse had to stay outside, for he was too tall. Geordie took off Falcon's saddle and bridle, and began to rub down my very wet beauty with a wisp of rough grass. (Falcon seemed quite happy, and to know that he was being cared for as well as could be.) The old woman followed Geordie, and they chattered to each other in the same low tone; I could not pick up a word, and even wondered if they were speaking in the Gaelic. Every now and then, as she asked questions or listened to Geordie's answers, she glanced back over her shoulder at me with a face full of wonder.

She had known my grandfather. It must be so. But where? The great ladies had known him in their great world – in cities, in castles, perhaps in England, or even abroad; Eugénie had so met him. Geordie Buchan had travelled widely as his master's groom; if, as I was sure, he too had known my grandfather, it might equally have been almost anywhere. Even Dandie Mc-Killop had lived his feckless life, in and out of prison, in many places. But this old wife? It was likely she had never left the glen in her life. Where else, then, did she see him but here?

I frowned, puzzling, while they chattered softly. Nothing linked my grandfather to this place, that I knew of. Had he, perhaps, visited the other Drummond branch, the General's branch, and become known in the neighbourhood? No – the General had only bought his place a few years ago. That would not do. The Countess had known him. Had he visited Glendraco? It seemed likely. But would a visit to friends leave so indelible a mark on the memories of the simple people? Would a grandchild's face, so many years later, cause the excitement I was seeing?

I do not know what welcome I would otherwise have had. The poorest crofters are some of the most hospitable people in the world, some of the greatest of natural gentlefolk; and I think the worn old woman would not have turned me away. As it was, she made me feel that my coming to her roof was the rarest honour and keenest pleasure she had ever known. She curtseyed. She bade me welcome in a stilted, formal, old-fashioned way, which maybe she had learned from a dominie half-a-century before. She ushered me into the croft, and begged me to sit down. Yet there was nothing obsequious in her manner; she did not whine, nor cozen, nor bow and scrape; she kept all her dignity, for she was in her own house, where she was mistress.

But what a house it was. One room; the hearth a hollow in the floor, in which smouldered a few blocks of peat, filling the small space with smoke that smelled very good, but made my eyes smart; the floor itself was trodden earth, now puddled and muddy from the rain which had poured in through the hole in the roof; there was a single rude bedstead, one rough wooden table, three stools, a chest, a shelf of cooking-pots. There seemed to be no other furniture; the Crombies seemed to have no other worldly goods; but it was hard to see quite clearly, as the only light came through the door and the hole in the roof.

Geordie came in from the byre, tugging off his bonnet as he ducked under the lintel of the doorless doorway. I noticed that his manners, usually most free-and-easy, were as formal in this impoverished hovel as those of our hostess herself. I made a resolution that I, too, would behave with strict correctness, which was not quite natural to me.

Geordie told me that the horses were perfectly well, and could leave at any time. It was a question whether it was better to dry ourselves by the peat fire in the croft, and risk the return of the storm, or to start straight back. I would rather have stayed to get dry, for my soaking and clinging clothes were most uncomfortable; the old wife, Flora Crombie, begged me to do so. But the fire was so wretched, and gave off so little heat in spite of all the smoke, that I despaired of ever getting dry from its warmth.

'I think we should start back at once, Geordie,' I said. To Flora Crombie I said, 'But I am very grateful for your kind offer of hospitality, Mrs Crombie, and hope I may visit you here another time.'

She nodded quickly, a dozen times, like a mechanical doll; there was a bright, sharp look in her old blue eyes which was not in the least like that of a doll.

Shortly after Geordie, Dugald Crombie came into the croft; he had been busy somewhere about his tiny holding. He wore a plaid over his shoulders like a shawl; his clothes and boots looked so rough that they might have been home-made. His face was so thin that the bones of his cheek and jaw seemed like to break through the skin. He had long, sparse white hair, and a long white beard, yet about him there was a neat and self-respecting look. He had nothing of Dandie McKillop's savage wildness – and nothing of Dandie's hatred, either. Like Flora's, his eyes were blue; like hers, his were full of bright interest and intelligence.

Like Flora, he stopped short when he saw me, and a look of joyful amazement spread over his face.

He made me welcome, as the wife had done, with dignified formality. I shook hands with him, and said we were leaving at once, but would come back to see them again.

We mounted, and rode to the bank of the burn. Geordie Buchan whistled when he saw it. Between its high, steep banks it had spated from a cheerful stream into a torrent. But I was not seriously worried, for I knew that a quarter-of-a-mile down stream there was the place where we had forded it before, with banks of more moderate steepness, and a smooth gravel bottom. Besides, Geordie's company on the homeward journey was as reassuring as Billy's had been on the outward.

We walked our horses down the hillside towards the wood, and to the place where we had crossed. Since the water was much broader, it was shallower, and did not roar at such an alarming pace between its banks. But of course there was far more water than the few inches of our earlier crossing, and it was rushing down, swollen with rain, at a far greater rate, and with far more noise. I did not like the look of it at all.

Geordie shouted, over the brawling of the waters, 'If we're tae gang, Miss Kirstie, we maun gang the noo. The burn wull rise a bit yet.'

I nodded. I knew that the important thing was to feel no fright, or my fright would be communicated to Falcon, and we should never get across. So I fought down the nervousness which was making a lump in my throat, and spoke cheerfully to my horse.

Geordie shouted that he would go first, and I was to follow close after. He would seize my bridle if Falcon was difficult.

Things went wrong almost from the first.

Geordie sent his horse scrambling down the bank and into the furious edge of the burn. Before he was more than a yard from the bank he turned and beckoned me to follow. Falcon, beginning his own nervous descent, slipped on the treacherous wet turf, and slithered all the way down on his hocks and tail. I clung on, by his mane, with the greatest difficulty, and we recovered ourselves at the bottom of the bank with no dignity and little confidence.

Geordie grinned at me encouragingly, and kicked his sensible old horse further into the burn. The water instantly frothed about his knees, and above, but neither horse nor rider seemed perturbed. I tried every way I knew to get Falcon into the water after them, but instead of going forwards he stumbled sharply backwards, tossing his head, snorting with alarm, terrified of the furious water. Geordie came back to us, and seized Falcon's bridle. He tried by main force to drag Falcon forwards into the burn, while I urged him forward too. Between us, at last, we got him down into the burn, and he found his feet on the gravel. Geordie grinned at me again. I thought we had won. But the water boiling round his legs, and plucking at my own boots, had lost none of its terrors for Falcon, and he rolled his eyes and snorted, and tried to pull himself backwards against the strength of Geordie's arm. I thought he was going to pull Geordie out of the saddle. Then I think Falcon stepped upon a loose stone (as Billy did, when he sprained his ankle) – he went almost down, half falling sideways. I clung desperately to his neck, but his neck, and my gloves, were slippery with wet, and I lost my seat and fell into the water with a monstrous splash. I went completely under; the water closed, for a moment over my head. I was on my feet in a second, spluttering, the water tugging violently at my habit-skirt; I found that I was holding Falcon's reins, and keeping hold even of my whip. Geordie had lost his own hold of Falcon's bridle, and Falcon now took it into his head to bolt not to the far bank, but to the one he had just left. He hauled himself up on to the bank, pulling me with him. I was wetter, wetter by far, than after the worst of the storm: every stitch of my clothes, every inch of my skin, every hair of my head, was wringing wet: and, most unpleasant of all, I could feel that my boots were full of water.

At this moment the rain chose to start again, heralded by a vicious squall which came lashing straight down the little glen.

While Falcon and I were scrambling out on to the near bank,

Geordie's horse, alarmed by the commotion behind him, bolted forward and pulled himself out on the far bank. Geordie turned him, and tried immediately to come back to help me. Every second I could see that the burn was rising, coming down faster, and blacker, and angrier. Perhaps it was this, perhaps the rain which now lashed at him, perhaps the memory of Falcon's near-collapse in the flood – something, at any rate, now got into Geordie's horse, and nothing Geordie could do would get him down into the water again. Geordie at last dismounted, splashed into the water (which came over his knees) and tried to pull his horse after him. The horse backed away, snorting, as Falcon had done, and pulled Geordie out of the water again.

So we stood on opposite sides of the burn, holding our horses, very wet, shouting at each other over the thrash of the rain and the roar of the waters between us.

I screamed, 'I'll go back to the croft! I'll be quite safe there! I'll get warm and dry! I'll put Falcon in the byre, and take his saddle off, and dry him too! You must go back, Geordie, and tell them I am quite well and safe!'

'Ye'll bide the nicht at the croft?' Geordie screamed at me.

'I have no choice!'

'Ay,' He shrugged. 'The diel drives.'

He did not like the arrangement. Nor did I, remembering the muddy floor, the rude furniture, the smouldering and reeking fire in the croft. But the devil was driving indeed.

I walked Falcon back to the croft through the coldest rain I ever felt, and found the warmest welcome I ever met.

eight

The old people did everything very slowly, as though they no longer had the strength or the will to move briskly. Yet somehow the things that had to be done were done more quickly, and with less fuss, than they would have been by a crowd of busy people rushing this way and that.

Dugald Crombie made a much bigger fire, and blew at it until I thought he would blow his lungs out of his chest. At first all he produced was an ever-denser cloud of smoke, which went not upwards through the hole in the roof, but all over the inside of the croft, and especially into my eyes and nose. The peat-reek was still a haunting and delightful smell, but it made the tears run down my cheeks.

Then Dugald went out to look after Falcon, which he said he knew well how to do.

'I warkit as a grum at the cassel, lang syne, wi' Geordie Buchan,' he said. 'The auld days war the gret days, the days o' the auld folk . . .'

He checked himself. His wife made a clang with the lid of a cooking-pot, looking at him fixedly.

'The old folk?' I asked.

'Ay,' said Dugald, 'the auld Airl o' Draco, granfaither o' the yin that bides there noo. Ay, an' the guid leddy, who bides there yet, wi' her mon deid an' her son deid . . .'

Saying no more, he stumped out to the byre.

While he was there, he could guard the doorway of the croft against any intruder: for now his wife helped me to take off my boots and every stitch of my clothes. She wrapped me in a great coarse plaid, and began to rub me as though it were a towel. It smelled most peculiar, of peat-smoke and fish and something I could not place, but did not like; and it was so rough that I thought it would scrape off my skin like a carpenter's file. But under her rubbing I was soon tingling and warm. She then unpinned my hair, and when it was all loose down my back she dried that also, with another piece of coarse woollen cloth from the chest.

'Eh,' she crooned, as she rubbed and tugged at my hair, 'I ne'er saw a heid sae bonny, syne . . .'

'Since when?' I asked. 'Who had a head like mine, Mrs Crombie?'

'Eh, I dinna mind. I'm an auld body an' ma mind wainders . . .'

When my hair was a little drier, we took turns dragging a

gap-toothed comb through it. Then Flora Crombie went once again to the chest by the wall, and found clothes for me – a woollen petticoat, a coat of her man's, and another rough shawl. The petticoat was much too short for me, reaching barely to my knees; there was nothing for my feet and legs, as my hostess possessed neither shoes nor any stockings.

My own dripping clothes were hung on a string close to the fire. I imagined they would never afterwards lose the smell of peat-smoke: and hoped they would not.

'Eh,' said Flora Crombie, 'I'll set aboot oor denner. There's naethin' but tatties an' a wheen salt fush. The morn we'll hae a gob o' aitmeal porridge, an' mebbe the burn wull be sunkit an' ye'll reed awa hame.'

'I expect the burn will be down,' I agreed, 'as it's a fine evening now. But I shall be very sorry to leave.'

'Eh! Yon's the kind word, an' nae surprees tae chiels that kenned the auld folk ... Losh, there's ma mind wainderin' – wha' cud I be ettlin' at?' She muttered and chattered to herself as she started getting the meal, as though she was giving me a performance that would make me think her mind was wandering. It did not make me think so. Words had slipped out, and she was trying to cover them up. They were not quite as careful as Geordie in guarding their tongues.

Yet, what had they let slip out? The man said he had been a groom for the old folk – for the old Earl, the Countess's long-dead husband. The wife said that, to people who had known the old folk, it was no surprise to hear a kind word. She had seen a head like mine, dark red hair like mine, long ago. It could all mean much or little: everything or nothing.

I sat on one of the little crude stools, stretching out my hands to the fire. I wriggled my toes on the damp earth of the croft's floor, and tried to pull the petticoat down over my bare knees. My shins were warmed by the fire, which burned steadily, but still sullenly and with more smoke than flame. I felt strange in the single, rough, short petticoat, the man's coat, the odd-smelling shawl. I was used to wearing so many clothes, and such different ones; certainly I was used to something beneath my skirts. I did not at all dislike the feeling of freedom; I was not at all worried by the possible immodesty, because I so completely trusted the Crombies, and I knew that no one else would come by this lonely place.

I was quite wrong.

Over the subdued clatter of Flora Crombie's simple cooking, I heard a greeting called in a gentleman's voice, a reply in Dugald Crombie's voice, Falcon's neigh and that of another horse, greeting each other as the men had done.

Suddenly I remembered what my parting from Billy had put quite out of my mind – the scarce-seen horseman on the hillside above us. This might be he. It must be he.

'My horse is lame,' said Lord Caerlaverock's voice. 'I've walked with him for close on a hundred miles. Well, perhaps two miles. Even if he could walk back to the castle, I can't. Besides, I doubt if the burn can be crossed until morning. Is it possible that you can give us both a roof for our heads for the night?'

Of course it was possible. The horse could be tied up in the lee of the byre, and the gentleman could sleep in the barn.

Lord Caerlaverock – my delightful friend Jack. I was bewildered. He had left the picnic party just after us, and ridden over the rough high ground. He had travelled furtively, trying not to be seen. Why?

I remembered the look he had given Billy Mainwaring, when Billy and I came out from behind the carriages at Lochgrannomhead – the cold and angry look, so unlike his usual happy expression. The sick thought occurred to me that he planned some mischief to Billy, as soon as Billy was alone. Billy would have ridden to the pass at the head of the glen, and then down into the grim solitude of the Dead Glen. There would be nobody there, except the throngs of reproachful ghosts of slaughtered robbers. The weather was thick and the visibility bad, so that even if there were some lonely herd, with his handful of sheep and his collie-dog, any dark deed could pass unseen. Would he ride up behind the unsuspecting Billy, his horse's hoofs silent on the wet ground . . .? Ah no, not he, a civilized man, a gentleman. And they were old friends, who made each other and everybody else laugh with their banter . . .

Well, then, why? What was he about? Why was he here? Was his horse truly lame?

In the two weeks and more that he had been at the castle, I

had scarcely been alone with him once. For most of that time, the castle had been full of guests, and nearly everything was done in large parties. Picnics, fishing expeditions, walks and rides were all great chattering collections of people. Since the crowd had become smaller, I might have been alone with him; but I seldom was, because Billy was always by. Thinking about it, by the smoky fire in the croft, I recalled an impression that Billy had made Caerlaverock sheer off. Caerlaverock had approached me, seen that Billy was there, and changed his direction – pretended that he was not intending to come and talk to us, but was on his way somewhere quite different. While Rollo Craker was there, he came to talk to me no matter who was already with me, or what we were doing; when David Baillie rode over from Inverlarig, he attached himself to me as eagerly as Rockfall himself, with an equal disregard for my preference, or anyone else's. But Caerlaverock was prouder than they, and invented urgent errands for himself, so as not to be part of a court.

The result of all this was that I had not got to know him any better. I knew no more about him than I had learned that first evening at Gaultstower – that he was sometimes very funny, in a mock-solemn way, that many females admired him, and that he thought, or said he thought, that I was beautiful. In fact, I felt that the longer he stayed at Glendraco the less I knew him. After that first half-hour, I felt that he was my friend, and I understood him. Now I was not sure if he was my friend, and I was quite sure I did not understand him.

I wondered if he would still think me beautiful, in a man's coat and a crofter-woman's rough short petticoat, bare-legged and bare-footed, with my hair damp and tangled down my back. I reached out to feel my own clothes. They were all still very wet. The thought of pulling on wet stockings and underclothes was most unpleasant; if Caerlaverock came into the croft, he would have to put up with the sight of a strange wild peasant-girl.

He and Dugald Crombie were talking quietly in the byre. I could not hear what they said, but I heard Caerlaverock's laugh. He did not seem depressed by wetness, or his horse's lameness. It was a most cheerful laugh. He sounded as happy as when he had been fishing for the Gaultstower trout. It was not the laugh of a man who had planned a desperate and violent act – still less that of a man who had struck down a friend from behind. I put that ridiculous thought out of my head. The question remained – why had he followed us, trying to be invisible, mile after mile up the glen?

At last it seemed that his horse was looked after, and some rough bed prepared for its rider by Dugald in the barn. In a moment, surely, he would come in. I tried to tug the petticoat down over my bare knees, embarrassed, a little nervous because I knew I looked so odd. I was glad for the first time that there were no windows in the low walls of the croft.

Caerlaverock came in. He saw me, and smiled. The smile deepened the dimple in his chin, and made his blue eyes very bright. His butter-coloured hair, usually so smooth, was tousled and damp. He carried his riding-coat over his arm; in his shirt-sleeves, slight as his figure was, he looked very wiry and well-muscled.

'Another orphan of the storm,' he said cheerfully. 'You look about twelve years old, Kirstie, and more beautiful than any human being has any right to look. You have never, I imagine, been caught in heavy rain while wearing tight buckskin breeches? I don't recommend it.'

He greeted Flora Crombie with proper formality, thanking her courteously for allowing him shelter under her roof. He made her laugh, as he made everybody laugh. He said that potatoes and salt fish were, of all foods, those he most wanted.

I noticed that, with his free hand, he was carrying something behind his back. He brought it out, as though deciding not to bother any longer with hiding it. It was a bottle, a plain heavy black bottle, crudely stoppered with a piece of wood. He pulled out the stopper, raised the bottle to his lips, tilted it, and drank deep.

Flora Crombie's smile faded. She looked at him in surprise, perhaps with alarm.

Lowering the bottle at last, Caerlaverock said to her, 'You have no cause to worry, Mistress. Banish that pensive frown, if you know what the words mean. Coming down to the croft from behind, I saw your man busy with some activity that did *not*

173

appear to me agricultural. When he removed himself, I came discreetly on, and found his illicit still. It is very well hidden – I have already congratulated him on his ingenuity. I cannot flatter myself that he was, at first, altogether pleased by my discovery, but now we have come to an understanding satisfactory to all parties.'

'Ay?' said Flora Crombie dubiously.

'Ay, indeed.' Turning to me, Caerlaverock went on with undiminished good humour, 'Whisky, you know, is the only manufacturing industry in this part of Scotland. On the West Coast they used to turn kelp into soap – and even into glass, I believe, though it is hard to imagine seaweed being transmuted into glass – but scientific progress has destroyed that trade. That is one reason why so many unfortunate West Highlanders have been compelled to emigrate. Landlords, of course, are the other – landlords, and their sheep and deer. Whisky remains, keeping a few folk busy. But it attracts a monstrous duty – ten shillings and fourpence per proof gallon today, and liable to be increased. Consequently a great deal is privily distilled by gentlemen like our host, out of grain and potatoes. Selling the product is the only way many crofters can pay their rent. Is that not the case with you, Mistress Crombie?'

'Ay,' said the old woman reluctantly. 'There's naethin' frae the land tae mak' eneuch siller tae gi' the Airl's factor.'

'As I thought,' said Caerlaverock, smiling sympathetically. 'Your corn and potatoes hardly feed yourselves. You burn all the peat you cut, and eat all the salmon you poach. Since your man has the art to distil good whisky, he has my warmest commendation. Many people, of course, would feel differently. Your friend Henry Cricklade, Kirstie, would be off in a lather to the Revenue Officers. Neil Draco, I imagine, also, although he benefits indirectly from the still. My clear duty, as his guest, is to report Dugald's industry to him, but I have allowed Dugald to persuade me to keep silent. I am shocked to say that I have allowed myself to be bribed.'

'What?' I asked, very surprised.

'With this,' explained Caerlaverock happily, raising the bottle again to his lips and taking a long pull. He turned to Flora

Crombie, and said with more solemnity. 'You must not imagine, Mistress, that I am taking the bread from your mouth, or his rent from the Earl of Draco. This excellent whisky is paid for. When more is required, as I sense it will be, from the store under the potatoes in the barn, that will be paid for too. This lays, I trust, the doubt I see in your face?'

'Ay,' said Flora Crombie without enthusiasm.

Caerlaverock produced a gold sovereign from the pocket of his waistcoat, and slapped it down on a stool.

'I know the laws of Highland hospitality,' he said. 'I would no more dream of offering you payment for our board and lodging than you would dream of accepting it. But your man's whisky is another matter. That you must allow me to pay for.'

Flora Crombie nodded, but her face did not altogether clear. I thought that what troubled her was, that she would much have preferred no gentleman, however friendly and free-handed, to know the secret of the hidden still.

Caerlaverock's eyes roved about the croft, taking in the crude furniture, the muddy floor, the smoking fire, the primitive cooking. They lighted on myself, and especially on my bare legs. Though Scotland was full of the bare legs of dairymaids and tinker-girls, no man – not even old Doctor Nicholson in Edinburgh – had seen my calves and knees since I was a little girl. I sometimes thought this was rather a pity, as I was proud of the slimness and straightness of my legs, but the rules of ladylike modesty were absolute, as much in Glendraco as in Princes Street. Now circumstances obliged me to sit with my knees shamelessly displayed, and permitted Lord Caerlaverock to inspect them.

His eyes roved further, to the string on which hung my wet clothes. All my underclothes were draped there, fully visible, unmistakable. He knew exactly what I had on, or, to put it more exactly, what I did not have on. I was thankful that the Crombies were with us, and would be all night in the croft.

I wanted to ask Caerlaverock if he had followed us. I wanted to ask him why. But I was frightened of the answer.

Dugald Crombie came in, very cheerful. He said the evening was set fair and the night would be braw, the burn would be passable to the horses the morn's morn, and his work outside was completed. He did not at all share his wife's disquiet, even though it would be he that went to gaol if the still was reported. In a moment I saw why he was so carefree. He, like Caerlaverock, carried a squat black bottle, and took regular drinks from it.

In answer to a look from his wife, Dugald said, 'Och, dinna luk lak an auld Meenister, wumman. The whisky's a geeft frae his Lordship.'

'That's true, Mistress,' said Caerlaverock cheerfully. 'No gentleman likes drinking by himself, so I bought a few drams of Dugald's own liquor for him to quench his own thirst.'

His wife pursed her lips and clucked.

'I'm blithe tae accept the geeftie,' chuckled Dugald, his sparse hair and white beard looking a little more raffish than before.

'Yince ye stairt yon ploy,' said his wife, 'there's nae end tae't, ma mannie.'

I began to feel a small twinge of uneasiness.

Our supper was soon ready, and, since it was so simple, soon finished. I wolfed, with a ravenous hunger I could not conceal, all that the old people gave me. They wanted to press more on me, but I saw that their own suppers would then have been meagre indeed, so managed to summon the strength of will to refuse. We ate off cheap, chipped stoneware plates, brought out, because there was company, from the recesses of the chest; tin knives were our spoons and forks. It was a far cry from the bewildering display of silver (which I had at last nearly mastered) on the Glendraco dinner-table.

'I compliment you on your salted salmon, Mistress,' said Caerlaverock. 'I am glad to see that you have a barrel of it in the barn. Lesser people make do with salt herrings from the market, but you offer your guests the king of fish. Lord Draco's water-keepers would be interested in your barrel, but they shall not learn of it from me.'

Yet, though he praised the food, he ate very little of it, preferring the contents of his bottle. His eye was very bright, and his face flushed. He glanced often at my bare legs and knees, which I was unable to keep covered up. I thought, in his startling blue eyes, there was a little look of Findlay Nicholson's eyes.

But all the while he kept up a flow of good-humoured chatter, making Dugald Crombie laugh loud and long, and Flora sometimes smile, in spite of her disapproval of the drinking.

He talked about their own lives, and those of other crofters and small farmers. He talked about the toll-roads, which provided the money for road-making and the building of bridges, and were so much a hardship to the poor of the Highlands that a Royal Commission (whatever that might be) had the previous year said that they should be abolished. Then he talked about the emigration of so many families to Canada and Australia. They hated to go, he agreed with Dugald, because of their passionate love for their own hills; but they were driven away by sheep and red deer.

'Ay,' said Dugald passionately, 'yon Drumlaw, yon bluidy Campbell, yon's an ill laird. He dispossessit a dizzen auld tenants, an' pit in yin Lowland sheep-fairmer. There's mair siller syne, nae doot, but shudna the laird hae mind for his ane? Ay, an' he claired the hull o' the auld crofters, an' let the richts to a fat body frae Embro for the deer-stalkin'. Siccan's the ploy o' yon Drummond, tu, the yin they ca' Janerel—'

'General Drummond is a connection of your guest's, Dugald,' said Caerlaverock, laughing.

'Ay, the wrang, ill sept. Lang syne we kenned the auld folk o' the leopard. Noo we hae anely their ill brithers o' the wull-cat.'

'The old folk of the leopard?' I asked breathlessly. 'A leopard with a rose in its mouth?'

Before Dugald could reply, his wife slammed down the metal lid on the pot where the potatoes had boiled on the peat fire. He looked at her owlishly; then his glazed eyes cleared.

He said thickly, 'Tuts, I ken naethin' aboot sic foolishness.'

Outside it was now full dark. Inside, the peat fire, in its hollow in the mud floor, glowed and smouldered and sometimes burst into small tongues of flame, when Dugald kicked it with his home-made boot, or Flora poked at it with a stick. One candle burned in the neck of a bottle – an expensive luxury which, I guessed, the old people only provided because Caerlaverock and I were there. Candle-flame and fire illuminated only a little island in the darkness of the croft; small as the house was, its corners were in deepest darkness.

The only sounds were the sleepy movements of cow and calf and two horses in the byre, and the hissing of the wet peat-bricks on the fire, and then, ominously, the chink of Caerlaverock's bottleneck against his teeth when he drank from it.

'Another casualty of the storm, Dugald,' said Caerlaverock, lowering the empty bottle from his lips. 'Will another sovereign produce a successor?'

'Ay,' said Dugald, getting unsteadily to his feet.

'Well then, let two sovereigns provide two successors, one for each of these dead soldiers, yours and mine. I still don't like drinking alone.'

Dugald giggled shrilly. There was little about him now of the neat, self-respecting, dignified Highlander who had welcomed me to his croft. 'There's twa ahint the tatties,' he said, 'wull cam oot togither.'

He took the candle and stumbled out to the barn.

It was an eerie little world that we were left in – old Flora, Caerlaverock and me – the glow from the fire just enabling us to see each others' faces. Flora's face was set, alert, tight-lipped; sometimes she looked at Caerlaverock or at the fire, but more often her eyes were turned upon me, intent, bright, in their deep sockets, in the little glare of an occasional flame from the peat; it was as though she were trying to read words which were written upon my face.

The animals were silent in the byre. Dugald was softly stumbling and muttering in the barn. There was no sound of wind or water. The only noise was the hissing of the fire. Time seemed to be suspended. Something was going to happen.

Caerlaverock said suddenly to Flora, 'Is this glen haunted? Are there ghosts here, like all those wretched fellows I've heard of in the Dead Glen yonder?'

'Ay,' said Flora shortly. 'There's mony a dolefu' speerit greetin' maist nichts.'

Caerlaverock asked about kelpies, brownies, fairies, speaking quite seriously, as though he fully believed in them, and wanted only to know which of the supernatural beings were about in the Monaidh glen.

I remembered what the Reverend Lancelot Barrow had told

me – how superstitious the simple people were, in spite of the teaching of the Church, how unshakeably they believed in the Little People, and how often it was reported that they saw them. There in the heavy darkness of the corners of the croft, in the glow and flicker of the fire, it was very easy to believe what the Highlanders believed.

Flora's answers to Caerlaverock were as serious as his questions. It was very strange to me. She was a sensible, clear-eyed, quick-witted old lady; and she talked of the kelpies as she might have talked of the sheep or the Chireachan shepherds. They were familiar neighbours, and part of her life in this wild and isolated place.

'You have the second sight, Mistress?' asked Caerlaverock softly.

'Ay,' came Dugald's voice unexpectedly from the darkness of the doorway. Bottles clinked in his hands. He said the candle had blown out, and he had dropped it, and could not find it in the darkness of the barn.

'There's nae anither in the hoose,' he said. 'But the fire maks licht eneuch for honest bodies.'

'Echt, echt, wae's me, ma anely caundle,' said Flora crossly.

'We'll fund it the morn's morn,' said Dugald. 'We'll nae fash oorsel's noo, wi' mair geefties frae his lordship.'

Dugald, I thought, came back from the barn drunker than when he went out there. He could afford to drink deep of his own whisky, as Caerlaverock was paying far beyond its value.

'Ay, the wumman wull hae the second sicht,' he said to Caerlaverock. 'Ay ay, she'll speir fine intil the days tae cam.'

''Tis lang an' lang syne I lookit,' said Flora heavily. 'There's nae future for sic folks as we.'

'But for Miss Drummond?'

The old woman's eyes turned, burning, upon my face. She looked at me with an intensity which seemed to light fires within her eyeballs, so that they glowed like lamps in distant windows. I pulled my own eyes with difficulty away from hers, and looked down at the duller glow of the fire.

'Ye'll tak a dram, then,' said Dugald to his wife.

To my surprise she nodded.

She took the bottle from him, and drank deep.

'It mebbe fogs the heid,' she said, lowering the bottle at last. 'But it clairs the e'es.'

She drank again.

She too, before my eyes, changed as Dugald had changed. The neat white hair, pulled back tight from the old brow, seemed to shake loose and rise up from the scalp, like seaweed on a rock at the changing of the tide. Bright spots of colour, the size of Caerlaverock's sovereigns, appeared on the thin cheeks. Her hands became talons, like Eugénie's, one clutching the bottle by the neck, one circling hazily in the near-darkness before my face.

She drank deep a third time from the bottle. Her hand shook; some of the liquor ran down her chin.

There was a little crackle from the fire. A tongue of flame, shaped like a crocus-bud, leapt upwards and danced on the hissing peat. The tiny glare cast shadows upwards across Flora Crombie's face. Her face looked like an eldritch skull. The atmosphere was charged with strangeness, thick with ancient mystery; to my frightened mind it seemed that the dark corners of the croft were thronged with creatures of another world that I could almost see and hear.

I shivered. The strangeness prickled at the back of my neck.

Flora drank a fourth deep draught from the bottle, then began to speak in a weird high sing-song. Part of what she said was in the Gaelic; part was meaningless rambling. On and on she sang, like a mad old bard reciting a mad old story. I tried to drag my eyes away from her face, but I could not, for they were held by some compulsive power in her own eyes.

A few scraps of what she said I could understand.

She saw a horse fall among rocks. She saw a boat on the sea, and a man jumping from it. She saw a soldier lying upon a floor. She saw an angry river, and people fighting for their lives among rapids and whirlpools.

All the while she spoke her eyes bored into mine; they were like gimlets, drilling holes into my brain; I could not have looked away if a pillar of fire had danced in through the doorway of the croft.

Her voice became higher and thinner, unintelligible, like a

crazy child mouthing gibberish. She dribbled at the mouth and her eyes were glazed. She dropped the bottle; it rolled, and a little whisky spilled on the mud of the floor. The spell was broken. She slumped forward on her stool. Dugald and I caught her before she pitched forward into the fire.

'Hauld her sae, Miss Kirstie,' said Dugald thickly.

I held her up, marvelling at the emaciated stringiness of her body, which felt too frail to support life. Dugald managed to spread a plaid upon the floor, and we laid her down on it, and covered her with another plaid. He said that it sometimes happened so; she would be recovered in the morning, forgetful of what she had seen and said.

'I could make little of that,' said Caerlaverock in a slurred voice. 'Horses. Boats. Dead soldiers. People drow-drowning. If that's your future, my dear, I don't envy you. Well, I shall em-emulate our hostess. Stretch out in a trance. Goo'night. I'll take my friend, my only friend, there's still two inches left.'

His friend was the bottle. He walked very carefully to the doorway, and a moment later I heard him stumble into the barn.

Dugald was even drunker than Caerlaverock. He could hardly walk, and his speech was hardly intelligible. I gathered he intended to sleep in the byre, among the animals, leaving the croft to me for decency's sake. I thought he might not get as far as the byre, but I heard him stumbling there, and muttering to the cow, and almost immediately snoring.

I took off Dugald's old coat, lay down in the petticoat on the rough bed, and spread the shawl over myself. I was very tired and very bewildered. There was no sense to be made of Flora's ramblings. What had I to do with soldiers, or a man jumping out of a boat? What she said was no more than the ravings of a very old woman who had drunk a quantity of whisky. It had fogged her mind indeed.

I sighed and yawned and settled myself to sleep, thinking that no one had ever spent a stranger birthday.

I was woken by a hand on my shoulder, and a reek of whisky on my face. I opened my eyes. I could see nothing; it was pitch dark; there was no glow from the fire. I had no idea how long I had been asleep. I found that I was no longer covered by the shawl; it had fallen off me as I slept, or been lifted off me, and I lay on the bed in nothing but Flora's short petticoat.

Caerlaverock's voice, soft and slurred, said, 'Dugald would not wake if your horse danced on his belly. Flora would not wake if you and I danced on her belly. We're alone, my dear. Isn't that agreeable?'

His face was close to mine as he leaned over the bed, his hand holding my shoulder. The whisky on his breath sickened me. I tried to wriggle out of his grasp, but he held me fast. The liquor had not taken away any of his strength.

'What do you want?' I asked loudly, trying to give myself courage.

'Hush! You won't wake the Crombies, and you might disturb the animals. Even if we choose to be wakeful, they deserve their sleep.' He giggled shrilly. He sounded very drunk. He said, 'What do you think I want, you witch? Why do you think I rode after you? What do you think brought me here? Why do you suppose I spent four sovereigns reducing our friends here to un-unconsciousness?'

'You'd – you'd use force?' I gasped.

'I'd rather not. If you're a sensible girl I won't have to. Don't be frightened. You might enjoy it. You're made for love. You've been asleep all your life, you modest little Edinburgh Miss – now I'm going to wake you up. Why should you worry? What's a little de-deflowering among friends? I'll give you some money, of course. Not much, but some. You won't be the loser. Except what you call your virtue, of course, but what good is virtue to a girl like you? You won't get a noble husband, not you, so you might as well have a noble ra-ravisher, eh? Stop struggling, slut! I won't hurt you. Relax. Yield, make the best of it. I can be brutal or gentle. It's all one to me. Be still! I'll have you whether you like it or not, so why not try to like it?'

'You'll have to kill me!'

'Oh no, dear no. Stun you, perhaps, but not kill you.' His voice softened, became cajoling, caressing. He said, 'Ah Kirstie, precious and beautiful Kirstie, do you think I'd willingly hurt a hair of your head?'

'Then let me go!' I sobbed.

'Ah, would you be so cruel? I have burned and sickened for you since I first saw you. I have been driven nearly mad these last days, watching you simper at the fat lout Mainwaring, watching the hounds run after you drooling and slobbering ... Ah, pity me, Kirstie! Pity me!'

He was sitting beside me on the bed now. I could feel his hip pressed against mine. I tried again to struggle free of his imprisoning hand, but he gripped me tighter, so that it hurt, and then took my other shoulder with his other hand, so that I was like a wrestler at a country fair pinned down by a stronger opponent.

My eyes were becoming used to the darkness now. There was, after all, a faint sullen glow from the fire. I could see Caerlaverock's face close above mine; I could see the faint gleam of the firelight in his eyes and in his teeth as he bared them in a wild laugh.

'You're caught, little animal,' he cried, 'trapped and tied up. Struggling will only hurt you.'

His face swam down upon mine. I felt the full weight of his chest upon mine, and then I felt his face on my face and his mouth on my mouth. He took one hand from my shoulder, since I was helplessly pinned under his weight, and seized instead a handful of my hair, and held my head still for his whisky kisses. I could not move my head without agony, without pulling out my hair by the roots, so savage was his grip of it. I could not fight clear from the strength and weight of his body. I could not free my mouth from the invasion of his. I was very frightened, and furiously angry, and utterly helpless.

He took his other hand from my shoulder, thrust it between my body and his, and put it upon my breast. I tried to scream, but he smothered the scream with his own mouth. His hand on my breast was like a clutching animal. Then that same hand went down my body to my leg, and found the hem of the petticoat. I felt the hand on my bare thigh. It was more than ever like an animal, a scuttling and disgusting rat. It moved up my thigh.

I struggled with new and furious desperation. My hands were imprisoned under his body, but I pulled one clear and seized his own hair. I pulled as hard as I could, jerking his head away from mine, making him gasp with pain. I struggled so violently that I was almost sitting up.

'Ah, would you, you bitch?' he screamed.

Keeping still his grip on my hair, he wrenched my hand away from his head. Then he grasped the top of the petticoat and pulled it violently. The cheap cloth rent. He tore the stuff right down to the hem, so that it was in two halves, falling clear away from the front of my body. His free hand was everywhere on my body, groping, scuttling over my skin like a crab, and then violently forcing my legs apart.

He was panting, groaning, mouthing obscene words. He was not a man but a mad animal. There was nothing about this dribbling beast of the gay, smooth-haired, mock-solemn friend I had known. I turned into a wildcat myself, to escape the disgusting explorations of his hand. I flailed out at him, I scratched at his arms and face, I screamed. The effect was to give him further mad energy and strength. Still holding fast to my hair, he jerked my head down on to the bed, and threw himself on top of me.

I felt utter, sickening horror at the bestiality, the indignity I was being made victim of. With my right hand, clear of his imprisoning body, I groped on the floor by the bed for any weapon I could hit him with. My fingers closed on something long and thin – a narrow flexible rod – my whip. I had dropped it, perhaps, when I pulled off my wet clothes. I grasped it, and brought it down as hard as I could on his back. His head jerked back. He was grinning like a beast, mouthing, frothing. I hit him again, with all my strength, full in the face.

He let go of me. One hand flew to his face. He moaned. He took his hand away. There was blood on it. There was a bright dark line where my whip had struck, full across his cheek from ear to mouth.

He began to cry. He sat on the edge of the bed, hunched up like a wretched child, sobbing into his hands. His shoulders shook. His sobs were dry, harsh, uncontrolled.

I picked up the shawl which had covered me, and pulled it about my body. I was trembling violently, not from cold but from shock and horror. My head was very sore where he had pulled my hair. I felt bruised and battered, sickened and defiled.

But I breathed a prayer of thankfulness that his wild onslaught had failed, that my whip had been within reach, that he was now broken and sobbing. I did not think he would attack me again. But, in case he did, I held the whip.

After a long time his sobs became less frequent, less desperate. His face was still buried in his hands. He was the most abject sight in the world. To my very great surprise, I found I felt sorry for him.

I got up and walked over to the fire, holding the shawl tight about me, holding the whip. My legs were trembling, but they carried me. My strength began to return, and my calmness. My heart thudded less suffocatingly in my breast, and my breath rasped less painfully in my throat.

I looked at the huddled figure on the bed not with revulsion but with pity. It was horrible that a man should give way to such animal violence; it was also horrible that he should give way to such shameless misery.

He sniffed and hiccuped, like a child whose only toy is broken. He stood up, trembling worse than I, and gathered up his own clothes, some of which he had pulled off. He staggered out into the thicker darkness. I heard him go into the barn, lurch and fall, and burst into renewed sobs.

I looked down at my whip, my deliverance, seeing it dimly in the firelight. It was so handsome, with its silver-mounted ivory handle. I remembered that Lord Caerlaverock had given it to me, not twelve hours before.

My clothes were not perfectly dry in the morning, but they were dry enough to put on. By the first light of dawn I dressed as well as I could, and did what I could to put up my tangled hair, Flora was moaning in her sleep; I put the shawl over her.

I went out to the byre. Falcon was his proud, interested, friendly self. I stroked his glorious silken neck. Caerlaverock's horse, tied up to the outside of the byre, seemed cheerful also. I wondered if he was still lame. Dugald was asleep on the bare earth. His mouth was open, his hair and beard wild. He looked incredibly dissipated, and his clothes reeked of whisky.

Holding my pretty whip, I went at last to the barn.

Caerlaverock was sitting on the floor, leaning against a sack of potatoes. He was fully dressed, though untidily. His hair was on end, his eyes bloodshot. The livid stripe ran, dark red, from ear to mouth where I had whipped him. There were scratches on his face, too, which I had made. His face was a pasty yellow instead of a sunburned brown; he looked ill and miserable.

He looked away from me when I stood in the door of the barn. He said huskily, almost inaudibly, 'Forgive me. Forgive me. I was mad. It was whisky. I love you too much. I wish I were dead. I wish I were dead.'

He got with difficulty to his feet, keeping his face turned away from mine. He said, 'I'll go away. You won't see me again. Tell Draco I'll send back his horse.'

He pushed blindly past me, and went unsteadily to the byre. Somehow, fumbling, he managed to saddle and bridle his horse. I thought I should help him, but I could not bear to go close to him, to this sick, whisky-soaked shadow of the man I had liked so much.

He had great difficulty mounting, and nearly fell off over the far side of his horse. He clutched the mane, and kept his seat; rolling in the saddle, he set off at a walk. He did not look back at me.

I noticed, as he went, that the horse was not lame at all.

The burn was down. Geordie Buchan came for me. He slapped the Crombies awake, and they stammered embarrassed farewells. Flora had no recollection of her soothsaying, but only of the whisky she had drunk, which she bitterly regretted. Dugald could hardly speak, and Geordie's laugh seemed to hurt his head.

We rode back gently, Geordie and I, Falcon stepping high and proud, and not a whit worse for storm or spate or his night in the byre of the croft. We rode together over the drawbridge into the outer courtyard of the castle.

The Earl strode out of a small door, moving more rapidly than I had ever seen him move. He seized Falcon's bridle, and looked at me searchingly.

'Falcon is well,' I said.

The Earl looked hard at Geordie Buchan.

'Ay, all's well,' said Geordie.

'I am to tell you,' I said, 'that Lord Caerlaverock will send your horse back.'

'Caerlaverock?' said the Earl, startled. 'He was at the croft?'

'Yes.'

'Alone with you?'

'Of course not. The Crombies were there.'

'He was at no time alone with you?'

'At no time.'

'Why was he there?'

'He was caught by the spate of the burn, as I was. He said his horse was lame, but it was not lame this morning.'

'He went away this morning?'

'At dawn, yes.'

'Why?'

'He did not say.'

'I was relying on him. He knew that. Why did he go away, Miss Drummond? Was he drunk last night?'

It was on the tip of my tongue to say: Yes, he was drunk; he was changed into a wild animal; he disgraced himself; I cut his face open with the whip he gave me; he went away out of shame. But this would give away the illicit still of Dugald Crombie, who could not afford a drop of whisky he did not make himself, and could not pay his rent without the still.

'How could Caerlaverock be drunk,' I said, 'in a croft where the people can hardly afford to eat?'

The Earl gave me a long, solemn, impenetrable look from under his heavy black brows; then he turned abruptly, and went back in through the little door.

Everyone was concerned about Caerlaverock. He was promised for the twelfth, for the first day of the grouse-shooting, and it was most unlike him to break his engagements, or to miss a chance of sport. The Earl looked grave, and stroked his chin. Lady Arabella sniffed and muttered, and whispered to Mrs Forbes. Angelica stared at me with large, soulful, solemn eyes. Someone was sent to the Monaidh glen to ask the Crombies what had happened; they knew nothing about Caerlaverock's departure, for they had been asleep, and they said nothing about whisky.

The Countess looked at me with a troubled face, but held her peace. Eugénie hissed and mumbled in the shadows.

After three days, a man brought the horse back. He took it straight to the stables, and only Wattie Dewar spoke to him. He was a servant of the inn at Lochgrannomhead; he rode the horse and led a pony, and rode away on the pony. He did not tell Wattie if he had seen Caerlaverock, nor if he knew where Caerlaverock had gone; the dour Wattie did not ask him. He brought a letter for the Countess, written by Caerlaverock at the inn. It contained only thanks and apologies; there was no word of explanation for his strange behaviour.

People looked at me oddly. Nobody said anything.

'Well, dear,' said Mrs Forbes comfortably, as we sat sewing in one of the silken rooms, 'it seems that everything is settled at last, and we are to be told the news! It is so exciting! I am sure that no two people were ever more ideally suited. So accomplished as dear Angelica is, with her music and her painting! And so concerned about the poor, and so forth. She will be the greatest help to Cousin Neil in his political life. Only imagine! A great London hostess! I should be thrown into palpitations if I had to stand at the head of a stairway, as hostess of an evening reception, but she will grace the rôle! All the friends of both, I am sure, will be enchanted at the news. Of course she was born into the purple, as they say, though I am never *quite* sure what that can mean. Purple long-clothes for a little baby? It seems hardly suitable. A purple cradle? Of course humble folk like us do not understand the ways of the great, even if they are, like myself, remotely connected to them by cousinship. The late Professor, I believe, *preferred* not to understand them. I do not know when the announcement is to be. I imagine we shall hear of it, officially you know, at the dinner-table one evening. What a moment that will be! We shall all raise our glasses and drink a toast to the happy pair! But I must be careful to raise my glass only once, of course, or my poor head will begin to spin, as it always does. And afterwards there will be a general announcement to the tenants and neighbours, and I daresay a party of some kind. Perhaps a bonfire! And then the announcement will appear in all the newspapers in London. It is a great event, you know, an important piece of news. The union of two noble families! Lady Arabella is so happy that matters are resolved at last. And so am I, and so must we all be! I am sure that Cousin Elinor must be delighted also, and thankful that one day the mistress of Glendraco will be someone so suitable as dear Angelica. Of course Cousin Neil could always be trusted to make a proper choice. He has a very keen sense of his duty. He much resembles the late Professor in that regard, though in other ways he is somewhat different. Dear Angelica has not much money of her own, but that scarcely signifies, since Cousin Neil has so much. She will bring him, as I was saying to Lady Arabella, gifts far more valuable than gold. Her accomplishments, her birth and breeding! She will grace the rank of Countess. Of course her grandfather was an Earl too, though her father was only a commoner. Still, he was a man of great eminence. Senior Steward of the Jockey Club, you know, which many people think higher than Prime Minister! I doubt if Mrs Carlyle would agree, but she is so serious. She and the late Professor would have had much in common. Perhaps it is as well that they never met! ... I wonder what can have come over Lord Caerlaverock? He rode away from your birthday picnic, you know, with such a strange look on his face. We miss him here, do we not? And Sir Hannibal too, but of course he will return. Like a bee to the honey-pot! Of course no one blames you for encouraging him, dear, as it is such a chance for you, though to be sure some of our neighbours have remarked ... Well well, I am not one to repeat gossip. Mr Baillie – I suppose I should call him Inverlarig, but it always seems to me so odd to call gentlemen by the name of their house, or estate, or whatever it is, instead of by their names, but in many ways I am still unused to the Highlands – what was I saying? To be sure, Inverlarig, but then he suffers so dreadfully from his gout. And General Drummond is so strict in his views of behaviour! One would think we were all soldiers under his command! ... I thought, you know, that Caerlaverock was sweet on your little friend Charlotte Long. Such a pretty little thing, so English rosy, with those golden ringlets! Lady Campbell and Georgina told me, oh, months ago, before ever you came here, dear, that they expected an announcement in that quarter. Perhaps that is why he went away. And yet, how could it be? ... Going away is a thing I myself will never do, because I have nowhere else to go! Of course I am imposing dreadfully on Cousin Elinor, as she allows me to call her, but there! I help all I can, in little ways, with a word here, and a stitch there, so I do not feel entirely useless ... One of our Lords goes, but another is to arrive. You knew that, I expect? That Lord Cricklade is awaited? He comes here nearly every year, at about this time. Cousin Elinor has known him from a baby, you know, so he is almost one of the family. Of course he is more serious than Lord Caerlaverock, or Sir Hannibal. To be sure he is a little older. He is cast more in the mould of Cousin Neil, perhaps. The late Professor was of the same stamp, a man of duty and conscience and deep thought. I used to see him thinking! Simply sitting and thinking! Can you imagine such a thing? I, for my part, am *not* given to deep thought. I am incapable of it! I would not know how to begin to think deeply! I do not suppose you will see much of Lord Cricklade, dear. He will not be a companion for you, as Lord Caerlaverock was, or Sir Hannibal. He will be on the hill, as they say, or by the river, and when he is here he will be discussing deep matters with Cousin Neil. I don't expect that you or I, dear, if we chanced to eavesdrop, would understand a word of what they said! I daresay, though, that dear Angelica will be included in their discussions, for she is so very clever, and well-informed, as well as everything else! But here is Mr Barrow, dear, calling you to your duties in the library.'

nine

'I can't believe it,' said Lord Cricklade. 'I simply cannot credit the evidence of my eyes. Is this really the little waif from Edinburgh whom I found sobbing by the drive at Lucksie? The dowdy little Puritan running away from home?'

'It is only,' I said, 'that I have nicer clothes now.'

'No, Miss Drummond, it is not only that you have nicer clothes, and a maid who is good at doing your hair. You hold your head up, and look the world in the eye. That is the difference. You look as though you belonged here.'

'I do belong among hills and rivers,' I said. 'I always knew that. I don't know why, because I come from a city.'

'You are well out of that city.'

'Oh yes. I like a large sky between mountains, not a small one between houses.'

He smiled, and said, 'We are two of a kind, I think.'

'I think that is flattering.'

'I am flattered you should think so. Actually, however, it is I who am outrageously flattered by the comparison. I have been used to riding all my life, but I have never come within a distance of your style on horseback. I have been used to big houses all my life, but I have never ventured your manner of entering a room.'

'Oh,' I said, pleased at what he said about my riding, but puzzled about the other. 'How do I enter a room?'

'As though all the people in it were at once your servants and your friends.'

'My servants! Oh dear. That is dreadful. I did not think I looked so conceited.'

'You didn't think you were beautiful, when we first met. At least, you said you didn't, and I did not think you made remarks like that in the way of fishing for compliments. I still don't think so. But you must know now that you are beautiful. Great heavens, girl, every man I hear of is desperate for love of you!'

He looked at me with such open friendship and admiration that, though I smiled, I blushed: and, though I felt myself blushing, I still smiled.

'But,' I said, 'you are the Rock of Gibraltar.'

'Am I? Who says I am?'

I remembered it was Charlotte Long who had told me Lord Cricklade's nickname. But I said, 'It was a great friend of mine. She tells me you are impervious.'

'Then she is a goose. I daresay I'm impervious to her, whoever she may be, but—'

'But she is much prettier than me,' I said. 'Truly she is. I shall not tell you her name, because that would be betraying a confidence, but if I did you would be obliged to agree at once that she is *much* prettier than me. Than I, I believe I should say.'

'Yes, I believe you should, but I always say "than me". Probably this ill-judging female *is* prettier than you, my wicked one-time passenger, because I don't call you pretty at all.'

'Oh,' I said, trying not to look as mortified as I felt.

'You are a raving beauty, which is a different thing.'

I blushed again; I could feel it; and I was still smiling; I could feel that too.

He had arrived five days before, in an open carriage with a pair of bright bay trotters. He complained that no railway came within seventy miles of Glendraco, but his mode of travel suited him. I could not imagine him sitting demurely in a train, like an Edinburgh advocate, or a wholesale grocer. He brought a quantity of gun-cases, and rod-cases, and two setter dogs, and a wizened little manservant, as brown as a nut, called Jewkes.

He said he found me changed. I found him marvellously unchanged. He was not quite as tall as the Earl, but more powerfully built. He had cut shorter his thick, curly light-brown hair, and shaved off most of his sidewhiskers, which had the effect of making him look younger. He still wore an old, neat knickerbocker suit and a tweed cap, and he still looked a man who never willingly spent a minute of daylight indoors.

He was not as *gay* as Billy (whom I remembered constantly) or as Caerlaverock (whom I tried hard to forget, but whose memory gave me nightmares). One was not always laughing at what he said. But he made me feel comfortable, and even sensible, and quite grown-up. I did not like him better than Billy, but I liked him in a different way. I could not tell what the difference was, exactly.

Billy had written to the Countess, to the Earl, and to me. He said that his business was a tangle, and would take longer than he thought. He was very cross about it in all the letters. His letter to me was a love-letter, the first I had ever had. It was very short, and I could hardly read it (his handwriting was dreadful, as bad as my own), but it clearly said he loved me, and missed me very much. I missed him too.

As Mrs Forbes had predicted, Lord Cricklade spent most of his time with the Earl. They shot grouse over their dogs, sometimes on foot and sometimes taking the shooting-ponies, and fished for the salmon in the Draco. They had long, serious talks, about politics and Ireland and the problems of the Highlands, of which I heard a few mystifying scraps. Angelica was sometimes with them, listening with her usual gravity, looking very beautiful and other-worldly.

The expected announcement did not come of the Earl's engagement to Angelica, but nobody doubted it was imminent. Annie Simpson told me that the Servants' Hall were all very excited about it: but her own excitement somehow seemed more dutiful than real. She knew she *ought* to be excited; she was so good and sweet and loyal that she *tried* to be excited; but sometimes a crack showed, and a sort of apathy came through. I wondered if Mrs Weir and Patterson and the others felt the same. Perhaps, I thought, it was all so predictable, so proper, so inevitable, that it lacked the thrill of surprise.

Lord Cricklade said, confidentially to me, treating me as an equal, which was so kind and clever of him, 'She will make an admirable Countess. Draco could not have chosen more – suitably. She will not be another Dragon, precisely, but a swan, serenely regal, white-plumaged, unruffled, graceful, silent ... Silent to a fault, perhaps, but then the swan is mute, isn't it, until it sings at the moment of death ... Do you like her, Kirstie?'

'Yes,' I said immediately. 'She is always kind to me. But – I don't seem to get to know her at all, which is strange, after all these weeks. Usually I do become friendly with people. One gets, you know, to guess what they are thinking, and to tell if they are happy or sad ...'

'I know exactly what you mean,' he said. 'I find the same. I am sure she would never willingly give pain, or cause any unhappiness to anyone – which I suppose is the highest praise you can give a person – but she gives nothing away, does she? She is a shuttered window, in contrast to yourself—'

'Am I so very transparent?' I asked, perturbed.

'Yes, very. While Angelica is, in my experience, uniquely opaque. That is rather pompously expressed, which is probably the effect of prolonged intimacy with Draco, but you know what

I mean. He, no doubt, can see into his loved one's soul, but I'm dashed if I can.'

'We are not required to see into Angelica's soul,' I said.

'Quite true, Kirstie.'

'In fact, I suppose we are required *not* to.'

'Quite true again. But I wonder why? Such opacity must be deliberate, at least partly. But why? I wonder why anybody wants to be so secret? To hide everything so completely?'

'Lord Draco is the same, I find.'

'Yes, so do I, but I used not to. He never wore his heart on his sleeve, you know, or shouted with maniac laughter, or burst into scalding tears—'

'As I do.'

'As you do, bless you. He never paraded his emotions, but it was possible to tell if he was joyful or angry.'

'It is still possible,' I said ruefully, 'to tell when he is angry.'

'Is it, indeed? Thank you for the warning. I want to stay here for a time yet, so I will be careful not to enrage the dear fellow.'

He waved, and climbed into a dog-cart in which he was going to a lower beat of the river. I went from the glare of the court-yard into the darkness of the great hall, and stood for a moment, blinking.

From just inside the door, by my shoulder, I heard a hiss, faint but angry, like that of an old snake which has lost much of its strength but none of its venom. Eugénie stood there, huddled as always in her shawl, mittened fingers clutching the shawl about her, staring at me with black unwinking eyes. She had heard – she must have heard – every word of my conversation with Lord Cricklade. I wondered if we had been indiscreet. I wondered what she would report, and to whom. I wondered for the thousandth time why she hated me. I wondered where Dandie McKillop was, with his fury and his threats and his idiot son.

As Eugénie hobbled away, Mrs Forbes came trotting like a plump duck across the hall. She, too, had been watching Crick-lade and myself.

'You're as thick as thieves, you two,' she said, 'you and Lord Cricklade. Whatever can he find to talk to you about, I wonder?'

'He once abducted me,' I said, 'and it makes a bond.'

She looked quite shocked.

Perhaps it was a silly remark, and liable to be misunderstood; but I could not have predicted it would have quite such frightful consequences.

Lord Cricklade treated me with unfailing friendliness. So did Mr and Mrs Barstow of Ardmeggar, Georgina Campbell and Charlotte Long; and so did Annie Simpson and Geordie Buchan.

But during the next days, it seemed to me that no one treated me quite as they had before. Men looked at me strangely, speculatively; women with a sort of fascinated aversion. The only other exceptions were the Earl, who did not notice me; Angelica, who looked at me exactly as she had always done, with solemn intensity; and the Countess, who, for some reason, I scarcely saw.

Mrs Forbes's good-humoured chatter quite dried up, as far as I was concerned. 'Oh,' she would say quickly, if I came by, 'just think! I almost forgot! A letter that must be written this instant, to ... to my nephew, in Ontario you know, an engineer ...' And she would hurry away, like an apple-dumpling on wheels, to whisper to Lady Arabella.

Lady Arabella herself simply got up and left any room I entered. General Drummond turned his back quite openly, when I met him in the village. I did not mind about them. If they removed the light of their countenances from me, I thought proudly, I would get on very well without. But I was sad and hurt when Lady Campbell of Drumlaw, who was my friend, twittered and looked over my shoulder and had an urgent errand.

Goaded by this unexpected unfriendliness, I asked one of the people I most trusted: I asked Mrs Barstow of Ardmeggar whether I had leprosy, or cholera, or what.

Her kind, weather-beaten face was more careful, more reserved, than I had ever seen it. She said, 'You do not know what is in their minds, Kirstie? What they might have heard?'

'No.'

'Your conscience is quite clear?'

'Well,' I admitted, 'no, not quite. I *have* committed sins. Almost all the ones my grandfather Strachan told me not to, I think. I mean, such as sloth. And then vanity, because people have . . . well, people have been so polite. And pride. And envy.'

'Whom do you envy, child?'

'Angelica Paston, for her piano-playing. Georgina Campbell, because she lives with her own family, who love her. Lord Cricklade, because he can do anything he likes, whenever he likes . . .'

'Yes yes . . . I cannot believe what I have heard. I *do* not believe it. I know, we both do, that you are all that we have always thought you . . .'

'What have you heard?'

'I don't think I can tell you. It would upset you to hear it, and me to say it. If your conscience is truly clear, Kirstie, then that is all that matters. And you may be certain that your true friends believe in you and trust you.'

She would not say what they had heard about me. She continued to insist that they believed the best of me. But her face was unhappy and embarrassed. She did not know what to believe. She did not want to talk to me very much.

After this, I wanted to confide in my friends Charlotte and Georgina. But somehow difficulties sprang up about their coming to Glendraco, or my going to Drumlaw. The days suggested were impossible; they had to do all kinds of things; they had cousins staying in the house who took up all their time. Lady Campbell it was clear, knew exactly what to believe.

I tried to confide in Lord Cricklade, but he would not take it seriously. He had heard nothing, because he had seen nobody, because he was always on the hill or the river-bank. In any case, he said he never listened to rumours. If there had been false rumours about himself, he would simply have ignored them, and simply despised the mean little people who believed them and passed them on. But I did not have his strength or his confidence. I wanted reassurance. But, when I showed this, he thought I was a silly schoolgirl, imagining plots and conspiracies. I saw that the more I talked about it, the more he would think so, and it was better to stop talking about it.

I would have confided, in desperation, in the Countess. But she was in one of her most frightening moods, cold and imperious and apt to make cutting remarks, and to send me away before I had opened my mouth. After a period of smiling blandness, the Dragon was the Dragon again, and it was safest to keep out of her way. Her dark brows lowered, her grey eyes snapped, and there was no lift to the corners of her mouth. Her moods were like the storms of the glen, coming suddenly out of a clear sky, hostile and chilling and frightening.

What maddened me was that I did not know what was being said, where it had all come from, what it was all about. Before I could tell them all it was a lie, I had to know what the lie was: and nobody would say. So, as far as I could, I withdrew myself from people, and spent my time with Falcon and Rockfall. *They* trusted me.

I got my first inkling of the truth from a most surprising source, in a way that would have been funny, if it had not been rather horrible.

I was still expected to assist the Reverend Lancelot Barrow with the new library catalogue. I worked with him three mornings a week, which was quite boring. It had been boring in the days when he talked, as he did at great length, teaching me many things I did not want to know; now it was still more boring, because he had given up talking. He was as silent as a coffin-bearer, except for the few instructions he was obliged to give me.

Often, in his pale soft face, there was a nervous flush, which looked like fever. Those long white hands, with their big scrubbed knuckles, seemed to shake whenever he took a book from me, or gave one to me. I was afraid he was ill, and afraid I would catch whatever illness he had. But he denied vehemently that he was ill, flapping his hands at me like the sails of a windmill in a tempest, and keeping his pale eyes downcast.

One blazing morning, when I yearned to ride my beloved Falcon, and hear my beloved Rockfall scampering and yapping behind us, I was perched on the top of the library steps, and handing down yet another heavy unread dusty mouldering book. The Reverend Lancelot Barrow reached up, and our hands touched. His hand felt like a fish – like Findlay Nicholson's. Mine seemed to give him a Galvanic shock, like those given to the insane in the Edinburgh hospitals. He dropped the book, which fell to the polished wooden floor with a crash like a caber landing on a drum. Suddenly he seized my hand in both of his. I was so astonished that I nearly fell off the steps. I saved myself from a horrid fall by putting my other hand on to his head, and so keeping my balance. Unfortunately, he took this to be a kind of response, or even a caress, and began kissing my hand as though he would gobble it. He was in a state of uncontrollable excitement, trembling violently, nuzzling at my hand exactly as Falcon did.

'Miss Drummond,' he mumbled into my hand, 'Christina, I can no longer keep silent! I will no longer try! To be so close to you, to be alone with you, has been daily torture to me—'

'Please, Mr Barrow,' I said, very distressed, 'I beg you to stop!'

I was sorry for him, because this was all very wrong and useless. It would leave an embarrassing shadow afterwards, and make it difficult for us to talk to each other. It was quite unpleasant, having him press his soft pale face against my hand, and smother it with kisses I did not want. The sad part was not that I disliked it, but that he was ridiculous. He was too soft and solemn to be passionate – it did not fit, it was absurd, it was disgusting.

Then he further lost control of himself, and tried to pull me down off the steps into his arms. This prospect was more than I could bear. I cried to him to stop, to remember himself, to respect my feelings.

'No,' he moaned, 'no. Always, from the first, I desired you, and lustful fires burned in my heart. But I believed you to be pure, and by a gigantic effort I held my peace. But now I know the depravity of your soul. Why should I not enjoy your favours too? Delilah! Jezebel! Am I not also a man?' He began to babble, in a ridiculous high voice, 'Yes, yes! A man, a man! This black coat conceals a heart – flesh – blood – fires – a volcano—'

Keeping hold of my wrist with one hand, he seized my ankle with the other. He tried manfully, grunting and panting, to pull me off the steps. But he was not at all strong, although he was so tall, because he had never done anything active in his life. Perhaps, if he had been more experienced, he might have found a better way than trying to pull a female off a step-ladder by brute force.

I could hold on to the post at the top of the steps with one hand, without difficulty. Although I was only a girl, I think I was stronger than he was. But my fear was that he would pull the whole thing, and me too, down on top of himself. He would probably be hurt, which would be a pity, although it was all his fault. It would take a lot of explaining, if he was knocked unconscious, and I would be blamed.

I dared not take away my hand from the post, to bring him to his senses with a slap, because then I should have been heaved off the steps, and there was no saying what he might not attempt. So, even as he wrenched at me, and I clung, I tried to think of words that would stop him.

'You are a *clergyman*,' I said, as sharply as I could for the effort of holding on. 'I am in your *care*.'

'You are in my power,' he moaned. 'Let go! Please! Why should I not, like other men—'

'Because it's a *sin*,' I said hopefully.

'Not to you! You have no soul! You are amoral – an animal – I know what happened – I have heard everything – do not deny – Caerlaverock – David Baillie has told me everything—'

I was so startled that I nearly let go. But I managed to grasp and cling. What story had the wretched man believed? What had poor David Baillie been led to believe?

Whatever the story was, it had induced this solemn flabby clergyman to behave like – like Caerlaverock himself. Because he thought I was Delilah, and all those other unpleasant things. He thought – what did he think? What *had* he heard?

It became important to me to find out, immediately. This horrid farce must end at once. I ended it. With a sudden violent jerk, I pulled my hand away from his grip, and my ankle from the grip of his other hand. I jumped down from the steps and ran out of the library. I heard a bleating cry behind me, but I ran to my bedroom to change into my riding habit.

Falcon was in his stall, because Geordie was expecting me to ride in the afternoon. Geordie was not about, and all the other men were at their dinner. By all the rules I should wait. But I was in no mood to wait.

I had never done it before, unaided, but I knew how it was done: I got my saddle and bridle from the great array in the room where they were kept, and put them on my horse. I talked to him all the time, as Geordie did. Falcon seemed quite content. I led him to the mounting-block, and climbed on, and set off for Inverlarig. By all the rules I should not have gone alone. There would be all kinds of disapproval and anger and unpleasantness. I was in no mood to care.

Inverlarig was a long white building, set on low ground among pine-trees. The present laird's father, Georgina had told me, had spent a lot of money on it, in the way of a new wing, and bigger windows, and a stately porch with stained glass, and a silly little tower at one end. All this made Inverlarig look not like a mansion, but like a farmhouse with inflated ideas; it was one of the reasons why the present laird required his only son to marry an heiress. The home-farm steading, which I rode by, had a squalid, abandoned look; there were gaps in the fences, and a tree which had fallen in full leaf still lay untrimmed in a paddock; the road between the steading and the house was full of deep ruts; it was a depressing place.

David Baillie saw me from a window and came hurrying out of the pretentious front door. His face was more purple than usual, and seemed almost to steam with embarrassment. Always before he had been excessively glad to see me, and had greeted me as Rockfall did; today he was astonished and dismayed.

He gabbled that his father was out, and his mother ill in bed.

I said, 'Please give them my respects, but it is you I want to talk to.'

'Me?' he said, in a strangled voice. He avoided my eye, and stared at a shrunken bush outside the house as though he expected it to save him.

Usually he was the first to rush forward to help me dismount (females are supposed to need help), but today he was frightened to come near me. At least the story – whatever the story was – did not have the effect on him that it had had on the Reverend Lancelot Barrow. I jumped down on my own, and looped Falcon's reins over my arm.

I said, in the sternest voice I could muster, 'David, I will have the truth from you.'

He made only a gargling noise, his back turned towards me. I felt my temper rising.

'The Reverend Mr Barrow,' I said, 'made some extraordinary remarks to me this morning. I could not understand him. It was a story he had heard about me. About Lord Caerlaverock. From you. What did you tell him? Why did you tell him? Answer me!'

'I . . .' said David, in a high, wretched voice. 'I had to talk to him.'

'Why?'

'He is a parson, a clergyman.'

'You had something to *confess*?'

'No! No! I needed advice.'

'From Mr Barrow?'

'He is a clergyman!'

'Advice about what?' I asked, my astonishment overcoming my anger. I could not imagine asking Mr Barrow's advice about so much as tying a shoelace.

'It was after,' David muttered, 'after what my father told me. He told me – told me to have nothing to do with you. But I thought – I thought I could redeem you—'

'*What?*'

'Save you,' he explained miserably. 'But I thought perhaps it might not work out like that – that you'd drag me down, instead of my pulling you up . . .'

'What,' I asked in a dangerous voice, 'did your father tell you?'

'About – about you and – you and Caerlaverock.'

'At the Crombies' croft, you mean?'

'Yes! Then it is true!'

'Some things are true,' I said. 'Some are not. I can't tell about this until you tell me.'

'It is true! I wish to God it was not, but my father says it is true! Yes, at the croft. That night, when you . . .'

'When I what?'

'You tried to . . . I can't say it!'

'Say it,' I said, 'before I thrash you.'

And I was almost in a state of mind to lash him and lash him again.

'You tried,' he gasped, 'to seduce Caerlaverock. My father has heard the whole thing! You wanted to be a lady, I suppose, a peeress. My father says you would have trapped Caerlaverock into marriage. But Caerlaverock refused . . . He rejected your – your advances . . . So he went away, to save you pain and embarrassment . . . But it has come out, in spite of that . . .'

Though I was beside myself with anger and shock, part of my mind continued to be cool, and to work in the normal way.

I understood that for David it must have been terrible, hearing that a girl he cared for had behaved in such a way, and for such a reason. He was very simple, and meant well. He must have been in a state of despair and confusion. So he went to Mr Barrow with his problem, trusting that a clergyman, because he was a clergyman, would tell him exactly what was right.

And I understood, now, the effect on the Reverend Lancelot Barrow. He *was* a man, as he said, at least in the way of instincts and desires. He would never have dared raise hand or voice to me, as long as he believed me virtuous; but as soon as he thought I was a trollop, he found courage to make his ridiculous advances. It was not pleasant, but it was understandable.

David had heard the story from his father. Where had his father heard it?

I asked David, who gasped that he did not know.

'Then I will ask him,' I said.

At last David turned to face me, his eyes wide and aghast.

'You can't!' he cried. 'He won't see you! He won't talk to you!'

'When do you expect him back?'

'Soon. Now. But – but you must not—'

Nothing would stop me now. I had heard the expression of one's blood being up, and I knew now what it felt like. My blood was so far up that it boomed in my head like a drum. I felt equal to any army of servants who tried to put me out, any company of men with pitchforks who tried to drive me away. Nothing would stop me getting the truth from Inverlarig. With this absolute resolve, my anger no longer made my hands tremble or my voice shake; I was no less angry, but I was calm.

Calmly I said, 'I will put my horse in your stables. He shall have water but no fodder. Then I shall go into the house and wait for your father, in whatever room he will go to. Nobody will put me out, and when I talk to him nobody will interrupt us. When I have found out what I want to know, I will leave.'

David became docile, like a dog that recognizes his master. He led Falcon to the stables, put him in a loose-box where there was a stone trough of water, and unsaddled and unbridled him carefully. Then we went back to the house, and in by the front door.

Inside, it put me in mind of my grandparents' house in George Square – everything was dark and ugly and uncomfortable. An old maidservant, who looked grubby, scuttled away at our approach, as though afraid of being asked to fetch something.

David showed me into his father's study, as that was where the old man would go directly he came in. Then David did not know whether to stay with me, or leave me alone; he stumbled uncertainly about the dark little room, between the desk and the fireplace and the window, avoiding my eyes, sometimes opening the door and shutting it again, dreading his father's arrival and yet hating the delay.

I ignored him. I did not care if he stayed or went away. My business was no longer with him. I felt supremely calm and determined. My purpose was utterly inflexible. It did not occur to me that it was strange in the least that a little nobody, an obscure girl just turned eighteen, should march uninvited into the house of a Highland laird, and wait in his own study, prepared to take a high and arrogant line with him, and whip the truth out of him if need be. For I had not left my whip in the stables. Instinctively I had brought it; now I held it like a talisman. Nothing would stop me getting the truth. I would go to any lengths. Nothing would make me leave until I had got the truth.

Though I told myself I was calm, I was not calm enough to sit down. I did not stumble about, like poor David, but stood inspecting old Mr Baillie's books and pictures. There were very few books, but a great many small pictures, dark, in dark frames, with dirty glass over them. One hung just beside the fireplace, an oval miniature in a blackened gilt frame, painted I thought on ivory. Its position beside the fire had made the glass that protected it blacker even than the rest. I could hardly see what lay behind the soot, but something in it aroused my curiosity. I unhooked it from its nail (it hung on an ancient iron ring on the back) and took it over to the window. David scuttled away, as though to avoid the contagion of being near me. I saw that the miniature was a portrait, a head; I could see a pale face, and a quantity of dark red hair. I took out my handkerchief, and scrubbed at the sooty glass.

I was looking at myself.

It was a young woman, no more than twenty, with high cheek-bones, dark straight eyebrows, dark red hair dressed in a long-forgotten fashion. There was a date, delicately drawn at the side: 1772. Below the head there was painted an heraldic device, a prancing leopard with a rose in its mouth.

David Baillie, when he first met me, told me he had dreamed of my face. I thought it was a pretty compliment, but it was the truth. What he had dreamed of was this picture, which hung in the house where he had lived all his life. Perhaps, when he was a young child, it was not dirty. Perhaps he was given it to play with, to keep him quiet. It was the picture he had dreamed of, not me. Yet he was right – it *was* my face. Painted a century ago, with a prancing leopard with a rose in its mouth.

We heard wheels and harness and an ill-tempered excla-mation. David turned to me, stricken, terrified. I hung the miniature back on its nail, and for comfort took a firm grasp of my whip; I faced the door, ready to do battle.

After a time which was full of bustling and shouts, I heard old Mr Baillie's voice just outside the door of the study.

'Young lady,' he was roaring angrily. 'What young lady? She should not have been admitted. I don't receive any young ladies. How dare you let her into my study?'

The door burst open. Baillie of Inverlarig came in like a limping whirlwind, as purple-faced as his son. He stopped dead when he saw me, and his face went almost black. For a moment he was too angry and too taken aback to speak.

At last he choked, ' *You*? How can *you* have the effrontery—'

'Because,' I said, cutting him short, 'I am very angry indeed.'

He stood gobbling at me, like the oldest and fiercest of the turkey-cocks in the Glendraco poultry-house.

I went on, 'Sit down, Inverlarig. Rest your gouty foot. David give your father a footstool. Then leave us alone.'

'How dare you?' shouted Inverlarig, 'You dare to give me orders in my own house?'

'Yes,' I said. 'Will you sit down!'

He was so amazed that he sat down, suddenly and heavily, in a black leather armchair. David stumbled forward with a footstool, and lifted his father's bad foot on to it.

I pointed at the door. David scuttled out. Inverlarig was still too startled to make any objection. David shut the door very softly behind him, as though anxious to prove that there was something he could do properly. I thought he would probably wait outside to listen, as I myself would have done. Perhaps the whole household was huddled outside the study door, all fighting to get an ear to the keyhole. I did not care. What was important was to get the truth. Nothing else mattered.

I stood over Inverlarig, which gave me a great feeling of power and authority. He stared up at me, his mouth having fallen open, as David's so often did.

Remembering his position as Laird of Inverlarig, and master of this house, he managed to say at last, in a rasping voice, 'What is the meaning of this outrage?'

'You talk of outrage,' I said, quite calmly, holding my whip before me in both hands. 'You, who spread scandalous lies.'

'*I? I?* I have never told a lie in my life!'

'You are either,' I said, 'very wicked or very stupid.'

It still did not seem to me in the least strange that I should talk like this to a laird of ancient family and estate, in his own house, standing over him; it seemed the right and proper thing to do, the only thing to do.

He gobbled up at me, more than ever like a turkey, deprived of speech.

'You do not like your son being in love with me,' I said in a cool voice, 'because you want him to marry a rich woman, to save yourself from beggary. Therefore you told him disgusting lies about me. I think you are too stupid to have made them up, so someone told them to you. *Who told you?*'

'I . . . I cannot tell you that.'

I lost patience. I raised my whip, and brought it down with all my strength on the leather top of his desk. It was a tremendous crack in the small room, like a heavy shotgun blowing a grouse into shreds. Pens and inkstands jumped on top of the desk, and some papers fluttered.

He jumped also, and his hands fluttered. He was quite helpless, below me in the deep armchair. He must have seen how very angry I was, how implacably determined. He must have pictured – anybody would – the whip coming down with equal ferocity on his mouth. But like many very stupid men, he was obstinate. He repeated, more firmly, that he could not tell me who had told him the story of Caerlaverock and myself.

'I was told it as the truth,' he said, 'and as the truth I felt it my duty to repeat it – to warn my son—'

'It suited you to believe it and to repeat it,' I said contemptuously. 'For the last time – *who told you*?'

He was not only obstinate, but also brave. I stood over him, holding the whip. He was at an utter disadvantage in the deep chair. He was already weakened and in pain from the gout. I was perfectly ready to cut him into ribbons with the whip, and he must have seen from my eye that this was so.

'Do your worst,' he said. 'I cannot tell you who told me the story.'

I raised the whip.

He said quickly – his courage faltering a little – 'I can tell you this much. I can tell you that the – that this report came from the inn at Lochgrannomhead. It came from someone who was there – that Caerlaverock spoke to. That is why I believed it to be true.'

I lowered the whip slowly. That was it, then – the story came from Caerlaverock himself. He had told it, with trembling sincerity, to one of our charming neighbours, who had been enchanted to believe it, and to tell everybody he saw.

Caerlaverock had overcome his self-loathing. No doubt it was a brief mood, brought on because he felt sick after drinking too much whisky. He had thankfully transferred his loathing to me – his furious resentment that I had had the impudence to refuse the honour of his favours – his vengeful rage that I had marked his pretty face, and humiliated him. He had got his revenge. Inverlarig was no more than his dupe, his tool.

I said slowly, 'You believed a lie, Inverlarig, because you wanted to believe it. Have you any idea what evil you have done? And how uselessly? Your son was always quite safe from me. I wish him good fortune in his search for a fortune. I do not aspire to his hand. I never did. Anybody but a fool would have seen so. You can give up hating me – there was never cause for it.'

He said, with difficulty, as though repeating a repugnant lesson set him by a hated schoolmaster, 'I accept that what you say is true. I find it impossible to disbelieve you. I have no reason to hate you, and I do not do so. If I have caused you pain, I am deeply sorry. I have no reason to hate you – but there are others—'

'Who hate me for other reasons?'

'Yes. You can have no idea of the – bitterness you have aroused.'

'Tell me the names of these others.'

'No. You have made me feel that I have very little honour. That little I think I must try to keep, for the sake of my son, my name, and forbears who were better men than I ... There are confidences which I cannot break. I am under your banner, Miss Drummond, if you will have me there – but I cannot betray to you the names of my old – my old allies. I cannot repeat the things I have heard said, nor reveal who said them.'

I nodded. He was a stupid and small-minded man, but he had put on dignity. He was speaking now as his conscience told him, and I could do no good with my whip.

The names flashed into my mind – General Drummond, Lady Arabella. Perhaps Angelica; perhaps the Earl. And always in the background, like a bitter-hearted crow, old Eugénie; and always, in the shadows of the rocks of the glen, the hate-crazed Dandie McKillop.

Inverlarig went on slowly, 'You are more of a man than any man I have ever met. I would to God you could care for my poor David – you would bring more to him than the heiress of the Duke of Renfrew. But he is not for the likes of you. You deserve a king. I never thought to speak like this to a young girl, and to you least of all. But I am being honest with you for the first time.'

'Thank you, Inverlarig,' I said. 'This is a turnabout.'

'Yes,' he said, 'it is a turnabout indeed. I dare not ask you to shake my hand, because you would be right to refuse to do so, but I would be proud if . . .'

I reached down, and we shook hands. David was called into the room, and I shook hands with him also.

Falcon was fetched, and I rode away.

When I had walked him a certain distance, past the miserable steading and clear of the sad Inverlarig farms, I found myself trembling. My anger was gone, and I felt a little sick. I was aghast at what I had done, at my crazy audacity. Of all the indiscretions people called so wild, today's adventure was the wildest. Even Lord Cricklade – even the Earl of Draco – would have hesitated to talk to a man like that in his own house, with his son outside the door, and his servants all about – would have shrunk from threatening a respectable old gentleman with a cutting-whip. Word of it would get about, and I would get still odder and colder looks.

I was pleased by what Inverlarig had said, but I was horribly depressed about Caerlaverock. His repentance can hardly have lasted an hour. His story about me would be believed by everyone. Why not? People loved to believe such things, and smack their lips when they repeated them. It was his word against mine – which would his old friends credit? Even the kindly Barstows of Ardmeggar were finding it impossible to trust me.

I was almost back to Glendraco when I remembered the little painting, which might have been of me, and had the prancing leopard with the rose in its mouth. I might have asked Inverlarig about it, after we became friends, but the talk we had put everything else out of my mind.

Rockfall reproached me, with a terrible look, for going off without him. So did Geordie Buchan.

Geordie said, in a graveyard voice, that the Earl wanted to see me as soon as I got back.

Fearing the worst, I walked into the castle. Patterson the butler told me that his lordship was in his study. It was a day for difficult interviews in studies.

In three and a half months I had never seen the Earl's study, which was part of a row of offices on the outer courtyard from which the estate was managed. It was most unlike Inverlarig's, and unlike my grandfather Strachan's, too. It was a big, bright, rather bare room, a place for working, with desks and tables, some upright chairs, large-scale maps on the walls, shelves of books and ledgers; everything was extremely tidy; I liked the effect; I thought that, if I had a great estate to rule, I would do it from just such a headquarters.

The Earl was in his shirtsleeves, studying some papers at a desk. He rose when I entered. I was struck, not for the first time, by the magnificence of his figure – the broad shoulders and narrow waist, the impression of great strength under great restraint – and by his startling resemblance to his grandmother, saving only that he lacked her bewitching smile. That he lacked, in fact, any smile at all.

'Please sit down, Miss Drummond,' he said (for he had only relaxed from formality to me that one time, when I was half-way up Meiklejohn's Leap).

I sat down. So did he. We faced each other across the desk.

The ledgers were not dusty, nor everything dark: otherwise I might have been in the study in George Square. My emotions were the same – nervousness, defiance which I was careful to hide, and a great wish to be somewhere else.

'You went out alone today, and were away for four hours.'

'Yes.'

'Have you no other answer than that? Simply "Yes"?'

'I am not a child. Falcon is my horse.'

'How came you by Falcon?'

'I am very grateful for such a wonderful gift, sir – but I think he *was* a gift?'

'Falcon is your horse. He is in my stable. He eats my grass when he is out, my hay and oats when he is in. His shoes are made by my farrier, and he is cared for by a groom whose wages I pay.'

'Well, yes,' I admitted. 'That is all quite true.'

'Does it give me any rights in the matter?'

'Yes, it does, but ... Do you not think I ride well enough to be allowed out on my own?'

He paused before replying, as though carefully considering what he thought on this subject. At last he said, 'Suffice it to say,

Miss Drummond, that you are not to go out without Buchan or some other responsible man. Is that clearly understood?'

'Yes,' I said sulkily.

'It is not always,' he said, 'either easy or pleasant to exercise responsibility. It would be more agreeable for me, as it would be for you, were I to say that you could go where and when you liked – were I to abdicate all responsibility, and ignore all possible consequences. This is not my way, Miss Drummond.'

'No,' I agreed.

'May I ask where you rode to today?'

'To Inverlarig.'

He looked startled. 'To see David?'

'To see his father.'

'On business so pressing that you could not wait for Buchan?'

'It seemed very pressing to me, at the time.'

'What was this overpoweringly urgent errand?'

'I wanted to know why he was telling scandalous lies about me.'

'Telling whom?'

'His son.'

'Does it greatly matter what David Baillie is told?'

'Yes, if he tells other people, and they behave like pigs as a result.'

'What you call the scandalous lies relate to Lord Caerlaverock?'

'Yes. I gather you have heard them too.'

'Are they scandalous lies?'

I stood up suddenly, maddened by this cool examination. I said hotly, 'If you believe that story, my lord, you had better order me out of your house.'

'I have known, Caerlaverock,' he said gravely, 'all his life and nearly all my own. I have heard an account of the events of the night you spent in Glen Monaidh. I believe I know quite well what happened.'

'Do you?'

'Yes. Some others do, also.'

'They do, indeed,' I said bitterly.

'Was Caerlaverock drunk?'

'How could he have been drunk, in that miserable croft?'

'He had no whisky?'

'Perhaps he carried a flask.'

'The contents of a flask would not make Caerlaverock drunk.'

'Then I do not see how he could have been drunk.'

'Think very carefully, Miss Drummond. Answer me as carefully, so that I shall know what to believe. Was Caerlaverock drunk that night?'

I did think carefully.

The Earl was looking at me gravely, without hostility, waiting for my answer. I was sure that, if I spoke honestly, he would see that I was doing so. He would believe me. He would make everybody else believe me – everybody I cared about – the Barstows, the Campbells, the Countess herself.

I had only to say: 'Dugald has a still hidden behind the croft. Caerlaverock found it. He paid Dugald four sovereigns, and himself drank two bottles of whisky. He was mad with the whisky, and tried to assault me. I beat him off with my whip.'

I had only to say that, and the filthy slander would be laid, and my friends would be my friends again.

And Dugald Crombie would go to prison.

'If you know the Crombies,' I said finally, 'you know that they are far too poor to buy whisky.'

The Earl nodded. He said, 'Thank you for your kindness in coming to see me, Miss Drummond. I expect now that you have pressing engagements, as I myself have.'

Dismissed, I walked out, feeling as though I had just committed suicide.

ten

Lord Cricklade took time off, from killing grouse and stags and salmon, to come riding with me. He chatted pleasantly, as always, about all kinds of things – it was the sort of conversation that one enjoys at the time, without remembering afterwards. He did not mention – he still would not discuss – the rumours being spread about me. He did wonder aloud why the castle chaplain had gone away on a sudden holiday: but he was not deeply interested in the reason, and rather pleased than otherwise to be relieved of Mr Barrow's pallid and deprecating presence.

He asked if I were going to Perth, in three weeks time, for the races and the balls.

'No,' I said, surprised. 'Nobody has mentioned it to me.'

'What a pity. What a great pity. The rest of us are going – Draco and Lady Arabella and Angelica to stay with Lord Mountfield, I believe, at Groyne Palace, and I to Sir Dundas Murray, which will be much less grand and much more comfortable ... We can't have you left behind, Kirstie! That will *not* do.'

'Lady Draco is not going, I suppose?'

'No. She is hardly of an age to enjoy a week of racing and dancing.'

'Then I daresay she wants me with her.'

'*Are* you much with her?'

'Yes,' I said slowly, 'in the ordinary way. Recently, not so much. But I expect her mood will change, as it does, you know, without warning ...'

'It does indeed,' said Lord Cricklade, smiling. 'The Dragon has not lost her fiery breath. By the by, I have been alert, warned by you, for signs of Draco's undiminished rages. But far from showing any anger about anything, he seems all the time to be – preoccupied. His mind is elsewhere, even when he's shooting grouse. It is, I think, affecting his performance.'

'Of course he is preoccupied,' I said wisely. 'He is about to announce his engagement. One *ought* to be preoccupied at such a time.'

'Ah,' said Cricklade. 'I must remember that, as a point of conduct. When I am about to announce my own engagement, I shall go about with an abstracted air, and miss my grouse.'

'Are you,' I asked a little breathlessly, 'planning to announce your engagement?'

'Yes,' he said. 'I am planning it.'

I looked at him, astonished. He was staring ahead, between the ears of his horse, with a bland expression.

'But,' he went on, 'I am still quite in the dark about the date. It depends on – the completion of a process so far incomplete. On the successful prosecution of a campaign so far in its early stages. I do things slowly, you know, not having a fine, fast brain like Draco's. But I make up for that by doing them carefully and thoroughly. My tactics are what are called Fabian – deliberate, unhurried, possibly devious. Do you understand me, Kirstie?'

He looked at me with such a smile that I could not have failed to understand him. A statue would have understood him. I blushed, which I seemed so often to be doing at that period. A statue, I think, would have blushed.

We stopped our horses, as though by unspoken agreement, at the same moment. He stretched out a hand towards me, and, without any conscious effort on my part, my hand went out to his. He pressed my hand briefly, then let it go. I thought (most immodestly) that it was a shame we were both wearing doeskin gloves. But, though it was through two thicknesses of leather, that squeeze of the hand spoke a library of words.

What were my feelings? I could not tell. They were in the completest muddle.

There were things about Cricklade that set him far above Billy Mainwaring. Beside him, Billy seemed a boy, a cheerful, unimportant urchin. On top of all else, Cricklade was much taller and handsomer than Billy. I was pleased and excited to be so much admired by Cricklade, and breathless to be told that, in due time, after a long and leisurely courtship, he meant to ask me to be his wife.

What would I say, when he did ask me?

Billy was dear to me. I remembered his face with affection, and his kiss with grateful emotion. He *was* dear to me. Boy he might be beside Cricklade, unimportant urchin beside this tall, handsome, powerful, smiling, serious nobleman. Perhaps I liked boys and urchins best. But did I? My head had swum a little that first day, in the gig; my hand had tingled at the memory of his.

What would I say, when Billy asked me?

*

Billy came back two days later, to make my emotions more complicated still. He rode into the stable yard, just as I returned from another ride with Lord Cricklade.

Billy's face lit up with such joy when he saw me that my heart gave a jump. Rockfall was overjoyed to see him. Billy and Cricklade were delighted to see each other after an interval of months – they had known each other, of course, for many years.

As the three of us walked back to the castle, Billy said, 'I came by Drumlaw, as I had a message to deliver to Sir Francis. Something about sheep, three-year-old wethers. The man's in love with the beasts – I suppose he'll evict some more crofters. However, that, though it raises my gorge, is not the point of this recital. He drew me aside, and regaled me with a story, Kirstie, which I found obnoxious and incredible.'

'Oh,' I said miserably. 'I might have known that you would hear it, as soon as you got within fifty miles of Glendraco.'

'I would not mention anything so contemptible,' said Billy, 'but I think you ought to know what is being said about you, and by whom. I have to add that Sir Francis quite evidently believed what he was telling me.'

'Caerlaverock could not have wished,' I said drearily, 'for a more successful revenge.'

'Was he drunk, that night?'

'How could he be?' I asked.

'As to that, I've no idea what liquor might have been available. He carried a flask, I suppose?'

'Lord Draco says a flask would not have made him drunk.'

'That's true,' said Billy. 'Jack's got a pretty strong head, much stronger than mine. But when he does get drunk he's a devil. I've only seen that happen once. It wouldn't be fair to describe it. The contents of a flask wouldn't do it. Anyhow, I told Sir Francis to take his miserable slander elsewhere. I suppose you've been saying the same, Cricklade?'

'I have not had the opportunity,' said Lord Cricklade. 'I have not listened to this story or any other. I never do. I will not attend to the malicious clatter of second-rate provincials.'

'Well, it would be the act of a friend,' said Billy, 'to thrust this lie down the throats of the miserable people who tell it.'

'I don't take quite the same view, Billy,' said Cricklade. 'The act of a friend, to my mind, is to ignore the rubbish completely. Kirstie knows full well that my opinion of her is unaffected. Since I know and trust her, I am totally indifferent to what happened, or what anyone says happened. I would rather not discuss it. I expect Kirstie feels the same.'

'I only wish,' I said, 'that I had made more use of my whip.'

I decided to go to a small room near the drawing-room, which I sometimes used because it was seldom used. It was a curious shape, made so that more important rooms would be a proper shape. It was a wedge, the blunt end all window, the furniture awkwardly placed. I would have filled it, if it had been mine, entirely with growing plants, with a single wickerwork chair in the middle, in which I could sit to water them. There were two doors, one to the Italian room, and one to a passage.

I wanted to be alone, and Annie was busy with my clothes in my bedroom. I wanted to think, to examine my feelings. Billy and Cricklade were both, in their very different ways, in undisguised pursuit of me. Both had declared themselves. Billy kissed me when he could, and poured out a muddled, enchanting song of love and praise. Cricklade was his pleasant, steady, sensible self; he was not seeking, like dear Billy, to sweep me off my feet, but to build love on a basis of friendship and trust and esteem. Oh, there was such a lot to be said for both methods! And the best of it was, that they remained firm friends, and spoke of each other with the greatest warmth. Of course it was all very bad for me.

Was it possible to be in love with two men? Was I depraved, unnatural, to be so happy in the company of both, to be so glad of the admiration of both? What did I want? Who did I want?

I went into the odd little room, from the passage, and at first could see nothing. The blind had been pulled fully down over the great window, so that the chintz on the chairs would not be faded by the sun. Like everything at Glendraco, the blind was heavy, and fitted perfectly.

There was a startled movement in the room, and a hissing noise. I knew the noise, for there was no other sound like it outside a snake-pit. Eugénie was not alone. Another figure, a slim tall woman, was sitting with Eugénie on the little brocaded sofa where I often sat myself. The other rose quickly out of the sofa, and stepped to the door into the Italian room. She opened it, slipped through, and closed it behind her. I heard footsteps hurrying away.

Eugénie sat where she was, hissing at me like a cobra disturbed, wrapped in her shawl, her mittened talons holding it about her. Black as her eyes were, they seemed to blaze in her chalk-white face with a malevolent light of their own, illuminating nothing except the bitterness within.

'I am sorry to have disturbed you,' I said politely, and went out again into the corridor.

I had seen Eugénie's companion, with whom she sat and whispered in the dark, as the other went through the door into the brightness of the Italian room.

It was Angelica Paston.

Old Mr Baillie was as good as his word.

He arrived at Glendraco one afternoon, in a shabby brougham with a shabby man driving, to pay a formal call. The Countess received him in the drawing-room; with her were Lady Arabella, Angelica, Mrs Forbes, and me.

'This is an unexpected pleasure, Inverlarig,' said the Countess.

'More unexpected than a pleasure, I daresay,' said Inverlarig, lowering himself with a grunt on to the sofa beside her. 'Only duty brings me here, ma'am.'

'Gracefully put,' said the Countess, with the ghost of a smile.

'Oh! Curse it – you're right – beg your pardon – didn't come out as I meant. Pleasure to be here, of course, honour to be received by your ladyship.'

'But you are combining duty with this pleasure?'

'Yes, I am. By God, yes. What I want to do is – ha – herumph—'

'Clear your throat?'

'To announce, – to, ha, place on public record – my conviction that the – the story being put about concerning Miss Drummond and Caerlaverock is – is an impudent and nasty-minded lie.'

'What changed your mind, Mr Baillie?' asked Lady Arabella, with a sneer on her face and in her voice.

'Hearing the truth, ma'am,' said Inverlarig, his face growing dangerously purple.

'"What is truth, asked jesting Pilate?"' quoted Angelica unexpectedly, in a low voice.

'Truth,' said her mother, 'is what you want to believe.'

'No, ma'am,' said Inverlarig stoutly. 'A lie is what many people have wanted to believe.' He turned to the Countess, and went on earnestly, 'She stood over me like a – like a warrior queen. What was the woman called? – Boadicea. Most magnificent sight I ever saw. Quite prepared to whip me until I screamed. In the middle of the enemy's camp, ma'am! Men have had the VC for less. Burning with conviction. I challenge anyone to have disbelieved her. Told me I was a fool or a rogue. Made me think I'd been both. Determined to make amends. Thought I'd come over and say so.'

Lady Arabella glanced at me, then back at Inverlarig. The sneer had not left her face. 'It sounds a wonderfully melodramatic scene,' she said. 'Quite theatrical. I confess I wish I had been in the audience.'

'So do I, Arabella,' said the Countess. 'Possibly for different reasons.'

'So do I,' said Angelica, surprising me again.

Patterson, with two footmen, brought tea into the room, and amidst the tinkling of cups and teaspoons the tense atmosphere relaxed. Lady Arabella found, as always, matters of absorbing interest to discuss in whispers with Mrs Forbes. Angelica looked with grave intensity at Inverlarig, the Countess, and me. My warrior-queen performance was not discussed again, nor the story which Inverlarig had declared he disbelieved. It was impossible to tell what the Countess thought of either, but she spoke with great friendliness to Inverlarig.

'I see there's a problem hereabouts which I'd hoped Draco had solved,' said Inverlarig, after talk on a variety of local topics.

'Oh yes?' said the Countess drily. 'I thought my grandson had decided on the solution to every problem, at home and abroad.'

'Not Dandie McKillop,' said Inverlarig.

'Ah! He is perennial.'

'Somebody told me he was back in gaol. Somebody else, it seems to me, got hold of an idea that he was dead. But there he is on the hill, large as life and looking as wild as a polecat. I asked my coachman about him. He knows all the local clash. He said – nobody knows where Dandie's living, or how he's living.'

'He lives in a hole in the ground, I'm afraid,' said the Countess, 'as no landlord will rent him a croft. He eats what he steals.'

'He's stealing from you, then, ma'am, for I saw him not half a mile from the castle.'

'Better he should steal from us than from a poor farmer.'

'Better he should go back to prison, where he belongs.'

'No doubt he will, in the fullness of time.'

Angelica did not look as though she had ever heard of Dandie McKillop. But I wondered; I wondered.

It was by pure chance – the luckiest chance – that I met Charlotte Long. I had been missing her gentle face and voice, and her funny little squeak of laughter, and her hint of a stammer, and her affectionate nature. I had loved her ever since she came to my room at Gaultstower, and I made the first real friend I had ever had. Getting to know her better, at Glendraco and at Drumlaw, I had grown to love her more, and it was a horrid deprivation when she and Georgina were forbidden my company by the Campbells.

She was driving a little basket-work pony-phaeton, like the one Eugénie sometimes used, with a tiny shaggy Shetland pony dwarfed by its blinkers and harness. Sitting in the little chariot, Charlotte with her golden curls looked like something from a picture-book of fairy-tales.

I was riding Falcon, with Geordie Buchan in attendance. I was thinking with gratitude of old Inverlarig – and of how little his conversion had influenced anybody else. We were not far from Drumlaw, at the foot of the great glen: but I was keeping well clear of their policies.

Charlotte and I called out to each other joyfully. I jumped off Falcon, and gave his reins to Geordie, and ran to my friend. I climbed up into the pony-phaeton beside her, and we embraced.

'Oh, how lucky, dear Kirstie!' cried Charlotte. 'I have missed you so d-dreadfully! I have *begged* Lady Campbell to ask you to Drumlaw, or let me go to Glendraco, but—'

'But I am not fit to associate with you?'

'Yes! No! I don't know! It is so odd! They will not say *why* you are suddenly beyond the pale – what is a pale? Never mind – but they look all strange and stern, even Lady Campbell, and Sir Francis grows as black as a th-thundercloud! What *is* it, Kirstie? What has happened?'

'You really don't know?'

'No! They won't say! They won't tell Georgina, either! Lady Campbell says it is too ⊥ well, dear – too *shocking* a story for our ears. As though we did not know *quite* as much about everything as they do! More, very likely. Because, you know, I have lived in London, where the most *dreadful* things happen, and one hears about them all . . . But whatever story they have got hold of, I *know* it is all nonsense.'

'Do you, Charlotte?'

'Yes, of course I do! How can you ask? Wouldn't you feel the same, if people talked so about me? I *know* you. You are *not* what they say you are—'

'What do they say I am?'

'Well, they *don't* say, precisely, that is what is so aggravating. But they *look* as if they would use, well, quite *strong* words.'

She told me all the things that she had been doing, and I told her some of the things that I had been doing. She was excited that they were all going to Perth for the balls and races, and very sorry that she would not see me there.

'Sir Francis says the races are not what they were,' she said, 'and I am not to imagine anything like Ascot, but I am sure it will be ex-exciting and beautiful. And the balls! I can hardly imagine it. Everybody in kilts and jewels, you know, and dancing reels and waltzes, whirling round. We are practising the reels at Drumlaw, so that I shall not get in a muddle and disgrace them. Of course Georgina knows how to do them already. They are such fun, and so elegant! But quite exhausting. I *do* wish you would be there, Kirstie! Really, it will *spoil* it for me, if you're not.

Can't we arrange it, somehow? I don't want to go nearly as much as I did.'

I was touched; I made her promise to enjoy herself as much as possible, even though I was not there.

On the lower slopes of Ben Draco, above a wall of green, there was a curious natural ledge. Lord Cricklade said it had been carved by a glacier in the Ice Age; Geordie Buchan said it had been put there specially for me. The ledge was a gentle curve, following the face of the mountain, nearly a mile long, at the east end as wide as a football-field, at the west end as wide as a bowling-green. Two hundred yards from the western end there was a narrowing, like the waist of an egg-timer, and the ledge was squeezed between two tall rocks no more than two yards apart; the rocks stood like sentries outside Holyrood, or like the footmen outside the great door of Glendraco. To the north of the ledge rose the steep, rock-strewn face of Ben Draco; to the south the ground fell away, here and there in precipitous rock and scree, towards the river.

The ledge was carpeted in springy turf, never hard nor boggy, kept short by sheep and red deer. It made the most wonderful natural gallop. Geordie Buchan said that any trainer at New-market would be delighted to exercise his racehorses on it. Falcon loved it, and so did I, and it was there that I first rode my beauty as fast as he would go.

We went there about once a week. I was passionately fond of the sensation of galloping at top speed on the perfect ground, in that perfect place. The wind blew not at me, but right through me. Geordie said it was good for Falcon to blow all the cobwebs out; it was good for me too. I forgot the tangle of my emotions about Cricklade and Billy. I forgot the sneering hatred of Lady Arabella; the unnerving, silent stare of Angelica; the whispers of Mrs Forbes; Caerlaverock's sickening treachery, and the way even the Campbells believed his lie; the hooded, taloned figure of Eugénie, crouched always in the shadows, watching and listening and hissing . . . All I knew was the steady drumbeat of Falcon's hoofs as he devoured that mile of turf, his sweet ears pricked, his enjoyment as keen and obvious as my own: all I knew was the heady rush of the Highland air, the brilliant sky, the empty immensity of the great glen.

There was never anybody on the ledge. That day there was nobody for miles.

'Awa' wi' ye, Miss Kirstie,' said Geordie with a grin.

And away I went! Falcon did not have to be told to gallop, nor told which way to go. He went like a bolt from a bow, nearly a mile, straight for the gap between the rocks. He would slow down, at the least pull of the reins, when we neared the rocks, and pull up comfortably in the last two hundred yards. He would be panting and blowing, and highly pleased with himself, and full of himself, and I would pat his neck, and pull his ears, and croon to him: and then Geordie would thunder up to us, with a grin that threatened to split his dear old face in two.

It was as glorious as always. I remember singing as we galloped – some snatch of old Scottish music, learned I knew not where – but the words were snatched out of my mouth by the wind, and I laughed aloud, and exulted in the speed and in Falcon.

We neared the twin rock-sentries, and I was not too intoxicated to rein back steadily. He slowed at once; his motion changed from the smooth rush of his gallop to the undulating grace of his canter, so that I was like a boat, rising with easy buoyancy to powerful, gentle rollers. Controlled, but still fast, we sped through the gap in the rocks. And as we did so, Falcon's head and shoulders seemed to disappear. There was suddenly nothing in front of me, as he was brought violently to a dead stop, and down on to his knees. I was thrown over his head. Sky and mountainside swung dizzily. Then there was blackness.

How long I was unconscious I do not know – perhaps it was no more than half a minute. I opened my eyes to find that I was lying on the grass. I felt ill and helpless, and my head hurt. I put a hand to my brow, and struggled to sit up.

Falcon stood quietly beside me, his reins over his head. There was blood on his forelegs.

I heard a noise of deep, harsh breathing, and turned, and almost swooned with horror. Geordie Buchan was locked, on the ground, in a violent struggle with a man. The other man was as old as Geordie, with wild white hair and a white matted beard. It was Dandie McKillop. As I watched, paralysed with horror, Dandie freed a hand from Geordie's grasp, and pulled a long knife from his tattered blouse.

I pulled myself somehow to my feet, staggering like a drunken man, like Caerlaverock himself, and tottered over to them. I think I screamed, but they were locked in the most violent and ferocious conflict, and neither heard me. The laboured breath rattled harshly from the throats of both. Geordie had hold of Dandie's wrist, but the point of Dandie's knife was creeping ever closer to Geordie's neck. The veins stood out on Dandie's face, and there was a look of triumph in his eyes.

Hardly knowing what I was doing, I picked up a rock the size of a football, and brought it down on Dandie's head. There was a most dreadful noise. Dandie went limp. Geordie heaved the unconscious man away from himself. Dandie fell backwards, and over the lip of the ledge hard by the sentry-rock. The ground was steep there – a slope of slippery dry grass, a patch of scree, then a jumble of dark grey rocks. Dandie rolled and slid, limp as a rag doll. He gathered speed as he went, and crashed among the rocks. He hung, at last, across a rock, like a dish-rag on a pump-handle.

Geordie struggled to his knees. He was panting with great, harsh, uneven breaths.

At last he managed to say, 'Ye sevvit ma leef, Miss Kirstie.'

I swayed, and sat down suddenly on the grass beside him. He kissed my hand, and repeated that I had saved his life.

'What happened, Geordie?' I asked tremulously. 'Why did Falcon come down? Why did Dandie McKillop—?'

'The black-hairted diel hae strungit a trip-line ahint yon stanes,' said Geordie. 'He kenned ye cam this road, an' gaun quick . . .'

'He wanted to kill me?'

'Ay. 'Tis an auld an' a bitter tale. Your gran'sire promisit tae Dandie McKillop a braw croft an' the job o' farrier tae the cassel—'

'My grandfather?'

'Ay, James Drummond o' Glendraco, Goad rest his soul. But he didna keep his cassel lang eneuch tae keep his word ... He lost a', ye ken, lost a' ... Lost the cassel and a' the lands, ay, lost a' ... Lost a' tae the mon Stewart, fifty year syne, ay, jist fifty year syne ... An' Stewart becam Airl o' Draco, ye ken, an' his Countess bides there yet ... Ah, wae's me! Dandie McKillop ne'er haed the croft, an' Stewart brocht anither chiel as farrier – he didna ken a word'd been gi'en ... an' Dandie McKillop's hairt hae been bitter an' black, aye syne, for Drummond o' Glendraco brak his word ...'

'Drummond of Glendraco,' I repeated unsteadily. 'And his arms showed a leopard dancing—'

'Ay, rampant, wi' a rose tae his mooth ... Yon's your ane, Miss Kirstie. Yon's your leopard.'

'My grandfather – sold Glendraco – to the Countess's husband?'

'Sold? Mebbe. I dinna ken.'

'And my grandfather – died – soon afterwards?'

'Ay.'

'How, Geordie?'

'I dinna ken.'

And so we sat with our hands clasped, with the horses grazing peacefully near us, until Geordie felt strong enough to do what had to be done, and my head, though it still ached horribly, had stopped swimming.

Geordie cried out again and again that I had saved his life. For this reason – only for this reason – he had broken his word to the Countess – he had told me who I was.

He told me the Drummonds had held Glendraco since the mists of earliest times. Before they built the present castle – itself, in part, of great age – they had had a still older fortress where the stables and steading now stood.

I remembered that Mr Barrow had said that there was an old castle there, and showed me ancient stones, and pieces of enormous wall. He said nobody knew whose castle it was. He lied, because he had been told to lie. It was the Drummonds' castle.

The Crombies had known my face, as Geordie had known my face, because they had known my grandfather, here in the glen, here in his own castle. They had all lied, because they had been told to lie.

Dandie McKillop had known my face, because he had known my grandfather. He had hated my face and me. A promise made by Drummond had been broken by his successor. Unwittingly – no one was to blame. But my grandfather was to blame, maybe, because he had not seen that his promise was kept.

Flora Crombie had seen a horse fall among rocks. She had seen a soldier lying upon a floor, people struggling in an angry river, a man drowning from a boat. What meant these sights? Were they past, or to come, or the ravings of a simple old woman?

Geordie did not know. He knew no more than he had told me.

But he had known my grandfather; had worked, and Dugald Crombie too, as a lad in the stables of the castle. He loved him. All his servants did. By Geordie's way of it, James Drummond was gay and just and generous; he rode the most difficult horse like an angel, ran up the steepest hill like a goat, drew fish from the river, and hearts from the breasts of women, as though drawing cards from a pack ...

We rode home slowly. Geordie Buchan had suffered no hurt beyond bruises; I had a lump on my head, but I was no worse than David Baillie the day I met him. Falcon's knees were barked, but he was not lame or sorry for himself; he wanted to run home much faster than I wanted to ride. Geordie said that he would bathe and bandage the places, and we must rest the horse for a day or two.

Over Geordie's pommel was the thin, harsh cord with which Dandie McKillop had brought down my horse. Over his cantle was the body of Dandie McKillop. Geordie said I had not killed him, but the fall among the rocks had killed him. I hoped he was right.

Annie Simpson very gently felt the lump on my head, and sent at once for the nurse Morag Laurie. Morag put me to bed, and said I must stay there until she allowed me up, in case I had damaged my brains, or split my skull. I knew I had done neither of these things, but I was glad to lie in bed, and eat my dinner from the second Earl's *porte-dîner*. I had a lot to think about.

'It is true,' said the Countess. 'And Geordie Buchan should be whipped for telling you.'

'I understand now,' I said, 'why you said in George Square that I had a right to be asked . . .'

'And you understand that it was madness to ask you.'

'Do *they* know all this?'

'Of course they do. When Glendraco was – forfeit to my husband, and James Drummond had – died, his widow lived in Edinburgh. Their son married your mother. Of course her parents knew. How could they not know?'

'I do not understand,' I said, 'why they never told me. Why nobody has told me.'

The Countess said, very gently and seriously, 'If you knew more, my very dear child, it would mean only misery. Let the dead past bury its unhappy dead . . . Wordsworth, sixty years ago, wrote a poem about the song of a girl who was cutting the corn, up here – do you know it? – she sang of "Old unhappy far-off things, and battles long ago" . . . Nothing, child, could be older, unhappier, or farther off than . . . than those things which happened, which should not have happened . . .'

After she left me, I began to weep. It was not because of the old, unhappy, far-off things, or the battles, or the things which should not have happened. They were not sad tears. I wept because she had called me her very dear child.

Geordie Buchan fought his way, almost literally, past Annie Simpson and Morag Laurie, to see me. He came in with his bonnet in his hands, shuffling and grinning. He said that Falcon had only broken the skin of his knees; after a day of stiffness he was longing for another gallop. And Rockfall, said Geordie, was pining for me.

Geordie himself had made a deposition, on oath, about the circumstances of Dandie McKillop's death. He said Dandie had stretched the rope between the rocks with the evident intention of bringing my horse down, and injuring or killing me.

Geordie, seeing this, had tackled him. During the struggle, Dandie had fallen down the steep slope, and cracked his skull on a rock. Geordie had told the story so, to save me from being bothered by questions. If I were asked about it, I was to remember that this was what had happened.

I thought it very likely that the Earl would bother me with questions – he seemed always so bent on knowing the truth about everything. But Geordie told me the Earl had gone away, summoned by urgent business. I was surprised; though so solemn, the Earl was a passionate sportsman, and as Lord Cricklade had long ago told me, this was the high sporting time of the year in our part of Scotland. But Geordie was not surprised; though indeed a passionate sportsman, the Earl would always put business before pleasure – unlike, he added, my grandfather.

'Sae,' he finished, 'ither folks wull no' ken the truth. But I'll no' sune forget ye sevvit ma leef.'

He kissed my hand again before he left, and made me feel like a queen.

'Who is the lady at Inverlarig?' I asked the Countess.

'Mrs Baillie? I forget who she was. Why ever are you interested, Kirstie?'

'No – I mean the girl in the little picture by the fire in the study. She was painted in 1772, and she looks just like me, and she has my arms, my leopard.'

'I did not know of this. It must be your great-grandmother, painted soon after her marriage. I never saw her – she died quite young, when James Drummond was still a child. She was French. Her father was the duc de Nonancourt. I believe he opposed the marriage, although there were still, in those days, strong links between France and Scotland . . . All the Nonancourts were murdered in the terror, killed by the guillotine . . .'

'Why is her picture at Inverlarig, I wonder?'

'Ah, why? When my husband became lord of this place, it was his – his whim to remove all trace of the Drummonds . . . He left the bindings on all those books, of course, which you discovered, but I daresay he never looked at them . . . As to that, I doubt if anybody has looked at those books, in all the fifty years since then ... Until you found them, and did not know what you had found, which is a very painful irony ...'

'My little silver looking-glass escaped also,' I said.

'Yes. That had been given to me. It was mine to keep and to give.'

'But there were other pictures?'

'All the Drummond portraits were sent to London to be sold. Some little ones, perhaps, did not go so far. I imagine my husband gave the one you saw to the Baillie of the time, who had, perhaps, admired your ancestress.'

'I would like to have that little picture,' I said.

'Inverlarig will give you anything you ask for.'

'Yes, I know he will. That is why I cannot ask him.'

'Oh Kirstie!' She looked at me with sudden distress. 'You are more like your grandfather, sometimes, than I can bear.'

'Why,' I asked, 'did Lord Draco empty the castle of – of Drummond things?'

'He was not Draco then. He bought his earldom from the government in 1816. They needed support after the war, and he had money and votes.'

'But why—'

'He would not knowingly have broken the promise to McKillop. There can have been nothing in writing—'

'Did my grandfather go away so very suddenly?'

'He had been away. He was away. He did not return.'

'Your husband came here instead?'

'You know that, and I cannot take that knowledge from you. But it is all you may know. Believe me, child, it is all you should know.'

'Why, when he came here, did he empty the castle of all—'

'Questions are tiring for you,' she said abruptly, 'and tiring for me too, after a long day. We will not talk more now. Try to sleep.'

Messages poured up from Billy. A message or two, more restrained, came up from Cricklade. Messages came from Inverlarig, from David and from his father; a message came, to my great pleasure, from the Barstows of Ardmeggar. A loving message came from Charlotte Long and Georgina Campbell, some-how smuggled, I suppose, out of Drumlaw.

I was bored after two days in bed. My brain was not squashed, nor my skull cracked; but Morag Laurie insisted that I rest for another full day, or I might have headaches all my life.

On the third afternoon, Annie Simpson, unusually awed, ushered in a totally surprising visitor. It was the Marchioness of Odiham.

The Snow Queen looked and sounded quite as terrifying as I remembered her. The temperature of my sunny room dropped ten degrees when she came in, and dropped further when she looked round it with icy pale eyes, and further still when she began to speak in her icy clear voice.

After congratulating me on my escape, she made conver-sation, graciously enough. She said that her husband was still off the coast of Norway in his yacht, and she intended to remain in Scotland for another month. She said that she was going to Groyne Palace, near Perth, for the race-week. The Earl of Mountfield was a widower, it seemed, and was her cousin, and she was to act as hostess for him at the Palace. She looked for-ward to entertaining there Lord Draco, Lady Arabella, and Angelica.

I thought they would all need extra warm clothes, to stay in a place where she was acting as hostess, for there would be icicles hanging from every ceiling.

'I arrived here yesterday,' she went on. 'I had a particular reason for coming, which concerns you.'

She paused and looked at me. I shivered.

'I find Elinor Draco in good health but low spirits,' the Snow Queen said, 'which she was unwilling to explain. You will not be surprised to hear, however, that I received an explanation, at great length, from Amy Forbes. I confess I stand amazed at Elinor's forbearance in continuing to extend hospitality to that poisonous woman.'

'Poisonous, ma'am?' I asked, startled.

'Venomous. She is Arabella Paston's toady and tale-bearer. If poor Arabella had been luckier in her life, she would not suffer so contemptible a satellite. However, this does not alter the distasteful shock with which I heard what Amy had to tell me. I am not surprised that Elinor is low in spirit, with such a story broadcast about her protégée. Are you?'

'No, ma'am,' I said dully.

The echoes of Caerlaverock's story were resounding far. Lips, no doubt, would be smacked about it at Perth; men would tell each other with sniggers over their port, and women whisper it above tinkling tea-cups in drawing-rooms . . .

'I told the detestable Forbes,' went on Lady Odiham coldly, 'that her story was an evil and impudent fabrication. I suppose Caerlaverock was drunk, although it is difficult to think where he could have procured enough spirits in one of those miserable cottages. I have never, I am thankful to say, seen Caerlaverock drunk, but Billy Mainwaring has given me an expurgated account of an occasion at which he was present. Him I believe, because Sir Hannibal Mainwaring is a man it is entirely safe to believe. I hope you agree?'

'Yes, ma'am, I do.'

'He is to be one of our party at Groyne. I am glad, since he is almost unique among young men nowadays in combining infectious gaiety with impeccable manners. You may be gratified, though you will scarcely be surprised, to hear that he most earnestly entreated me to invite you to Groyne also for the races and balls. His entreaty was quite unnecessary, as I had already decided to do so. Will you honour me by accepting this invitation, Christina?'

'*Honour* you?' I gasped.

'You have twice shamed me – twice reproved me, firmly and in public, for my ill behaviour. I should not have stared at you as I did at Violet Bodmin's house. It was unforgivably rude, and you were quite right to tell me so. I should not have spoken as I did in this house. It was unforgivably cruel, and you were quite right to tell me so. You have earned my highest admiration, for what little that is worth. Will you come? Billy will be so pleased, but no more so than I. Will you come? Oh, Kirstie! Are you going to be as rude as I, and disdain even replying to my invitation? Are you so unforgiving?'

'I – I'm sorry, ma'am. I am speechless!'

'Then I will take silence as implying consent. Elinor will tell you what you need, and you will bring your maid. I shall ask Elinor to send you to Groyne a few days early, so that we can practise the reels. A very high standard is required, if you wear the tartan sash. One warning I should give you. My cousin Mountfield, though an old man, is quite certain to fall in love with you. That will not, of itself, discommode you unduly. But he will prove his devotion by giving you a wealth of secret information about the races, and my warning is that you should ignore it. The horse he says will win is invariably last. The man to consult about racing is Lord Cricklade, but I expect you know that. Goodbye, dear.'

And she was gone.

Annie came in with eyes like saucers (I am afraid she had been listening at the door), and we began to discuss what clothes I should take to Perth.

Morag Laurie allowed me up, but I was not to ride for another two days, or do anything rash.

I came downstairs to an empty house. Mrs Weir told me that the Countess had gone off to Ardmeggar, taking Lady Arabella and Angelica, and Mrs Forbes was off on a day-long errand of charity. The Earl had not returned; the Reverend Lancelot Barrow was still on holiday; Sir Hannibal was after a stag on the Dalnabeith ground; and Lord Cricklade was fishing, with his luncheon in his pocket, on the topmost beat of the Draco.

I went to the stables, to see Geordie and Falcon and Rockfall, who were all in even better health than I was. We might have disobeyed Morag Laurie, but I knew Wattie Dewar would report us.

As I walked slowly back towards the castle, a carriage came towards me. Lord Cricklade was driving; beside him was his little brown servant Jewkes. It was the open carriage, with the bay pair, that he had arrived in: but they had closed it, by pulling the folding roof over the top.

As they neared me, I saw that Lord Cricklade was not dressed for fishing at all. He wore a tall black hat and a black cutaway coat, as though he was on his way to visit a bishop.

He pulled up the pair, handed the reins to Jewkes, took off his hat and his gloves, and jumped to the ground.

'I abandoned the river,' he said unnecessarily.

'That was unlike you,' I smiled.

'Not altogether. I try to retain a sense of proportion. I was coming to look for you – will you come for a drive with me, Kirstie?'

'I should like to very much,' I said truthfully, 'but you know I cannot, and you know you should not ask me. My reputation is already so low that I daresay another crime could not make it worse, but – well, you know, it is simply not allowed!'

'I know it is not allowed, but I think you should come, just the same. Do you remember driving with me in my gig, from Lucksie almost into Edinburgh, and then full-tilt in pursuit of the Dragon's coach?'

'Yes, of course I remember. I will never forget that drive.'

'Nor will I. *That* was even more improper.'

'Yes, it was, dreadfully improper, but it was necessary.'

'I hate to remind you, but had I not driven you that day, you would not be here now.'

'That is quite true.'

'You would be affianced, or perhaps married, to the creature you told me of – the one with wet hands, who lectured you.'

I shuddered. 'Well, it was because of those things, that I *had* to – to behave in such an unladylike way, and rush about the Lothians in your gig. Now there is no threat, at least of *that* kind, so you see—'

'There is no threat, but there ought to be gratitude, I think?'

'There is! There always will be!'

'Then I think I have a moral right to ask you to drive with me, and I think you have a moral duty to accept. Come, Kirstie! You trust me, surely?'

'Yes, of course I do ... Well, I shall say I was compelled by moral arguments, and superior strength, and so forth ... Why have you put up the top of the carriage?'

'In case it rains.'

'But there has never been a finer day!'

'Jupiter thunders out of a clear sky. Or, to put it another way,

231

if we are doing something the Dragon would think improper, we are best to be discreet about it. And, thirdly, it is better for your poor head not to be in the full glare of the sun.'

Rather dubiously, I let him hand me up into the carriage: and, as he followed me up, he kept hold of my hand. Neither of us was wearing gloves. The pressure of his fingers was strong on my own. I knew that I should draw my hand away. Part of me wanted to, but part was more than content that it should stay where it was. The modest and ladylike part won (somewhat to my own surprise) and I pulled to free my hand from his; but he held it fast, and smiled at me, and the carriage rolled forward.

'Where are we going?' I asked.

'Wait and see. I have planned a surprise.'

Something in his voice – something of quiet determination – rang little bells of alarm in my head. I looked at him, frowning. He met my gaze with a smile. He was more deeply sunburned than when I had first seen him, and his hair was bleached paler by the sun; he looked supremely sane and reliable, a true friend, a man to trust implicitly. The little alarm-bells fell silent. The surprise, perhaps was a picnic, or a view of particular beauty.

We chatted about our first drive, and about all that had happened since. He was as pleasant and informative as always. But he kept hold of my hand.

We went down the glen, at a surprising pace, and took the turning towards Lochgrannomhead.

'What is the surprise?' I asked him again. 'Where are we going?'

'Trust me, Kirstie,' he said gently.

We did not go into Lochgrannomhead, but turned up a different road which I did not know. We were going a long way, and still travelling briskly. I was puzzled. I could not be frightened or suspicious, with Cricklade, but I was puzzled.

I said, 'I am sorry to be so – earthy, but it must be luncheon-time—'

'Are you hungry, Kirstie?'

'Yes, very!'

'Good. That is provided for.'

I was still expecting a picnic at a beauty-spot; but instead the carriage drew up outside a small, lonely whitewashed farm-house.

I stared at it, not understanding why we should have come to such an uninteresting place.

'Some friends of mine live here,' said Cricklade. 'Not polished people, but discreet, and somewhat in my debt. They have undertaken to let us stop here for an hour, and eat our luncheon in comfort. I have something to show you, Kirstie.'

'Something here?'

'Something here,' he said tapping his pocket.

Full of wonder, I let him hand me down from the carriage, and we went into the farmhouse. The wife, a plump woman of late middle age, bobbed and disappeared. Cricklade showed me into a parlour, very clean, full of overstuffed furniture and pious pictures.

'I doubt if they use this room twice in a year,' said Cricklade. 'I would have preferred to sit in the farm kitchen, but we do need privacy.'

'Why do we?' I asked stupidly.

'Let us eat and drink first.'

Jewkes had seen to the horses; now he brought a basket in from the carriage, which was full of cold food, and a bottle of white German wine. Jewkes waited on us with a sort of brusque efficiency, no expression on his little wrinkled face. He banged the plates and forks about, as though to show he knew exactly how it was done, but deplored having to do it. Cricklade continued to chat pleasantly, discussing the depressing pictures in the parlour, and going on to other pictures and painters, of which he had wide knowledge. I scarcely spoke. I was bemused by this strange expedition. I wondered very much what surprise Cricklade had in his pocket, which he said he would show me when we had finished. When I asked him about it, he only laughed, and filled my glass with wine.

He finished the last of a bunch of the Glendraco hothouse grapes, and drained his glass, and signalled to Jewkes. With much banging Jewkes cleared away the luncheon things, and took them out. I heard voices in another room, and then Jewkes whistling outside.

'Now, my dear,' said Cricklade pleasantly, 'the hour has come.'

'The hour for . . . ?'

'Revelations. Don't look so tense – John MacLaren and his wife are not five yards away. Are you sitting comfortably? Your head is not troubling you? What I have to say will take a minute or two.'

'What you have to say? The surprise?'

'That, also, will take a few seconds. Now – I told you, did not I, that I was a slow and careful man, methodical, exact, painstaking? I compared myself, rather vaingloriously, to the Roman general Fabius. He was known to his impatient compatriots as the 'Delayer', and even accused of cowardice. He withdrew, you know, and circled, and kept everybody guessing, and avoided battles, and became quite a bore – but he won. Oh yes, he won. When I spoke to you about this, I imagine you thought I was talking about my – my unhurried pursuit of yourself. Well, so I was, in part. But I was also referring, less obviously, to another campaign I have been waging, on another front. A more elaborate affair, that other campaign, and I have been engaged on it since early June.'

I looked at him blankly. I had no idea what he was talking about.

'Immediately after our ride together in my gig,' he went on placidly, 'I went into Edinburgh. I called at George Square, and was granted an interview with Mr and Mrs Strachan. They were in a state of the most lively anxiety, which I was able to assuage. I spent a long time with them. I flatter myself that I impressed them favourably. I did not dwell on my sporting tastes, but rather on my legal duties as a Magistrate, my participation in debate in the House of Lords, my regular attendance at places of worship – in short, I presented myself to the Strachans as everything that was mature and dependable. Don't look at me like that, Kirstie! All that may be only a part of me, but it is a large and perfectly authentic part. Well, I went there again the following day, by which time they had heard from the Dragon. They were upset by the prospect of your removal to Glendraco, here they suspected that all was libertine indulgence. I assured them that the Dragon's household was extremely well-conducted, and

Draco himself a man of the highest gravity and principle. Partly for this reason, they decided to take no legal action to get you back. Partly it was - though I do not fully understand this myself - to avoid a great scandal, and the publication of matters which they wished to remain unpublished. Though curious, I was unable to learn from them what scandal they feared, nor what dark secrets they were so anxious to keep secret. I fancy you don't know either? Be that as it may, they were for these two reasons resigned to your remaining at Glendraco, though hardly overjoyed about it. And meanwhile they had come to trust me, as you do.'

'As I did.'

'*Touché*. This trust, this esteem, I was careful to foster during the following weeks. I called at George Square whenever I was in Edinburgh, confirming, at each visit, the favourable impression they had formed of me. You were discussed, I should tell you, at great length and on many occasions. They are deeply concerned about you, you know. I put it into their minds, very tactfully, that what your wild and rebellious spirit required was not a somewhat flabby husband, like your medical admirer with the damp hands, but a man of strength, spirit and experience. The sturdy oak, you know, rather than the flexible sapling. I should say that these discussions were entirely objective. I did not identify myself as the required oak-tree. There, perhaps, I was less than frank with the Strachans, because I was determined to have you the first time I met you, and my determination has never wavered. You have no comment?'

'Not yet,' I said in a stifled voice.

'How ominous that sounds. Am I so repellent, really? Have you detested my company, or screamed when I took your hand? Have you frowned or sneered when I told you how beautiful I found you?'

I had not. I had revelled in his compliments, basked in his admiration, enjoyed the pressure of his hand. He knew it as well as I did.

He looked at me searchingly, and then laughed. 'You do not grow any less transparent, my dear.' he said. 'You see that this situation is of your own making. Had you been visibly revolted by me, or bored by me, then I might have abandoned the whole

235

attempt. I doubt it, but we must admit the possibility. So far from that, you have been transparently – always transparently – happy in my company, and gratified by my devotion. Well, now! I had for many weeks continued to assure the Strachans that the propriety of life at Glendraco was quite as strict as in any other great house, though not in all details, perhaps, what they themselves would have approved. I was able to tell them, with perfect honesty, that as far as I knew you were behaving with decorum and modesty. Until recently. Until honesty obliged me to report to them that a monster of indecorum, a nightmare of immodesty, had made your name a byword for fifty miles.'

I looked at him in stupefied silence.

'I wrote the Strachans a letter,' went on Cricklade seriously, 'in which I said, with perfect truth, that a respected local land-owner, a baronet, had forbidden his daughter and her friend to associate with you, for fear of moral contamination. That a dis-tinguished general would not be in the same room with you. That your continued presence at Glendraco was an embarrassment to your host and a scandal to the neighbourhood. All true, you will agree? A letter of impassioned appeal came back to me from George Square. They wrote to me because they did not expect truth from you, or help from the Dragon. What should they do? How could they remove you without the odious publicity of a legal action, without uncovering those secrets which they were so desperate to keep hidden. Well, I was able to suggest a remedy. You will note how adroit my strategy had been. Until this junc-ture I had not revealed, in person or on paper, my own intentions with regard to yourself. I now did so, in a measured and sober fashion. I have not got a copy of my letter, but I expect one day to be able to show you the original in George Square. You will not fail to admire it. To give you the essence of many pages, I said that I was prepared to accept responsibility for you. I said that it was incumbent on me, as I had inadvertently subscribed to your removal from their care. I said that I would make an honest woman of you, and keep you honest by a judicious com-bination of strictness and Christian charity. I was not so much asking for your hand, you see, as producing myself as a *deus ex machina* – the one solution to an intolerable problem.'

'Very clever,' I said, through clenched teeth.

'Yes, very,' he agreed mildly. 'At that stage a remark came to my ears which at once stiffened my resolution and showed me my method. You told Mrs Forbes that I had once abducted you. Oh what a rash jest, Kirstie! How ill-advised and foolish! She told a number of people, with baited breath, and they all told me. I was not best pleased, you know, for a day or two. But then I thought – shall my bride be a liar? No indeed! We will make the story true, but prospectively, instead of retrospectively, if you understand me.'

'You are abducting me now?' I asked with difficulty.

'Yes and no. In one sense I am unquestionably abducting you – here you are, after all, in the remote house of people who are obliged to do what I want, with only myself and my servant, who is also obliged to do what I want. We go where I choose, and do what I choose. To that extent I am abducting you, and shall continue to do so. But in another sense it is all, I'm afraid, less dashing and romantic than it seems. "Abduct" implies some measure of illegality. But the whole police force of Scotland could only approve what I am doing. I am acting, Kirstie, not merely with the permission but at the urgent request of your legal guardian.'

'Oh God,' I said.

'*He* is your guardian, my dear, only in a remote and unhelpful sense. Your grandfather's letter has more immediate pertinence. This is the surprise I promised you.'

He drew a letter out of his pocket. I recognized my grandfather's cramped and angular hand. I took the letter from Cricklade. Because my hands were trembling, I spread it out on the table in front of me.

George Square

My dear Lord Cricklade:
This is a brief communication, written in the Utmost Haste, to express our Thankfulness to God, and Gratitude to you, for your Undertaking in respect of Christina. It comes as the Answer to heartfelt and incessant prayers. You have my Authority to take Christina from Glendraco, and to marry her by whatever Rite is acceptable to you. I bless the Forbearance and Christian spirit in which you shoulder this Burden,

and rest assured that in your charge lies the unhappy child's best prospect of Salvation.

I have the honour to remain, dear Lord Cricklade,

Your Lordship's deeply obliged servant,
S. Strachan, Writer to the Signet

'You see,' said Cricklade, 'The Magistrate in me is greater than the sportsman.'

'I did not like Caerlaverock's way,' I said slowly, 'but I much prefer his way to yours.'

'Ah, you do not have my regard for the law. Well, my dear, shall we go? The rings are in my pocket. I have arranged for us to be married in Aberfeldy, and there is still a long way to go.'

eleven

Lord Cricklade took me firmly, very firmly, by the arm, and led me out to his carriage. There was nothing I could do. He was much stronger than I; the walnut-faced Jewkes stood by; the farmer and his wife were within call. If I pulled away and ran, where would I run? Up the bare hillside? Along the road? There was no other person in sight, no dwelling for miles. There was nowhere to hide on the bleak, treeless ground. I was very far from my friends, if I still had any friends. I had no money. I did not know where I was.

I hung back at the step of the carriage, but Lord Cricklade's great strength compelled me up and on to the leather cushions. He followed me up instantly, and took my hand and held it fast, while Jewkes shut the door on us.

We were going into a town. I could appeal to someone. To whom? Cricklade was a lord, a man of high position, well-known and respected, a Magistrate. He carried a letter from my grandfather, my legal guardian, not merely approving what he was doing but begging him to do it.

My face must have shown my feelings to Lord Cricklade, who found me so very transparent.

'Is it so terrible, Kirstie?' he asked gently. 'You will be Lady Cricklade. You will be treated like a queen in Wiltshire, you will conquer London. You will be the mistress of a beautiful house and still more beautiful stables. You will have fine jewels to wear, though you may not care about them. You will have fine horses to ride, and I think you care about them very much indeed. My dear, what do you *want* out of life?'

'Freedom,' I muttered.

'But my love, you shall have it, as far as becomes a wife and a peeress. I am not a Turk, you know. I do not want to tyrannize over you. I would hate to live so. I love you dearly and devotedly, and I fully intend to prove so today and every day as long as I live. You *shall* have freedom, Kirstie. You shall do exactly as you like, because I know that the things you like are good things, and I like them myself. Falcon is yours; you shall have him at your own home. You love that disreputable dog of yours; you shall have him at your own home. I do not flatter myself that – that your feelings for me are a tithe of mine for you, but I *do* think you have been glad of my friendship? At the risk of sounding vain, I think you have been – perhaps – half, or a third, or a quarter in love with me?'

'Well,' I said slowly, 'if I have been a little in love with you, why do you need to be so – so cold, and devious, and calculating?'

'*Cold?* To go to such lengths to make sure of the girl one loves – do you call that *cold*?'

'Yes, yes! Cold! Like a machine, not like a man! Why couldn't you just *ask* me?'

'Because I knew you would have said no.'

'How can you know that?'

'Because I can read you, Kirstie. You would have thought of Mainwaring, and said no.'

'How can you know that?' I asked again.

'I know it no better than you yourself know it. Look into your own mind and heart. Be as honest as I know you always are.'

I did as he said. I looked into my mind and heart. And it was true – Cricklade was right. I would have thought of Billy, and said no.

'If I do prefer Billy,' I said slowly, 'how can you want me?'

'How can I not, my foolish darling? Have you any idea what love is?'

'Yes,' I said passionately. 'I have, but you haven't! To go secretly about it like this, with all these clever stratagems, getting yourself legal rights, behind my back – it may be greed, or passion for possession, like a – collector staring through the window of a shop – but it is not love!'

'It *is* greed for you,' said Cricklade earnestly. 'It *is* passion to possess you. I hunger and starve for you. But I am *not* thinking only of myself. I love you, Kirstie, and therefore I deeply and seriously wish that what comes to you is what is best for you. I know, from your grandparents in Edinburgh, a great deal about you. Your childhood rages, your disposition to wildness and rebellion . . . Your grandparents are strait-laced, but they are not stupid, and they are very far from uncaring. Honesty obliges me to accept the truth of much that they said about you, and honesty will oblige you to accept it, also. Well, then! What kind of man should such a girl marry? What kind of man will look after her as she needs? What *is* best for yourself, Kirstie? Passionately in love as I am, I might have deluded myself in this regard. I might have convinced myself, falsely, that I was what you needed. But I have examined my conscience, believe me. You know me well enough to know that I *have* examined my conscience. And I do *not* delude myself. I *am* what you need. I am deeply and sincerely convinced that your happiness lies with me. I understand your affection for Mainwaring. I can see that he is easy to be fond of. But I do profoundly believe that your union with so – lightweight and flexible a character – would be a disaster for you, leading ultimately only to misery and waste. I cannot expect you to agree with all that I say on this subject – not yet. But I beg you to try to believe that I am not cold, not wholly selfish and cynical. I love you. I want what is best for you. I could not – *could not* – risk your acceptance of Mainwaring. I could not risk your refusal of myself.'

'But you don't mind if I refuse you now?'

'Now your refusal has become irrelevant.'

'My feelings, too? You call *that* love?'

'I am not in despair about your feelings. You feel outraged at the moment, because all this has been too great a surprise. I should have softened the shock, prepared your mind, but I could not risk everything by forewarning you. You must see that? I am not depressed about your mood. I think you have felt – been prepared to feel – warmly about me. I shall be a gentle and thoughtful husband, Kirstie – I swear it. I shall earn your love. You've submitted – you've welcomed – the pressure of my hand. You'll submit to – ay, and welcome – my embrace as a husband—'

'You'll have to force me,' I said.

'So be it. I shall have marital rights, and I shall exercise them. Remember that I know the law. My God, girl, do you think that I have taken all this trouble – waited all this time – taken so many pains to be certain – to leave untouched the sweets that are mine to taste, to deny myself what I want so dearly and deeply?'

'I did not like Lord Caerlaverock's way,' I said for the second time. 'But if I am to be forced to submit to a man. I prefer his way to yours.'

Cricklade shrugged. 'Your taste in love-making,' he said, 'must be distressingly squalid. I hope I shall teach you better. Our first lesson will be tonight, after we are safely and decently married, at the house of a friend of mine. He is away, but his servants are warned and all preparations made. Our dinner is cooking at this moment, our champagne cooling, and our bed airing.'

I choked at this. He put it down, I think, to prudery; but it was not: it was revulsion.

How could a man, who had been so attractive to me, fill me now with such feelings of disgust and fear? He was quite right in all he said – the position he was taking me to would be envied by any girl in the three kingdoms; he would be attentive and thoughtful; I had welcomed the squeeze of his fingers on my own, and yearned for more than hand-holding. It ought to have been flattering that so great a gentleman went to such trouble to be sure of me. But it was exactly the sort of trouble he went to that filled me with loathing.

We rattled into the small grey town of Aberfeldy. Ordinary people on their ordinary business walked up and down the streets. I saw a pretty, bare-legged girl, in shawl and bright petticoat, her hair drawn back into a net. She saw me at the window of the carriage. A little look of envy crossed her face, because I was a lady in a carriage, and she was a poor girl with no shoes to her feet. If she had known that in a few minutes I would be Lady Cricklade, with a mansion and jewels and a stable of beautiful horses, and a popular, respected and handsome husband, she would have been envious indeed. But ah God, how I envied her! She could run away down the street without a hand or a voice raised to stop her.

We trundled to a halt outside a bleak little grey house at the edge of the town.

'The Manse,' said Lord Cricklade. 'The Reverend John Sinclair is expecting us. I have spoken with him long and earnestly; he knows me well, and I think respects and trusts me. He has also received a letter from your grandfather, written at my suggestion. I have seen the letter, which is quite explicit. Your grandfather writes to Mr Sinclair both as a Writer to the Signet and as an Elder of the Kirk – he warns the good Minister to ignore any display of girlish reluctance you may make. There now! My faithful Jewkes has made all ready for you to get down, so let us lose no time. The ceremony will be quite brief. Scottish law is much simpler than English in regard to marriages, you know, which explains the popularity of Gretna Green. We shall not, of course, have a glass of wine with Mr Sinclair, as he shares your grandfather's convictions on that subject – but we will have one as we go along, perhaps, to my friend's house. To be sure we shall be man and wife by then, and may be in a mood for other things than drinking . . .'

Numb, I allowed myself to be helped to the gritty pavement by Cricklade and Jewkes. Cricklade jumped down after me, and took his firm grip of my arm above the elbow. His fingers felt like iron bands – not gripping painfully, but imprisoning utterly. He was a big, powerful man, supremely active and healthy; I am light and slim; he could have picked me up and thrown me over the roof of the Manse.

And he was armed with all legal powers. And the Minister esteemed and trusted him, and was warned to ignore my reluctance.

Slowly we walked towards the door of the Manse. Jewkes was just behind me. The door opened. A tall, spare man, quite young, appeared in the doorway; he had a white, bony face, hard pale eyes, and hands that looked as well-scrubbed as the Reverend Lancelot Barrow's.

'This is Mr Sinclair, my love,' said Cricklade, 'the Parish Minister, who is being so kind as to marry us.'

'Gud day, your lordship,' intoned the Minister, as though conducting a service on his doorstep. 'Gud day, mem,' he added to me grudgingly: for to Scotsmen of his background and belief, at that time, women were at best chattels and at worst the instruments of Satan. He looked at me warily, thinking (I suppose) that I might scream hysterically, or struggle, or faint.

And I was very near doing all those things.

'Five minutes should see us to the end of our business, I think?' said Cricklade cheerfully.

'Ay,' said the Minister, turning back to the man he so greatly esteemed and trusted. 'Nae mair. An etairnal bond is forged in the wink o' an e'e.'

'An eternal bond,' murmured Lord Cricklade, smiling at me, 'forged in the wink of an eye. Come, let us proceed at once to the anvil. I want to hear the hammer strike the metal that hoops us together for eternity, Kirstie. And of course, speaking of metal hoops, I have provided myself with a small gold one for your finger.'

He produced it, as he spoke, with the hand that was not holding me to his side: a gold wedding ring, that had lain in his waistcoat pocket. It glinted in the afternoon sun.

In five minutes that ring would be upon my finger. I should be Lady Cricklade, married for eternity to a man with a soul like a legal textbook, like an emotionless machine, like a greedy collector of jewels or porcelain.

Suddenly, from the side street by the corner of the Manse, came the most welcome sight in all the world: the dear round face of Billy Mainwaring. He looked tired and dusty; the grime on his cheeks and brow was streaked with the sweat that had run down them. He led a big brown horse, with foam about its bit and its shoulders dark with sweat. His face was grimmer than I had ever seen it.

My heart blazed with joy and relief.

Cricklade stopped short when he saw Billy. His jaw thrust out and his brows came down.

'What are you doing here?' he asked abruptly.

'I came to find out what you are doing here,' said Billy through clenched teeth. Turning to me, he said, 'Is everything all right, Kirstie?'

'Everything is as wrong as it can be,' I said.

'Then we will put it right,' said Billy grimly.

'Mr Sinclair and I are about to do that,' said Cricklade mildly.

'Oh no,' I said. 'Not now. Why did you follow us, Billy? How did you find us?'

'Wattie Dewar told me you had gone off with Cricklade in his carriage,' said Billy. 'I thought that strange, but – no more than strange. Then I went to the gun–room to put away my rifle, and noticed that Cricklade's guns and rifles had gone. I ran to Cricklade's room. His things were gone – everything. He had packed up and left Glendraco, suddenly, when I knew he was expected to stay for another week. My first thought was that you had gone willingly – eloped – without telling me or anyone. I was hurt, but not so very surprised. Cricklade is, in the eyes of the world, a – desirable match, I suppose.'

'Thank you,' said Cricklade mildly. 'Kirstie has been in the way of thinking so too.'

'I found Annie Simpson, your maid,' said Billy, looking steadfastly at me and ignoring Cricklade. 'She said you had taken nothing – no clothes, brushes, things for the night – nothing. I ran back to the stables, and found that you had not taken Rockfall, either. I could imagine you leaving of your own free will without taking your nightdress, Kirstie, but I could not imagine you leaving without taking your dog. So I was nearly sure that you had gone unwillingly. But, in all Scotland, where had you been taken? Then a most lucky thing happened.'

'Most lucky,' I breathed.

'Draco's butler, old Patterson, had seen a letter on the salver in the hall, waiting to be taken to the post – a letter addressed in Cricklade's hand to a Reverend Mr Sinclair here. I could think of few reasons why a Church of England peer should suddenly be in correspondence with a Free Church Minister in Aberfeldy. One reason seemed more horribly obvious than any. It was a long shot. But it came off, eh? *Did* you come here willingly, Kirstie?'

Before I could reply, Cricklade said sharply, 'Mr Sinclair!'

The Minister looked at him, eyebrows raised.

'Before Miss Drummond subscribes to whatever childish nonsense this rash young gentleman may propose,' went on Cricklade solemnly, as though he were on the Bench in his own Courtroom, 'may I know if you have received a letter from a Dr Findlay Nicholson in Edinburgh?'

'Findlay?' I gasped.

'Ay, ma Lord, I hae received an epeestle frae Dr Nicholson.'

'Saying?'

'Writ at the instance o' Mr Simon Strachan o' George Square. Sayin' the doctor was the maydical adveeser o' Miss Drummond, an' gi'in' me solemn warnin' that the girl was subject to veesitations o' Satan, takin' the form o' rebellious outbursts contrary tae duty an' tae her ain better inclinations.'

'Oh God,' I said drearily, 'you thought of everything.'

'Ye'll no' tak the name o' the Lord in vain in this place,' thundered the Minister. To Billy he said, 'We'll have nae interruptions, young mon. This is the Lord's work we du.'

Billy's face darkened with rage. He dropped the reins of his horse and took a step towards Cricklade. Cricklade glanced behind him at Jewkes. I looked back at the little servant, following Cricklade's eye. Jewkes's hand was in the pocket of his roomy groom's coat, holding some large, heavy object which thrust forward. I realized it was a pistol. Billy saw it, too.

'I shall give evidence at the Inquest,' said Cricklade equably, 'that Jewkes was obliged to fire to protect my life against a furious assault, of which the apparent motive was insane jealousy.'

'Is that what brocht the mon here?' asked the Minister.

'He is, or thinks he is, in love with my bride,' said Cricklade.

'Thou shalt no' covet thy neighbour's wife,' trumpeted the Minister.

'She's not your wife yet,' cried Billy hotly.

'No,' agreed Cricklade. 'But five minutes will put that right.'

'I'll fetch a constable—'

'Do, my dear fellow, and I'll be delighted to show him the documents in my pocket. Your arrest is much more likely to follow than mine, I assure you.'

'Is that true, Kirstie?' Billy asked me.

'Yes,' I said in renewed misery, hope having flared only to be extinguished.

Lord Cricklade towered beside me, gripping still my upper arm with fingers like steel bands. Behind him stood Jewkes, his pistol in his pocket. In front stood the Reverend Sinclair. Lord, lawyer, Minister, Magistrate, guardian, doctor – all, with the massive forces which they represented behind them, were united in carrying me into the drab little Manse and marrying me to Cricklade. And a man stood by with a pistol, in case dear Billy tried anything foolish and heroic. He was little needed! Billy was no weakling, but Cricklade could have smashed him senseless to the ground with a single blow – and both of them knew it as well as I did.

I saw that, in five minutes, I would be Lady Cricklade. And that, in five hours, I would be stripped and ravished by Lord Cricklade. What had been – sometimes, in my daydreams – a heady and enchanting prospect, had become an odious and hellish degradation. Because he was a lawyer, not a lover: a calculating machine, not a man: a strategist, not a wooer: a devil, not a god: an enemy, not a friend. Because I did not want to be his wife. I did not want his hands on my body. I shuddered at the thought of his cold hard lips on mine . . .

I saw, as I stood there, three futures in front of me – just three, no others. I could kill myself. I could kill Cricklade. Or I could submit. The last I could not. The first I would not. It was the second, then. I would make myself a widow, as soon as might be, after he had made me a wife. Of course I would be caught and tried and hanged. So be it. My long neck would suit the noose, and make the hangman's task an easy one.

'Come,' said Lord Cricklade, 'we have kept Mr Sinclair waiting long enough.'

Then my plan came to me.

It depended on an appalling number of things. On my being able, somehow, to wriggle free of Cricklade's grasp. On Jewkes not catching hold of me. On Billy holding his whip loosely, or realizing in time what I was doing. On my being able to jump, in a long skirt not at all made for jumping . . .

I composed my features into an expression of obedient resignation which I was very far from feeling. I realized that I had been standing very tall, in an attitude of defiant arrogance; now I let my shoulders sag forwards; I lowered my head submissively; I relaxed the muscles of my arm so that, to Lord Cricklade's imprisoning fingers, it would feel limp and defeated.

I said quietly, 'If it must be, let it be quick. Go back to Glendraco, Billy – you can do nothing here except get yourself killed or hurt. We must all do our duty. Jewkes has his, and Mr Sinclair has his—'

'Ay,' said the Minister gravely.

'You have yours, Billy, which is to go away and forget me. And I have mine.'

'Ay,' said Mr Sinclair again.

'May I see my ring again?' I said humbly to Cricklade.

'Yes, my love, of course you may,' he said, smiling, indulgent, tender.

The grip of his fingers on my arm had already relaxed a little, owing to the new docile character I had assumed. Now he was preoccupied for a moment, groping with his free hand into his waistcoat pocket for the wedding ring.

It was the moment – the one and only, unrepeatable split second in which I could save myself.

I wriggled and snatched my arm from Cricklade's grasp. I sprang towards Billy's horse. As I passed Billy I snatched the whip from his hand. I ran full tilt at the side of the tall brown horse. As I came to it, I jumped wildly upwards and forwards; I grabbed a handful of mane with my left hand, and the cantle of the saddle with my right, which already held Billy's whip. My feet swung clear of the ground. I heaved myself further on to the saddle, and at the same moment smacked the whip upon the horse's quarters. He snorted, bucked, and started forward. Confused shouts and running footsteps were following me. I felt clawing hands. I lashed out behind me with the heavy horn crook of the whip. Hanging like a sack of potatoes across a pack-horse, clinging for dear life to the mane, I hit the poor horse again with the whip. He broke into a canter. I was almost bounced from my ridiculous and precarious position. I knew that I must fall – that I should be married as Cricklade planned, but with a broken shoulder or a cracked skull. I clung still, somehow, the horse swinging and bouncing below me. I dared not take hold of the reins, to slow him down or steer him, for that would mean letting go of the mane, and I knew if I did that I must fall. So we bounded on, going wherever the horse chose, and at whatever speed he chose.

We rattled madly along the road. I had a vague sense of staring faces and mouths agape, of shouts behind and wild waving arms before; but all my attention was concentrated on staying on the horse.

I felt my hat fall off, in spite of pins. My hair came down, and blew all about my face, so that I could see nothing and could hardly breathe for it. I dropped the whip – but it had done its duty nobly.

At last Billy's horse slowed to a trot, which was worse than the canter: and then to a walk, which was much better. And then he stopped. He tossed his head and neighed. I think he was greatly puzzled by carrying a sack across his back, which clung to his mane, and shouted, and whipped him, and by being ridden without a hand on his reins. Mercifully, both reins had stayed on his neck, and not slipped over his head to trip him up.

When he stopped, I managed at last to get a foot in a stirrup, and heave myself astride the saddle. This was no easy matter, for my long tight habit-skirt had to be pulled up almost to my waist, before I could sit cross-saddle. The effect was not indecent, as I wore the usual trousers under my habit, strapped beneath my boot-soles with leather thongs: but it must have been highly absurd. And I was hatless; my hair fell wildly about my face and shoulders, and my face, I daresay, was purple from effort and from my sacklike position.

Once sitting up and holding my horse's reins, I looked round. I was out of sight of the town; no one visible was in pursuit of me. I had no idea by what road I had left Aberfeldy. I had no clear idea how far I had come. I knew, for the moment, only that I had escaped – for the moment.

What would Cricklade do? Follow me in his carriage? Then I must go where the carriage could not follow. Follow me on one of his carriage-horses, or on a borrowed or hired horse? Then I must go faster than he went.

Which way? From my study of the Atlas with the Reverend Lancelot Barrow, I remembered that the approximate direction from Aberfeldy to Glendraco was west. That meant keeping the sun on my face, while there was a sun, and the North Star on my right cheek, if I was benighted.

It occurred to me that the police might have been warned to look out for me. Cricklade and the Minister between them, out-shouting Billy, would command total belief, blind obedience. I must avoid any person I saw. And any croft or farmhouse might have been visited, or be visited soon, by a galloping mounted messenger. I must steer clear of villages and towns, and of all houses, however great a detour I had to make.

And so I started the longest, weariest, maddest ride that can ever have been taken by the intended bride of a rich and popular Peer of the Realm.

During the remaining hours of daylight (I had no idea how many) I rode on, walking and trotting, keeping my face to the sun as steadily as I could. It was not so very steadily, for I had to avoid the high tops, and go instead round the shoulders of hills, and skirt park fences, and avoid farms; three times I had to go far out of my way to find bridges so that I could cross rivers; so my course was a sort of wide, wild zig-zag: but I thought I was going always more or less westward. The country was far from that I knew, and utterly unfamiliar; most of it was awesomely empty. The sun went down, but I could still steer by the peach-coloured glow which it left in the western heavens. Then that, too, darkened into purple and then into black. I was alone on a strange horse in a strange country, not knowing what direction to travel in, or what traps and hazards lay before my horse's feet. I guessed I would go round in a circle, and perhaps kill myself and maim my horse, if I tried to go on. So I stopped, and scrambled off (most awkwardly, because of my long tight skirt), and sat on the ground with the horse's reins in my hand, talking to him to keep my courage up.

I did not dare to think what would happen, if I did reach Glendraco. Would not the Earl, and the Countess too, support Cricklade exactly as my grandfather had done? And for the same good and generous reasons? To see me well and safely married, far beyond my deserts of fortune or of character? Perhaps Lady Odiham would want to help me, or Mrs Carlyle, or the Duchess of Bodmin. But how could I appeal to them? How could they answer my appeal, when law and authority stood fast at Cricklade's side?

I was very stiff and sore and tired, from riding in an unfamiliar way, in most unsuitable clothes. I was hungry and very thirsty.

The moon rose, a little short of full. I thought – the new moon rises in the west, and the old moon in the east, and the full moon in the south; this great golden autumn moon would guide me, if I kept it to my left; and it would soon give me light enough to show me how to go, if I went slowly.

I had a struggle as great as before to get myself up into the saddle. In one way it was easier, because there was no hurry, and the horse knew me now; in another way it was harder, because I was so tired and stiff.

The horse was well rested, and anxious to get home to his stable; he stepped out briskly, seeing quite well in the brilliant moonlight where to put his feet down.

On we went, slowly, never out of a walk – for my sake, and the horse's sake, and safety's sake – crossing strange country that looked stranger in the moonlight. A few watchdogs barked, at long intervals, from lonely crofts. I could steer no more regular course by night than by day: for although I was not so frightened of going close to human habitations, I was more frightened of broken ground and holes and natural hazards. The course I steered varied almost between due south and due north. But at least I was putting always more miles between myself and the

Manse of Aberfeldy: between my finger and Lord Cricklade's hateful ring.

The moon sank. It became impossible to see, to go further in safety. Clouds covered the stars to what I thought was the northwards. It was impossible to steer. I climbed down from the horse, sat myself on dew-soaked grass, and waited for dawn. I had never felt more utterly weary in my life, more drained of strength, more achingly in need of sleep . . .

I was wakened by a strange noise – a high, rapid piping, something between the babble of a young child and the cry of an exotic bird.

I opened my eyes.

A pale sky arched above me as I lay on the ground. In it, hanging above my head, was a blurred black mass. I blinked and the mists of sleep cleared from my eyes. The black mass was the head and shoulders of a man, who knelt beside me and looked down at my face. The head was covered with long, matted black hair, and much of the face with a heavy black beard. The mouth hung open, revealing a graveyard of blackened teeth. The little eyes, like an insect's, stared down into mine with an expression in which no intelligence, no human feeling showed. The man was enormous, a giant; huge limbs, like trees, were covered with black hair and with ancient filth. He was dressed in desperate rags.

The giant held the reins of Billy's horse, which was grazing quietly on the rough hill grass. The saddle had been taken off.

My mind rose sluggishly from the depths of exhausted sleep, and then grasped the terrifying reality of what I saw. This was Adam McKillop, the untamed idiot, son of the man who had hated me so much that he had tried to kill me: son of the man that I had killed.

Of all the people in the whole world who might have found me, helpless and alone on the hillside, this was the most catastrophic. He would know – he must know – what had happened to his father. He had been without doubt a witness of that dreadful scene, hiding in a peat-hag or behind a rock. He had seen – he must have – the furious struggle between the two old men, seen me pick up the stone and smash it down on his father's head. He knew, too – he must know – that Drummond of Glendraco had sworn to give his father a house and a fine position, and the promise had been dishonoured, and Dandie McKillop had been driven to a life of vagrancy and crime . . .

I was filled with fatalistic despair. My helplessness was so complete that I did not scream, or even tremble. I would be stabbed through the heart with the long knife which, long before, I had seen in Adam's hand; or my skull would be smashed with a stone, so that I met the death I myself had meted out. I hoped that his aim, with knife or rock, would be good.

'Please God,' I said, 'let it be quick.'

I realized that I had spoken aloud.

A look approaching understanding came into Adam's little black eyes, and from his gaping mouth came a torrent of the shrill, piping gibberish which was the nearest he came to human speech.

He stretched out an enormous hand to my head. I closed my eyes, not wishing to see the face of my murderer at the moment of my death. Waiting for the blow, I felt instead a very gentle stroking. I felt the hair being stroked from my brow. I heard the shrill jabbering soften to a bird-like twitter.

I opened my eyes again. I searched the savage and terrifying face which now hung inches above mine. I thought I saw in it a look of curiosity, of anxious concern. That look vividly reminded me of something. My fogged mind groped for a moment, and then remembered.

The look on Adam McKillop's face was the look I had often seen on Rockfall's face. When my adored and adoring dog thought, with his precious animal instinct, that something was wrong, that I was worried or distressed or hurt, then into his soft brown eyes came this look that spoke of his anxiety as clearly as a man's words.

Adam wished me no ill. He was sorry for me, worried about me. He wanted to help me. I was sure of it. Those eyes could not lie. The savage idiot could hide his feelings no more than Rockfall could.

I find it hard to understand, now, the completeness with which my terrors departed – the strange, immediate certainty with which I knew that Adam was my friend. But so it was. He looked at me with Rockfall's eyes, and twittered like an anxious bird, and stroked the hair from my brow. He could have broken me into pieces with one vast hand, and then stolen the valuable horse he held by its reins – but he would not; he would take me safely home.

I smiled at him, and sat up.

It was very early morning still: the sun was already bathing the high tops to the west with pinkish radiance, but its rays had not yet come down into the broad glen where I lay. We were on low ground, a great slow shoulder of sheep-pasture below the purple heather and granite outcrops of a hillside. Below us ran a small burn with a track beside it. There was no house in sight, nor the smoke from any chimney.

I stretched out a hand to Adam, and he helped me to rise. It struck me how much gentler his fingers were than Lord Cricklade's. He looked at me anxiously when I was on my feet; I smiled, to tell him that I was well.

I said, 'Can you lead me to Glendraco, Adam?'

I understood, from his piping voice and from the look in his eyes, that he would.

I pointed to the saddle. I struggled to understand his response to this; he pointed to the horse, to the saddle, and to my skirt: and at last I saw that he meant me to sit the horse aside, as though with a side-saddle but bareback, which would be more comfortable for the horse and for myself. He showed me a mark on the point of the horse's withers – a saddle-gall. He was quite right. Without a sheepskin or a soft pad, the saddle would have pained the horse.

He lifted me on to the horse's back as though I were a child's doll stuffed with straw. But, though he was so hugely strong, his hands were so gentle that I hardly felt their pressure. He gave me the reins. He put the saddle over one arm, and took the bridle with his other hand, and began to march with great strides towards the pink-washed western hill-tops.

And so we came at last to the great glen, and past the waking village, and into the stable-yard of Glendraco Castle.

The first people I saw there were the two I most wanted to see – Geordie Buchan and Billy Mainwaring.

Geordie did the last thing I could have expected. He burst into tears. He hobbled forward, patted the horse on the neck, pumped Adam McKillop's hand so that Adam dropped the saddle on the cobblestones, and reached up to help me down.

But Billy was before him: Billy with a bandage about his head. Billy lifted me down, and I came down into his arms; and we embraced each other shamelessly, before Geordie and Adam, speechless with happiness to find each other safe.

'Your head?' I asked at last, speaking muffled into his dear shoulder.

'A misunderstanding with your friend Cricklade,' said Billy cheerfully. 'He thought you ought to be stopped, and I thought he ought to be stopped from stopping you, and we argued about it for the space of two seconds. He terminated the argument rather abruptly.'

'He *hurt* you, Billy!'

'The paving-stone did more damage than his fist, I think.'

'I am sorry!'

'I'm not.'

'Those two seconds – they were what I needed to get away?'

'Well, it was a briefer delay than I expected, but—'

'You saved me.'

'Thank God I was there.'

'I hit someone with your whip.'

'Jewkes.'

'I am sorry. I hoped it was Cricklade.'

Someone had let Rockfall out of his kennel; he came into the stableyard, and saw or scented me, and came at me like a bullet from a rifle. Only Billy's arm kept me, weakened as I was, from being knocked to the ground by the passionate impact of his greeting. He rushed to Geordie, as though to report to the old man that I was back; he rushed barking to Billy; he rushed to Adam, and licked his hand; he rushed back to me.

I choked to think that, all undeserving, I should have the devotion of three such living creatures as Billy, Geordie, and Rockfall.

Geordie satisfied himself at last that none of my bones was broken, and the horse had nothing worse than his gall. He began to lead the horse away.

I called after him, 'Can you look after Adam? He found me and brought me home.'

Geordie nodded and grinned, and spoke to Adam in Gaelic. Adam twittered back, stroked the horse's nose, and followed Geordie away.

'I think Adam is good with animals,' I said to Billy. 'I think he would be good with a sick or frightened animal. Do you think Lord Draco would give him some work here?'

'I wouldn't care to have a creature like that in my own establishment,' said Billy. 'He might comfort the animals, but the sight of him would drive the milkmaids into hysterics. And yet, I don't know. Medieval Lords used to have a dog-boy, you know, who lived with the hounds in their kennel and spoke to them in their own language. An idiot, a "natural", far better than any normal man at pulling the thorns out of their pads ... Leaving that subject, my precious girl, tell me what happened to *you*.'

And so we told each other our adventures. Cricklade had tried to have Billy arrested for assault, and for impeding a Magistrate in the execution of his duties, and for a time this had looked all too likely to succeed. But Billy was able to show that the horse I had taken was his, and he was glad to have me take it; and the Reverend Mr Sinclair had surprisingly announced that Cricklade had struck Billy during the course of a brief argument, and not the other way about. Billy had found a doctor to bind up his broken head, after Cricklade had driven off in his carriage with a face like thunder. Later Billy had managed to hire a gig, and drive back to Glendraco. Now he, Geordie, and a dozen others were about to set out to search for me.

But the horses which were being brought out, from stables and loose-boxes, to be saddled, were led in again, or taken out to their paddocks. We had the stable-yard to ourselves.

Billy took my arm, and drew me under an archway. He looked at me somewhat uncertainly, his eyes very bright, his breathing uneven.

I felt a wave of love and gratitude towards him. No woman

could have more devotion than Billy's; no woman could have the devotion of a greater darling than Billy.

He took me into his arms. I threw mine round his neck. I felt him trembling. I was trembling too. He kissed me. I responded to his kisses with an emotion which almost frightened me. Our bodies were pressed together, and our mouths locked together. Once again – as, once before, in the rain-swept glen of Monaidh – I felt like a leaf on a rapid river, swirled and swept by a rushing torrent of passion.

He whispered into my cheek, 'Will you marry me, darling Kirstie?'

I could not reply.

He drew his face back from mine, and searched my eyes with his own.

I wanted to say, 'Yes, dearest Billy, of course I will!' But the words would not come. My throat would not let them pass, nor my tongue form them.

He muttered again, huskily, 'Darling Kirstie, will you marry me?'

My mind screamed at me: 'Say yes! This kind and gallant man is all that you could wish for, more than all you could ever have hoped for, and he will make you happy, and you love him dearly, and his kisses fill you with joy – say yes!'

But I could not say it.

I shook my head, dumbly.

A stricken look came into his face. He whispered a third time, 'Kirstie, my darling girl, will you marry me?'

I shook my head, and tears started out of my eyes and rolled down my cheeks.

He took his arms from about my waist, and stepped back, and gazed at me. Then he turned and walked away, slowly, his shoulders bowed.

My own heart felt like cracking. Was I mad? How could I shake my head at him? Deny the love I felt for him? Refuse what I wanted so much?

I sat down on an upturned bucket, buried my face in my hands, and wept long and miserably.

I could not understand myself. My mind, my thinking brain,

mocked and jeered and railed that I was a fool, demented, madder by far than the gentle idiot Adam McKillop – that I was acting with the insane perversity of which I had so often been accused, in George Square, in my turbulent childhood.

But 'yes' could not be driven from my lips; and my head, which wanted to nod, found itself shaking.

Later in the morning (when I had eaten, and changed, and looked respectable again) I sat with the Countess in her boudoir.

She heard all my story in silence.

At the end she said, 'Henry Cricklade has never in his life, I think, done anything he considered wrong. Anything incorrect, anything, as the French say, *louche*. What antagonizes you is not his motive but his method. You are childish enough, Christina, to want tears and tempests and sighs and declarations – which are all, I admit, highly gratifying – but aside from your taste in modes of courtship, has the man done anything *wrong*?'

'Well,' I said slowly, 'it depends what he thinks.'

'Of what?'

'Of me. Of truth. Of the stories about me. Of Sir Francis Campbell, and Lady Arabella, and the rest. Of Caerlaverock.'

'What has all that to do with Cricklade's motives?'

'Everything!' I said. 'Do you think he believed Caerlaverock's story was true? If he did, then he thought the same of me as Lady Campbell ... Did he think a girl like *that* would be a good Lady Cricklade? Could marrying such a person be his idea of acting correctly? Would it be a – a responsible thing to do, in regard to his servants, and tenants, and friends, and brother Magistrates, and so forth?'

'I see what you mean,' said the Countess gravely. 'Do you take it then, child, that he did *not* believe the – story we have heard about you?'

'If he did not believe it,' I said, 'then he lied to my grand-parents, to trick them into – supporting his noble sacrifice. And he made sure the lie was spread to the Nicholsons in Edinburgh, and the Minister in Aberfeldy. Don't you see, ma'am? He was either marrying a harlot, or spreading a cruel lie so that he could force into marriage a—'

'A nice girl?' said the Countess. The corners of her mouth lifted; she smiled slightly. 'An obedient, dutiful, mouselike, well-conducted little Miss?'

I smiled too. I could not help it, though the thought of Billy made me feel so far from mirth. 'Not exactly that,' I admitted.

'There is much we shall never know,' sighed the Countess. 'Passion makes men behave – very oddly – as I have reason to know . . . Cricklade fell in love with you when he first drove you in his gig. *I* saw that at the time. I even remarked on it, I think? I warned him it would not do – though, in retrospect, I scarcely know why I did. I suppose, if things had been different, it might have done very well, if only he had had the sense to behave more – romantically, less cautiously and legalistically and – what was your word? – deviously.'

'His word,' I said.

'As though he were proud of it? How more than strange.'

'He *was* proud of it, ma'am. He didn't exactly boast, but he thought he'd been *very* clever.'

'So, in his way, he had. He very nearly succeeded, did not he? I can understand what he was about, given his obsession with you, child. He saw that, for all the esteem you felt for him, you would have refused his offer.'

'Then he knew that before I did.'

'I don't doubt it. He could see, better than you, the effect on you of our little Billy. Hence . . . all that happened.'

'Yes,' I agreed uncertainly. 'I was not sure for a long time, but I would always have refused his offer.'

'Thrice fortunate Billy. And how has *he* contrived to remain silent?' She looked at me sharply with those clear, wide grey eyes, that gazed with such childlike wonder, and saw so much. '*Has* he remained silent? I don't think he has! My dear child, Billy proposed to you today! I can see it in your face!'

'Yes.'

'And?'

I felt tears start again out of my eyes.

'You refused him?' murmured the Countess.

'Yes.'

'Why, Kirstie?'

'I don't know, ma'am!'

'You surely love him? Is it possible not to?'

'Yes, I do love him! But ... I could *not* say yes. Try as I might, I could *not*.'

The Countess looked at me long and sadly. She looked as though she understood what was making me behave so idiotically: but I could not see how she understood, as I did not understand myself.

She asked me no more, but talked instead of her grandson and Angelica Paston.

'I think,' she said, 'you will hear the announcement at Perth.'

Billy left the castle later the same day. He said the estate of which he was Trustee had run into new trouble with its tenants. No message, as far as anyone knew, had come for him, so I did not see how anyone could have believed him. I did not know if anyone knew the real reason for his abrupt departure, even before the Earl came back, beyond the Countess and myself. Perhaps Angelica: but it was impossible to guess what went on behind that solemn, perfect mask. Perhaps her grim mother. Perhaps the garrulous Mrs Forbes. Perhaps Annie Simpson, from whom I had few secrets; perhaps Geordie Buchan, from whom I had even fewer.

I knew that Billy was promised to join our party for Perth. Part of me badly wanted to see him there, as part of me hated to see him leave Glendraco; but part of me dreaded his being there, as part was thankful he was leaving.

When we said goodbye to each other – shaking hands, with great formality, in the outer courtyard – we were both on the edge of tears.

'Our party is quite reduced,' said Mrs Forbes to me, confidentially, in the Italian room. 'All the rank and fashion has deserted us, except Lady Arabella and her dear daughter. But for them, we should be humble indeed, should not we? With only nobodies like ourselves to welcome my cousin Neil home. What a mercy it is that the dear Pastons still honour us. And how curious and unfortunate it is that two such splendid gentlemen as Lord Cricklade and Sir Hannibal Mainwaring should leave *so* unexpectedly! And on successive days! First one, and then the other! One stands amazed! It is quite as though, is not it? something were driving them away! Of course, they are both gentlemen of the *highest* reputation. That makes them, I daresay, more fastidious than some others can afford to be. Neither has ever been linked to scandal, or to the *slightest suggestion* of anything peculiar. They are concerned, I daresay, not to touch pitch . . . If a roof shelters someone of whom they cannot approve, someone of dubious or notorious reputation, then they simply leave! And go elsewhere! To find more congenial, more suitable companionship! So fortunate. I myself, of course, cannot afford to be so nice. I am obliged, by sheer poverty, to stay where I am, *whatever* I think about things, and at *whatever* outrage to my conscience!'

Two days later I came back from a ride on my beautiful Falcon, with Geordie beside me and Rockfall racing round us with a ceaseless energy I found astonishing. He had become a very handsome dog, with feeding and brushing and exercise, though of what mixture of breeds I do not think anyone could have told.

As Geordie and I rode into the yard, Rockfall gave a sudden excited bark and shot on ahead of us. A tall black horse, one that I did not know, stood in a corner of the yard, held by Wattie Dewar; its rider was out of sight in the archway where I had refused Billy's offer. Rockfall rushed up to the invisible rider, and gave him an uproarious welcome.

I was completely puzzled. Rockfall was joyous in his greeting to his friends, but he was very shy of strangers, no doubt because of the way he was ill-treated before we found him.

Out from the archway into the stable-yard came the Earl of Draco, impeccable as always, serious as always, just returned.

'His Lordship hae a new horse,' murmured Geordie, with eyes only for the black.

The Earl pulled off a glove and held out his hand to Rockfall. Rockfall licked it with passionate enthusiasm. The Earl submitted gravely to this loving attention. And then there happened something I thought I had never seen before, and thought I should never see. The corners of his mouth lifted, like the ends of a recurved longbow, and he smiled at the dog. His face, for a moment, was lit by the sweetness of the smile. It was his grandmother's smile. The resemblance, always startling, was miraculous.

My heart jumped like a young salmon in the river. My head spun. I rocked in the saddle, and clung to Falcon's mane to steady myself.

All was clear to me.

Stupidly, disastrously, calamitously, I had fallen in love with Lord Draco.

When Billy offered me his well-loved hand, my head said yes, but my heart said no, because my heart was already lost.

It took that one brief, sweet smile to make me realize – to pour light into the troubled darkness of my feelings – to make me curse fate for a cruel joker, and myself for a susceptible fool.

I had as much chance of Draco as the Reverend Lancelot Barrow had of me.

He would be announcing, at Perth, his engagement to Angelica Paston.

And I did not even *like* the man.

'I happened,' said the Earl to me in his big, white, cheerful study, 'to meet Caerlaverock while I was away. He was staying, as it chanced, in a house in Strathearn which circumstances caused me to visit.'

'The circumstance of his being there?' I asked. 'Did you go to find him, sir?'

'He did not want to see me, or to see anyone,' said the Earl, ignoring my question. 'His hosts were allowing him to be a recluse. It was said that he was convalescent from an illness, which was in a sense the truth. I persuaded him to see me, and we had a long talk, in private. He expressed himself with great bitterness, even violence.'

'Oh,' I said drearily.

'Bitterness against himself. Violence against the way he behaved to you. He was very drunk that night. Why did you not tell me that, Christina?'

'I had a reason,' I said.

'Yes. You were protecting Dugald Crombie, who needs the illicit still to pay his rent. I have known that for years. The Crombies are good people. You need not have lied to me.'

'I – I wish I had known that.'

'You could have cleared up the whole affair, simply by telling me that Caerlaverock had drunk a bottle of Dugald's whisky! That you did not, out of concern for an old crofter couple, does you infinite credit. I am proud to have you as my guest in the house.'

I was too amazed to reply: but simply goggled at him, like a frog.

'Lord Caerlaverock told me that he went to the inn at Lochgrannomhead,' Lord Draco went on gravely, 'and there spoke to nobody.'

'*Nobody?*'

'In a relevant sense, nobody. Of course he commanded hot water and coffee from a servant, and made arrangements about sending back the horse, and paid his reckoning. But he saw nobody he knew. He confided in nobody. He gave no account to anyone, true or false, of the events of the previous night. He has not done so since. I am satisfied that he was telling me the truth. Caerlaverock is, as I said, passionately repentant. If he dared, he would come to you and beg your pardon on his knees.'

'He told no one,' I gasped. 'Then . . .'

'Then some person unknown,' said Lord Draco without expression, 'has maliciously fabricated an utterly fictitious story, falsely giving Caerlaverock as the source, with the sole object of making you despised and hated.'

I tried to digest this. It was hard to do so.

At last I said slowly, 'I think – this person you speak of – is much worse than Caerlaverock.'

'I entirely agree. Caerlaverock is not all evil. He has weaknesses, but nearly all his qualities are good. When sober he is, as you know yourself, the most delightful of companions. To behave like a rabid animal after too much drink is – unattractive. To do this other must earn, I think, eternal damnation.'

'No,' I said, 'not quite. Dandie McKillop hated me enough to try to kill me, but he had a reason I can understand, and now that he is – dead – I am sorry for him.'

'And when you know who has tried to ruin your life, will you be sorry for him?'

'If I know *why*, perhaps . . . I am so glad it was not Caerlaverock. Inverlarig would not tell me where he heard the story—'

'Nor me,' said Draco. 'I asked him, as you did. But he had given his word that he would not tell, and he *will* not tell.'

'I would like to know,' I said thoughtfully. 'I would like to know very much . . . Oh, sir, mentioning Dandie McKillop has put something into my mind—'

'You recommend Adam for some position in my stables or farms?'

'Well, yes, because I am sure, in spite of looking as he does, and the way he talks, or rather doesn't talk—'

'It is done. He has always been perfectly harmless, you know, and only in trouble of any kind because his father led him into it. I have been looking for him since Dandie died, to make sure he was safe and fed. He cannot manage on his own. People took him in whenever his father was in gaol, and some hoped to keep him. I did myself, after he was most patient and skilful putting a splint on the leg of an injured calf. But as soon as Dandie was free he whistled, and off Adam would go to his poaching, thieving life. Well, that will happen no longer. When you saved old Geordie you saved Adam also.'

'And you have saved me,' I said. 'I am so grateful.'

For the second time I saw his smile. And this smile was at me, not at my ridiculous dog. And so I was lost beyond salvation.

For now, I not only loved him, but I liked him too.

twelve

There was a long, barbaric opening blast from the bagpipes. I curtseyed, as I had been taught, to my partner Sir Duncan Raden. He, like a very well-dressed giant bear, bowed and grinned at me. His full Highland evening dress almost confused the eye with its complicated richness; Cairngorm stones gleamed from his doublet, and the glass eyes of the otter which made his sporran winked at me, giving back like the thousands of lustres above us the blaze of the enormous chandeliers of the Assembly Rooms.

The piper swung into the jigging, hypnotic music of the eightsome reel. We circled to left and right, and swung with our partners, and then Lady Odiham, a skyrocket of diamonds in the tiara in her hair, was slowly revolving in our midst with an expression of amused detachment. She danced with Draco. As they set to each other they seemed both to belong to a world far removed from earth and passion and fatigue. If Sir Duncan was the world's most elegant bear, the Earl was the dancing leopard on my own coat of arms, more superb to my helpless, infatuated eye than the whole of the rest of the ballroom put together. Lady Odiham set to Sir Duncan – Beauty and a supremely magnificent Beast – and they swung; and then the three of them went into the mazy figure-of-eight. Lady Odiham set to young Torquil Bruce, who laughed with the unaffected enjoyment of the moment which was his great charm, and then to her cousin, the elderly but merry Earl of Mountfield, of Groyne Palace; for once his face was solemn, because to him reels were a deeply serious business; his legs were as thin as the skean dhu which was thrust into the top of one checked stocking, but he pranced about like a grasshopper taking part in an ancient ritual.

We circled to left and to right, and now Angelica Paston was solemnly gyrating in the middle, the Marble Goddess after the Snow Queen, her cool, grave beauty wonderfully framed by her soft hair and the perfect simplicity of her pearl-coloured silk dress. All the men – even the high-spirited Torquil Bruce and the emblazoned giant Sir Duncan – treated her as though she was made of the most delicate porcelain.

The third lady was little Catriona MacLaren, whom I loved after knowing her for two days, for she laughed at the same things that I laughed at; and when she saw a cab-horse being whipped she tried to buy it, on the spot, out of the shafts. When Sir Duncan swung her round, he lifted her clear off the floor, and she squealed with excitement, and Lady Odiham smiled her cool smile, and Angelica watched gravely.

And then I went into the middle, in my hooped dress of filmy white silk, with the tartan sash over one bare shoulder, with the broad choker of pearls the Countess had lent me, and with the heartening knowledge that, thanks to silk gown and jewels and Annie Simpson, I looked better tonight than ever before. I knew just what to do, for Lord Mountfield had sedulously taught me during the two days I had spent at Groyne before the rest of the party assembled there. He, and Lady Odiham, said I took to the dancing naturally, and it was true. As soon as I began to move my feet to the music of the pipes, my whole body seemed to float and whirl and spin to the rhythm. Now I spun one way, in the opposite direction to the dancers circling round me, and then the other way, when they turned. The chandeliers spun above me, like moons in a mad dream, in the immense vaulted roof; all about, filling the ballroom, there was a bewildering pattern of brilliant colour, swinging and swaying, a glorious living tapestry of jewels and bright hair, white shoulders, rich velvet, tartans, laughter.

I set to Sir Duncan Raden; he grinned, and swung me dizzily off my feet; I heard a high laugh of pure joy, and realized it was my own. I set to happy Torquil Bruce; his face was pink with exertion and delight, and his curly hair stuck up on end like a brush. As he swung me he murmured, 'Oh, I do love you, Kirstie!' I spun again as they circled, and spun as they circled back. I set to Lord Mountfield, who pranced on his old stick-legs, and almost flew through the air himself when we swung. I set to the Earl of Draco, who smiled broadly, and said, as we swung, 'You look very beautiful, Kirstie.'

I scarcely, after that, remembered anything clearly of my first great Highland Ball.

I was aware of faces, hundreds of men's faces, the cheerful, open, weathered, healthy faces of the cream of Scotland, the faces of all the men I danced with, for my card was somehow completely full – of smiles and warmth and delightful admiration – of murmurs of how beautiful I was, most encouraging murmurs about my eyes and hair . . .

I was aware of animosity and malice, and disapproval and whispers, and staring eyes that swivelled away the moment I turned to meet them . . .

I was aware, half-consciously, through the blurred colour and moving glitter and soaring music, of friends and enemies, of love and hatred, of intoxicating success and miserable failure . . .

And all the time I saw that smile, broad and sweet, lighting up the grave, handsome, hawk-like face, the corners of the mouth lifting like the ends of a recurved longbow. And all the time, every moment of that hectic and miraculous night, I heard those words spoken just loud enough for me to hear over the scream of the pipes and the laughter of the dancers: the words, spoken gravely though the face was smiling – 'You look very beautiful, Kirstie.'

We trundled home, exhausted and wilting, in a fleet of carriages, from the Assembly Rooms to Groyne Palace.

'I hoped you would enjoy it, dear,' said Lady Odiham. 'I thought you would be admired. But I did not expect you to be the unquestioned queen of the ball.'

'Why did you not expect it?' asked Lord Draco. 'I did.'

I could not see, in the dark carriage, the look Angelica gave him.

Most of the others said the races were a disappointment and a bore. I found them neither. Of course the others had been to Edinburgh and Ayr races, and some of them to Ascot and New-market and York, but I had never seen a race or a racehorse before. The horses were more beautiful than anything I had imagined on four feet; and I loved the bright silk jackets and coloured boot-tops of the little wizened jockeys, and the solemn formalities of the start and the unsaddling and the weighing-in, and the scarlet coats of the Caledonian Hunt Club, who had a gay striped tent of their own, to which I was several times taken for refreshments, and the kilts and plaids, and bonnets of the Perth Hunt Club, who had another special tent, to which I was also repeatedly taken; and I loved the ballad-singers, into whose tambourines the pennies tumbled, and the 'gymnastic exhibition tent', where a man with fierce moustaches tied himself into remarkable knots, and the waxworks housed in a great closed wagon on wheels, and the company of the Groyne Palace party.

I had a parasol, and twirled it, and needed it; but a cloud came over the sun of my enjoyment. Torquil Bruce, whom I liked very much, proposed to me for the second time just after the first race (the first time had been in the Supper-Room, during the ball) saying, among many much nicer things, 'I don't care what *any* of them say about you—'

'I know what they say,' I said flatly. 'But will you tell me who's been saying it to you?'

'I can't very well do that, Kirstie,' he said, looking unhappy for the first time in the three days I had known him. 'A confidence, you know . . .'

I could not be bothered with this, not at such a time. I seized his shoulder and shook it as hard as I could. 'Who told you?'

'I daresay, really, you have a right to know,' he said. 'Anyway, I can't refuse you anything. It was General Drummond.'

'Will you do something for me?'

'Of course I will! Anything within my power!'

'Ask General Drummond where he heard the story.'

'Well, yes, if you wish. But he may not tell me. He may keep confidences better than I do.'

But I was determined to track the story back and back, step by step, to the poisonous spring which was its source. I said, 'The General will tell you who told him, if you say you don't believe the story. He'll tell you, to convince you that the story's true.'

He nodded, unconvinced but anxious to please me; he smiled a little bleakly, and went off in search of my distant and disagreeable connection.

The next race had a most close and exciting finish – although I was afterwards told that the result had been arranged in advance by the owners and trainers and jockeys. As three horses flashed past the winning-post together, amid a great roar from the crowd, Torquil touched my arm.

'You were quite right, Kirstie,' he said. 'The General did tell me where he got the story, because he knew that would convince me the story was true. It almost does.'

'Almost?'

'Almost. It was Sir Francis Campbell. All your neighbours, you see.'

'Oh yes, it started in the glen, of course it did.'

I thought that if Torquil Bruce asked more questions for me, people might realize he was asking questions, and I should learn no more. So I went in search of Sir Duncan Raden.

Sir Duncan, at my request, asked the Campbells of Drumlaw where they had heard the story. They would not say; they would not tell even him.

Sir Duncan came apologetically back to me, more than ever like a bear with a very good tailor, but softened my disappointment by asking if he might call on my grandfather.

'Which one?' I said, which must have been the most stupid question ever asked.

'I have enquired about Mr Strachan, in George Square,' said Raden. 'Can't you understand why, Miss Drummond?'

'Oh,' I said, understanding very well.

'As you may know, I am a bachelor, though so very advanced in age.' (He was about thirty-two.)

I blushed, flattered and gratified, because Sir Duncan was an entirely delightful bear. Catriona MacLaren had told me that the Raden estates in the far north made even Glendraco look like a pocket-handkerchief.

'But,' I said, 'you have only known me for two days.'

'Henry Cricklade had only known you for two minutes before he decided to marry you,' said Sir Duncan.

'When – when did he tell you that?'

'In July, when we were fishing together on the Spey.'

'Oh . . . Where is Lord Cricklade now?'

'I wish I knew. I hoped you did. I like knowing my enemy's position.'

'Enemy?'

'Rival. My plan is to beat Cricklade to it, even though he's had a deuced long start . . .' He stopped and looked at me. 'It's no good, is it, Kirstie?'

'No,' I said, looking at the ground. 'I wish it was. Truly I do, but . . .'

'Your heart is another's,' he said, making a melodramatic joke of it, but serious below the joke.

'Yes, unfortunately.'

'Why unfortunately?'

'Because it is no good.'

I suppose he thought I was in love with a man who was already married. He said, 'Then we are companions in misfortune. That should make us friends, Kirstie.'

'We are!' I said.

He pressed both my hands in his, which were as big as dinner-plates, and we smiled sadly at each other, and we were friends.

It was flat, rich lowland country round Perth, startlingly unlike that of the Draco glen, with broad cornfields, and lush pasture grazed by Leicester sheep and Ayrshire cattle, and great Clydesdale horses pulling the wains. Of all, no part was so lush and green as the garden of Groyne Palace. And of all the great garden, which thousands of visitors came each summer to see, the greenest and dewiest place was a strip of billiard-table lawn in the midst of an army of topiary yews.

In the early evening, after our return from the races, Angelica Paston surprised me by suggesting a stroll in the gardens. It was to this spot that she led me, and we sat on a white wrought-iron seat, and watched white fantail doves going in and out of the holes of a dovecote among the yews, and a white peacock, which strutted with trailing plumes among the giant, green, living statues of himself.

Angelica talked of Billy Mainwaring, making the nearest I had ever heard her make to idle conversation. She regretted that he had not joined the party, that the injury to his head, caused by a fall from his horse, obliged him to rest in seclusion for a week or two.

This subject was soon exhausted, as she did not want to talk about it very much, and I did not want to talk about it at all.

I wondered what she really wanted to talk about.

'Do you like being an orphan?' she asked me suddenly, turning her grave eyes from the fantail doves to my face.

'No,' I said, startled, 'of course not. Of course I wish I had known my parents.'

'I wish I had never known mine,' said Angelica.

I looked at her, stupefied.

'I have just had the millionth conversation with my mother on the only topic which interests her,' went on Angelica, as solemn as ever, with no change in the marvellous marble gravity of her face, or in her low, perfectly modulated voice. 'The brilliant marriage she requires me to make.'

'To Lord Draco?'

'We had a sort of quarrel, except that we are too well-bred to raise our voices . . . Yes, with Draco. That has been the plan all my life. It would not have been a matter of life and death, however, if my father had not been completely selfish and irresponsible. I admired him enormously as a child – he seemed so very gay and dashing, and he was so very handsome. He spent all his time at the races, or his trainer's stables at Newmarket, or his stud in Yorkshire. It all gave my mother a great detestation of horses.'

'But he was so grand,' I said, 'He was – what was it he was?'

'Senior Steward of the Jockey Club. Yes, immensely grand. I believe his tenure of that exalted office postponed his bankruptcy.'

'Oh . . .'

'In the event he died before he was bankrupted, but I understand it was a damned close-run thing.'

Seeing the amazement on my face – which was not shock at the words, but merely astonishment at her using them – she smiled gravely. 'A phrase of the Duke of Wellington's,' she said, 'and so hallowed by strawberry-leaves, history, and association with a national hero. Well, after my father died of brandy and debts, what had been a pleasant dream of my mother's became a condition of survival. My marriage had to provide her support, you understand – it was that or a rooming-house in Boulogne.'

'But – she has relations? She is a Lady—'

'Oh yes indeed, a galaxy of the most resplendent relations. Unfortunately, they do not like her. As she has no claim on them, charity would be inspired only by affection. There is one she does have a claim on, her nephew, my cousin Benmore. He was at the races today, but not often visible. It was interesting to see the hunted look that came over his face whenever he saw my mother or myself. Benmore spends a great part of his energy avoiding his poor relations. I see his position. He inherited a large fortune, but he has only got a small one now. He is no relation of my father's, of course, but they might have been twins.'

'He likes racing?'

'He buys far more horses than he can afford, and enters them in races they cannot win, and backs them as though they could not lose, and flies into a rage when they do lose, and shouts that his jockey has cheated him, and dismisses his trainer, and complains to Tattersalls ... I can understand an evil man,' said Angelica, frowning slightly, as though in contemplation of an important philosophical point, 'and I can understand a very silly one. But it is hard to understand a man being both evil and very silly. Don't you think so, Christina?'

'Yes,' I said, not knowing what else to say, and wondering what was coming next.

'My mother,' went on Angelica, 'was the dearest friend of the late Countess, Neil Draco's mother. Or so she has always said. It may be so, but I must say I find it astonishing.'

'Why?'

'How could Draco have had a mother who was a great friend of my mother's? How could anyone capable of producing *him* have an intimate friend such as her?'

'But – your mother produced *you*, Angelica?'

'Yes. That is the difference. That shows you how different the two mothers must have been.'

'I don't understand. You and Lord Draco—'

'Draco is what he is,' said Angelica gravely. 'He is high-minded, honest, public-spirited, philanthropic, genuinely concerned about suffering and misfortune.'

'Yes.'

'Above all, he is true to himself. He is exactly what he appears to be.'

'But you?'

'I,' said Angelica, 'have been playing an uncongenial role for so long that I scarcely now know who I am.'

'Playing a . . . ?'

'My mother made it clear to me, after my father died, and she had seen the lawyers and bankers. I think she was not welcome in many houses, but she was welcome at Glendraco. Or at least, they did not turn us out. It had to be Draco, then. As an objective, he was chosen by circumstances. What did he want? What would attract him? What sort of female would seem to him a suitable consort? Someone of education and accomplishment, someone with a deep and heartfelt concern for the great issues of the day, someone serious, who would never seem frivolous or flighty, someone very feminine, who would never do anything wild and hoydenish . . . Very well, the last available shillings were squeezed from Trustees and unwilling relatives, and spent on music-masters and drawing-masters, on tutors and professors, and I laboured to turn myself into what you see.'

'Well, it may have been a labour,' I said, 'but now it is done, and you *are* what I see.'

'I am a false person,' said Angelica. 'I do not exist. I do not know what I was, or what I might have been, but I know that now I am – something my mother invented, a lay-figure in an artist's studio, a dressmaker's dummy. Well, it might have done. There is a great deal in Draco that I unfeignedly admire.'

'There is a great deal in you,' I said, 'that he seems to admire.' (I did not risk 'unfeignedly', because I was not quite sure what it meant.)

Angelica nodded seriously. 'In any case,' she said, 'as a man of honour he is committed.'

'He *has* offered?'

'My mother says so. He has allowed her to convince him. Possibly things he said to me and to her could bear a less binding construction. But he believes me to feel myself bound to him – so, being Draco, he believes himself bound to me.'

'Then,' I said slowly, 'the Grand Design has succeeded. I wish you happy.'

'There is, ironically, a fatal objection,' said Angelica. 'That is what my mother and I have just been arguing about. I cannot contemplate the prospect of marriage without a feeling of physical illness.' The strange girl said this with just such quiet, regretful seriousness as though she were refusing, at the dinner-table, some rich dish which she knew disagreed with her.

Changing the subject abruptly, she said, 'You are a person like Draco.'

'*I?* Oh no, I am not at all public-spirited, or high-minded, or phil – the other thing you said.'

'You are like him in a more important way. You are true to yourself. You are what you are.'

'I have no choice,' I said ruefully. 'I am told I am quite trans-parent. I am not nearly clever enough to deceive anybody for a moment.'

'You do not want to. You have no need to. You have inter-ested me – no, fascinated me – by your certainty, your consistency. Have you sometimes caught me staring at you?'

'Well, yes,' I said. 'And I wondered how I could possibly in-terest you.'

'When you climbed the cliff for that dog. Your scrapes and spills with the horses. That night you spent in the awful croft, when Caerlaverock got so drunk—'

'Do you think that is what happened?'

'Yes, of course. I always knew. My mother liked to believe that other story, but it was only because she wanted to. I tried to argue with her about that, but you can perhaps imagine trying to make my mother see reason, and admit that she has been wrong—'

'Why did your mother want to believe the other story?'

'The cliff, and the horses, and so forth,' said Angelica, ignoring the question to which I very much wanted the answer, 'all those things were things that belonged to *you.* They were natural to you. They would not have happened to me in a million years. I would not have wished them to, you understand. I am a complete coward. I am frightened of heights, and of all animals and most people ... You fascinate me because the real always fascinates the spurious, the certain the unsure, the substance the shadow. And because you are so beautiful that, when I think of you in the middle of the night, I bite my pillow to stop myself screaming . . . Tell me, have you read Greek lyric poetry?'

'Not *extensively*,' I said, dismayed by this odd turn in the conversation.

'Have you read the poems of Sappho?'

'Not – not deeply.'

'Have you heard of the island of Lesbos?'

'Er, no.'

'Of a way of life, and a rite of love, at once more pure and more passionate than anything our civilization knows? A life and love miraculously free of the gross intrusion of the masculine . . .' She laid a cold hand on mine and looked searchingly into my eyes, so that I blinked, baffled and embarrassed. 'Have you heard of these things, dear Kirstie?'

I said awkwardly, 'I expect I am more at home in Scotland than I would be in Libya, or wherever it was you spoke of . . .'

She looked away, and bent her great solemn eyes on the white fantail doves.

'Of course you know, Kirstie,' said Catriona MacLaren, 'that the first ball was only a kind of overture.'

'Just a little informal gathering of friends,' agreed Torquil Bruce, 'come as you are, take us as you find us.'

Lady Odiham smiled that utterly misleading glacial smile. 'Hardly to be dignified by the name of "Ball",' she said. 'Just a romp among a few local people. The *real* ball is tonight, Kirstie.'

Lord Draco, who had re-acquired the habit of occasionally smiling, smiled. My heart turned over, and I felt a little sick, because that was the stupid effect his smile had on me.

Then Angelica came into the room, solemn white marble, glacially perfect, carrying a book which I knew to be printed in German. The Earl's smile disappeared. His face resumed its usual gravity. He rose at once, and went to her side, and they drifted to a corner; she opened the book and indicated a passage; they discussed it with each other in low, serious voices.

I thought they were teasing me, but they were not. I could not have imagined greater splendour, but here it was – a brilliance of colour, a dazzle of jewels, almost painful to the eye, and with this an atmosphere somewhat more grand and formal, so that I felt I was taking part not only in a gorgeous celebration, but also in an ancient ceremony.

Once again, miraculously, my programme, with its little golden pencil on a silken string, was half full before ever we arrived, and full a moment after we arrived.

I was to waltz with Lord Draco. I was not at all sure that I could feel his arm about my waist, for the length of a waltz, without swooning. Perhaps he would wish to sit the waltz out. I was not sure I could survive that without swooning, either.

I was angry with myself, and contemptuous, and impatient. I had thought I had *some* strength, *some* independence. I had thought myself in love with Billy, and with Cricklade, and even with Caerlaverock; and I had thought I could master my emotions, and behave rationally. Now I faced the uncomfortable truth that I was a lovesick ninny, as undignified as a nursemaid holding hands with a soldier in the Princes Street Gardens. My attachment was idiotically fixed on a man who was pledged to another woman: who knew himself to be pledged: who could not extricate himself, even if he wanted to, without a dishonour of which he was incapable: and who showed no sign of wanting to extricate himself, but, on the contrary, every sign of being entirely happy with his commitment. Oh God! He had given me two polite compliments, and half-a-dozen smiles. His choice of a wife was someone as different from me as a Grecian statue from a back-street urchin. Angelica truly said he would be revolted by a female who did wild, hoydenish things. I did them constantly! It did not seem to me that I *chose* to do them – they were all somehow forced upon me by events – but the miserable effect was the same. To Draco I might have some good qualities, as might a terrier, or a vigorous pony, or a schoolboy, or a jockey, or a chimney-sweep. But I was not a thoroughbred, and I was not a Grecian statue, and I was not what he liked. I thought there might be something to be said for life on Angelica's peculiar island.

Meanwhile the pipes skirled and the kilts swung, and I tried to forget my despair in the swirl of the dances.

*

'The Dashing White Sergeant' is one of the gayest and simplest of all the Scottish country dances. Two men, with a girl between, or two ladies, with a man between, go all the way round the ball-room, dancing with each set of three that they meet, and then going on to the next.

According to my programme, I was promised for this dance to David Baillie and a young man equally pink and wordless called Hugh MacLeod, whose lurid tartan did not at all match his complexion. But, as we formed ourselves into our sets, Sir Duncan Raden came hastening up, and asked Hugh MacLeod to relinquish me. Hugh MacLeod went pinker, and stoutly refused. Sir Duncan whispered to him, frowning. Hugh MacLeod went so pink that I thought he would begin to sizzle, like chopped salt beef in a pan.

He said reluctantly, 'Oh, very well, if that's the case, if Draco says—'

'He does. Thank you, my dear fellow. If Miss Drummond consents, you may have my Number Twenty-three with her. Is that agreeable to you, Miss Drummond? Do you mind being bargained for, like a block of railway shares or a German Principality?'

'No,' I said, 'but—'

Sir Duncan gave me a meaning look, but I did not know what the meaning was. But I knew that he was my friend – we had decided so at the races.

David Baillie held my right hand, thinking, as I did, that we should start to dance where we were standing. But the place did not suit Sir Duncan. He took my left hand, and led me at a great pace to a different part of the ballroom, David panting behind like a packhorse at the tail of a wagon. I could see no special merit in the new place Sir Duncan found for us. In fact, I did not like it as well, because the three in front of us, and going in the same direction, were Sir Francis and Lady Campbell and General Drummond. Of course, since we *were* going in the same direction, we would not be obliged to dance with them, but merely follow them round the ballroom. But all through the dance I would see the backs of their necks, and sometimes their faces when they swung round, and I knew they would look as cold and contemptuous as possible whenever they caught sight of me.

Sir Duncan grinned at me encouragingly. 'That's right,' he said. 'All according to plan.'

'Your plan?'

'You'll see. Ingenious fellow, Draco.'

'But what—? Why—?'

'Don't worry, Kirstie, Draco knows what he's doing.'

I looked round for the general whose orders my genial giant bear was so obediently carrying out. I did glimpse him, far away at the other end of the ballroom, visible because he was taller than most of the men in between. He was between two ladies whom I could not see, facing in the opposite direction to ourselves, so that eventually we would come face to face, and I would set and swing with him.

Please God, I prayed, don't let my face show that I feel sick at the thought.

The fiddles struck up (for the pipes played only for the reels) and I was almost able to lose myself in the strenuous enjoyment of the dance. Three, four, five, six, seven, eight different three-somes we danced with, Sir Duncan and David and I, as we worked our way round the ballroom. Then we swooped beneath the arches formed by the arms of the eighth set, and met our ninth, and I was face to face with the Earl of Draco. On his right was Lady Odiham, with her cool detached smile, in a dress of cold steel grey; on his left Catriona MacLaren, apple-cheeked and dimpled and excited, who gave a little hoot of joyful greeting when she saw Sir Duncan and myself. The Earl's face was grave. I waited dizzily for his smile, but he did not smile. While I waited, as the others set and swung, I saw the backs of the heads of Sir Francis and Lady Campbell and General Drummond. Even the backs of their heads seemed tense and creased with outrage that an abandoned creature such as myself should come dancing along behind them. I noticed, fleetingly, that the three they were dancing with, whom we should shortly dance with, included Georgina Campbell and Charlotte Long; it was a family reunion. I could not see the man between Charlotte and Georgina; it seemed he was a little man, and hidden behind the height of Lord Draco and the bouncing bulk of Sir Francis Campbell.

To my relief and misery we danced between the arched arms of Draco and his partners; Draco and I stood back to back, each ready to dance with a new face; and the face that faced me was Lord Caerlaverock's.

Caerlaverock stopped dead, a yard from me. His face was as white as paper, as white as old Eugénie's. Across it, livid still, was the mark left by the whip he himself had given me. Georgina and Charlotte looked at him, and at me, wide-eyed. Bright spots of colour appeared in Caerlaverock's cheeks. Sir Duncan also froze into immobility, an enormous oak-tree, rooted in the polished wooden floor of the ballroom.

Suddenly the gay, jogging music whined to a halt. There was an outcry from all round the ballroom. I heard a murmur, 'Draco!' Glancing behind me, I saw that the Earl had his arm raised, as a signal to the fiddlers. He had stopped them. It flashed on me that he had arranged to stop them, on this signal. It flashed on me that my coming face-to-face with Caerlaverock was the moment he had planned for the music to stop. And he had planned that Sir Francis Campbell should be by, and that he himself should be by.

There was an indignant babble and buzz from all around us. David Baillie was pop-eyed with astonishment at this unheard-of interruption to the ball; so, I think, was I.

I was aware that Draco had turned. He stood behind my shoulder, looking fixedly at Caerlaverock. The three on the other side had turned also, the Campbells and General Drummond. Sir Francis looked over Charlotte's shoulder, frowning, angry, puzzled; Lady Campbell looked over Caerlaverock's; General Drummond, close to an apoplectic fit, looked over Georgina's.

A shrill babble of complaint and amazement and outrage came from all parts of the ballroom, but this part, this centre of the storm, was still and silent. The stage was set. Draco had set it. He had persuaded Sir Duncan Raden to partner me, and to take position just behind the Campbells. He himself had taken position just ahead of Caerlaverock. This conjunction of persons was no coincidence. Using the simple mechanics of 'The Dashing White Sergeant', Draco had organized a face-to-face collision between Caerlaverock and myself, with the others standing by.

Caerlaverock's white face turned bright red – not a healthy flush, but as though he were struck by a fever. Beads of perspiration stood out on his brow. He dropped the hands of Charlotte and Georgina. He recoiled a step, bumping into Lady Campbell. He did not notice her. His eyes were fast on my face. All other eyes were fast on his face.

He said huskily, so low that I could hardly hear, 'I want to beg your pardon, Miss Drummond.'

'Louder!' barked a voice behind me. I jumped. It was Draco.

'Ay, louder,' muttered Caerlaverock. He raised his voice, so that it cut through all the hum and hubbub nearby. He cried, 'I tried to assault you when I was drunk, in Dugald Crombie's croft by the Allt Monaidh. I have been bitterly ashamed and disgusted with myself, and I humbly entreat your pardon.'

Somehow I said, 'You were drunk. You – you were not yourself. Let us forget it.'

'Can you?' he cried. 'I cannot, nor ever shall. I tried to force you, to rape you, like an animal. You treated me as I deserved, with your whip.' He touched the livid weal on his face. 'This is the mark,' he said, 'of my infamy and your purity.'

It was fustian stuff, perhaps. Lady Arabella would have sniffed, and called it melodrama. But it had a striking effect. There was a huge collective gasp, all about us. Silence had spread from Caerlaverock outwards, as more and more people realized that a disgraceful scene was being played on the stage of Lord Draco's setting. There was still a clatter and chatter from far away in the ballroom, but every second the waves were spreading outwards from the impact of Caerlaverock's words, which had fallen into the midst of the ballroom like a stone into a mill-pool, rocking the gorgeous dancers out of their merriment into shocked attention.

Suddenly I heard a voice upraised in cold fury. It was my voice. I said, 'Sir Francis Campbell, you have spread a venomous lie that you now know to be a lie.'

His face was suffused with blood so that it turned almost black. He said thickly, 'Do you wish me to apologize? I will—'

'I am not interested in your apologies,' I said, still so burning with an icy fire of anger that I scarce knew what words were coming out of my mouth, 'since no one will ever again believe anything you say. Make your apologies to God, on your knees. What I want is the name of the person who told you the lie about me.'

I heard a whisper close above my ear, 'Well done, Kirstie!'

It was Sir Duncan Raden. I glanced at him. He was wearing an excited half-smile, and his fists were so tight-clenched that the knuckles showed as white as bone through the leathery brown of his hands. I wondered, fleetingly, idiotically, why he had taken off his kid gloves. Perhaps to strangle someone. I hoped not. I wanted to do that myself.

'Perhaps,' I said to Sir Francis, astonished at the note of bitter contempt in my own voice, 'you amused yourself by yourself inventing the story you have told so widely?'

'No! I – I d-did not invent it!' he stammered. 'I was told – assured – it was the truth! In all honesty I believed it! I was – was told it was the gospel truth—'

'Who told you?'

His eyes fell away from mine. They fell to the jewelled buckles of his shoes.

Lady Campbell's voice cut in, unexpectedly, from behind Caerlaverock. 'It was Charlotte, wasn't it? Charlotte, you had been talking to—'

All eyes were suddenly on Charlotte Long, who looked more bewitchingly pretty than ever, pink and white, with cornflower eyes, and bright gold ringlets, altogether like an exquisite Dresden figurine.

'Yes,' she said, in her little high breathless voice. 'I had been talking to – to a person who knew Jack – who had been with Jack at the inn – and J-Jack had told him . . .'

'Who?' came a voice like a whiplash cracked in a small room. It was Draco, behind me. I jumped. Charlotte jumped. She turned great frightened eyes on Draco, and caught her bee-stung lip in little white teeth.

'I spoke to no one,' said Caerlaverock, in a voice suddenly stong and confident.

The import of his words did not strike everyone at the same speed. Some faces – Lady Campbell's, Sir Duncan Raden's –

showed immediate and total understanding; others – David Baillie's, Catriona MacLaren's – showed that they were slower to digest the implications. But after a moment of heavy, breathless silence, all eyes were turned again on Charlotte: and there was a dark look of indignation and disgust on every face; and her own face was crimson and contorted.

'It was Georgina's idea,' she cried.

'Liar!' screamed Georgina.

'It's you who are lying! Own up! The whole scheme was yours!'

Georgina screeched like a wildcat, and seemed like to throw herself on Charlotte, to scratch her face and pull her golden hair; but her father grasped her arm.

Georgina began to sob hysterically. Through her sobs we could make out a wild and bitter indictment: 'You hated Kirstie from the first moment you saw her, because she took Caerlaverock from you! You wanted him, because he is a Lord—'

'I loved him!' shrieked Charlotte.

'Yes, and he loved Kirstie!'

'You wanted Draco,' sobbed Charlotte. 'That's why you hate Angelica P-Paston. That's why you hate Kirstie e-even more than I do!'

Some sense of shame seemed suddenly to strike them both. They had lost all control of themselves, because each had lost what she most wanted, and each had tried to betray the other, and it had all failed, and tumbled about their heads, disgracing them utterly before the face of hundreds of people. Both had scarlet and crumpled faces; both were sobbing uncontrollably. If looks could kill, their looks at each other and at me would have slain and horribly mutilated.

Sir Francis Campbell, with a face of thunder, led his daughter and her one-time friend away. Lady Campbell followed. She still reminded me of a bird, but a crippled and pinioned bird, with bedraggled wings and dragging feet.

'That was well done, Jack,' said Draco gravely to Caerlaverock, over my shoulder.

Caerlaverock blinked at him, gave me a crooked and miserable smile, and pushed away blindly through the press of people. They parted to make way for him, their faces full of astonishment and pity.

'You can hold your head high, Kirstie,' said Lady Odiham.

'She has never for one second ceased to do so,' said Draco.

He signalled to the fiddlers. The music started. Dazed, I found myself dancing, as though nothing had happened.

I did not waltz with Lord Draco. We sat out, on little gilt chairs at the edge of the ballroom, under the eyes of half Perthshire.

I tried to thank him, but he brushed my thanks aside.

'But to get Caerlaverock here—' I said.

'I told you that most of his qualities were good.'

'I know that, but—'

'Give him some credit.'

Credit himself he would not take. All was due to Caerlaverock's self-disgust and very considerable courage, to Sir Duncan Raden's tactical skill in placing us where we were, and my own haughty challenge (at the thought of which I now almost sank through the floor) to Sir Francis Campbell.

'It is very strange and horrible to me,' I said. 'Do you know, Charlotte Long was the first person who ever kissed me good-night—'

'Have many people done so since?' he asked, with the ghost of a smile.

'Only your grandmother. But Charlotte was the very first . . . and all the time she hated me already!'

'Yes. I think she really did love poor Caerlaverock. Perhaps she does so still. It was unfortunate, from many points of view, that he should have been so deeply struck by you the first time you met at Gaultstower, and still more so that he should have confided it to Charlotte. That was typically honest of him, and typically imprudent.'

'What a good actress she must be,' I said.

'No, not really.'

'But to convince me so completely that she liked me – loved me!'

'You are easy to convince. You believe the best of people. You reach out to the world, and believe that it is reaching back, equally trusting and affectionate.'

'I do seem to have been a little blind,' I said ruefully. 'What with Charlotte and Georgina, and Lord Cricklade, and Mrs Forbes—'

'Sometimes,' said Lord Draco, 'your judgements have been just as ill-considered and just as wrong, the other way about. You have judged coldly people who felt warmly. Lady Odiham, for instance—'

'Yes indeed, that is quite true,' I said. 'Her manner completely misled me. Angelica is another—'

A quick, dark frown came and went on his face, like a cat's-paw of wind crossing a smooth hilltop lochan. He scraped back his chair and rose abruptly to his feet. He said I should have some lemonade; he meant that by saying the wrong thing, I had ended the conversation.

After a furious foursome reel, Catriona MacLaren and I took refuge in the room where grim Perth ladies'-maids put the pins back in descending hair, and stitched up the descending hems of gowns.

'I really want a bath,' sighed Catriona, 'or a swim in the Tay.'

I laughed and agreed.

'At a moment like this,' she said, 'all hot and bedraggled, I long to be a fish. So perfect always, so beautiful and fashionable! Never a worry about things falling down, or falling off, which I thought my bodice would do in the last reel. And always cool. But people would come after one with dreadful barbed hooks, disguised to be delicious . . . Like Charlotte. She is like a salmon fly, don't you think? So attractive, and so deceptive! Fancy the horrible creature being so jealous of you, and you never guessed it at all.'

'People say I am too trusting.'

'Yes, you are. That is why you are so nice. I am, too, which is why *I* am so nice . . . You know, I expect Drumlaw always hoped Georgina would catch Draco. Did *they* pretend to like you, as she did?'

'Yes,' I said, remembering. 'But what has that to do . . . Of course, I can understand Georgina hating Angelica, if Georgina wanted Lord Draco for herself . . .'

'Can't you understand more than that, my dear goose?'

'Oh,' I said.

'They hate *you*, all of them. Why do you suppose they should do that? Why do you think that odious Lady Arabella goes out of her way to be horrid about you?'

'But – but they have no need to worry about *me*. Draco has never so much as . . . I mean, it is all arranged between him and . . . What do you *mean*, Catriona?'

'For a clever girl,' said Catriona, smiling, 'you are a great fool, Kirstie.'

After this second and grander ball, dawn was well broken before we got back to Groyne. The sky was clear and pearly, and the ground wet with dew. When we climbed out of the carriage, the little box hedges of the parterres in front of the Palace were festooned with autumn cobwebs, each gossamer strand a string of lucent diamonds.

I felt terribly tired, and wide awake, and elated, and horribly confused.

Sir Duncan Raden, whose energy was as boundless as Rockfall's, proposed a stroll in the famous gardens before we went to our beds. 'For it will clear our fogged brains,' he said. 'And gardens look best in the early morning, even if some of us do not.'

The older people, of whom there were a great many, sighed or smiled or frowned at this ridiculous project, and went off to bed. Old Lord Mountfield, whose eyes were red-rimmed with fatigue and champagne, made an effort to join the stroll, but was led firmly away by his cousin.

Angelica said that she was tired, and would go to bed.

Lord Draco, to my surprise, said that he would stroll in the garden.

We started in a group – Sir Duncan, Torquil Bruce, Catriona, Lord Draco, myself, and half a dozen others who do not come into this tale. We spoke in hushed voices – even Torquil and Catriona – so as not to disturb a sleeping world, and because the cool dawn seemed to reprove loud chatter and silly laughter.

I lingered behind the others, looking at jewel-strung cobwebs in a hedge of lavender. I felt my arm taken. I was drawn into that same secret glade, in the midst of the fantastical yews, where

Angelica had talked to me so oddly. Now I was alone with Draco, on the same white seat, in the dew-wet silence.

I looked at his face, a little frightened. There was that in it I had never seen before – an expression I could not fathom.

There was a kind of anger in his face. But I had seen him angry, and with myself, and it was not anger only. There was a kind of sickness, and a kind of ravenous hunger.

He kept hold of my arm, just as Cricklade had done outside the Manse in Aberfeldy. It was an uncomfortable reminder. He reached across with his other hand, and took my left arm; so that I was twisted on the seat, half facing him. I thought: if I pull away, he will let me go. But I was incapable of movement.

I thought: he is going to kiss me. My heart rose up into my throat as though it would choke me. He pulled me towards him; his dark, grave face swam towards mine. I felt his lips, first gentle and then brutal and bruising. I abandoned myself utterly to his kiss. I felt one of his arms go about my back, and strain me towards him. I felt a hand on my breast, which seemed to spring into fierce independent life, and to writhe and burn against his palm.

He released me. We drew away from each other, and stared into each others' faces.

He began to talk in a low rapid voice which was as strange as the look in his face. 'I had heard little about you before I saw you,' he muttered. 'I knew only that my grandmother had brought some girl to Glendraco. I was quite glad. She had been often lonely since my mother died. Apart from that, it did not matter to me one way or another, until I saw you.'

'You were very rude,' I said, choking, 'about my hat.'

'Of course I was, you witch! I wanted you the moment I saw you. Wanted, lusted for. Slavered for, God forgive me, like a hungry dog divided from its meat. I was one with Cricklade, Caerlaverock, Baillie, all your panting and slavering adorers – no better, no more dignified, no more discriminating, as near reverted to the animal that blindly obeys every filthy physical impulse . . . Of course I spoke to you sharply! The sight of you – your face, your hair, your walk – the first glimpse of you nearly knocked me out of my saddle. Me! I, whom pride and position obliged to link myself only with the highest, sick like a rabid dog about a little miss from the city – I, who was already irretrievably committed to the Pastons. Of course I was rude! I struck back at the threat you posed to my peace of mind and my duty – struck back like a fencer, or like an angry child . . . And I had to build, then at once, such a wall between us that we could scarcely see over, so that we should not touch each other, or make any contact. I had to make my heart feel about you as my mind thought about you – that you were an impertinent, intrusive nobody who could cozen my grandmother but not me. I had to despise you. I had to dislike you. You must not be admitted to the level of my friends and equals.'

'You made that clear,' I managed to say, 'but you apologized after.'

'And after that you climbed Meiklejohn's Leap, and I was distraught with anxiety for your safety.'

'You showed that in a strange way.'

'What would you have had me show?' he burst out. 'Was I to reveal anxiety for you so intense that I was almost physically sick? Was I to display *that* in front of my affianced bride? Her mother? My grandmother? Our friends? Why do you think I would not let you ride that headstrong pony that threw you? Why do you think I forbade you to go fishing by dangerous waters?'

'Oh,' I said. 'I thought . . .'

'And now, here, I have been subjected to the sight of men in hundreds fawning and grovelling about you. And you smile at them, and you hold their hands, and they put their damned arms round your waist in the dance . . . And you whisper to Raden, and clasp hands with Bruce . . . And I can stand it no longer. I want you. I must have you. Do you understand?'

'Yes,' I said dizzily, his face a stern and beautiful blur a foot from my own.

'I would to God I could marry you, but you know that is impossible. I am bound. My word is given. You know that as well as I. We cannot have our hearts' desire, Kirstie, but we can make the best of things, and it is a good best. You will stay at Glendraco as my grandmother's companion. You will have respect, always after tonight. You will have honour. You will have all the horses you want, and everything else you want. Money, if you need it. Jewels, clothes, everything of the very best. You can travel. Would you like that? You can go, with any female companion you choose, to Paris, Rome, Vienna . . .'

He was smiling now. The horrible irony was that his smile was as broad and sweet as though he was not breaking my heart.

He talked on, and on and on, rapidly and urgently, about my beauty of face and figure, and the yearning desire he felt for me, and the respectable position I would seem to occupy, and the rich bribes he was dangling before my eyes.

Of course, no one had said 'No' to him in all his life. He was not simply accustomed to having his way in everything, he regarded it as part of the natural order of the universe. What he desired he had a right to – it was merely a question of arranging the best way to enjoy it. He had arranged that, to secure his free enjoyment of my body, he should fix me in a position of public respect and private shame.

It was not outraged virtue that filled me with sick rage. Where he was concerned. I had no virtue. I would have submitted to him then and there, anywhere, at any time, because I loved him, without sin. No – it was not my virtue but my pride which he was casually, comfortably offering to destroy. I would have given myself to him, joyfully, and asked nothing in return: but he wanted to buy me. The thought of the life Draco was proposing for me filled me with disgusted humiliation: the thought that he thought he could buy me with money and jewels and horses.

A life of furtive passion, of creaking midnight floorboards; of hot, guilty groping in dark rooms, with servants exchanging knowing glances in the morning. Worse – a life on a salary, a paid servant working for wages, available on the employer's demand, as obedient as a chambermaid; an hour of fornication paid for by a necklace or a gown.

He said softly, 'You look distressed, my little love. I am sorry. I have shocked you, because what I am proposing is not moral as your Edinburgh grandparents understand morality. Should you be bound all your life by *their* rules, Kirstie? Should we? If all happens as I suggest – as I beg – it will be because we love each other, you and I. I do not think the merciful God in Whom

I believe would want us to be divided, although, because of my promise to the Pastons, we cannot be publicly united.'

I did not think so either. He was finding better words.

Gently he went on, 'I am afraid I have hurt you, as well as shocked you. It is the last thing in the world I would wish to have done. I have said insulting things, because I have tried to convince myself. I have tried to fall out of love with you, Kirstie. I failed. I never in my heart believed any ill of you at all, and never could.'

He leaned forward to kiss me again, smiling, with an air of ownership. It was that air that broke the spell of his words and snapped my self-control.

I struck him in the face.

I had never slapped anyone before, in the face, with my hand. I had imagined, I think, that one would do it with one's open palm. But my right arm lay across my breast, and I hit him back-handed, as hard as I could.

It would not have hurt him very much. But outside my glove, on the third finger, I wore a ring. The Countess had lent it to me. The stone was a single large garnet. It was not very valuable, but the colour matched the red in my tartan. The stone gashed his cheek, cutting it, so that it bled.

The mark on Draco's face was almost exactly like the mark on Caerlaverock's.

With my head on a tear-wet pillow, I realized that I must go back to George Square.

thirteen

Later in the day I wrote a letter to the Countess of Draco. I tried to thank her for her kindness to me. I said I would not return to Glendraco. I did not say that I could not live in the same house with a man I loved to distraction who wanted me to be his private whore. I thought it better that the Countess should be hurt by my ingratitude than by her grandson's arrogant cruelty.

I wrote to Geordie Buchan, with messages about Falcon and Rockfall. Lady Odiham came into my bedroom, and found me weeping over the paper. She embraced me as I sat, cradling my head against her breast.

My parting from Annie Simpson was almost more than I could bear. I was succeeding, by heroic effort, in keeping my eyes dry; but when she burst into tears, and clung to me, I broke down myself.

Lady Odiham took me to Edinburgh. It was kind of her. She asked me no questions. I thought she knew part of the truth.

And so, at the end of September, I was back in my own bleak bedroom in George Square. I dressed myself in dowdy and all-concealing clothes, and drew worsted stockings up my legs; I pulled back my hair into the unbecoming knot which my grandmother thought respectable; I resigned myself to the study of the Prophet Jeremiah.

I might never have been away.

My grandparents greeted me with so little demonstrative welcome that I might have been out for no more than an hour, matching darning-wool in the shops. Within seconds I was back in the iron routine of the household. The one change was for the worse – my friend little Janet the under-housemaid had been dismissed for impertinence – not to my grandmother, but to the grim old parlourmaid Carstairs.

My return was mentioned in family prayers. It was as though they all prayed for strength to deal with the added burden of my presence.

After a few days I plucked up courage, and said to my grandfather, 'The stories you heard from Lord Cricklade were false.'

'Were they so, Christina?'

'Yes! Yes, they were! At Perth, ten days ago—'

'Sir Francis Campbell of Drumlaw forbade his daughter to associate with you. Is that false?'

'No, but afterwards—'

'General Drummond, to whom you have the honour to be distantly related, refused to speak to you. Is that false?'

'No, for a time he did, but—'

'By your own admission, then, Lord Cricklade's reports to us were true.'

'But other people—'

'We know nothing of other people. We know only, from Lord Cricklade, about the reactions to your behaviour of Sir Francis Campbell and General Drummond. That is enough. We were indeed, grateful to be spared more revelations which could only have grieved us. You have confirmed that the two gentlemen I named so deplored your conduct that they refused social intercourse with you. That is the sum of what Lord Cricklade told us. We marvel the more at his charitable forbearance in accepting the charge of your redemption. No act of perverse rebellion has more distressed and grieved us than your ungrateful escape from that worthy man. He is at home now, in the South of England. I have written to inform him of your return here, but I do not entertain the serious hope that he will renew a project for which we gave heartfelt and repeated thanks to the Lord.'

A few days later again, in the second week of October, my grandfather announced in the drawing-room that the ways of the Almighty were inscrutable, but that the workings of the Divine Will tended always towards ultimate rightness.

'Had your marriage to Lord Cricklade resulted, in the fullness of time, in the generation of issue,' he went on in his courtroom voice, 'one cannot but stand dismayed in contemplation of the effects, both immediate and remote. It has been put to us by Dr Findlay Nicholson, and we accept the justice of his words, that we should never have permitted you to entertain hopes of matrimony. Although I never expected to say these words, I am now of the firm opinion that it would be best, Christina, if you did not marry. You should compose your thoughts towards a life of service to others, perhaps in a hospital or school, rather than a career as wife and mother. Such a life will be equally rewarded in Heaven, if not on earth, and will free humanity of the infection which it would otherwise suffer from the proliferation of a strain of which, as things now stand, you are the sole representative.'

'I daresay Lord Draco agrees with you,' I murmured.

'I have no doubt he does, since by all accounts he is a serious and high-minded man. We disagree with him profoundly in point of politics as of theology, but we can respect the honesty of the position and the uprightness of the man.'

Bad blood. A tainted name. As Lady Arabella said.

'Why did my other grandfather sell Glendraco to the Countess's husband?' I asked. 'What did he do that marked me with this – this scar that everybody talks about but no one will talk about?'

'When he rode to Newhaven,' my grandmother burst out, with something like passion, 'he rode out of the world of decent, God-fearing folk into the pit of everlasting damnation and torment.'

My grandfather looked at her sharply, with one of his blackest frowns. She put a hand to her mouth.

'The subject,' said my grandfather, exactly as long before, 'will not be discussed in this house.'

But my grandmother, in her emotion, had given something away.

Newhaven. Immediately after he sold or gave away Glendraco, it seemed, James Drummond rode to Newhaven, the little fishing-port on the Firth, the home of the mad, bad fishwives. Immediately after that, he died. How? Why? Of what? Why was the blood bad? Why was the name tainted? What did he do, there in Newhaven, that removed him from the ranks of the God-fearing, and damned him eternally – and damned me too?

It was so very long ago. Would anyone in Newhaven remember?

Newhaven was notorious, scandalous, dangerous. Decent people never set foot there – it was the realm of the dregs, the loud, foul-mouthed fish-women, all savage and promiscuous, all as strong as strong men. Dared I venture there?

Well, I had met dregs among fine ladies – perhaps I would meet fine ladies among dregs. I could not find greater hatred and treachery than Charlotte Long's, greater malice than Lady Arabella's, more beastly drunken violence than Lord Caerlaverock's, more insolent lust than Lord Draco's. I could not encounter greater hazards than the rocks that tumbled down Meiklejohn's Leap, or the rope stretched between the boulders on the hillside. There would scarcely be a Dandie McKillop at Newhaven; there would be no Eugénie.

I told myself Newhaven held no terrors for me. I could walk there in little more than an hour. But, as a matter of fact, I was very frightened at the thought of going there. My grandparents and their servants spoke of it with revulsion: it was a sink of iniquity, a very Sodom-and-Gomorrah, a jungle of wild animals.

I wobbled in indecision, torn between burning curiosity and serious alarm.

Two things made up my mind for me.

The first was a moment I relived, from almost five months before. I was sitting in the parlour, in the middle of the morning, darning a hateful black worsted stocking. Jennie Ross, the usual fishwife, crossed the square to our door. She looked as splendidly strong and healthy as ever; her skirt was kilted up, as ever, over her bright striped petticoats which fell no lower than the middle of her calf; below that her legs and feet were bare. Her basket was strapped to her back, with a band round her forehead to take some of the weight from her shoulders. She looked magnificent – as free as I had been for a short time: as free as I should never be again.

Jennie Ross descended the area steps to the kitchen door. I heard her bargaining shrilly with the cook. 'Saxpence!' she cried, outraged. 'Saxpence for ma bonny caller ou? Ye sud be ashamed o' yersel' in sic weather. There was nae a haddie nor an ou in a' Newhaven the nicht! Saxpence! My certes! I'll no' sall two sullin's worth for saxpence!'

I heard our cook's voice, raised to almost equal stridency, 'I'll no pay a ha'penny mair than saxpence.'

After a long, loud wrangle, Jennie Ross sold her 'caller ou', her fresh oysters, for ninepence. 'Hey, mem,' she said, 'tak' yer ou. Ye're a guid customer, but it's no tae ilka ane I'd gie sic a bairgain.'

Jennie ran up the steep steps, as though her basket was weightless and the steps flat. She heaved her basket on to her shoulders, and pulled the broad head-strap on to her forehead. As five months before, she glanced up and saw me at the window.

As before she waved cheerfully, shouted something I could not understand, and roared with laughter.

I thought: she is no more than forty. She is far too young to remember. But she may have heard – there may have been stories – she may know if there are old, old people with good memories . . .

I dropped my darning and ran downstairs. I ran through the hallway, past the astonished Carstairs, and ran out into the square, hatless as I was, against all my grandmother's rules.

'Jennie!' I called. 'Jennie Ross!'

She turned, and gave me a surprised grin. 'Ye'll no' be seekin' mair fush, Miss?'

'No,' I said, 'no – it's something else I want from you.'

I wondered how to go on – it would sound so very ridiculous, asking this woman about something that happened ten years before ever she was born.

I said, 'Fifty years ago something strange – something horrible – happened in Newhaven to – to a man of my name. I don't know *what* happened, exactly, but he died. He came down from Edinburgh, and died in Newhaven—'

'There's a' mony dee in Newhaven as onywhaur,' said Jennie Ross, looking more surprised than ever.

'Yes, of course, but if there's anyone in Newhaven old enough to remember, then perhaps they *will* remember, and I – I would like to ask them about it.'

'A body o' yer nem? A mon ca'd Strachan?'

'No! I am Drummond.'

'Whisht, I didna ken. Aweel, I'll speir aboot in the toon, there's a wheen auld bodies wull mebbe mind yer fellie. Fufty year syne? Ay, ilka auld Don o' saiventy wull mind, I doot. An' me an' ye wull hae anither crack in twa-three days, hey?'

'Yes! Thank you! Thank you!'

'Drummond, is't? Ay, ye hae nae luk o' the Strachans. Dod! Ye're owr bonny tae spring frae yon forefeuchan, draigled stirp . . . Guid day, Miss Drummond!'

She laughed, turned, and strode away, like a glorious savage: and in a moment raised her voice in the eldritch cry of her kind: 'A caallerr owhoo-oo-oo! A caallerr owhoo-oo-oo!'

Carstairs was waiting for me just inside the front door, her face like outraged granite.

'Jennie Ross,' I said mildly, 'is in need of spiritual guidance.'

'Ay, an' she's no' on her lane,' said Carstairs grimly.

I knew that she would tell my grandmother about my indecorous sortie into the square, and my conversation with the dangerous and abandoned fishwife. But, to my surprise and relief, my grandmother said nothing to me about it.

I waited impatiently for Jennie's next visit, haunting the parlour window at her usual hour on her usual days. But it was a week before I saw her again, striding across the square with her creel on her back.

Someone else was watching out for her, besides me.

When Jennie was still some way from our door, the kitchen-maid ran up the area steps and hurried to meet her. The kitchen-maid was a sour-faced creature called Mary Watson, with a perpetual snuffle in her red nose; her responses during family prayers were raucous with obtrusive piety. She wrapped a shawl about her head as she crossed the square, for she would not commit, as I did, the immodesty of going out of doors bareheaded.

Mary Watson stopped in front of Jennie Ross, who stopped also, and grinned. They began to talk. Jennie's grin vanished. She gestured angrily. Their voices were raised, but I could not hear what they said, for a carriage went by, drowning their words. By and by Jennie turned, her face angry. She strode away, her back to our door, and I heard her cry 'A caaller owhoo-oo-oo!'

That afternoon my grandmother ordered fish to be delivered from a shop in Princes Street. It was more expensive than if she had bought it (as the shop itself did) direct from a fishwife. But it kept Jennie Ross, or anyone else from Newhaven, away from our door.

My grandmother said only that she did not want fishwives at her house.

Well then, I thought, if Newhaven will not come to me, I must go to Newhaven. But I was still frightened of going there, and torn by indecision.

*

In the first week of November, when dead leaves swirled through the streets, or lay in blackened and soddened drifts in the gutters, and the choking Edinburgh fogs seeped through windows, and set the whole city coughing, I sat in the parlour, by the window, thinking with misery about my disreputable dog Rockfall, and aching to see him again.

A brougham, exceptionally smart, rattled up to our door. It was dark blue, picked out in gold. The lamps and harness-brasses gleamed – in the murky Edinburgh air, which tarnished all bright metal in minutes, they must have been polished moments before. The horse was a fine iron grey with a thoroughbred look. The coachman wore top boots and a tall hat with a cockade. The Edinburgh streets were full of broughams, but this was the smartest I had ever seen. For a moment I thought it must be the town carriage of some high legal luminary come to confer with my grandfather (who was at home, in his study); but vehicle and horse and coachman all had a more glossy and fashionable air than went with any gentleman of the law.

Just as he stopped his horse, the coachman looked up. It was Wattie Dewar. He was transformed by his smart clothes, but looked quite at his ease in them. I thought: it is the Countess, my Dragon. Hamish has retired, or is ill, and Wattie is her coachman now. Then I thought: but she would never go on wheels without groom or footman, for who will hold the horse while Wattie helps her down? It must be, not the Countess, but . . .

My heart pounded, and I put a hand on my breast.

The near door opened, and a tall man in a beautifully-cut broadcloth coat jumped down and strode to our door. The Earl of Draco's face was as grim as my grandfather's. There was a mark on his cheek – the scar of the wound gouged by the stone in my ring.

Wild explanations raced through my head for this extraordinary visit. Was he imitating the devious, the grimly unromantic strategy of Lord Cricklade? Ah no – for my name was tainted and my blood bad, and if he had me at all it could only be illicitly and surreptitiously; and he was promised to Angelica Paston. Was he expecting to buy me from my grandparents, as though I were an unwanted Turkish daughter to be sold into the seraglio of a Pasha? Did he hope to lure me back to Glendraco, enlisting the help of my grandparents? Was he coming to repossess the few things I had brought with me from Groyne – my clothes, my brushes, my little silver looking-glass?

He pounded the knocker. I looked down at him with hatred, for the insufferable assumption he had made that I would gratefully rush to be his secret, back-stairs whore, prepared to accept whatever payments he doled out to me. I looked down at him with helpless and overwhelming love.

I did not know why he was here. I knew only that I could not meet him face to face.

I ran to the parlour door, opened it softly, and crept to the head of the stairs. My grandfather was in his study, my grandmother in the kitchen with the cook: but perhaps he would ask not for them, but for me.

I heard his voice, inside the front door, which had already been closed behind him.

'I would be most grateful,' he said, 'if either Mrs or Mr Strachan could spare me a few minutes. Ideally both, if they will be so kind.'

'Please to wait in the parlour, my lord,' said Carstairs.

'Is Miss Drummond at home?'

'Ay, my lord.'

'I shall hope to be permitted to see her also.'

I tiptoed the two flights of stairs up to my bedroom, as Lord Draco climbed the main stairs to the parlour. I slipped into my room, shut the door, and sank trembling on to my bed. Whatever he had come about, I could not face him. Whatever he wanted to say, I could not listen. I was frightened by the tempest of feeling in my breast, and contemptuous of myself for not being mistress of myself, and furious that I should still be so affected by a man who had made me so insulting a proposition, for such insulting reasons.

Bad blood, a tainted name. *My* blood was known to be bad, *my* name was tainted, because of what had happened at Newhaven. That had become clear with my grandmother's incautious outburst; it was now clearer still, with the way Jennie Ross had been forbidden our door.

I could go to Leith by train – a journey of a few minutes. I could get an omnibus there, from the centre of the city, for a few pence. Then it was not a great walk along the Firth to Newhaven. I could: I would: my indecision suddenly disappeared.

I put a shawl over my head, so that my excessively recognizable hair was hidden. I counted the pennies in my purse (there were very few), and put my purse in a basket. I crept downstairs, and past the parlour door.

Once again I was reliving a moment of five months before.

Once again I heard the interminable rumble of my grandfather's voice, the bleating echoes of my grandmother's.

I heard Lord Draco say, 'You understand that this is a matter of the most crucial importance to me.'

Rumble from Grandpapa; bleat from Grandmamma.

'Yes,' said the Earl, 'that is quite true, Mr Strachan. All my own plans for the immediate future *are* intimately affected. In fact, as you will have realized, my whole future is conditional, in large measure, on your permitting Miss Drummond to return to Glendraco, and on her own willingness to return. As to the last, I am in hope that her reluctance may be overcome when the full situation is explained to her—'

Rumble. Bleat.

In a moment they would ring for a maid, who would be sent to fetch me.

Alert for signs or sounds of Carstairs, or any others of my grandparents' unwinking old spies, I tiptoed on down the stairs. I slid back the bolt of the front door, blessing the diligence of the maid who kept it oiled. I slipped out. Keeping my back to the house, so that I should not so readily be noticed from the parlour window, I went round to the other side of the Earl's carriage.

I called softly, 'Wattie! Wattie Dewar!'

Since he was alone, without groom or footman, Wattie was waiting on his box-seat with the reins in his hand. He was staring into the distance, as though dreaming of his own faraway places. He looked down, seeming to wake up slowly from his dream. His face showed astonishment and (to my surprise) delighted greeting.

'Miss Kirstie!' he exclaimed.

'His lordship,' I said, 'sent me out with a message for you, Wattie.'

'Hae yon folk nae sairvants,' he asked indignantly, 'tae ca' ye tae tak' maissages intil the streets?'

'The message concerns me,' I explained. 'It saves time if I come myself. His lordship asks if you will kindly take me at once on – on an urgent errand I have, to – to a place a short distance away.'

'On yer lanesome, Miss Kirstie?'

'Yes, of course. You know very well I am quite accustomed to doing things by myself. Geordie Buchan could look after me – don't you think you can do as well?'

'Hoots!' he cried. 'I'll tak' finer care o' ye than auld Geordie, wha mad' ye gellop owr a bit cordie – clemb ye in, Miss Kirstie, an' I'll blithe gang onywhaur ye send.'

A coal-wagon rumbled along the side of the square behind a pair of dispirited cobs. The noise, I thought, of its wheels and hoofs would drown the noise of the light brougham and its single high-stepper. I jumped in and shut the door, which had a catch like the door of a room, and did not need to be secured from outside. Through the speaking-tube (something I had never used before) I directed Wattie to York Place, and so to the Leith road.

If there were shouts behind I did not hear them.

To hold a proper conversation through a speaking-tube is not easy, especially if one has to interrupt oneself constantly to tell the coachman how to go – and especially if one is not very clear oneself how to go. I would much have preferred to sit beside Wattie on his box, but he would have been gravely shocked by such a proceeding (he was very strict in his views about practically everything) and I needed his help and therefore, as far as possible, his approval.

In spite of all difficulties, I managed to hear the important news from Glendraco.

My best friends were well – Geordie Buchan, Annie Simpson, Mrs Weir, Morag Laurie, Patterson.

Falcon was well, being exercised against my return, under

Geordie's eye, by a boy from one of the farms who would not damage his mouth or mar his temper (for Geordie, by Wattie's way of it, would not have it that I would never return to Glendraco, although I had written to tell him that I would never see him again). Adam McKillop sometimes strapped my horse, which, being both stronger and gentler than anybody else, he did better than anybody else.

Rockfall had pined, but recovered his spirits a little when Geordie Buchan took him out of the kennel to live with him in his croft. But still, Wattie said, Rockfall would look up and wave his tail hopefully when he heard footsteps crossing the stable-yard; and he whined and moped over some things he knew were mine, like an old cloak, and a saddle, and my whip.

The Reverend Lancelot Barrow had come back – having been told, I suppose, that the castle was safe for him, now that the evil invader had fled. His return was a matter of the utmost indifference to Wattie Dewar, a Wee Free as staunch as my grandfather Strachan.

Lady Arabella Paston and her daughter had gone away, but it was thought they would be coming back. The Earl's engagement to Angelica was still not announced; although he was far too discreet to say so, I had the feeling Wattie thought it never would be. I did not ask him about this, though I burned to – he would know little, and say less.

Mrs Forbes was still there. Wattie snorted when he mentioned her; they had had a theological argument, it seemed, during which she had tried to thrust Episcopalian tracts at him, to his scandalized indignation.

Wattie had seen the Ardmeggar and Inverlarig families. The Barstows of Ardmeggar were as hale and popular as ever. David Baillie was well, his father's gout no better, his mother's nerves worse.

Sir Francis and Lady Campbell had gone away into England, hurriedly, and their factor was trying to let Drumlaw to a merchant from Glasgow. Wattie had heard rumours of a scandal involving Georgina, but he would not repeat them to me; I who knew the whole unpleasant truth, would not repeat that to him, either. Charlotte Long, it seemed, had been sent back to

London. I knew enough about the ways of the world, now, to know that reports from Perth would have preceded her. She would meet some very odd looks. I knew exactly how it felt. I was sorry for her; but I hoped devoutly that I would never see her again.

There was no news – at least none had reached the coach-house and stables – of Cricklade, or Caerlaverock, or Billy Mainwaring.

Nor had Wattie any information about the Countess. The autumn storms had kept her indoors – he had not set eyes on her for three weeks. A few gentlemen had been to stay in the castle for the grouse and the last of the deer-stalking, but there had been no large party.

'An' yon auld maid,' bellowed Wattie down the speaking-tube, 'Jennie they ca' her, a daft-like nem for a Frenchwumman – she'll hae been puirly.'

Eugénie ill? I felt terribly untouched by this news.

Suddenly he stopped the horse. The speaking-tube crackled with his horror. 'Ye'll no' gang intil siccan toon, Miss Kirstie?'

'Have we got to Newhaven, Wattie?'

'New, is't? Haven, is't? I ca' it auld pairdeetion. Och, wull ye smell the fush?'

I lowered the glass in the carriage door, and leaned out to sniff. He was right. I had once heard Billy refer to 'a very ancient, fish-like smell' – that was Newhaven. Although we were only at the edge of the place, the road was strewn with bits of fish – heads, tails, entrails, oyster and mussel shells – much ancient, much the offering of the last hour or two. I leaned out a little further, to look ahead. Our road turned, just in front of us, into one of the narrow streets of a straggling, dingy village. Though the houses were stone-built, and some of them whitewashed, they looked no bigger or more luxurious than the croft of Dugald Crombie. Old women in garish clothes stood, in twos and threes, in the doors of some of these tiny dwellings; they called to each other in voices as shrill as cats, as raucous as starlings. I could not understand half the words they used – but Wattie could, for he glanced at me from his box with a face scarlet with scandal.

Wattie said he would go no further. He would not risk his

lordship's new carriage or the fine new trotting-horse. I thought he was afraid the fishwives would steal the splendid brass lamps of the carriage, and the smell of fish and crunch of shells would make the horse bolt – and I thought he was probably right.

'Wait, then,' I said to him, and climbed down from the carriage.

My feet immediately crunched on shells, and slithered on the heads and guts of fish. I was glad, for once, that I was wearing clothes of my grandmother's choice, and not my Glendraco finery. I picked my way gingerly over to the nearest group of old women, three crones in white caps and gaudy short gowns revealing layers of striped petticoats. As I neared the hovel by whose door they were standing, I saw that it was even poorer and rougher than I had supposed – a small byre, a pigsty, a prison cell with a roof. The road, which became a street between such houses, was even filthier than I had supposed. Yet the old women were as 'trig', as neat and clean, as fine ladies taking the air in Princes Street Gardens. The contrast was startling. Only the ruined teeth in their mouths, and the broken veins on their faces (that spoke of strong liquor), fitted at all with the squalid place where they lived.

These old matriarchs might be the very people I was looking for: but I thought that, before asking, I had better have the one fishwife I knew as a kind of ambassador to this wild unknown country.

I said, rather shyly, 'Can you tell me, please, where Jennie Ross lives?'

'Whilk Jennie Ross?' asked one of the old women, looking at me with little, red-rimmed, suspicious eyes.

'Oh,' I said, 'are there several people of that name?'

'Ay. I'm ca'd Jennie Ross mesel'.'

'I mean young Jennie Ross.'

'A bairn?'

'No – about forty years old, I think.'

'Whilk Jennie Ross o'sic yearn?'

'Oh – there are several of the same age?'

'Ay. There's lang gleed Jennie Ross, an' fou Jennie Ross—'

The one I wanted was tall, but had no squint; she was certainly not mad. I said uncertainly, 'The one I'm looking for is big and strong, very handsome, with black hair, and a red-and-white petticoat, and she goes to George Square—'

'Och, ay, gret black bonny Jennie Ross ye sud hae speired after. She bides in the farrest awa hoose in the back raw, whaur ye see the lum reekin'.'

'Oh – thank you – I'll go and find her.'

I called to Wattie to wait. He nodded glumly. I set off for the farthest house in the back street, followed by the cackling laughter and lurid language of the strange old women.

I picked my way through the disgusting alleys, trying to keep the hem of my gown out of the bits of fish which were strewn like snowdrifts everywhere. I was not at all beginning to get used to the smell. As I went, I was aware of hostile and suspicious eyes from doorways; when I passed groups of women, some fell silent and watched me, while others screeched at me in what sounded like a foreign language. I saw very few men, and supposed they were all fishing. I came at last to the house at the end, nearest the beach and the waters of the Firth of Forth; its smoking chimney made me sure Jennie must be at home. It was no bigger or better than any of its miserable neighbours.

I had raised my hand to knock, when the door opened. A big man with a red beard stood there, with an apron about his waist, and a cooking-pot in his hand. One of his legs was bare, the rough canvas trouser having been chopped off at the knee; the leg was swathed in a dirty bandage.

I asked for Jennie Ross, and satisfied her husband that it was 'great black bonny' Jennie Ross I sought.

'She's no hame,' said Ross. 'She's no retarnit frae Embro.'

Unable to go out in his boat because of his injury, Jennie's husband was doing the scullion-work for her. Seeing this, I learned in a second much about the strange world of Newhaven. Ross said his wife might be back in an hour, or two, or three.

I bit my lip, wondering what to do.

My first thought was to climb thankfully back into the brougham, and go home to George Square. I thought I could get off just outside the square, and watch our door until I saw the Earl leaving. It was infinitely tempting to leave the noisome alleys and hostile glances of Newhaven, and to get back to the safety and comfortable upholstery of the carriage.

But that would be absurd – to come so far, and then immediately to run away again, having found out nothing. Were a few fish-heads and unfriendly looks to frighten me away from the place, when I wanted so badly to find answers to my questions?

Jennie Ross might be three hours – perhaps more. It would be dark in three hours. I could not ask Wattie to wait so long, and he would not, even if I asked him.

I had only a few pence in my purse. I could not wait three hours in an inn, even if there was an inn in Newhaven into which I dared go.

I asked Jennie's husband if I might wait for Jennie in his house. He rolled his eyes, deeply shocked. A man and a woman, unless married, could not spend three minutes together alone in a house. That was the law of the place – morality was as rigid as speech was loose. There would be an outcry among the neighbours if I went into the house, said Ross, and a terrible storm from Jennie when she came home. He was a big, powerful man, but he was not going to risk Jennie's wrath. Nothing I said would shake him; he barred my way into the house. I could go in after Jennie had returned, if she asked me in.

The alleys seemed more disgusting than ever as I picked my way despondently back to the carriage, the eyes that followed me more hostile, the screeching voices more derisive.

'I must wait for my friend,' I told Wattie Dewar. 'I suppose you must go back, in case his lordship needs you.'

'Ye'll no wait in this sink o' ineequity?' asked Wattie, his eyes goggling with horror. 'Ye'll no bide here on yer ane?'

'Yes,' I said firmly. 'There's something I must do here, and now that I'm here I shall do it. But please, Wattie, I beg you—'

'Ay?'

'Don't tell anybody where you brought me. Say you took me to – anywhere you like – but please don't mention Newhaven.'

He nodded glumly, touched his hat-brim, and began to turn his horse.

I stood uncertainly, watching him, wondering if there was anywhere I could so much as sit down to wait. The horse and carriage rattled away, south towards Edinburgh and a familiar world. I could see the back of Wattie's head over the roof of the carriage: it was eloquent with relief at leaving the stink and threat of Newhaven. I wished violently that I was safely within the carriage; but I wanted the answers to my questions.

I turned to face the sea again, and the loathsome alleys and hostile eyes and shrill derisive voices. I felt very alone and unsafe, among foreigners with strange ways, who despised and resented me. All the stories I had heard flooded back into my mind – the drunkenness, the savagery, the wildcat violence of these eldritch women.

Lord, Lord, I thought, what have I got myself into now? Impetuous folly had got me into all kinds of trouble before – now it was like to have got me into a scrape I would be lucky to get out of.

The old woman I had first spoken to – old Jennie Ross – began to walk up the street towards me. Although she looked as decrepit as her own hovel, she walked with surprising strength and grace; she moved like my friend the other Jennie Ross. She was not, perhaps, as old as she looked; whisky had aged her face, but her body was still vigorous.

She stopped, and stood with her arms akimbo, and looked at me narrowly.

'Ay,' she said flatly, as though making an accusation. 'Ye'll be the lassie. Gret black bonny Jennie Ross hae been speirin' after a mon ca'd Drummond, wha cam' an' deed here fufty year syne.'

'Yes,' I said, 'it was for me she was asking. Do you – do *you* remember his coming?'

'Ay, I mind it. I was a wee bairn, but I mind the clash.'

I said unsteadily, 'What happened? How did Drummond die?'

'Whaurfo', lassie, sud ye seek ahint the stanes o' the grave? 'Tis fufty year syne. The deid sud bide in peace.'

'But I cannot live in peace!' I cried.

''Tis an auld, ill tale, lassie, an' I nae mair'n a wee bairn yon tide . . . No! No! I'll no spake the words – ye're owr bonny to hairk siccan tale . . . No! Let the deid bide in their lang hame.'

She would say no more; but she looked at me kindly, and asked me into her house to wait for my Jennie Ross.

304

The house consisted of two tiny rooms, as rough within as without, but snug against the weather, and not without comforts. An old man was busy with a besom in a corner. Old Jennie Ross ordered him out; he went, with the humble air I recognized in Newhaven husbands. The two other old women came in with us, called Phemie Johnstone and Mirren Carnie. They also knew something of James Drummond's fate; they also had heard, as ten-year-olds or thereabouts, the gossip among their elders; they also refused to tell me anything about it. I battered against their obstinacy: it was infuriating that they *knew* but would not say. But again and again they said, not unkindly, that it was an old and ill tale, and the dead should lie in peace.

But they saw – these smartly dressed, foul-spoken, outlandish, domineering old women – they saw that my desperation to learn the truth was as strong as their determination to keep it from me. They became most curious about me, and answered my questions with a torrent of questions of their own. I had nothing to hide from them; but I did not think it sensible to prattle to such people of Earls and Countesses and castles. They asked if it was my coach I came in, and the driver my coachman. I told the story of my coming. Somehow it sounded much more flagrantly impudent, in the telling, than it had seemed to me at the time – much more audacious, and even dishonest. It delighted them! They cackled and screeched with laughter, and their strangled speech, as they laughed, was larded with words I *did* know, which made me blush, and (I admit) giggle.

Still laughing, old Jennie Ross brought down from a shelf a squat black bottle, from which she filled four chipped enamel mugs. It was whisky. I pretended to sip, out of politeness. They all swallowed at an amazing rate, and the highest good humour filled the tiny room. They patted my arm, and called me to empty my cup so that it could be filled, and bared their dreadful teeth at me in the warmest smiles. They said I was a lass of their own sort (but they said it in words which I could not write down); and I understood that this was the highest compliment they could pay me.

But still they would not tell me what had happened to my grandfather.

My Jennie Ross came in, great black bonny Jennie Ross as they called her to distinguish her from all the other women of the same name. She was astonished to find me in Newhaven, greeted me with cautious joy, and accepted a mug of whisky which she threw down her throat as though it had been warm weak tea.

I said, 'I saw Mary Watson order you away from our door. I am so sorry if I was the cause of that.'

'Are ye so?' she said, her face suddenly sober. 'But Mary Watson hae the richt o' it.'

'What?'

'Ay. They kent fine ye were speirin' after yon auld tale, an' they didna wush ye to ken wha' cam' tae yer gran' sire. They'll hae the richt o' it, lassie.'

There was a chorus of agreement and approval from the older women. The tale was to be kept from me. Even the fishwives of Newhaven had joined the conspiracy.

It was more than I could bear. I burst out, 'I *will* know! Somebody *must* tell me! I shall go mad if nobody answers my questions!'

I saw a troubled glance exhanged between them all. I heard the whispered word 'fou'.

Was that it?

Pieces clicked together in my mind, making a pattern which was horribly, terrifyingly clear. Bad blood, indeed. I had better not marry, said the Strachans. Bad blood in every generation, said Lady Arabella. My grandfather had been insane, and I had shown, all too often, signs that I had inherited his insanity. . .

The women saw the stricken look in my face; Mirren Carnie patted my arm; old Jennie Ross poured whisky into my mug, which overflowed, because I had drunk none.

Into this moment of tense and troubled hush, there came from outside a shout in a man's voice, and the sound of wheels and hoofs.

'Hout! Anither cairt?' murmured old Phemie Johnstone. 'Twa in a day is a strange-like veesitation.'

The older Jennie Ross went to the door and opened it. It was full dark outside, and had been for a time. She stood in her doorway, looking out suspiciously, a candle in her hand.

A voice I knew, a clear strong voice like a trumpet, called, 'Mistress – have you seen a young lady here this evening, a stranger from the city?'

'Hey, ma Lord,' came Wattie Dewar's voice, 'yon's the auld yin Miss Kirstie haed her clash wi'!'

Wattie had betrayed me, as once long before. In spite of my urgent appeal, he had told them where I was. By his lights, no doubt, it was his duty. I cursed his lights and his duty.

'What became of her, Mistress?' called Lord Draco. 'Is she there behind you?'

'No, no!' I whispered, in agony lest he should find me.

He would be armed, like Cricklade, with heaven knew what permissions and authorities from my deluded grandparents. Such was his air and manner and rank, they would believe anything he said; and he had the reputation – partly deserved! – of a serious and high-minded man. I would be wholly in his power. There would be no wild escape, like my ride from the Manse at Aberfeldy, and no Billy to delay the pursuit. Draco could make of me what he liked – which I could have borne, perhaps, if I had not loved him.

'Please!' I whispered fervently. 'He mustn't find me!'

''Tis tru I clashed wi' a lass frae Embro, three-fowr hour syne,' called old Jennie Ross from her door. 'She was speirin' for a wumman ca'd Jennie Ross – gret black bonny Jennie Ross, ye ken, no' lang gleed Jennie Ross, nor fou Jennie Ross, nor auld trig Jennie Ross, whilk is masel' – I dinna ken if she fund the wumman. I doot she didna, for the chiel's awa tae Embro wi' her creel. The lassie set off doon the road tae Leith, or mebbe wastward tae Granton. Ay, I mind the noo, 'twas the Granton way she tuk.'

'Are you sure of that, Mistress?' said Draco, who had approached much nearer, and spoke more gently and courteously.

I trembled, for he was only three yards away, the other side of the wall, with an open door between us.

'Ay,' replied old Jennie Ross crisply. 'I'm naithin' mair'n an auld fushwife, but I ken ma laift frae ma richt. Gang the Granton road, ma mannie, an' ye'll mebbe see her wi' the gran' lichts o' yer cairt.'

The fishwives were no respecters of persons. The old woman must have realized Draco was a gentleman, a personage, yet she called him her 'mannie', as she might address a labourer or an urchin.

'Thank you,' said Lord Draco gravely. 'I hope to God that I do.'

Old Jennie Ross shut the door on him, and came back sighing to the little circle round her kitchen range.

'Heuch, heuch, yon's a purpose-like mon,' she said, 'ta' as a rowan-tree . . .' Turning to me, blinking owlishly in the candle-light, she said, ' 'Twas his cairt ye tuk?'

'Yes. And the coachman gave me away, though I begged him not to.'

'Whaurfo' d'ye seek tae flee, lassie? Whaurfo' wud ye skulk ahint owr petticoats?'

'Because,' I said bitterly, 'they think I've inherited my grand-father's madness. Oh, I beg you, I beg and implore all of you, tell me – tell me – *what became of James Drummond?*'

Into a long and heavy silence Mirren Carnie said, 'We were a' barins, yon tide. But auld Eppie Dundas . . .'

The eyes of all four looked inwards, considering this sugges-tion, weighing the rights and wrongs of it. I waited in breathless anxiety, looking at their faces in turn. It was strange how their attitude to me had changed, gradually but unmistakably. First they had sniffed at me contemptuously, as a patronizing outsider. Then they had taken pity on me. Then, absurdly enough, they had come to admire me, because of the way I had borrowed Lord Draco's carriage. Now . . . well, what now?

'Mebbe,' said Phemie Johnstone slowly, 'the lass hae a richt tae ken the tale o' her ain gran'sire . . .'

'Ye'll no' brang Eppie Dundas here the night,' said Jennie Ross crisply. 'I'll no' hae her in ma hoose.'

'We'll gang tae her hoose,' said my great black bonny Jennie Ross.

'Whisht! Ye'd tek an Embro leddy tae siccan meeserable stee?'

'Yes!' I said, 'Take me there! Sty, stable, anywhere, do you think I care where I go, if I can only hear the truth?'

'Och, Eppie'll no' lee. Mebbe she'll no' spake, but she'll no lee. She haena a' her wits, puir body.'

It was a sudden change of heart with them all. I thought it was brought about by that passionate outburst that was forced out of me. And that was brought about by Draco's coming. Perhaps, after all, he had made a little bit of amends, all unconsciously, for tearing my heart in two.

The women wrapped their shawls about their heads. Old Jennie Ross picked up a bull's-eye lantern. We went out into the narrow street, and buffeted our way along it against a brisk wind from the sea. I was glad of that wind, for though it stung my eyes to tears, it blew away with its clean salt breath the stench of the fish that strewed the ground.

We came, very soon, to a smaller hovel, hideously dingy even in the light cast by the bull's-eye lantern. Mirren Carnie knew old Eppie Dundas best, being the closest relation (all the women – all the people of Newhaven – seemed to be related, for they never married out of their own kind); Mirren Carnie, therefore, went first into Eppie Dundas's hovel, and shone the lantern-beam about it.

'Ma Goad,' I heard her say, 'the auld coo's fou wi' the whusky.'

We all followed her in. I was disheartened to the point of weeping; the others, perhaps, were relieved. Somebody lit a candle. It was a place of abject penury, dirty and almost unfurnished, cold, damp, full of the fish-stink and the smell of new-spilled liquor.

'Och,' murmured Phemie Johnstone. 'Wha' an *awfu'* shame.'

Candlelight and the beam of the lantern disclosed a dismal little heap of old clothes: which turned out to be a half-conscious old woman, very skinny and frail, dirty, ugly, toothless, with tufts of yellow-white hair on a grey scalp, and a dribble of whisky on her chin. The old eyes blinked redly, stupidly, trying to focus. I could not imagine how so pathetic a creature could survive in such a house. Perhaps whisky kept out the wet, as it helped her forget the stink and cold and discomfort. Temperance tracts seemed to have little bearing on life in Newhaven.

The women sat Eppie Dundas up, and pulled her ragged costume straight. They did not make her trig, but they made her almost decent. Her mouth was open and dribbling; her eyes seemed like to shut again; I saw no hope at all of getting any sense from her that night.

But, in the simplest way, the others worked a transformation in the poor old creature. The method was to pour some of the whisky old Jennie Ross had brought, into a mug she had also brought, and hold the mug just out of Eppie Dundas's reach. Her hands, blackened and black-nailed, clawed for it, but they tantalized and teased her, until she was screaming with indignation, wide awake, perfectly aware of all that was going on.

They gave her a little whisky. They said she could have more when she had answered my questions.

I was pulled forward into the candlelight, and the rheumy old eyes blinked up into my face. My shawl had slipped back from my brow; she could see my hair also.

Into the terrible old face came that which I had seen before – how many times? – on the face of the Countess, Eugénie, Dandie McKillop, Geordie Buchan, Dugald and Flora Crombie – the unmistakable look of astonished recognition. In Eppie Dundas's face there was neither joy, nor hatred: but naked terror.

'Wae's me,' she moaned in a very faint and stifled voice, quite unlike the screeching she had just been doing, when she clawed for the whisky. 'Sic a braw laddie, an' he droont hissel' in the morn, ravin' an' greetin' wi' meesery … Aie! Aie! The ghostie hae cam' tae tormint puir Eppie! … '

Little by little the story came out, with the whisky as a carrot to pull the old woman along, and to give her courage to face my face, which she thought was James Drummond's, come to reproach her for lending him her man's fishing-boat …

Whiles Eppie Dundas relapsed into maundering and whimpering; whiles she wailed and trembled, as horrors came at her from the darkness beyond the light; but at last the story came out, all of it, all I would ever know.

There was little enough.

James Drummond had ridden down from Edinburgh, in the first light of dawn, in full military evening dress. He was a man possessed. He raved and wept, he cursed himself, he did not know what he said or did, but he had a single firm purpose. He hired Jaikie Dundas's little boat, with its oars and its single sail. He paid a silver shilling. He helped Jaikie push the boat down the sandy beach into the water, and splashed aboard, regardless of seawater on his gorgeous uniform. At that moment Jaikie and others divined his purpose, and tried to stop him by force. He hit one man with his fist, and broke the head of another with an oar, and threw the anchor into the belly of a third, the madness of his grief giving him a strength an army could not have withstood. And so he took himself far out into the calm dawn sea, as the sun was peeping up over the Lothian coast.

They found the boat near Cramond, five miles up the coast. In it were his cloak and his bonnet and his sword. Jaikie Dundas had kept the sword, hidden in a safe place, because he had lost a day's fishing, and the silver shilling was not enough payment. Eppie had long ago pawned it to buy her whisky. The sword was a grand one, a dress sword, with a device engraved on the blade, near the hilt, of a leopard dancing with a rose in its mouth.

They could not tell, Eppie said, from James Drummond's ravings, why he was in a state of such violent misery, such utter despair. But it was himself he cursed.

There was no doubt in the minds of the five fishwives – none – that James Drummond when he died was insane, possessed by demons of his own making, demented and witless: and there was no doubt in their minds that, for this most horrible of reasons, he had committed a mortal sin.

Ah God, there could be no doubt in my mind either.

fourteen

My grandmother took one look at my face. She said, 'You know, then.'

'Yes.'

'All your life we have tried to protect you from that knowledge. And from . . .'

'From my inheritance. From myself.'

'Yes, Christina. But ...' She spread her hands helplessly, looking suddenly years older than she had looked the day before. 'Your marriage to a doctor, who could keep you always under observation, seemed to us a wise arrangement. That Findlay Nicholson should himself have urged the match seemed to us a merciful dispensation of Providence, and the answer to our prayers. We learned from Lord Cricklade how repugnant the contemplation of this marriage was to you—'

'*He* told you that?'

'Yes. He led us to suppose, however, that marriage to himself was not odious to you, and his own claims to be a suitable husband for you, though less obvious than Findlay's, were not contemptible. He has the duty of inspecting insane asylums in his County, together with medical men of specialized experience—'

'So he would make a good keeper for a madwoman.'

'There is no purpose in bitterness, Christina. It is God's will.'

'Yes,' I said submissively. But I was unconvinced that God would will such a thing. I went on, 'Why, knowing how – how James Drummond died, and in what state, did you let my mother marry his son?'

'We did not know. We knew only that he had been drowned. His widow was highly respectable, and lived simply here in Edinburgh. Though Episcopalian, she was a woman of the strictest moral principles, and her life was in all regards a model of frugal propriety. She brought up her son, an only child, according to those principles. His remarkable physical resemblance to his father, which astonished many people, was all that we knew, in that regard ...'

'Was my father insane?'

'That is a very brutal and importunate question, Christina.'

'I am sorry to be brutal. I do not know what the other word means. *Was* he insane?'

'He was brought up, as I have told you, by a woman of strict principles and frugal life. He married another such woman. He had no opportunity for the licentiousness, extravagance, dissipation, wildness, of the kind which ...'

'Destroyed his father.'

'Yes. Since you know that, we need no longer blink the fact.'

'How did *you* find out about – his death, and so forth?'

'His widow told us, Mary Drummond, on her own deathbed.'

'My other grandmother.'

'Yes. It was shortly after her son's marriage to our daughter: your parents' marriage. Conscience obliged her to tell us – to say what should have been said before, which should have prevented the marriage. The shock to us was very great. I do not think your grandfather and I have ever quite recovered from the agony of that moment.'

'Knowing that your daughter had married ... Yes. I understand how you must have felt. I am sorry.'

'Your mother's decision to urge her husband to emigrate, to start a new life among strangers, seemed to us eminently wise.'

'You must have been sad to see her go.'

'We were broken-hearted when she went,' said my grandmother steadily, 'and overjoyed at her return.'

'And then broken-hearted again.'

'A bare three months later. Yes. When the Lord saw fit to take her from us.'

'It would have been better,' I said bitterly, 'if He had taken me, and left her.'

My grandmother looked at me with a face so crumpled by sudden misery that I found myself embracing her, as I had hardly done in my life. In that moment I realized how deeply she loved me, and how totally she had been guided by concern for me.

Later I said, 'I hope you were not worried about me last night.'

'We prayed. It was all we could do, when Lord Draco told us you were not to be found.'

'Why did he come here?'

'He desires you return to Glendraco. Old Lady Draco is very ill, and wants you by her.'

Wattie Dewar had been right that there was illness in the castle; but he had been wrong about the invalid.

'Oh,' I said, stricken. 'I should go there. But ...'

'Should you go, Christina?'

'Yes, Grandmamma. It must be my duty to – to repay some of her kindness, by being there, if she wants me ... But I cannot go.'

'Lord Draco was most urgent that we should permit you to

go, and that you should overcome a reluctance which he understands you may feel.'

'He should understand it, indeed,' I murmured.

'Unless you go to the castle, he cannot leave it. It is highly necessary to him that he *does* leave it, as he has been offered a portfolio in the government. He cannot accept this deeply gratifying offer from the Prime Minister if he stays at Glendraco with his grandmother; and he says that he feels obliged to stay, unless you go there.'

'You mean,' I said stupidly, 'if I go, he won't be there at all? Well then, if the Countess wants me, of course I will go. Will you let me go?'

'I agree with you that it is your duty to go, Christina. We therefore acknowledge that it is our duty to send you.'

'Grandpapa too?'

'We discussed the matter at length with Lord Draco yesterday, while you . . .'

'I was quite safe, you know. The people at Newhaven are kind, and quite strict about some things.'

'Our prayers for your safety were answered. But not our prayers for—'

'My ignorance. Well, I prayed for knowledge, Grandmamma, so we were pulling in opposite directions. How confused the Lord must be in a war, with both sides praying for victory . . .'

'The shock you have received, Christina,' said my grandmother, with a return to her usual grimness, 'does not excuse blasphemy.'

'That was a theological point, Grandmamma, not blasphemy . . . What did Lord Draco say about Cricklade?'

'That without precisely lying to us, Lord Cricklade had given us a misleading impression. That your own behaviour had been exemplary.'

'Oh! . . . That was nice of Draco . . . Do you still want me to marry Lord Cricklade? Because, you see . . .'

'It is now Dr Findlay Nicholson's considered opinion, after study of recent articles published in *The Lancet* concerning the heritability of—'

'Insanity. Findlay's view is that I should not marry anybody.

314

Yes, I had forgotten that. I expect he is right. It would not do to have children who . . .'

'No, Christina, it would not do.'

I looked at my grandmother as though for the first time: and saw, beneath the grimness, the misery and the infinite compassion.

And, for myself, I looked greyly into a grey future.

'I kent ye'd be hame, Miss Kirstie,' said Geordie Buchan comfortably, helping me up from the cobblestones of the stable-yard: for Rockfall had knocked me clean off my feet with the hysterical enthusiasm of his greeting.

Oh, my heart overflowed with joy at returning to so much love and goodwill, at my reunion with Falcon, and Annie Simpson, and the old servants whom I liked so much, and who were so glad, seemingly, to see me back – my heart and my eyes overflowed. My happy tears would have filled the Draco, if all its tributary burns had dried up.

Until I saw the Countess. The change in her terrified me.

I had been forewarned, by each of the many people who interposed themselves between myself and the sickroom.

First there was Dr McPhee from Lochgrannomhead, a little grim man with a shock of untidy black hair. He said that he would have forbidden me to see his patient, as nothing should be allowed to excite or exhaust her; but she had been so anxious to see me that to keep me away might have a worse effect than to let me in. But I was not to worry her, or let her wear herself out with talking.

Then I saw Morag Laurie, who loudly thanked God (to the scandal of Patterson the butler) that I was back, as her ladyship had been fretting for me. But Morag warned me that I would be shocked when I saw her ladyship.

Then I saw the Reverend Lancelot Barrow. He kept his eyes averted from me, and dodged to the far side of an oak table in the great hall; he seemed to be afraid either that he would otherwise be tempted to pounce on me, or that I would pounce on him. He waved his long, over-scrubbed white hands, which seemed to emit an odour of carbolic soap, and talked in his whinnying voice about our allotted span, and the will of God, and divine rewards. This seriously frightened me, as the others had not spoken as though the Countess were truly dying.

Then I saw Mrs Forbes.

'So,' said she, 'the profligate has returned. I daresay Edinburgh was very dull, was not it, after your taste of life at Glendraco? And after those extraordinary happenings at Perth, of which everybody was talking. Everybody said it was so noble of dear Lord Caerlaverock to have spoken as he did, even though everybody knew that he was telling a dreadful fib. Well well, you will not be allowed into my Cousin Elinor's bedroom, you know. Even I, who am a relative, am not allowed there, so you see it would be quite wrong for an outsider to attempt to gain admission. I do not really know why you have come back. I would leave instantly, myself, to save everybody trouble, if only I had somewhere else to go ... Fortunately Lady Arabella and dear Angelica will be returning before long, to lend a certain radiance and elegance to our life here ... Why are you going upstairs, Christina? You may *not* go near my Cousin Elinor's room. Whatever that impertinent Morag Laurie says, *I* say that you must not disturb my Cousin Elinor, since even I, who am a relative, am not permitted to do so ...'

Then I saw Eugénie, who was coming out of the Countess's bedroom as I approached the door. She was cloaked as always, with misshapen claws in woollen mittens holding her cloak about her. Her black eyes burned, when she saw me, in her paper-white, wrinkled face. But, instead of giving me her usual malevolent stare, she looked away as I approached. I suddenly realized that she had been crying. I had not imagined her capable of tears. A new, cold finger of fear probed at my heart.

I tiptoed in. The Countess was lying back on her pillows, her eyes closed, her lips slightly parted. Her face was completely bloodless, as pale as Eugénie's. It was much thinner. It was only two months since I had seen her, but illness and fatigue seemed to have ravaged and wasted her, so that she was as frail as a straw. The deep lines on her brow and about her eyes, which had spoken of thunderous frowns and a high commanding temper, and those other lines about her mouth which had spoken of laughter, looked now as though all had been etched by suffering.

She looked terribly weak and old and ill. She did not move, or open her eyes. At the sight of her, I sat down on a stool by her bed and began to weep.

She had often been hard and distant with me, when the mood took her, or when I had done something outrageous to bring her anger down upon my head. She had been infinitely generous, thoughtful and loving, too. She was a great lady. I would never meet anyone like her again. I did not believe the world held another like her. Perhaps she was a survival from a grander and more heroic age. She had become a great part of my life – the greatest part. I was proud to have been part of her life, her household, and grateful that I had had the privilege of knowing her. The world without her would be a drab place.

I wept for her and for myself; and then I felt a hand, light as paper, on my hair.

A faint voice whispered, 'Kirstie, dearest child, now you are back I shall get better.'

Until I came, Eugénie and Morag had shared the nursing between them. But Eugénie had come to the end of her strength; she was too frail herself to lift her mistress on the pillows, or help her eat, and her hand had begun to shake, so that she could not wash the Countess, or brush her hair. She was violently possessive; she did not want me in the sickroom, and hissed that she would manage. But Dr McPhee ordered her away, to her own bed. So the nursing fell on Morag and me. We had a hard winter of it. The castle was like a tomb, grim and quiet. No company came at all. The neighbours who called for news left their cards in the hall, and went away saddened by the look on Patterson's face. Maids crept in and out of the Countess's room, to clean and do the fire and bring food: I saw only them, the doctor, and Morag.

After a week's enforced rest, Eugénie came back to the sickroom. She did nothing, because she could do nothing, but she would not be anywhere else. She sat in a corner, silent, wrapped always in her great cloak, her eyes fixed unblinkingly on the Countess's haggard face, or flickering after me as I moved about the room.

The doctor said I must get out sometimes, for exercise and fresh air; so I rode Falcon, with Geordie Buchan on his cob, and Rockfall racing round us. But I never dared stay out long, for terror of what might happen while I was away.

At first the Countess did seem better: a little feverish colour came into her cheeks, and her eyes were as clear and impudent as when I first knew her. She would talk to me for a little while, before her eyelids sagged again, and she sank back exhausted on her pillows. She knew about my Newhaven escapade. Draco had told her, before he left for London, the story of my borrowing his carriage. The Countess laughed when she asked me about this – her first laughter, Morag said, for six weeks. But the laughter turned to a cough, and she lay back in great distress, and Morag was very angry with me.

Then, after this appearance of greater strength, and of interest in things and people about her, she relapsed again into lethargy. She was too weak to speak, and would eat and drink almost nothing, and spent most of each day asleep. Sometimes, when she had been sleeping all day, she would be wakeful at night; and then Morag or I, who took turns sitting up with her all night, would hear strange rambling stories of fifty and sixty years before, of wars and love, balls and gambling, and the 'old, unhappy, far-off things, and battles long ago' which the Countess herself had told me of.

In the middle of December Lady Arabella and Angelica came back from extended stays in other houses. I understood that, like Mrs Forbes, they had nowhere else to go. I hardly saw them. The Countess was barely aware that they were under her roof; she was not interested in them; she did not want to see them; and Dr McPhee, I think, told them to leave her undisturbed.

A few days later I was sitting, exhausted, at three o'clock in the morning, beside the Countess's bed. I had slept for an hour or two during the day. I dared not sleep now, in case the Countess had one of her terrifying coughing-fits, or slipped sideways on her pillows, or needed a drink or one of her medicines. It was deathly quiet. A north wind had blown all day, and the ground was frozen like iron; a few flurries of little dry snowflakes had hurled themselves across the glen; but now the wind had dropped, and outside there were frosty stars in a sky of black ice. There was a little fluttering noise from a baby flame on the coal in the grate. The only other light in the room came from a night-light on the table by the bed.

I saw that the fire was burning low. I tiptoed over to the fire-place, and put more coal on the fire, delicately, lump by lump, so as to do it with no sound. But I was clumsy in my fatigue – my fingers were awkward and my brain slow – and a lump of coal fell out of the grate on to the hearthstone with a small clatter.

The Countess stirred. Her eyelids fluttered.

In a slurred, blurred voice she began to speak, as she so often did in the middle of those endless nights.

She said, 'We do not need a fire tonight. It is hot. It is mid-summer, after all. I do not know why the servants have lit a fire. It makes the room stuffy. The gentlemen look overheated. Of course, they have drunk too much Burgundy . . .'

This was another of the dreams which visited her, a picture in her mind of some hot night in the distant past.

'Are you bringing out the dice-box?' her faint voice went on from the pillows. 'There is grudge here, so there will be trouble. Hazard? Shall you play hazard? I wish you would not. How grim your faces are! What stakes are you playing for? I beg you, not high, not too high! Are you mad? Are you both mad? So many fortunes have been lost at hazard, you know, and people have fled abroad, and people have killed themselves . . .'

There was a little hiss from the fresh coal on the fire. Very faintly, from the mantelpiece, I could hear the ticking of a French clock in an intricate gilded case. The flame of the night-light stood up as still and straight as a sentry, so quiet was the air of the room.

'Oh God!' came the Countess's voice suddenly, loud, de-spairing, heart-broken.

I started forward to the bedside. But she had not moved; her eyes had not opened. The cry came out of her dream.

Her voice came again low and blurred, heavy with misery. 'He has thrown and lost, and thrown and lost again. He has thrown and lost everything. Oh God, what madness! What wicked and insane folly! He has thrown and lost, and thrown and lost again, and he has lost Glendraco ... Cursed dice, cursed table! He is leaving the room with a face like stone, without a backward glance, even at me ... What is that? That noise? A horse? He has taken a horse? Where is he going? Where is he riding to, at this time of night? Is it daylight yet? Is it dawn yet? Where is he riding to? Ah, he is riding north, north to the coast, to Newhaven, Newhaven, Newhaven...'

A week before Christmas the Earl came home. He spent a little of each day with his grandmother. She was unmistakably glad to see him, though she hardly spoke to him. I tried to be out of the room when he was in it, but Morag was sometimes in an exhausted sleep and I could not bear to wake her: and then the Earl and I looked at each other across the Countess's bed. I saw the grief in his eyes. We exchanged no words at all.

Then the snow came.

Christmas and Hogmanay went by, almost unnoticed in the little enclosed world of the sickroom.

More snow fell, snow on snow; as far as we were concerned, Morag and I, there might have been floods, drought, or heatwave.

A week after the New Year, the Earl came out of his grandmother's room, where I believed that Morag was on duty. He went away down the stairs with a frown that had something else in it than worry.

To my surprise, Morag approached along the landing. She said the Countess had asked her to leave the room while she talked to her grandson. It was that talk which had put the frown on the Earl's face.

Morag and I went into the bedroom together. The Countess was lying back on her pillows, her eyes closed and her lips parted, looking hardly strong enough to sustain life for another day.

'You must take things more easy, Miss Christina,' said Dr McPhee. 'What you and Morag are doing is superhuman – flesh and blood won't stand it. You must ease up, my girl. That old Frenchwoman is stronger now – she can't do very much, but she can sit with her ladyship part of the night.'

'But, doctor—'

'I have come to the conclusion that it would be good for her to do so. She wants to feel useful. Her whole life has been devoted to her ladyship, you ken, and it's important for her own peace of mind that she is helping her ladyship now. You can spend a few hours each night in a proper bed, your own bed, instead of camping hereabouts, within call of the patient.'

'Well, but—'

'It's an order, Miss Christina. I won't answer for the consequences, unless you do as I say. We'll have another invalid here, if you go on as you are, and that would not be convenient, would it? Think of me, please!'

'But I am quite all right, doctor—'

'You are not. How could you be? You're exhausted. Have you looked at yourself lately, my dear girl? Thin, and with black circles under your eyes – you look like something between a witch and a workhouse waif. You're far too bonny to be doing that to yourself. If I could, I'd make you take a complete rest for a fortnight, but we can't spare you. I've tried to persuade her ladyship to let me find a trained nurse – there are excellent, reliable women to be had in both Edinburgh and Glasgow – but she won't hear of it. She won't have a strange face in the room. She won't have anybody but you, Morag and Eugénie. Well, we can't risk upsetting or distressing her, so you must go on bearing the brunt. But you *must* take things more easy. You must get right away from this sickroom, out of the house, out into the fresh air.'

I nodded. I felt uneasy, leaving the Countess for any length of time, but Morag and Eugénie were with her, and Dr McPhee was very earnest in what he said.

And the world outside beckoned to me irresistibly – crisp snow under a bright sun, a strange, silent, transfigured world.

I went to my own room, of which I had seen so little since I came back to Glendraco. My way took me past Lady Arabella's room, which, with Angelica's room beside it, was in the broad passage which led from the main first-floor landing.

Lady Arabella's door was shut; but even through the heavy and snug-fitting wood I heard voices raised.

'You stupid, ungrateful idiot,' rasped the parade-ground voice of Lady Arabella. 'Go to him at once – beg his pardon – say you were thrown into confusion by his proposal—'

'I was not thrown into confusion, Mamma,' said Angelica coldly. 'And well Draco knows it. I am not confused, and I am not changing my reply to him.'

I hurried on, because I thought the sound of Lady Arabella being thwarted in her heart's desire would be very undignified and disagreeable.

On my way out across the great hall, I glimpsed Mrs Forbes disappearing into one of the drawing-rooms. She looked as though she had been made to take poison, which had not yet killed her, but shortly would.

I walked over to the stables, a broad track having been scraped clear of snow. It was heaven to be out in the brilliance and dazzle of the sunlit snow, breathing the clean cold air, striding instead of tiptoeing, coming alive after the exhausting half-life of the airless sickroom. I tried to obey Dr McPhee, and put everything out of my mind except my intense enjoyment of the moment.

Geordie Buchan said I could not ride. The snow would ball in Falcon's feet, and the drifts hid all the traps and pitfalls of the ground. Rockfall rushed up joyously, begging for a walk. Geordie wanted to come with me, but I needed to go faster and further than his stiff old legs would carry him.

'Rockfall will guard me,' I said.

The old man started to object that I could not go tramping about the hillside on my own, but before he could finish we were off, Rockfall and I, crunching through the frozen crust of the snow. The dog was mad with joy, and I with the sense of my brief liberation, so we both behaved idiotically, running, and falling down, and getting covered with snow.

Rockfall barked, and sped back along our tracks to another solitary walker: a tall figure, fifty yards away, who was following us with giant strides. Rockfall jumped up at him. Draco laughed, and pushed him away, and then threw a snowball for him, which Rockfall chased as though it had been a fresh steak.

Draco strode on. I wanted to run away. But he was crossing the ground twice as fast as I could.

All the same, I turned and started away, but I tripped, and fell into the snow again, and by the time I had scrambled to my feet Draco had come up to me.

His face, usually pale, had a high colour from exertion and the freezing air; the scar across his cheek showed up vividly. I had always thought him handsome. Now, against the huge unbroken slope of dazzling snow, he looked like a god.

He said abruptly, 'Nothing I do or say, in this life will atone for the insolence of the suggestion I made to you at Groyne.'

'Oh – it's forgotten,' I stammered, aware of my hair being full of snow, and my face scarlet.

'Of course it is not forgotten. Every time I see myself reflected in a piece of glass, I am reminded.' He laughed briefly, without humour. 'Caerlaverock's scar has almost disappeared, I believe . . .'

Oh, people are so oddly constituted – I wanted so badly to reach out and touch his scar with my fingertips, that I had to clutch my hands together, to make them behave. I wanted to kiss the scar. I wanted, and felt ill with wanting, to . . .

'But there has been a change in my situation,' Draco went on gravely, interrupting the dizzy sequence of my thoughts. 'As you yourself have known for a long time, I have been obliged in honour to make an offer of marriage to Angelica Paston. I postponed performing this duty, which was an absolute duty, on a variety of pretexts. Although I esteem Angelica's character and the quality of her mind, and greatly admire her face and figure . . . Well, I did not fervidly want her to be my wife. I did do so at one time, or fancied that I did so, years ago, and unfortunately told her mother so. I think I asked her to put in a good word for me. Those words have been spoken, and to Lady Arabella of all people . . . At any rate, I could postpone my proposal no longer—'

'Because your grandmother asked you to ask her,' I said.

He looked surprised. 'Yes. And in view of her state, I had to accede immediately to her wishes. But Angelica has refused me.'

'Her mother must be displeased,' I said stupidly.

He smiled slightly. The smile lifted not only the corners of his mouth, but also the end of his scar. I did not know why that scar should make him so much more handsome than he was before –

how it should make me feel helpless, hopeless love for him even more dizzily than before . . .

'I am to understand,' Draco went on, 'that Angelica's refusal is final and irrevocable. That while she hopes always to be allowed to regard me in the light of a friend, any warmer or more intimate emotion, etcetera, etcetera.'

Rockfall whined at us, wanting more games, thinking it stupid to stand talking when there were snowdrifts to plough through, and snowballs to be made and thrown.

'I am free, Kirstie!' said Draco. 'My dearest love, will you marry me?'

The bright sky swung above me. I put a hand to my head. I turned away from him, because I could not guess what emotions would be showing in my face.

Struggling to keep my voice steady, I said, 'I bear a tainted name. If you went to Newhaven, you would know why. If you asked my grandparents, you would know why.'

'What does your name matter to me? To anybody? We'll change your name, Kirstie! You'll take my name!'

'My blood is bad,' I said in a muffled voice.

The tears were beginning to spill out of my eyes.

'No,' he shouted. 'It can't be. Not yours. I've seen you these last weeks, working yourself to the pitch of collapse, like a saint . . . Whatever happened in the past, the distant and forgotten past—'

'It is no more forgotten than your scar,' I said flatly.

He argued and pleaded. He spoke sternly, then cajolingly, then passionately. He begged me to turn to face him, but I would not, because he would see my tears, and the love I knew I could not keep out of my face: and I would see his face, and the scar of the wound I had made, and my resolution would crack . . .

I could see no way of ending this horrible, heart-rending conversation.

At last I could bear his pleading and his passion no longer. I said, through the hands which covered my face, 'Lord Draco, I have not forgiven you. I shall not forgive you. I do not love you. I do not like you.'

I heard his sharp intake of breath, like that of a man who suddenly and unexpectedly cuts himself on the blade of a sharp knife.

I said, 'How do – do you expect me to – to feel about you? You are vain, arrogant, and boring. I was enjoying my walk. I think I have earned it, looking after your grandmother. You have spoiled it. I wanted to be alone with my dog, who to me is worth a thousand conceited prigs like you. I wish you would go away.'

He gave a deep, uneven sigh. I think it was the saddest sound I ever heard. Then his footsteps crunched away, at great speed, through the frozen crust of the snow.

Rockfall whimpered, aware of something terribly wrong.

I stood in the brilliant sun, blinded by tears. I knew that I had thrown away my one chance of happiness, and that I was right to do so.

And so I returned Rockfall to Geordie Buchan, and myself to the sickroom, and slipped back into the routine. I felt that, where my heart had been, there was a cold stone in my breast.

Weeks slid by, their passage hardly noticed upstairs in the quiet, insulated rooms. The iron frost kept its hold of the great glen. I ventured out, when I could, for long, solitary walks with Rockfall. As the days lengthened the cold, if anything, intensified.

The Earl of Draco went away, back to his government duties in London. He took a prolonged farewell of his grandmother, and a brief one of me.

'Goodbye, Miss Drummond,' he said abruptly in the great hall, as he paused on his way out, in riding-boots and greatcoat. 'I know I leave my grandmother in the best possible hands. I am to be told immediately, please, if her condition gives rise to anxiety.'

'Yes,' I said: and the stone in my breast turned back into a heart.

The scar on his face was white against the high colour of his cheek.

Lady Arabella and her daughter found somewhere else to go. I was surprised, as Lady Arabella was not welcome anywhere. I later learned that the Duchess of Bodmin arranged something (which probably no one else could have managed) out of concern not for the Pastons but for the Countess.

Angelica, who had been my friend for a few minutes, was my friend no longer; I never saw her; and I was told about her departure after it had happened.

With March, the bitter winter at last began to loose its hold on the glen. The Highland winter is more dour and obstinate than that of the south, and the Highland spring is shyer and more nervous; but when April came the ground was soft and wet, and Rockfall and I, on ever longer walks, disturbed the red grouse sparring and displaying; and the warm air was full of the trill of meadow-pipits, the uncanny dog-like bark of the sinister raven, and the wild haunting cry of the whaups returned from the sea-shore to the hilltops.

As the year mended, so did the Countess.

Her eyes grew clearer and her voice firmer. There was more colour in her cheeks, and a livelier interest in things about her. Her appetite improved. She thrust away the slops we brought her, and called for meat; and Dr McPhee was full of approval when she demanded a glass of wine with her dinner.

On the first of May she left her bed, and, with Morag Laurie on one side and myself on the other, took a few faltering steps about her bedroom.

'My legs feel like hazel-twigs,' she snorted indignantly. 'And my head swims. Deposit my carcase back on that loathsome bed. I'll try again this afternoon.'

Eugénie, with bright unblinking eyes, watched us from the corner of the room.

Dr McPhee, that afternoon, drew me aside, and said, '*Now* will you rest, Kirstie? You've been for weeks, for months, like a young tree on which an old one leans. That's very well for a time, for you're not exactly brittle, but at last even a strong young tree bends to snapping point. *Rest*, girl! Have you no consideration for me at all?'

I tried to do as he bid me, but the Countess wanted to try to run before she could safely walk, and Morag and I were hard put to it to keep her behaving sensibly. Her convalescence was extraordinarily rapid, considering her age and the Valley of the Shadow of Death through which she had passed.

In the second week of May we helped her downstairs, and in the drawing room she received Mrs Barstow of Ardmeggar. Mrs Forbes was also there, twittering and fluttering like the meadow-pipits on the hill, and the Reverend Lancelot Barrow, flapping his white scrubbed hands like a windmill hung with washing, and Dr McPhee. We made a dowdy enough little gathering, but the Countess's great spirit and gaiety made of the occasion a blazing celebration of her return to the world. The Dragon had recovered her fire: but it was a merry fire, all sparks and fireworks, and instead of scorching us it warmed and delighted us, and filled the room with laughter.

At five o'clock we helped her back to her room, where Eugénie was waiting. I thought the Countess would wish to sleep, but, when we had helped her to bed, she took my arm; I sank on to the stool by her bed, wondering what she was going to say.

Morag went out, to see Dr McPhee before he left. The room's other door, into the sitting-room where I had spent so many parts of nights, was ajar. I heard Eugénie moving about in there, hobbling stiffly in the evening sunlight, as heavily swathed in her great cloak as in the bitterest depths of winter.

'Things have been going on,' said the Countess, 'which I was in no condition to observe. I received only grossly inadequate accounts from my grandson, who adds secretiveness to solemnity to produce a style of report I find intensely irritating. He appears to regard me as a Parliamentary Committee, to which very little must be revealed, but that in proper form ... What *has* been happening, Kirstie? Why is my grandson not affianced to Angelica?'

'I ... He ... If he did not tell you, I am not sure I should.'

'Probably you shouldn't, but I trust you will. I *commanded* him to get things straightened out at last. I was bored with waiting. I thought he had shilly-shallied too long. Her mother, I daresay, thought so too. So, child? Have I not been through enough? Are you going to torture me with unsatisfied curiosity? What is the good of curing me, if you then kill me by not answering simple questions?'

'Well, she refused him, ma'am,' I said.

'I know that, but *why*?'

'She told me once she did not – she could not think of marrying anybody.'

'Oh. Is the silly chit infatuated with some married man? I did not think she had the spirit to do anything so *outré*.'

'No, it was not that . . . She told me she is not – not drawn to any man.'

'Not drawn to *any* . . .? Oho – I think I see. Yes, how much that explains. Dear heaven, what an irony! The hapless Arabella has dangled the child – who *is* very beautiful – like a carrot or a toffee-apple in front of the boy's nose – *and* she was armed with some kind of schoolboy protestation he made years ago . . . and all the time her runner wouldn't come up to scratch! What a pity. I'm bound to say, I derive a certain unforgivable satisfaction from the thought of Arabella's chagrin, but, all the same, it's a pity. They would have suited well . . .'

There was no reply I could make to this. I attempted none.

The Countess turned her head on her pillow and looked at me intently. Her grey eyes had never been so clear, so sharp, so unnerving.

She said, 'Why did you refuse Billy Mainwaring, Kirstie?'

I suppose my wretched transparent face, as always, gave everything away; for she stretched out a hand and put it against my cheek and said softly, 'Oh my dearest child, I was afraid it was so. What have I done to you? I should have foreseen, but I never thought . . . should I have left you alone, left you in Edinburgh to marry that worthy doctor?'

'No,' I said, my face lowered almost to the sheet. 'Not after he read some articles in *The Lancet*.'

'You know too much, Kirstie.'

'I do not know enough, ma'am.'

'One or the other, perhaps . . . James Drummond lived here like a king, you know. He was worshipped, venerated like a king. Things were more feudal then . . . The wild things he did made him the more admired, the foolhardy, harebrained things, like your own climb up that cliff . . . His wife was well-respected. I did not like her myself. She had been chosen for him, I suppose, not altogether well-chosen. She was suitable, eminently suitable, but only in the obvious ways. She did not match his spirit. She did not meet his flint with steel, or his thunder with lightning—'

'Or his dice-box with a pack of cards.'

'*How do you know about his dice-box?*'

'You told me, ma'am, how he lost Glendraco.'

'*I* told you?'

'Yes. And then he rode to Newhaven in the dawn.'

'And you know . . .?'

'I know everything. But I do not know enough.'

'There is no more to know, dearest Kirstie. Believe me, there is no more to know! I brought you here to make . . .' She gestured helplessly, 'some kind of restitution. It was an insane idea – a well-meant gesture, with consequences of endless grief and tumult, endless dissatisfaction and yearning, endless, endless crying for the moon . . .'

'I know why you brought me here,' I said. 'I am so glad you did, in spite of everything. I would rather cry for the moon, than never have seen the moon.'

'That is either very wise or very foolish, dearest child,' she said in an exhausted voice. 'But I am too old and too distressed to make out which . . .'

I tidied up the room, and hung up some clothes, and put more coals on the fire. Morag returned, and told me to go away for a rest; I remembered that she had been talking to Dr McPhee, and heard his words in her voice.

I went, with dragging steps, to my own room, thinking about how things were turning out. I was no longer needed here, with the Countess recovering. I did not think I could bear to stay, crying for the moon, even if the moon were crying for me too. I would go back to Edinburgh, and embark on the sedate career my grandfather suggested, in a hospital or school. If Rockfall pined Geordie Buchan would comfort him; and if Geordie and the others pined, why, Rockfall would do his best to comfort them, with his ridiculous plumy tail, and his pink tongue, and his great liquid eyes . . .

Thoughts such as these had their usual miserable effect on me;

so that when I opened the door of my room my eyes were brimming.

Annie Simpson stood there, by the door, her face startled. She gestured wordlessly towards the armchair by the window.

There, to my amazement, sat Eugénie.

She looked more than ever like an old black crow, huddled in her cloak, her misshapen claws curling out of her woollen mittens. Her wrinkled chalk-white face looked infinitely old; but her black-button eyes stared at me with bright intensity.

She made a sharp gesture to Annie, ordering her out of the room.

Annie looked at me, her eyes wide with unspoken questions, her mouth agape with outraged astonishment.

I nodded to Annie that she should go. I could not begin to imagine what Eugénie wanted with me; I could not wait to find out.

Annie went out, her face dubious, with a long backward glance. She closed the door behind her. I did not know if she would linger outside the door to listen; I would have done, but Annie had much higher principles than mine.

I had known Eugénie for almost a year. In all that time, except for the two months I was away in Edinburgh, I had seen her every day, and often many times a day; but in all that time I had scarcely ever heard her speak. I knew she *could* speak, and in English of a kind – she spoke to the Countess, and to the servants; she had spoken to Dandie McKillop. But to me she was a creature of hissings and mutterings, which sounded like no language at all.

Now she began to speak, in a queer clipped sing-song voice with a strong French accent; she spoke quietly, rapidly, as though she had little time, and much to pack into it.

She said, without any preamble, 'Many years ago I 'ave been nurse for the children of miladi. It was a 'appy family, *vous comprenez*? I was proud and 'appy to be there. All was well. We were calm, like a ship in a tranquil sea. Me, I 'ad escape from Paris, from the Revolution, as a very young child. I 'ave been taken out, *en contrebande*. 'Ow is that? I 'ave been smuggle away by a friend. My family were all killed. We were *aristocrates*. But that

330

'as been no good to me, in England. I 'ave become *nourrice*, a nurse, for little children. I must eat, yes? I 'ave become a nurse for my bread, and I 'ave care for the little children of miladi. *Bien.* It was not what I 'ave been born to, but I was 'appy.

'Then I was more 'appy. Love came to me. That is *extra-ordinaire* to you, eh? The ugly old woman 'as been one time in love with a fine young man. 'E was not noble, but a common soldier, a young man of the people. *N'importe*, 'e was very gentle and kind. Per'aps 'e was weak. That was not important, in the life together that we 'ave planned, because I was *not* weak. Ah, *bah*, it is a lifetime ago . . .

'At the same time as my soldier 'as come into my life, another soldier 'as come into the life of miladi. Yes, 'e was *officier*, very fine and gallant, rich, of ancient line. My soldier, my poor John Anderson, was 'is servant. That was 'ow we 'ave met. My John and I, in Edimbourg . . .'

The bright black eyes seemed to turn inward, for a moment, seeing her young soldier, remembering their love.

She went on, still more quietly and rapidly, so that I had to lean forward, and strain to hear her words, 'Into our tranquil sea, that fine gentleman came like a *baleine*, a whale. *Il était très beau. Mon dieu, qu'il était beau, avec la beauté du diable.* That face, 'is face . . .'

Eugénie looked searchingly at my face, and seemed to be reading her next words from the page of an open book which was my features.

She said, ''Is brow was 'igh, and 'is *joue*, the bone of 'is cheek was 'igh, like an *indien* of America, and 'is brows very dark and straight, and 'is eye dark, dark blue, like midnight, but blue, not black . . . 'is skin was pale, fine, like the petal of a flower, like a white *camélia*, like a *magnolier* . . . ah, *il était trop beau*, 'e 'as come in our quiet lake like a *baleine*. 'E was mad, you understand, *une bête sauvage, une fauve* . . . 'E 'as want miladi. To get 'er, to 'ave 'er, even one time, 'e will destroy everything, the 'usband, the little children, and miladi too . . . I tell you, 'e was *diable*, a thing from 'ell. 'E die as 'e live, and as 'e deserve. 'E die a terrible death, alone, in the sea, mad . . .'

'You hated him,' I said dully.

'*Bien sûr! Je l'ai détesté!*'

'And when you saw my face . . .'

'Your face! It is not your face! It is 'is face! 'E is reborn, the devil who 'as try to destroy miladi and the little ones! And *you* 'ave come to destroy miladi, and the little one of the little one . . .'

'So,' I said, 'you tried to kill me. Knowing what I know about myself, I wish you had succeeded.'

'I try to kill you, *bien entendu*,' said Eugénie rapidly. '*Of course* I try, to save miladi and the young one.'

If I had expected any trace of regret, apology, repentance, I would have been disappointed. There was nothing in Eugénie's face, or in her rapid sing-song voice, that conveyed anything but the certainty that she had acted rightly – acted in the only logical and moral way.

I remembered Dr McPhee's words: Eugénie had devoted her life to the Countess. The Countess's welfare was her obsession, her religion. Like other obsessed souls – like Dandie McKillop – she had gone to the brink of sanity, or beyond it. When she saw me, she was seeing not a raw girl from Edinburgh, but a devil reborn – a devilish threat, reborn, to her beloved mistress. Ah God, of course she tried to kill me!

'Why are you telling me this?' I asked suddenly.

'*Ah, pourquoi*? But it is clear, yes? You mus' understand? Well now, I am old *très faible*. I cannot 'elp miladi when she is sick. My arms are weak. My 'ands – *regardez* – they cannot 'old a spoon, or a small glass. That Morag Laurie, *cette espèce de vache*, she 'as not the brain. It is you who mus' look after miladi. *Voilà tout*. That is quite clear?'

'But,' I said, dumbfounded almost beyond speech, 'if you think I came here to destroy—'

'*Bah*. I do not think so. I did think so, yes of course. Now I 'ave seen. All winter I 'ave watched, and I 'ave seen. You do not look after miladi so well as I did, but you do better than the cow Morag Laurie. So, miladi need you.'

'But – if my grandfather was—'

'*Idiote*? Well, if you like, you 'ave say to miladi just now, you did not know enough. *C'est exacte*. I do not know enough. I 'ave say James Drummond was *un fou, une fauve sauvage*. But I do not know enough. I 'ave watch you, and you are not the *grande-fille d'une bête sauvage*. So? So I see that I do not know enough, and I am too old to go to find. The game with the dice—'

'The game of hazard, when he lost Glendraco—'

'*C'est ça.* I was not there, *bien entendu.* I was guarding the little children, *à l'autre côté de la cité.* All the others who 'ave been there, all are dead. All except miladi, who will not talk about the game, I think. And one other.'

'Who?'

'My poor John Anderson, my *bien-aimé*, my lover. 'E was there. 'E was James Drummond's servant. 'E was there to pour the wine, yes? 'E saw the game. 'E was *épaté*, struck with thunder, filled with 'orror. I 'ave seen his face after, it was the face of a ghost. 'E would not tell me about the game – *me* 'e would not tell. Well, then, 'is master died in the sea. John Anderson 'as go into the Scotch Brigade, and go to Spain. 'E there 'as a bad wound, many wounds, 'e is *mutilé*. 'E gain a pension, a little money every month, as long as 'e live. 'Is wounds are never truly cured. 'E 'as always a piece of lead in the *poitrine*, in the chest, and a piece of wadding in the leg. They pain always. 'E cannot sleep. 'E is no more a whole man, but a broken man in pain. Whisky, that dulls the pain of those old wounds, so 'e spend the pension all on whisky. So I do not blame 'im, but I do not marry 'im.'

'But – with all that – he's still alive?'

'Nine months ago 'e was alive. I 'ave 'ear, from a doctor. John Anderson was not in good 'ealth, but 'e was alive.'

'Where can I find him?'

'*You*? You cannot find 'im, mamselle. You cannot go more near than one mile from where 'e is. You may send a person, per'aps.'

'Where is he, Eugénie?'

'In Glasgow. In the worst part, in a place full of murderers and thieves. 'E can per'aps still tell to *quelqu'un* – not you, but to someone – what 'as 'appen when they throw the dice for the last time . . .'

'Then what?'

'It 'as a value, to know. A value to me. I do not talk to you *pour m'amuser*, but because there is a value to me to know. You understand?'

'No,' I admitted.

'I wish to know if you are *idiote*. Per'aps James Drummond 'ad a reason to play with the dice as 'e did, to wager as 'e did. Per'aps 'e 'ad a reason to ride to the sea to die. If 'e 'ad a good reason, per'aps 'e was not *fou*. If 'e was not, per'aps you are not. If you are not, you shall stay 'ere to look after miladi. If you are, I must find another. *C'est tout.*'

I gasped. I had always heard that the French were a very practical race: but this took my breath away.

Her obsession with protecting the Countess from harm was as overmastering as poor crazed Dandie McKillop's obsession of ancient hatred – and as near tipping her over the brink into the cloudy whirlpools of insanity. It must have been, to drive her to trying to kill a young strange girl. Yet, with all this, the extraordinary old woman was being totally practical. She was making her arrangements for the future, as coolly as an Edinburgh lawyer drawing up a will.

Eugénie gave me the address which she had been sent by the doctor who wrote to her. I realized that, all down the years, she must have kept a kind of remote eye on the broken-down soldier she had once loved. Perhaps she was not altogether hard and practical.

I wondered who would go to Glasgow for me, to find a drunken cripple in the middle of the worst slum, and ask him about a game of dice that had been played more than fifty years ago.

fifteen

The person I most trusted was Dr McPhee. So, when he next came to the castle, I asked him for a talk in private. He sniffed and snorted, as he always did, with an appearance of angry impatience; and then suggested a walk. We collected Rockfall, at the sight of whose ridiculous caperings the grim little doctor almost laughed. We walked uphill through the wet spring grass, Rockfall finding a million scents to send him wild with excitement, and Dr McPhee complaining that his boots would be soaked and ruined.

I asked him if insanity was hereditary.

'Why do you ask that, Kirstie?'

'It concerns – it partly concerns someone I know. It's really a high – hyper—'

'A hypothetical question? Very well, I'll answer it as such. There is no single answer, of course. It entirely depends on the type of insanity, on the causes of it. If a man gets a blow on the head which damages the brain, he may be a hopeless idiot thereafter. But his son, who has not had a blow on the head, can be as sane as you or I.'

'Yes. But a man who all his life shows signs of – of wildness, and who behaves in an unbalanced way—'

'If he's wild all his life, from infancy, then there's a presumption he was born wild. His wildness then is likely inherited, like the colour of his hair or the shape of his nose. And if he passes those things on, as we see every day among families we know, then he can pass on other things likewise – temperament, talent, any of the things that go to make up what we call a human being. You'll be understanding anything about horse-breeding, Kirstie?'

'Not much,' I admitted.

'Nor I, but I've heard a lot of expert talk on the subject. Some stallions, so the experts tell me, have a remarkable propensity for transmitting their own characteristics to their descendants. If it were not so, then Mr Weatherby's Stud Book would be only of the purest academic interest, which the experts tell me is by no means the case. A stallion regularly hands down, for example, his size, conformation, colour, ability, his speed or staying-power, his gentleness or savagery. Now, an interesting thing is this. I was hearing some weeks ago, from a racing man, about a stallion he owns. I forget the name. It won the Derby, or some such. It was a big, tall chestnut, with great speed but a difficult character. It has had – how many foals would it be? Thirty or forty a year?

Something of that order, and for many years in succession. Of all those foals, a proportion have inherited the chestnut colour and general appearance of their sire. And those – mark this, Kirstie – have inherited with the colour both the ability and the difficult character. Some, by my friend's account, have been very fast runners, but so difficult in character that no one has been able to train them. Do ye follow? Other offspring have been bays or greys or blacks – skewbald or spotted, for all I know – and they're apt to be quite different. They've taken after their mothers, I daresay. Now, if it can happen so with horses, I see no reason in nature or logic why it cannot happen so with men.'

'But people are more complicated than horses.'

'Ay, to be sure they are. But some of the attributes of a person are simple enough to identify. A green eye is a green eye. If we see a child with a bright green eye, and a father with a bright green eye, we leap to the conclusion that the child has inherited the colour of his eyes from his parent. And I don't doubt we're right. If we see a long thin child, or exceptional musical talent, or a violent temper, then commonly we make the same assumption. Again, I don't doubt we're right. A violent temper is a violent temper . . .'

'And insanity is insanity.'

'It is that. There's been an interesting series of articles in *The Lancet* on this very subject. After my study of those, I came close to feeling that the – if you'll forgive the word – that the mating of human beings should be as carefully considered and controlled as the mating of thoroughbred horses, or saddleback pigs, or prize poultry. It's a morally unacceptable notion, of course, but it would save a terrible lot of human misery.'

'Yes. I understand. Thank you.'

'Why *do* you ask, Kirstie? What friend does this concern?'

'I was thinking of Adam McKillop,' I said. 'Can I ask you another high – hyper—'

'Hypothetical question? Ask on. But I must turn back now, or my boots will fall off my feet.'

'It's about—' I thought quickly for a moment. 'It's about Adam's father.'

'I ken the story. That was the man who was killed last year, falling down the hill?'

'Yes. You see, he had – fifty years ago – a sort of blow on the head, which sent him insane.'

'Ay?'

'But it wasn't a blow on the head. It was a shock. It was a sudden, terrible disappointment. Could that send him mad, like a blow on the head?'

'Hm.'

Dr McPhee stopped to consider the question. Rockfall circled round him, first very slowly, then very fast.

He said at last, 'I have been in practice too long to say that anything in medicine is impossible. But I never saw a case of the kind you describe. Literature, mind you, is full of it. Classical drama more so, I fancy, in the persons of such characters as Orestes. It would be a favourite device of those gloomy Jacobeans – you can imagine the dramatic effectiveness of a man sent raving by some horrible revelation. *The Duchess of Malfi*, I mind from my student days, has some such device ... Ay, it's strong dramatic meat, but I don't know of any well-attested case in real life. I doubt it would be unheard of in Scotland, the sober life we lead. No, on reflection, I do *not* find myself able to believe in a shock rendering a man insane who was not, in a true sense, insane already.'

'I understand,' I said again. 'Thank you.'

He had answered both my questions: and given me, to both, the answers I least wanted to hear.

'How did my grandson acquire a long and deep wound on his cheek, Kirstie?' asked the Countess.

'How should I know, ma'am? But I expect he can tell you.'

'He can tell me, no doubt. I am not convinced he has done so. He has given me an account of it, since I naturally asked him about it the moment I saw it. His account was a perfect example of what I meant about all his reports to me. He tells me nothing, but he tells the nothing in a very solemn and formal way ...'

'What account *did* he give you, ma'am? I was wondering myself how it happened.'

'Were you, child? Were you indeed? He says that he fell, while walking alone in the gardens at Groyne, after the second Perth Ball. He struck his face, he said, on a sharp stone. He says the ground was slippery with heavy dew, and he was tired, and preoccupied, and careless ... He blames himself entirely. He says – and this is the part of his story which I find particularly unsatisfactory – he says he is glad of the scar, because it will remind him all his life never to make such a wretched mistake again. Did you know that, Kirstie? Did you know that he blames himself entirely?'

'Who else should he blame, ma'am, for – for making a false step?'

The Countess sighed, and turned away from me. I turned also, and went softly out of her bedroom.

I studied the maps in the library, and saw that it was about a hundred miles from Glendraco to Glasgow, going by Loch Lomond. Though Glasgow was served by the railway, the railway did not extend north towards us; the whole journey would have to be done by road. Well, a hundred miles in a light travelling carriage was nothing to a man who had such a thing. Who had, that I could ask such a favour of?

Then I sighed for my friends, or the people I had thought my friends.

Billy Mainwaring would have gone to Glasgow for me. Without conceit, I knew that he would have gone to the ends of the earth for me. But Billy had gone abroad, to India, in October; he had gone to the ends of the earth, and was there still. I knew why he went; so did the Countess. I thought he was right to go; so did the Countess. But I longed for his help now.

Lord Cricklade was at home in Wiltshire. Now that foxhunting had finished for the season, he divided his time (I supposed) between the Magistrates' Court, the County Asylums for the Insane, his farms, and the river. I would not have asked *him* for a handkerchief to staunch a bleeding wound; but, even if I would, I could not.

Caerlaverock so the Countess told me, was in London for the season. (I could not picture the 'season' in a place like London; for the matter of that, I could not picture London, except as a larger and dirtier Edinburgh.) I thought Caerlaverock and I could have been, with caution, friends again. But he was too far.

I could hardly imagine myself writing to him to say, 'Please go to the slums of Glasgow, and ask a drunken old soldier . . .'

Who, then?

The Reverend Lancelot Barrow would be protected, in the slums, by his cloth. He could go by the public coach in two days, perhaps three. I could give him the money, having borrowed it from the Countess or from Dr McPhee. He *ought* to be willing, after what happened between us, to do me such a trifling service . . . Well, yes, he ought – but the thought of Mr Barrow flapping his hands and bleating in the Glasgow wynds was so utterly absurd that, in spite of everything, I found myself laughing.

David Baillie would go without hesitation, and his honest and stupid and spirited old father would urge him, if he needed urging. He was strong and active enough to come to no harm, perhaps, among the thieves and murderers. But David would lose the address, and miss the way, and forget the name of the man he was looking for; and if he found him he would get the story wrong, and bring me back a rigmarole of jumbled rubbish . . .

I could not send any servant on so delicate a mission. Geordie Buchan, perhaps, who had loved my grandfather: but Geordie was far too old to make such a journey by himself. Besides, I could hardly send away a Glendraco servant for a week.

I could trust Dr McPhee, more than anyone I knew. But there was no question of his being able to get away for a week, nor his young assistant in Lochgrannomhead. No doubt Dr McPhee knew doctors in Glasgow, to whom he could write on my behalf. This was the most practical idea I had had – the *only* practical idea I had had. I was almost at the point of asking for another confidential interview with the doctor. But, after deep thought, I gave up the idea. I could not bear the thought of a stranger, a brisk, businesslike, insensitive, disapproving Glasgow doctor, becoming involved in my most personal affairs, and learning my family's most hideous secrets.

I did not want a stranger telling me that my grandfather was a madman when he diced away Glendraco.

The Countess had been there, in the stuffy room with the fire unseasonably lit, when the dice-boxes were brought out for the last, mad game.

What need to send to Glasgow, to interrupt the drunken dreams of poor John Anderson?

I asked the Countess, delicately, about the game of hazard. Into her eyes came such pain, into her face such a wave of age and weakness, that I was frightened of what I might be doing to her. She was not herself for the rest of the day, and would not eat that night.

I knew I could never raise the subject with her again.

So I enquired, very innocently and privately, into the possibility of going to Glasgow myself. Once there, I could not venture alone into the wynds. No one could, not a policeman, not Draco himself. But I would find a doctor or a constable or a Minister who would seek out John Anderson for me, and take me to him, or bring him to me.

I found there was a weekly public coach from Lochgrannom-head to Killin, and a coach of unknown frequency from Killin to Crianlarich, and other coaches, of uncertain number, from there to Helensburgh, Dumbarton, Clydebank, and so to Glasgow. An inside seat all the way would cost me four guineas or more. I might be three or four or more nights on the way, depending on the days when the infrequent coaches ran. That meant nights in inns, on my own: impossible – they would likely not even admit me, thinking I could not be respectable, to be travelling so. Well then – I would take Annie Simpson. That meant eight guineas to get to Glasgow, even without the reckoning at the inns, and what we should need to spend in Glasgow itself; and we must still return.

In fact, I needed at least twenty-five sovereigns before I could think of setting off. I could not beg or borrow so daunting a sum without giving a reason. What reason could I give? The true one? Anyone I asked would think me as insane as . . .

Except Eugénie. She would well understand. And it would suit her coldly practical French mind to have the last great questions answered. It occurred to me that she must have savings. She received a wage, I supposed; I could not imagine that she spent

340

anything, as she never went anywhere, but lived her whole life within a few yards of the Countess. I pictured a woollen stocking full of golden guineas under the mattress of her bed.

But Eugénie had had a change of heart. Perhaps she regretted talking to me as she did. Though I sought her out, and spoke pleadingly to her, she hissed and coughed and barked at me in rapid French I could not understand, or spoke so low I could not hear, or hobbled away without saying anything at all.

Days went by, too many days. I had a feeling time was running out. There was no reason why, since John Anderson had survived his broken life for fifty years, he should not survive for another month or year: but I had a nagging fear that he might not. I wanted to run to Glasgow at once. I felt it vital that I should do so. But there was no possibility of my going there and I trembled to think that if, by some miracle, I ever got there, I should find that John Anderson had been laid in a pauper's grave.

Near the end of May, the Duchess of Bodmin came to Glendraco Castle. She was to stay for a fortnight. She said she was tired of her little house, and her garden and gardeners, and wanted to look at wider skies. Her broad cook's face, and hearty cook's laugh, cheered everybody up. She was like a cordial tonic to the Countess, and she was very kind to me.

We strolled by the river bank one afternoon, she and I. Rockfall plunged into the water after a bird, or perhaps a fish; he scrambled out and shook himself, so that we were showered with river-water, and screamed at him; this caused him to rush at us with his tail a-wag, for the praise and petting he was sure he deserved.

The Duchess said, 'One is obliged to pretend to like dogs, in this country. In the ordinary way I have learned to tolerate them. But *yours* . . .'

'He has *no* manners,' I admitted, 'but—'

'But you love him besottedly. I know. *Le coeur a ses raisons que la raison ne connaît pas*. Which is, I suppose, the story of most lives . . . On that subject dear, Alicia Odiham gave me a fascinating account of your adventure at Perth. Well, to be sure, you may have had a dozen adventures at Perth, but I expect you know the particular one I mean. You were all dancing "The Dashing White Sergeant", I think she told me. The last time I was induced to perform that bumpkin bouncing, my tiara fell off, and landed with a crash on the floor. Diamonds flew about like rice at a middle-class wedding. They were swept up, but do you know what? Some of the best stones were never recovered. The flower of the Scottish aristocracy had pocketed them . . . In spite of that humiliating memory, I wish I had been there on *your* night. Alicia painted it as a scene from melodrama – *The Rake's Confession*, perhaps, or *Virtue Triumphant*. I hear little Charlotte Long met a very chilly reception in London drawing-rooms. Letters, of course, flew south like snowflakes. I do not suppose she had been absolutely ostracized, but there are certainly houses, the best ones, to which she would not be admitted. Alicia spoke of her *very* severely, calling her a scheming minx, and using other terms which you are too young to listen to. I take a much more tolerant view, having been a scheming minx myself, at her age. I had to be, you understand – I was neither rich nor beautiful, my mother was a widow, and I had five sisters. But I was lucky. I got my Duke, while she lost even poor Caerlaverock . . . There is no justice, dear. At least, not much. Which is so fortunate, for people like myself . . .'

Then she said she was going, when she left Glendraco, to a great house near Paisley, and then home in time to welcome Lady Odiham.

'Paisley,' I said. 'Is not that near Glasgow, ma'am?'

'Too near. Barely six miles, I think. It may have been a convenient place when the house was built, but now it is all set about with iron and coal and tall chimneys and men with dreadful black faces. Of course the Kilwillies profit to a hardly credible degree from having all those things on their land, or under it, but it does *not* make for a restful or elegant countryside.'

'Even so, I – I would like to see it,' I said. 'Out of interest, you know.'

'Then come with me, dear. Elinor Draco can spare you, now that you have made her well. The Kilwillies will love to have you for a week. Even if they did not, they would pretend to, since you are a friend of mine. Being a Duchess, you know, gives one all kinds of monstrously unfair advantages ... Osbert Kilwillie will bore you dreadfully about his minerals and canals and railways, but he is a good soul, and his cellar is the third best, to my mind, in Western Scotland. Elinor can send to fetch you back. That excellent Mrs Barstow, who looks like a horse, was saying this morning that a change would be good for you. I doubt it, myself – if you looked any better than you do now, the trees would begin to bend down and worship ... That's settled then, dear? I always prefer company on a journey, and I can think of none I would prefer to yours.'

'It is – hum – a sort of charitable duty,' I said. 'He is an old servant of my family, fallen on evil days. I expect he should be put into a hospital, or – something.'

'That sounds quite right and proper, my dear,' said Lady Kilwillie. 'But there is not the least need for you to go personally into the city. The Saltmarket, did you say, down near the river? You should certainly not go to such a place.'

'Oh, but ma'am,' I said, 'it is surely my duty to go. I daresay he will take help from me which he would refuse from anybody else. And if there is need to put him into a hospital I think it must be me who puts him there. People like that are so frightened of hospitals, you know, that if a stranger tried to make him go—'

'The child's right, Isabella,' said the Duchess. 'If a stranger tried to haul one of my gardeners off to hospital, he'd have his arm cut off with a scythe before he would sign the papers.'

'If somebody could very kindly show me the way . . . ' I said.

'I'll do better than that,' said Lord Kilwillie. 'I'll send two men with you. Robbie Murray shall drive you, and Mungo Dick shall go too. I'll see they both carry good stout cudgels. You'll be as safe with them as taking tea with a Judge in the Queen's Hotel.'

So it seemed that, thanks to their kindness and the kindness of the Duchess, the insoluble problem had been solved, and everything was suddenly easy.

The journey had taken two days: though, at the breathtaking speed the Duchess travelled, it might have been accomplished in one. We went through the middle of Glasgow, which had broad streets far cleaner than Edinburgh's, and fine buildings all of white stone.

'Why are people frightened of Glasgow?' I asked the Duchess. 'I never saw such an orderly place.'

'There are parts not *quite* like these parts, dear,' said the Duchess. 'I have never seen them myself. From what I've heard, I trust I never shall.'

Then, by an enormous bridge, we crossed the Clyde, and I begged that the carriage might be stopped for a moment. The river seemed to me huge (of course I had never seen the Thames) and was packed with shipping of all kinds. To the mile of docks of the Broomielaw were tied up ocean-going steamers, larger than I had ever seen in the Firth of Forth, with flags that showed them (as the Duchess's coachman explained to me) to have come from all corners of the world. Other ships, of all sizes, were creeping to and fro, so close to each other that I thought they must collide. Little gay-painted river-steamers, and sailing boats and skiffs, bustled among the giants. I could have watched them for hours, understanding what I have heard about the romance of the sea, imagining huge languorous voyages under the Southern Cross.

'Very picturesque,' said the Duchess, 'but a lot of foreign sailors don't make for a peaceful town. Come along, dear. I want my tea.'

So we came to Kilwillie, built during the Regency from the profits of the mines, which had also paid for the first Lord Kilwillie's title. It was called Kilwillie House, but it was a palace. Trees had been planted to hide from its windows the source of its wealth; but the Duchess was right – it was *not* set in an elegant landscape.

Nor was Lord Kilwillie elegant, though he was the soul of kindness. He was a little bustling, bristling man, like a mongrel terrier-dog; he wore a cutaway tail coat made out of a fierce tweed, and yellow leather gaiters like a country groom. Lady Kilwillie came from Edinburgh. She had not heard of the Strachans, and I could see that their paths would never, never have crossed. They were very welcoming, though my arrival was a complete surprise to them. To them the Duchess could do no wrong, and they would have put on a welcoming face for anybody that she brought; but they were truly friendly and openhearted people, and I believed their welcome to me was genuine.

So it was not pleasant to mislead them about my reasons for finding John Anderson.

The Duchess knew James Drummond had died a horrible death. I remembered her telling Lady Odiham so, while I stood outside the window in her dark garden. She knew little more. I did not want her to know any more. I did not want the Kilwillies to know anything about it at all.

There were social engagements and expeditions arranged for the next two days; so my visit to Glasgow was fixed for the third day, Thursday. The drive would take less than an hour. It was agreed that I should leave immediately after luncheon, and so be back comfortably before dark.

Yes, the insoluble problems had been solved, and everything was suddenly easy.

After a spell of brilliant weather, the sky on Thursday was full of low, dark clouds hurrying up from the south-west. Lord Kilwillie said the glass had fallen and was falling still. He predicted heavy rain. I thought it wise to dress for this weather, in stout shoes. I thought it even wiser to dress inconspicuously: I did not want to attract attention in whatever strange world I was venturing into. I wore drab, dark clothes, and wrapped myself in a long cloak with a hood, provided by Lady Kilwillie's maid, which made me look like a conspirator, and feel like a piece of cheese from the grocer.

Robbie Murray was the Kilwillie under-coachman, a stocky, sturdy countryman of about forty in a neat coat and gaiters and a billycock hat. Mungo Dick, though named for the Patron Saint of Glasgow, was also from a farming family, and looked it; he was a sort of superior groom, and looked as though he lived in the stables. He was wiry and agile, a few years younger than Robbie and a few inches taller. Both carried stout, heavy-knobbed sticks, as Lord Kilwillie had promised. After I took one look at them, my vague fears vanished.

The rain began as we drove, in the early afternoon, from Paisley to Glasgow, By the time we crossed the bridge over the Clyde, it was thundering down on the roof of the closed carriage, soaking poor Robbie and Mungo. A curtain of rain almost hid the massed shipping by the Broomielaw. It bounced on the paving-stones of the bridge, hissed in the river, and drowned all the clamour of the teeming dockside.

A few hundred yards beyond the river, we came to a broad fine street of stone houses and public buildings. There were a few closed carriages, many cabs, and a three-horse omnibus like that which had started my escape in Edinburgh a year before, all with rain-darkened, steaming, unhappy horses. People on foot were huddled in doorways, or scurrying for cover with coats held over their heads. The bare legs of the girls were mottled blue with the cold rain, and splashed with muddy water from the wheels of the cabs.

Robbie Murray told me, by the speaking-tube, that we were crossing Argyle Street; if we went on we would come to George Square (another George Square!); he assumed that was our way, since his mistress had never been any other way. But I called to him to turn right, towards the Trongate, as Eugénie's directions told me. Lord Kilwillie had often been to the Trongate Bank and the Tontine, which I understood was some kind of business centre, so that, for the moment, Robbie and his horse were still on familiar ground; and for several hundred yards our way was still a broad, safe street, peaceful, magnificently clean.

We passed the Gate, and came to the Cross, which was dense with cabs and omnibuses and scurrying people. Robbie's voice called to me again on the speaking-tube. Were we to go left up the High Street (which he did not like the idea of), on to the Gallowgate (which he liked less), or down into the maze of the Saltmarket (which he liked least of all)?

'The Saltmarket,' I said.

'We'll no' tak' a horse an' carridge by yonder, Miss. We maun gang on owr ain feet, wather or nae wather.'

'Can we leave the carriage here?'

'Ay, we'll seek a coach-hoose wi' a ruf.'

Robbie drove the carriage into the forecourt of the Tontine Hotel, an opulent building by the Cross. Mention of Lord Kilwillie's name was all that was needed. Cheerful ostlers un-harnessed the horse and put him in a dry stall, with straw on the floor and hay in a rack and a rug over his steaming, rain-blackened quarters. There was no need for money to change hands – the people of the hotel knew that Lord Kilwillie was not only very rich but also (which did not always follow, they said) very generous. This was fortunate, as I only had three shillings, Robbie about the same, and Mungo a few pence.

The ostlers and porters thought, no doubt, that I was going into the hotel. We did not tell them we were going into the Saltmarket: they might have doubted if the carriage was truly from Kilwillie.

We started down the Saltmarket, back towards the river. To go from the tidy opulence of the Tontine into the teeming Saltmarket was to jump from a known world, full of safety and certainties, into something completely strange. The houses were tall and black with lofty gables, once the houses of rich merchants, but now decrepit, dirty, windowless, patched, crumbling, rickety. At street level the houses had been turned into an infinity of tiny shops. A very few sold meat or tea or cottons; most sold whisky or tobacco, with a few old-clothes shops and many pawnbrokers. The reek of cheap tobacco filled the narrow street, in spite of the rain, but it did not hide the worse stench of human filth and poverty and misery. People pressed about us, as though no one in this part of the city had anything to do but stand about in the street. Nearly all were in tatters, and their skin dark with dirt. The shrill jabbering all round us was almost impossible to understand. There was very broad Scots, with a strange twang I had not heard in any other place; Gaelic, from wretched Highlanders evicted from their crofts by sheep, who had come down from their hills and settled at last, like silt in a river, in this very lowest and most miserable of all places; and much Irish. The Scots speech was quite as strange and uncouth as the others. The greatest noise came from pedlars and drunken women. The pedlars shrieked about their 'harrins', old clothes, and dead men's boots. A fat old woman with a stall of bannocks was suddenly assaulted by a mob of near-naked little boys, who managed to knock her over and steal most of her wares. I started after them furiously, but Robbie Murray gripped my arm, muttering nervously.

Robbie and Mungo were both looking about them, ill at ease, gripping their cudgels firmly. I realized that all this was as strange and alarming to them as it was to me.

I felt eyes upon me. Turning sharply, I saw a big man with a purple, bloated face covered with red stubble, and little red-rimmed eyes like a pig's, and a greasy greatcoat with most of the buttons missing. He had a short clay pipe in his mouth, and a bottle in his huge red hand. He was staring at me fixedly. He turned to nod to another man, whose cadaverous face was smeared with dirt, and who wore a blackened Highland bonnet over lank, dirty black hair.

Whatever was in their minds, they could attempt nothing in the midst of the crowd – even this crowd. But I was glad of the cudgels Robbie and Mungo carried.

We pushed and wriggled our way through the crowd, going always down towards the river. I had a sense that, with every yard, we were getting further from any contact with sanity and safety, deeper into horror. The buildings were yet more decrepit, the broken windows stuffed with rags, the doors hanging off their hinges. The street was full of broken glass, excrement, bones, disgusting rubbish of all kinds. The rain did not have a cleansing effect on the street but, instead, turned all its filth into a kind of loathsome broth, through which we almost had to wade. Still all the women and many of the men had bare legs and feet. They, like the buildings, looked even further down the scale of degradation than those near the Cross – their language was shriller and more uncouth, more of them were drunk, especially the younger women, their clothes were more tattered, and their faces and limbs more heavily smeared with the grime and slime of years. The stench was worse, too.

We came to a pawnbroker's shop, bigger than any of the rest, with a whisky-cellar on either side, and a roof half fallen-in far above in the weeping sky.

'This is the place,' I said, remembering the directions. 'This is where we turn off.'

Sure enough, opposite the pawnbroker's there was a narrow gap between the buildings, the mouth of one of the wynds, the little back-alleys of the quarter.

Robbie, with an uneasy face, started ahead of me into the alley. Something, before I followed him, made me glance round. Ten yards away, looking at me as fixedly as before, was the bloated man with a greasy greatcoat, and the gaunt man with the dirty lantern jaw and dirtier bonnet.

I was more than glad of the cudgels of my escorts; I thanked God for them.

The wynd twisted, narrowed to an arch no wider than a small doorway, and gave on to a little court, with a dunghill reeking and steaming in the centre. A dozen entrances gave on to the horrible little open space, either of houses or of other wynds. We were to take the second from the left. Dark faces looked at us from doorways, slatternly women, haggard and half-naked children, men skinny or bloated, maimed or dangerously powerful. I could see apathy and greed, misery and malice in their sick eyes.

As we threaded the entrance of the next wynd, I glanced back again. The bloated man and his thin black friend were there, at the edge of the court. What could have been chance could no longer be chance. They were following us. But there were only two, and I did not think they were a match for my sturdy guardians. Then, as I peeped round the corner, two other men shambled out of doorways to join the first two. The bloated man said something, and laughed, and all four followed us with their eyes.

We came to the next stinking little court. Beside the dungheap in its midst, full in the pelting rain, lay the body of a baby, unmistakably dead. I screamed, overwhelmed by the horror of the tiny blue-white body abandoned in the rain by the dungheap. Robbie Murray took my arm and hurried me past the body into the next wynd.

The four men behind us had become five. Robbie and Mungo knew they were there. I had a feeling that, though they were strong active men with sticks in their hands, they were becoming as frightened as I was. They would not have come, had they known where we were going. The Kilwillies would not have allowed us to go. We had stepped off the map into uncharted jungle. The men were frightened. I did not blame them then, and I do not do so now. Apart from the silent, savage band dogging our footsteps, we were in a world where ordinary human laws had no meaning: where, if a woman had a dead baby to dispose of, she dropped it by the dungheap in the nearest court . . .

We had to ask our way now, for Eugénie's directions were confused and sketchy, and the labyrinth of twisting wynds and little filthy courts was utterly perplexing. We asked an old woman, toothless and hairless, in rags, who only dribbled at us drunkenly. We asked a young girl, who was nursing a baby in a doorway from a breast as dirty as the ground at her feet. She replied indifferently; Robbie and Mungo had as much difficulty understanding her speech as I did, and they lived a bare ten miles away.

She sent us wrong, or we misunderstood her. We doubled back, and wearily explored wynd after wynd, court after horrible court, all looking very much alike in the rain and filth. We asked directions a dozen times. Twice I was spat upon. Eyes glared hungrily at my cloak and boots. The five men following us had become six or seven, as far as I could tell. They made no attempt to come closer, and none to hide themselves from us.

It was in my mind to give up, to run back to the comparative safety of the crowded street. But it seemed the greatest folly, the greatest waste, to go back after coming so far. I was sure that if I left Glasgow now I would never talk to John Anderson, and the most important question of all would remain for ever unanswered.

So we went on, and came at last to a court where a leaning gable almost cut out the sky, and a door with a sort of double arch had the dungheap as its mat. This was the place. This was the house described by the doctor in his letter to Eugénie.

A man in sea-boots came out of the double-arched door, and I asked for John Anderson. Without replying, he pointed up a flight of dark and narrow stairs immediately inside the door. My heart jumped. I put the men following us, the terrifying stench and squalor of the place, my fear and disgust, out of my mind, and started running up the stairs to get answers to my questions. Robbie and Mungo pounded after me. Almost at once we gave up any attempts at speed, for the stairs were so slippery with wet dirt that it would have been very easy to fall. Even indoors water seemed to pour everywhere. Moisture ran down the inside of the walls. There was a heavy, pervasive smell of rot, as well as of human filth and cheap tobacco and vermin.

We looked into successive rooms as we went up through the tall house, for the people here lived one above the other, like the drawers in a chest of drawers, instead of in cottages side by side. The first room I saw I thought must be a stable or pigsty, until, after an instant, I saw the absurdity of getting animals up such stairs. But it was impossible to believe that it was an apartment where people lived. A mass of stinking, filthy straw, mixed with a few greasy rags, covered part of the floor. That was all. There was nothing else. There was no furniture. Some of the rooms boasted a stool or two, but most had only the piles of straw, from which a pig would have recoiled.

In one room there were three emaciated children lying huddled together on the straw. I started in; Robbie pulled me out, muttering of fever. In another, an old man sat amongst the straw coughing painfully and endlessly. The stench in that room was very bad.

I called to him, nervously, 'John Anderson?'

He could not speak for his terrible dry cough, but he pointed upwards with a pipestem arm.

And so we came at last, at the very top of the house, to a little room under a steep-pitched roof. Its only window was a small skylight, a pane of glass in the roof, through the sides of which the rainwater dribbled. One wall sloped to within a foot of the floor. There had been a door in the doorway, but all that remained of it was one broken hinge.

On the floor lay a man whom I immediately, in despair, took to be dead. His eyes were closed. His face was unimaginably old, a dirty white curiously blotched with brownish patches, with here and there on face and skull a wisp of straggling white hair. He did not seem to be breathing. He was almost covered by the straw, with only his head clear of it, as though someone had pushed it over him out of respect for the dead.

'John Anderson,' I said drearily.

'Ay,' piped a thin high voice at my feet.

I jumped.

The eyelids flickered and opened. Understanding came slowly, slowly into the glazed old eyes. He sighed with infinite weariness, mumbled complainingly, and passed a trembling hand, thin as a skeleton's, over his face.

At last his eyes focussed on my face, as I sank to my knees by the straw. And then I saw it once again – the shudder of astonishment, the start of unmistakable recognition.

I forgot everything – Robbie and Mungo standing awkward and nervous behind me, the horror of what I had seen, fright of what was to come.

I pushed the hood back from my head, so that the old man could see the colour of my hair. He gazed at it. His eyes wandered over my face. His hand began to shake so badly that I thought he was falling into a fit.

I took his hand, and said, 'I am James Drummond's granddaughter.'

He nodded, almost imperceptibly. His face was full of wonder, and his hand shook in mine.

I asked him about a game of hazard, fifty years earlier, in a stuffy room with an unnecessary fire.

He looked bemused. He did not speak. His eyelids sagged over his eyes, and rose again reluctantly, slowly. He made no effort to lift his head from the straw. He did not know what I was talking about. He heard my words but he could not understand them. He had forgotten. His mind had gone, after half a century during every day of which he had deadened the pain of his ancient wounds with whisky bought by his pension.

Urgently, desperately, I reminded him about James Drummond, about Edinburgh, about that last awful night.

Robbie and Mungo shifted their feet behind me. They were nervous and impatient. The afternoon was wearing on. This was all taking far longer than any of us had expected.

John Anderson's face flickered when I mentioned Eugénie, but still he said nothing, but only stared at my face with a look of wonder and despair.

'There was a last throw,' I cried, almost in tears with desperation. 'A final throw, with a huge, mad wager. You were there! You were his servant! You were filling their glasses with wine! You saw! You heard the wager! You were frightened, horrified – you would not tell Eugénie . . .'

'Ay,' piped the old voice suddenly. 'I was there. I haird the wager Glendraco made. The cassel an' the lands an' the siller –

a' bet on yin thraw o' the dice. It mebbe seemit creeminal folly, but 'twas nae siccan thing. I kenned Glendraco! He was no' fou, the laird. For the ither mon, he bet a strange bet. Ay, he mad' a great wager, a monstrous wager. Glendraco cudna refuse yon bet, for he was wishfu' wi' a' his soul tae win wha' the ither wagerit . . .'

'What did the other wager, John?'

'His wumman.'

'*What?*'

'His wife. I dinna mind his name, nor hers. But I mind her. She was the mistress o' my French lassie, an unco' bonny leddy wi' een like a bairn's . . . Her mon wagerit *her*, tae match Glendraco's bet o' cassel, an' lands, an' siller . . .'

'James Drummond,' I faltered, 'would have won his opponent's wife . . .'

'Ay, an' blithe tae tak' her. But the dice fell wrang an' wrang. The ither held the wife, an' gainit Glendraco an' a' . . . Sae Drummond o' Glendraco rid doon tae the strand, an' sought obleevion in the waves o' the sea . . .'

'It was mad,' I murmured, 'but it was not *mad* . . .'

John Anderson began to whimper, and to struggle with the hand I was not holding under the filthy straw. I helped him, and presently he drew the hand from beneath the straw, holding a bottle he had been hiding there. But he was too weak to raise his head to drink, or to carry the bottle to his mouth.

I called to Robbie and Mungo, who hurried up and crouched by the straw.

'Sud the auld yin drink, Miss?' asked Robbie dubiously.

'Perhaps not,' I said, 'but he wants to.'

So between the three of us, we lifted him to a sitting position, and held the bottle to his white lips. Some of the whisky ran down his chin. Some went down his throat, so that he choked.

Over the dreadful rattle of his choking I heard a noise in the doorway. I looked up.

The bloated man with the greasy greatcoat stood, filling the doorway, with other men just visible behind him. He said something I could not understand. He advanced into the little room with a long knife in his hand. The others came and stood, in a tight pack beside and behind him. One or two grinned wolfishly, but most had an expression of cold indifference.

The leader was staring at me with his little red-rimmed pig eyes. He barked some kind of order, gesturing with the point of his knife. I could not understand what he said, but his meaning was clear. He was telling me to stand up and walk over to him. Had I been willing, I could not have done so, for terror had taken all the strength from my limbs.

Robbie Murray and Mungo Dick knelt, frozen into immobility, by John Anderson's pile of straw. Both looked frightened but defiant. Both had their cudgels ready to their hands.

In a body the newcomers crossed the little dark room, which now seemed packed with people. They brought with them a wave of acrid animal stench. They surrounded us as we crouched on the floor. The leader no longer had a pipe in his teeth or a bottle in his hand, but only the long wicked knife. He reached down and took hold of my arm, just below the shoulder. He began to pull me to my feet.

Robbie and Mungo both jumped to their feet, holding their cudgels. Robbie, brandishing his cudgel, shouted to the bloated man to release me. One of the newcomers hit him behind the knees with a club, so that he yelped with pain and collapsed backwards. Then all the newcomers except the leader hurled themselves at my guardians. There was a wild, brief struggle, almost in silence. John Anderson was underneath it all. His straw was hurled everywhere. The bloated man had both my arms twisted behind my back, so that I could not move without agony. I screamed and screamed again. He clapped a forearm over my face, without releasing the grip of his other hand on my wrists. His great arm, like a ham in the greasy coatsleeve, hid the fight from my eyes. I heard desperate grunting, whimpers of pain, blasphemy, a high thin cry like that of a wounded hare . . . then silence.

The bloated man took his arm from my face. I screamed again, but it was a little scream of utter despair. Robbie and Mungo both lay in horrible, unnatural attitudes, very still and quiet, among the straw and rags of the bed. Robbie's face was a mask of blood. Mungo lay half across the skinny, tattered figure of John Anderson. The old man lay flat on his back, as still as they. His face looked as though it had been crushed by an enormous rock.

The attackers were panting and dishevelled. None seemed hurt. The two who had grinned wolfishly were still doing so; the rest, who had looked coldly indifferent, still did so.

One of the pack picked up John Anderson's bottle and raised it to his lips.

They began to strip the bodies of Robbie and Mungo, mouthing comments about the quality of the clothes and the contents of the pockets. They stripped the bodies naked, and divided up the clothes among themselves. The coins they found, one silver snuffbox, and one leather-covered flask, they surrendered to the leader, who grunted and dropped them in the pocket of his greatcoat.

He never loosed his grip, all this time, of my wrists behind my back. It was very painful, but I was so sick with horror that I hardly felt the pain.

Most of the band now left, carrying clothes looted from the bodies of Robbie and Mungo. Two carried also their useless cudgels.

Three men remained – the bloated leader, the cadaverous man with the dirty lantern jaw, and a small man with quick black eyes and black curls.

They took me downstairs. The small man led, going cautiously, spying out the ground as he went, and turning back to gesture that all was safe. We reached the court. It was almost dark, and still raining. My captor pulled me hard against his flank, so that as we crossed the court we seemed to be lovers. I tried to pull away, sick with revulsion, but he twisted my wrists behind my back so that I sobbed with the pain.

They took me a short distance, along wynds like all the others, across courts like all the others, to a house like all the others. It came to me then, with a dizzying shock, that an army could search the Saltmarket and never find me.

We went up two flights of stairs, and I was pushed into a room where there were a dozen people. One candle lit the room, which had straw and rags on the floor, and nothing else. There were two men, eight or ten women, and a few children.

My captor called a name. A big woman dressed only in a ragged shift came forward. He told her, in words and in a dialect that will not go down on paper, to make sure that I did not get away. He would come back for me, the next day or the day after, with a purchaser. As payment for this task, she and the others could have my clothes.

There was a subdued, animal growling from the others in the room. With the most shocking oaths, the bloated man promised disgusting mutilation to all of them if I was allowed to escape. The three men left. The room had a stout door; the big woman in the shift closed and bolted it.

Then all the women crept forward, and once again I was surrounded. They said that they would take my clothes now, as payment in advance for guarding me. They laid hands on me, and tried to strip off my cloak. I struggled, pushing away their hands, twisting and turning. One woman seized handfuls of my hair, and jerked my head backwards; at the same moment the big woman slapped me hard across the face with her open hand. They threw me down upon the straw. Though I struggled still, they were far too many for me. They stripped every stitch of clothing from me, chattering and screeching all the time, stinking and verminous, greedy and cruel.

When I lay panting, sobbing, exhausted, as naked as the day I was born, I remembered that there were two men in the room. One, an old man, seemed to be asleep. The other was looking at me with a lop-sided smile, wet-lipped. He was a tall, gaunt, big-boned man, with a shock of red hair, about thirty. He seemed, like some of the others, to have undressed for the night, for he was wearing only a long shirt. He looked strong. He looked drunk.

I covered myself, as best I could, with straw and rags. I could hardly bear to lay my head on such filthy material, but there was no choice. I cringed at the greasy touch of the bedding on my bare skin, at the loathsome straw pressed against my thighs, my breasts, my stomach.

The others settled themselves all about me on the straw, screeching to each other about my boots and silk underclothes. They would not keep them to wear, but sell them to buy whisky and perhaps food.

I wondered, numbly, in utter despair, what was to become of me. The bloated man had said he would return with a purchaser. Not of my clothes. Of what?

I remembered Lord Kilwillie quoting a conversation with a Sheriff of the city, who said that in the slums of East Glasgow the main sources of revenue were theft and prostitution.

Theft I had seen – theft and bloody murder.

But prostitution? Was somebody being brought here to purchase – me?

sixteen

I had had occasion, during the previous extraordinary year, to think myself unhappy. I had railed at my ill-fortune, and thought myself the most wretched creature on earth. How stupid! How little I had really to complain of – how supremely lucky I really was! Marriage to Cricklade would have been tolerable. Marriage to Findlay Nicholson, even, would have been paradise compared to *this*. Rape by Caerlaverock – humiliation and disgrace at the hands of Draco – I would have submitted to gladly and thankfully, if it meant escape from *this*. Death among the hurtling rocks on Meiklejohn's Leap, death when hurled from Falcon's saddle on the hillside, I would have welcomed with joy, if it meant escape from *this*.

The others in the room settled themselves to sleep all round me – men, women, children, filthy and evil-smelling, disgusting as rats, dangerous and merciless as wolves. I peeped through half-closed lids, seeing my unspeakable prison through wisps of greasy straw. In the dim, flickering light of the single candle my captors looked like creatures of hell, scarcely human, goblins and devils, obscene animals. The harsh chatter of the women was gradually stilled as they settled their division of my clothes. The old man was snoring. A child whimpered in its sleep. The women laid themselves down to sleep in the straw, some still fully dressed in their rags, some in shreds of dirty underclothes, some naked. The tall man in the shirt sat in a corner, looking fixedly in my direction, wearing still his lascivious lop-sided smile. The big woman who had hit me snuffed out the candle. I heard her settle herself across the door, to bar my escape.

Numbly I mourned for Robbie Murray and Mungo Dick, whom I had led to their deaths. I mourned for John Anderson, who had died because of me. I mourned for myself, for I was as good as dead.

James Drummond had killed himself in despair, in a dark night of the soul, because he had lost everything he had, and lost the woman he loved to distraction. Like grandfather, like grand-daughter. I had inherited his face; I would inherit his death. He was not mad; nor was I. He faced the future with repugnance, and preferred to end his life; so did I. Whatever God's law about self-destruction, whatever punishment awaited me for my presumptuous sin, I would kill myself. I faced the thought calmly. The dark unknown of death held no terrors for me, compared to what life promised. If there was a knife in the room, I would use that; if a bottle, I would smash it, and use a sliver of glass. If there was no sharp weapon I would throw myself out of the window, and smash my skull on the greasy stones of the court, and there would be another dead naked body in the rain beside a dung-heap.

So be it. I prayed for resolution. I prayed for speedy opportunity. I prayed that my body would be smashed or pierced before it was defiled. I did not pray for forgiveness, but only for a clear chance and a steady hand.

The child whimpered again, hungry in its sleep. The room was pitch dark, full of the sound of breathing, muttering, bodies shifting amongst the straw. There was a cold, damp draught from the broken window. I felt the filthy bedding between my bare legs and between my bare breasts and against my cheek. I decided, suddenly, that I could not and would not wait until morning. The bloated man would be back – who knew when? – with a purchaser for my body. Perhaps early. I must be dead before he came.

I could not search for a knife in the dark, nor for a bottle to break into needle-sharp slivers. There might be no such thing in the room. If there were, I would not find it. If I hunted about, they would realize what I was planning, and tie me up.

It was the window, then. I planned, coldly, how I would manage it. I lay eight feet from the window. Between the window and myself lay two women, the whimpering child, and the old man. There was no glass in the window; once there had been small leaded panes, but now there was only a piece of sacking. I thought deeply, to remember exactly what I had seen of the window before the candle was snuffed out. It was high, but I could reach up and grasp the sill and pull myself up, and wriggle through. I was sure of that. It was a small window of the antique sort, with a pointed top like a church door, but there was room for my slim body to go through. If I grazed the skin from my hips and shoulders, it was no great matter. It was no matter at all. I must go through head first, and when my weight was far enough out I must dive, head first, to the ground. It was not a great height, but if I fell right it would be enough. My head must strike the ground first. I was quite clear about that. The stones of the court would do the rest.

I began to tremble violently. I felt sick at the prospect. My resolution wavered. I was very frightened of what I was about to do. But then, inside my head, I shouted my weakness down. The thought of life was far more dreadful than the thought of even so horrible a death.

The big woman who was guarding the door was much stronger than I. I knew that from the size of her arms and shoulders, and from the weight of her hand when she slapped me across the face. If she caught me, she could pull me back and toss me across the room. But she was by the door, at the farthest point from the window. It was not so very far. She could cross the room in a few strides. Once I started, then, I must be very quick. I decided to wait a little, until they were all more deeply asleep. The man in the shirt – where was he? He had been by the door, too, sitting against the wall. Probably he was still there, as another guard on the door.

I knew I was right to wait, but, as I waited, my courage drained away. My whole body trembled in the straw, my heart thudded in my throat, and I could scarcely breathe. I could not do it. I did not dare. No matter what nightmares tomorrow promised, I could not push myself out through the window to my death.

Then, as I thought about the morrow, a succession of obscene images gibbered at my mind. What would happen? The possibilities gaped at me like half-seen monsters in a swirling fog, so that I writhed and trembled and cringed as I lay. And so my courage returned, because the alternative to death was worse than any death.

The room was quiet. The whimpering child was still. All about me was the slow breathing of deep sleep. I was frightened of my own fright – frightened that, if I waited any longer, my courage would desert me again.

Now.

I got carefully to my feet, making no more than a faint rustle in the straw. The damp air was cold on my bare skin. I stepped the three paces to the wall where the window was, going delicately, avoiding the sleeping people. I groped upwards in the dark. The wall was wet, and felt greasy. I felt the window-sill. I blessed the pitch darkness of the rainy night. My resolution was firm. I tensed myself to jump up and on to the window-sill.

I felt a hand seize my ankle. It was the hard, painful grip of a hard hand. It was the grip of a man's hand – of the gaunt man in a shirt who had looked at me with a drunken, lop-sided smile.

The hand let go of my ankle, and instantly two arms went about my waist. The arms pulled me away from the wall, and threw me violently down on to the straw on my back. Then the owner of the arms was on top of me. His breath reeked of whisky and cheap tobacco, and his body smelled rancid with sweat and dirt. He still wore his shirt, but he had pulled it up round his shoulders. The rest of him was as naked as I. I struggled madly, but he was far too strong for me. I felt a knee thrust itself between my knees, then two knees, pushing my legs apart. A hard hand was across my mouth, hurting, me, gagging me. I scratched and tore at the hand across my face, but I could not move it. I felt his other hand thrust between his body and mine. I felt it go over my breast, gripping and squeezing painfully. The hard, bony knees were forcing my legs further and further apart, while the weight of his body kept me pinned down upon the straw.

I fought insanely, ferociously, with mad fury, scratching and tugging at the hand on my face, trying to twist my hips away from his. But he seemed not to feel my teeth or my fingernails. The acrid, animal smell of his breath and his unwashed body filled my nostrils, in spite of the hand across my mouth, filling me with sick disgust. I could hear his heavy breathing. My own sobs and cries were stifled by his hand. I expected at any second the stabbing, tearing invasion of my body.

There was a spark of light, then a flame. Flint-and-steel had lit tinder, and tinder the stump of a candle. Immediately there was a big, solid crash inches from my face. The body which lay on top of mine went limp. I felt something warm and wet upon my cheek. My face was freed from the throttling hand, my breast from the horrible grip of those bruising fingers. The body was pulled off mine. It was the gaunt man, unconscious, his shirt under his armpits, bleeding from a wound on the back of his head. It was that blood I had felt on my cheek.

The big woman in the shift grunted with satisfaction, and rolled the unconscious man over, away from me. I wondered if he were dead. I did not care. She still clutched the bottle with which she had clubbed the man. Beside her was another woman, a hag in a shift so ragged that she might as well have been as naked as I was. The hag held the candle. Her face and the big woman's were ghastly in the candlelight.

'I'll no' hae ma mon plaisuring anither,' said the big woman in a surly and threatening voice. 'Tak' heed, or I'll dint yer heid for ye.' She gestured with the bottle towards my own head.

I sat up slowly in the straw, bruised and panting, the sobs jumping in my throat. I wiped the man's blood off my cheek with my forearm, and looked at it stupidly.

There were complaining murmurs from all about the room, from women whose sleep had been disturbed. The whimpering child was whimpering again. The old man snored on.

The big woman said something to the hag with the candle. The hag cackled and nodded, and somewhere found some strips of rag. The big woman tied my ankles together, and then tied together my wrists behind my back. She made no further remark, to me or to any of the others. She grunted again, satisfied with her knots, and the hag blew out the candle.

The room settled itself to sleep again. Apart from complaining about being disturbed, none of the other people made any comment, or seemed in any way surprised by what had happened. None did anything to help the unconscious man. None had given me more than an incurious glance. To them, to women and young children alike, an unconscious man with a bloody head, a naked girl prisoner lashed at the wrists and ankles, were part of an ordinary night.

I lay back in the filthy straw, the bonds painfully tight. I was trussed like a chicken for whatever 'purchaser' was brought to inspect me.

My state was worse than before. Even the alternative of death was now denied me.

Dawn peeped through the sacking on the unattainable window. I had not slept, but lain in miserable discomfort of body and agony of spirit. I prayed for a miracle, because nothing else would save me.

My companions woke slowly, reluctantly, to the new day. They rubbed their eyes, spat, yawned, pulled on their clothes. By daylight they looked even more wretched, even more menacing, than by night.

Some looked at me as incuriously as before, some ignored me. The gaunt man groaned. His hair matted with dried blood.

After a time most of the women went out, some to steal food, some to sell my clothes in the mean little shops of the Salt-market, some (as I realized from their talk) to sell their bodies, for a few minutes and a few pence, to foreign sailors on the Broomielaw.

I was to be of their sisterhood. By nightfall, no doubt, I would have earned a shilling or two for my new owner. But by that time, if my most heartfelt prayers were answered, I would have found a new chance of killing myself.

It was still raining outside. The room was damp and, in spite of the season, cold. My wrists and ankles were still tied up. The physical discomfort would have been intolerable, but it was swamped by the spiritual agony.

Hours passed. People came and went. Some of the women who had gone out with my clothes came back with food and whisky and snuff. The food was of the cheapest kinds – sowens made from husks of oats, and the kind of brose called crowdie, a thin distasteful gruel of meal and water. I was not given any food. I could not have eaten. I could feel, on my cheek some of the dried blood from the gaunt man's head which I had not wiped off on my arm. I could see, on my breast, the bruises left by his hand, and on my thighs the bruises made by his knees. I was dirty from the greasy straw in which I had spent the night; I could feel straw clinging to my hair, and see blackish wisps clinging to my legs and loins.

The man with the bloated face came into the room. He looked round quickly, with vivid suspicion, and a hand hidden under his greasy greatcoat. I was sure the hand held the knife I had seen. He saw me and his face relaxed. He called to someone outside. A stranger came into the room, a dark-skinned man with thick lips, and with eyes as bright and black as Eugénie's. He was much better dressed than anyone I had seen in the slums, with a tall silk hat and shiny boots. He came and stood over me, licking his thick lips. His eyes flickered up and down my naked body. He seemed to approve of what he saw, for he grinned and licked his lips again. He squatted down beside me, and inspected me with his hands as well as with his eyes. He prodded and squeezed my body, every part of it. He even forced open my mouth, and inspected my teeth. I wanted to scream; I cringed away from his lascivious exploring fingers, but I was still helplessly trussed like a chicken, lying naked on my back on the straw.

At last he went away into a corner of the room with the bloated man who was selling me. They had a long discussion in low voices. Constantly their eyes flickered across the room to where I lay. The bloated man seemed to be holding out for more than the swarthy man would give. At last the bloated man shrugged. Coins changed hands. I watched, with horrified fascination, wondering numbly how much I had fetched.

So it was that I did not see the door open quietly again, nor see that a newcomer stood in the doorway with others behind him until I heard a grave voice say, 'That looks like your man, Inspector.'

Draco had found me. My heart was flooded with joy and thankfulness. I almost laughed aloud, but instead burst into tears.

Draco came a pace into the room, looking about, frowning. Five men, neatly dressed but powerful looking, came in after him. Four made straight for the buyer and seller in the corner, while the fifth remained on guard by the door. The bloated man drew his knife, but before he could use it a truncheon descended on his wrist. He shouted an oath and dropped the knife. Within seconds handcuffs were on both men.

There were screams and ape-like chattering from the women in the room. Half a dozen rushed at the policemen, clawing and screeching. They were subdued, pushed aside, with calm severity.

Draco saw me as I lay. In two strides he was beside me. I thought he would look away, from delicacy, when he saw that I was lying naked on my back. But he did not. He devoured me with his eyes. I felt my whole body blushing in furious embarrassment. I burned for my hands to be free, so that I could cover my nakedness with them: but I could do nothing but lie as I was for his eyes.

He said hoarsely, 'My darling girl, are you hurt? What have they done to you?'

'Tied me up,' I sobbed happily.

He knelt down at once, taking out a small pocket-knife. In a second my ankles were free. I rolled over, so that he could cut the rags that bound my wrists. I felt them freed.

Now I would have expected myself, as soon as I could move, to hide myself in some way – to cover my nakedness before the Earl of Draco – to spread my open hands, at least, over my body. I blush even now to think what I actually did. I rose to my knees on the straw, turned to face him, and threw my arms round his neck. We embraced long and passionately, and he kissed my brow and my hair and my lips, and I felt his arms blessedly about me and his hands on my back.

'I am all right,' I managed to tell him between our desperate kisses. 'I have not been hurt, or . . . anything.'

'Come,' he said into my cheek. 'I'll take you away, darling Kirstie.'

'Oh yes.'

'On one condition.'

'Anything.'

'That you promise to marry me.'

'Oh well,' I murmured, 'if that is the condition, I shall have to say yes.'

So he wrapped me in his greatcoat. He said my feet would not get any dirtier than they were, from walking barefoot as far as his carriage. He had a few words with the Inspector of Police, thanking the men and congratulating them. He said I would be available to give evidence at the trials. I nodded, but I could not see or speak for my tears of happiness.

'I came home,' said Draco in his carriage, 'to find that you had gone to Kilwillie with the Duchess. I thought nothing of that. Everyone seemed to agree that you would be better for a rest and a change—'

'I am,' I said. 'Much better.'

He laughed and kissed me. At last he said, 'Then Eugénie mentioned something to my grandmother.'

'Ah,' I said. 'Thank God she did.'

'I do so,' said Draco gravely. 'I persuaded the two of them to tell me – a number of things I did not know. I also induced Dr McPhee to commit a certain breach of professional confidence. So I realized, my beloved girl, that you were afraid you had inherited . . .'

'Yes.'

He burst out, 'How could you think such a thing? How could you possibly be such an idiot as to think . . .'

Realizing how absurd his remark was about to turn out, he checked himself and smiled. The smile lifted the corners of his mouth like the ends of a recurved longbow, and his grey eyes, as he smiled at me, had the sweet directness of a child's.

Without thought, modesty, hesitation or any dignity, I flung my arms round his neck, and he kissed me, and I kissed the corners of his mouth, which were still lifted by his adorable smile.

'At any rate,' he went on at last, sitting with his arm about my shoulder, and my head against his shoulder, 'I realized you were desperate to learn from old John Anderson what happened that dreadful night to – cause the events of the following dawn. That, in fact, you were proposing to venture into the worst and most lawless slums in the world – you, the most beautiful girl in Scotland!'

'Am I?' I asked innocently.

'Quite how beautiful,' he said gravely, 'even I never realized until today.'

'It was very rude of you to stare.'

'I know. But after we are married I intend to do it a great deal of the time.'

This thought was too much for me. I buried my face in his chest. It was some little time before conversation could be resumed.

'I followed you down here,' he said at last, 'and arrived at Kilwillie yesterday evening to find them in a state of some anxiety. The three of you had disappeared, the carriage was still at an hotel, nobody knew where to look for you ... Of course Kilwillie should never have let you go without a dozen men, but he simply did not know – none of them knew – what conditions prevailed in that hellish place. It happened that I did know. I had never been into the worst slums – I had scarcely ever been to Glasgow – but I had read an official report about them, written only a few years ago. I was therefore even more alarmed than the others were.'

'But how did you find me?'

'It took all night. Fortunately the police employ a number of informers, who are quite happy to betray their friends for a shilling. One of these estimable people heard your red-haired friend boasting in a whisky-cellar about a girl he had found ... That information led us, ultimately, to the house where John Anderson lived—'

'Oh! Are they ... Were they ...?'

'He is dead. I am very sorry. He had only a short time to live, I think, at best.'

'But – the others?'

'Alive. Robbie Murray was hit on the head, no more. He was already conscious, though not rational, when we found him. He will need a long rest, but he is in no danger. Mungo Dick suffered a stab-wound in the back – a typical injury in that quarter of Glasgow – but he is strong and healthy, and the surgeons are confident about him.'

'I must see them both.'

'Yes. And now tell me, my precious love, *did* you find out . . .?'

'I found out,' I said, 'that my grandfather was mad, you understand, but not *mad*. He was desperately in love with your grandmother—'

'My God,' said Draco, very startled. 'Are you sure?'

'Yes, quite sure. That is what I found out. It was losing her, as well as everything else, that sent him . . . into the sea at dawn.'

'And now,' said Draco, 'her grandson is desperately in love with his granddaughter.'

'And,' I admitted, 'his granddaughter is desperately in love with her grandson.'

'Your heart, Kirstie, has it – truly changed so much?'

'It hasn't changed at all,' I explained.

'But you told me I was . . .'

'Yes, but I thought I was bound to go mad, you see.'

'That is what I still cannot understand. *You*, the bravest, sanest, clearest-headed—'

'I am not clear-headed just now,' I said into his shoulder. 'And I was not feeling very brave last night.'

'But *how* could *you* have thought—'

'Well, it is how I was brought up, you know, with a terrible stigma, a horror that must not be mentioned. And they said, and truly believed, that I must never marry, that I must never have children . . . I believed it, too. That is why I was so horrid to you in the snow, when Rockfall wanted a game . . .'

So we bounced along in his carriage, with the rain beating on the roof and the windows, locked in each others' arms. I think he kissed every bit of my face, and I think I kissed every bit of his. I was decently wrapped in his enormous greatcoat, and had a rug round my legs also: and although it is dreadful to admit it, there was a longing in me to be embraced by him as I had been in

367

the horrible room in the slum, with his arms round my bare back, and his shirt-front pressed into my bare breasts.

They were all very kind to me at Kilwillie. Draco managed to smuggle me upstairs (I think he gave a sovereign to a housemaid) in my peculiar clothes, and barefooted, and by the time the others saw me I was a respectable young lady again. At least outwardly.

We did not precisely announce our betrothal. That would have been premature. Draco's grandmother had to be told first; and he had to approach my Strachan grandparents also, and reassure them about my mental state. We did not announce anything; but I do not think we were good at concealing our feelings. I was not surprised at myself – I knew that I had never been good at pretending, or dissimulating. But I *was* surprised that Draco allowed himself to smile at me so constantly and so lovingly, and to take my hand, at every chance that offered, with such poor attempts at hiding what he was doing.

I went to bed early, cooed over by the Duchess, and Lady Kilwillie, and a number of maids. I convinced them all at last that I had come to no harm, and needed no doctors or physics, or a week in a darkened room, or a medicinal visit to Harrogate or Scarborough.

I remembered my prayers, and wept long and happily into my pillow.

I went to see Robbie Murray, who lived in an apartment in a wing of the coach-house. His wife looked at me reproachfully, but Robbie was composed, though quiet, and said his head had almost stopped aching. Mungo Dick had been brought into the big house itself, to be nursed better. The surgeons had wanted to keep him in hospital in Glasgow, but he wanted none of that, and Lady Kilwillie supported him. He was much worse hurt than Robbie, but much more cheerful. He would not have it that I was in any way the cause of his wound. He was delighted that the bloated man had been arrested, and said he looked forward to the trial.

I thought the Kilwillies were lucky in their servants, and the servants were lucky in the Kilwillies. Each had earned the affection and respect of the other. I hoped that, when the time came, I would do as well at Glendraco. I mentioned this to Draco. He replied, 'You have already earned much respect, my darling, and I am sure you will earn much more. But it's nonsense for you to speak of earning affection. Other people may earn it, but not you. You don't need to. It comes to you, floods at you, from men and women and children and animals, Duchesses and mongrel dogs. People open their hearts to you, as morning-glory flowers open to the sun. That is because you are not a person at all, but a cross between an angel and an urchin—'

He went on like that until, tired of talking, he kissed me instead. It was an intensely agreeable way of passing the time. I would never have suspected that my solemn beloved was so good at pretty speeches; I would never have suspected he was so good at kissing, either.

We went home to Glendraco. The weather had cleared, and we had a golden journey. But, as we covered the last miles down the Draco Glen, clouds hurried up from the west and one of the sudden summer storms threatened. The heavens opened just as we crossed the drawbridge, in the evening, and we ran, laughing, through sheets of rain into the great hall. We were not expected until the next day; there were no ranks of smiling and bowing servants welcoming their master home; the great hall was dark and deserted. Draco and I smiled at each other; and he helped me off with my wet cloak.

Then he seized me, as though bent on murder, and kissed me with an almost brutal ardour.

'In my own house, darling,' he murmured into my cheek. 'In your home, my darling Kirstie.'

I tightened my arms round his neck. I, too, was getting very good at kissing, owing to intensive practice over the last few days.

It was, perhaps, unfortunate that Mrs Forbes and the Reverend Lancelot Barrow, together, should have crossed the hall at that moment.

They disappeared clucking in dismay, like hens in the stable-yard chased by Rockfall, until I taught him better.

Draco grinned at me ruefully. 'I meant to keep the secret a little longer,' he said, 'as we did at Kilwillie.'

I laughed outright. But though he pressed me, I would not tell him why I laughed. I loved him with all my soul, but ... I did not think it wise to tease him about the smiles he had given me at Kilwillie, not one of which went unobserved by the others. Of course, I knew by now that he was by no means as depressingly solemn as I had first thought him. But still, he had solemn patches. He was a great nobleman, and a figure in the government. He was important; he was, perhaps, self-important. He could not be blamed – only very gradually changed. He must have been told a thousand times, by toadies and women, that he was extraordinarily handsome; he was far too intelligent not to realize that it was true. He must have been deferred to a thousand times, his opinion asked and treated with exaggerated respect; he was far too intelligent not to realize that his opinions were entitled to respect – but not always, perhaps, as Holy Writ. In spite of his scar, and the reason for his scar, he was entitled to have a high opinion of himself. I could *come* to laugh at him, and make him laugh at himself – but not all at once. We loved each other very much, but I knew I must still be careful, and treat him with respect, and tread gently.

We later sat, with the Countess, in her sitting-room upstairs. Outside, rain borne by a gale-force wind hurled itself at the windows. Inside, golden lamplight gleamed on the two marvellous faces which I loved so well – which, although separated by nearly fifty years in age, were so startlingly alike.

'So,' said the Dragon in her most terrible voice, 'you model your behaviour on stable-boys and scullery-maids, and steal furtive kisses behind doors. Is that the example of behaviour you contemplate setting?'

'If we have set a shameless example to Cousin Amy Forbes,' said Draco mildly, 'I hope she will not be tempted into some scandalous indiscretion.'

The Dragon's terrible frown seemed to waver, and then to disappear from her brow. The corners of her mouth rose, and she stretched out her arms to me. Then she joined our hands, and held them between her two hands, and said she was truly happy for the second time, only, in her life.

'Of course I should have foreseen this,' she said. 'I daresay, in my heart, I did. You, darling child, are the image of your grandfather in soul as you are in face. Neil here is said to be very like me, although I have never found the comparison so very flattering ... What could be more natural than for history to repeat itself? You have clearly inherited from your grandfather, Kirstie, an unfortunate disposition to fall in love with anybody who looks like me. And you, my dear sobersides grandson, have inherited from me a disposition to fall in love, desperately and violently in love, with anybody who looks like James Drummond ... Oh yes. Did not Eugénie tell you? Did she say only that *he* ...? Did not John Anderson tell you? The soul-consuming fire of his love for me was matched, ay, more than matched, by my love for him. What romantical stuff I am talking! But ordinary words are no good to me, if I am to make you understand ... I do not know what would have happened, if he had lived. A terrible scandal, even in those days, when behaviour was freer than it is now ... We both bore famous names. He was one of the richest men in Scotland, as well as the handsomest and bravest and best-loved. I was – not unknown, not unwelcome where I went. Marriage between us would have been almost miraculously suitable. But we were both married before we met – we both had young children ... He was thirty-two years old, I five years younger, when we met, in Edinburgh, for the first time. It was strange we had not met before. If we had met, at any time, in any place, we would have loved one another at once ...'

Still holding our clasped hands between her hands, the Countess leaned back in her chair and closed her eyes. I thought she was tired, and should rest by herself. But she started speaking again, with her eyes closed, in a low, clear voice.

'My husband,' she said, 'was an amiable but weak man. You get from him, Neil, nothing whatever, that I can see. He inherited a moderate fortune but not a great one. Both he and the fortune needed looking after, and for a few years I had done my best. I had looked after him, moderately well. His reputation and his health were both better than he deserved. But, as to the fortune, that I could *not* protect. Of course he dealt with the bankers and lawyers and men of business – I never saw them. He dealt with the money-lenders, too, and mortgaged his estate, and pawned my jewels. Like many people at that time, he gambled. Horses, gamecocks, boxers, dice, cards – it was the passion of that age. He was in desperate straits at the time I met James Drummond – I did not learn till afterwards how desperate. That is his excuse for what happened. *And* he saw what was in James Drummond's eyes, and what was in my eyes. He thought he was losing me. He was right. He thought he was losing me because Drummond had a great fortune, and he had only debts. He was quite wrong . . .'

She did not move. Her voice did not change. Her eyes did not open. The grip of her hands on our hands tightened.

'We were in despair, all of us,' she said. 'My husband, who had lost everything, and was losing me. James Drummond, who would come to me from his young wife and baby son, cursing himself, for his treachery. I, who would go to him from my own nursery, disgusted at myself, but powerless to resist my love for him, and glorying in his love for me . . .'

Her voice rose to a wail of misery, and her hands began to tremble.

'Oh then,' she cried, 'in an overheated room, when they had both drunk too much wine, the dice-boxes were brought out—'

'Stop,' I begged her. 'I know what happened! I know what the stake was! Don't torture yourself—'

Her voice sank to a whisper. 'Ay,' she murmured, 'you know the stake my husband wagered, against the castle I am now living in, and the jewels I am now wearing . . . You know that he was so desperate for money, that he bet – what he bet. What you do not know – what only I know, because I was at my husband's side at the gaming-table . . .'

Her voice came to a low and breathless stop. Her eyes were open now, but looking blindly inwards at the scene she was re-living.

She said, 'My husband cheated.'

The rain had stopped; but a still more violent wind battered at the windows of the quiet, dim-lit room.

I glanced from the Countess's face to her grandson's. I found his eyes fast on mine; but he turned from me, with the black frown I had grown to know so well, and thought never to see again; he stared at his grandmother.

He said, 'Knowing this, how could you live at Glendraco?'

She said, in a weary voice, 'It belonged to my husband. It was his house. How could I not live here? James was dead. I was ill, with the shock of the game and the shock of his death – I was delirious for days and nights. I was – quite as distraught as my lover – but I was not a man – I did not have his courage ... When I came at last truly to my senses, I found myself in a bed here. The papers had all been signed. There were witnesses to the wager. The details were kept secret, but the legal title was good. James's widow never returned here. She did not want to, without him. She never had liked living in so remote a place. She stayed in Edinburgh, becoming pious and something of a recluse ... My husband paid her a pension which, as he often said, he was in no way legally obliged to do ... He himself was – transformed by those events. Wealth does not bring happiness, they say. Perhaps not. But to him, great wealth, great responsibilities, brought a new way of life. He never touched a card or a pair of dice again. He scarcely drank. He scarcely went to the cities, or even the small towns. He worked hard. He lived in and for Glendraco—'

'And bought an Earldom,' said Draco quietly, 'with James Drummond's money.'

'It cannot be justified,' said the Countess in an exhausted voice. 'None of it can be justified. He, my husband, suffered agonies of remorse for what he had done. But – he kept what he had won. And I – I kept silence. I was mistress of Glendraco. I became a Countess. I became the Dragon. Oh yes! I know my name. All my life since, I have tried to do right. But ... I kept silence, and we held what we had, and we hold what we have.'

Draco pulled away his hand from mine and from his grandmother's. He said, 'But it is not ours to hold.'

'Yes it is,' I said. 'If it is mine, I give it to you. Will Glendraco do, as a wedding gift from bride to bridegroom?'

'You see,' said the Countess gently, 'justice is done at last. That is why I have told you what I swore I would tell no one.

You two may know, you should know, because Christina Drummond of Glendraco has come back to be queen of the kingdom of her ancestors. Justice is done. The dancing leopard with the rose in his mouth has come home, at last . . .'

But Draco was staring at us both as though we were speaking in a language he had never learned.

He said suddenly, 'Please excuse me,' and strode out of the room, closing the door softly.

The Countess sighed. 'It has been a shock to the poor boy. He has very rigid views, a very high notion of honour. He is suddenly faced with the realization that we have been living here for fifty years by fraud, and it – upsets him.'

'It need not,' I said. 'He did not cheat. He would not, in a million years . . . I wish you would tell me more about James Drummond – if you can do so without grieving yourself?'

'I will do so with joy, darling child, but there is simply no need. Inspect yourself, inside and out, and you see your grandfather. Look about you, at the effect you have, and you see the effect he had. Because he had a strong will and a mind of his own, people thought he was perverse. Because he was brave, people thought he was mad. Because he was beautiful, people thought he was dangerous. Because he was generous, people thought he was extravagant. He aroused envy and resentment, but I have never known anyone who aroused so much love and admiration . . . at least, until I came to know you.'

Then she began to say, with far too much generosity, how happy she was that I was marrying her grandson: not only, she said, because I was getting back my own, but also because I myself was . . . well, the things she said were so kind and loving that I wept for only about the tenth time that day.

'Where has the boy gone?' murmured the Countess fretfully. 'There are a lot of things I want to say to him tonight—'

'My God,' I said. 'I don't know where he's gone, but I know why he's gone.'

The awful and obvious truth had blazed into my head like a skyrocket. Glendraco had been won and lost by cheating. The Earl had no moral right to a stone of the castle, a yard of the estate, a penny of the fortune. Morally, all was mine, and he a pauper. Since it was so morally, he would make it so legally. I knew this with instant and blinding certainty. He would rush to Edinburgh, perhaps to London, to see lawyers and sign papers, to turn me into a great heiress and himself into an abject starveling. He would do this because it was morally right to do. His conscience would give him an absolute command.

Very well. Let him do all that. I would bring it back to him as a dowry.

Then he, a pauper, would be marrying a woman of enormous wealth. Would he? Draco? With his notions of honour, and his notions of pride? A new certainty gripped my heart with cold, clutching fingers. Draco would not marry for money. As a poor man, he would not live on the wealth of a rich wife. Honour, pride, conscience would all forbid it.

Saying I know not what to the Countess, I jumped to my feet and ran out of the room.

I ran along the passage, and up the stairs of the tower in which Draco had his suite of rooms. His manservant MacDougal was standing in an open doorway, a stunned expression on his face.

'I'm tae say naethin', Miss,' said MacDougal. 'An' I wudna if I cud, for I ken naethin'.'

I did not think this was quite true; but it was true he would say nothing. He was very puzzled, but he was very loyal.

So I did what I should have done at once. I ran down to the hall, and out into the courtyard, and across the drawbridge, and along the road to the stables. The battering wind had blown the rainclouds out of the sky. Now it raced a few clouds across the moon, which was half full, and high in the southwest. The wind plucked at my clothes. I wore no coat, hat, gloves or boots. When the moon was clear of clouds, everything was sharp and brilliant in the rain-washed air; and in the bright moonlight I saw Draco, with a horse, outside the stable arch.

Draco wore a coat, and riding boots. A satchel was slung across his shoulder. He was doing something to the saddle of the horse – perhaps adjusting a stirrup-leather – while a groom held its head. I realized he had sent a servant, running, to have a horse got ready, while he changed his clothes and packed his satchel. While they were his servants and his horses, he was using them, for all they were worth, to help him make sure they ceased to be his servants and horses. This thought, for some reason, made me furious with anger. How dare he use *my* horses and servants – to make them mine? Anger gave wings to my heels; I pulled my long tight skirt clear of the ground, and ran as fast as I could towards the stables.

Suddenly Draco was up in the saddle. The groom let the bridle go, and saluted. Draco turned his horse, and trotted briskly down the glen, away from the castle and from me.

I screamed his name, but the wind plucked away my voice, and I might as well have been whispering to myself.

I ran: how I ran. I tripped and fell on the road, which the rain had made slippery. I was up and running on before I had time to notice if I was hurt or not. The wind seemed like to pick me up and throw me into the river.

Even as I reached the stable arch, I could see Draco clearly in the moonlight, trotting purposefully down the path beside the river. I thought of the bridge six miles below, where the road rejoined the river, and the ford two miles below. The ford might be unpleasant, after the heavy rain.

I ran into the stable yard. It was dark. The groom had disappeared, going thankfully back to his fireside and his pipe. Almost certainly he would have no idea where his master was going; and certainly, if he did know, he would have been told not to say.

Well, I could make do without a groom. The stalls and loose-boxes were not locked up – I could get any horse out. But the rooms where the saddles and bridles hung *were* locked. I could get hold of a groom, and have the doors unlocked, and saddle and bridle Falcon – and by then Draco might be five miles off, going in any of five directions.

I knew where Falcon was, but I did not want to risk his legs hurrying on wet ground in the dark. Besides, I was not at all sure I could manage him unbitted and bareback. I opened the upper half-door of the first loose-box. The moon, clear of cloud, shone in through the window at the back. I saw the gleam of a silvery flank. Was there a grey in this first box? Then I remembered – it was the dun Connemara called Malachi, a strong, lively pony who had once thrown me off.

I opened the lower half of the door, and ran into the loose-box. Malachi was sleepy, and surprised to be visited. I was thankful he was not lying down. He showed some dislike of the noise of the wind. I knew there should be, hanging from a brass hook, a leather head-collar, which would have to do instead of a bridle. I found it almost at once, groping with my fingers over the stable wall. The moon washed in through the window again, to help me. I slid the leather loop over Malachi's nose, and buckled the strap behind his ears. To my joy there was already a four-foot cord attached to the head-collar, for the groom to lead him by. It would not make the best rein in the world, but it would help.

I led Malachi out of the loose-box, and ran with him to the mounting-block. The wind thrashed my skirts about my legs, and blew my hair all over my face. With the rope in one hand, and a good handful of mane in the other, I managed to haul myself on to Malachi's broad back. My skirts and petticoats were almost round my waist, for I was wearing an absurdly close-fitting gown, quite unsuited to this kind of thing . . .

Of all the ridiculous sights I ever presented, I suppose that night's was the most ridiculous – hatless, virtually skirtless, blown about by a gale-force wind, trying to steer a headstrong pony with a single rope to a nose-band, trying to keep my seat on his broad, muscular back while he broke into a trot and then a canter . . . But he was a good pony, and had a brisk, purposeful canter, and I began to hope that I should catch the beloved fool who was running away out of pride and conscience.

At any other time I would have exulted in that mad ride. We scurried along beside the river, which gleamed and swirled and chuckled in the moonlight; although I was constantly blinded by the loosened hair which blew across my eyes, I loved the boisterous playfulness of the wind; Malachi was splendid, and seemed infected by my urgency.

And then I saw them ahead of us, the horse walking. Far ahead, but only walking. I kicked Malachi – a strange and satisfactory movement to a sidesaddle-rider like myself – and nearly fell off when he spurted forward. I screamed at the fugitive, but the wind swept my voice away, and the only effect was to excite my pony to a perilous tendency to buck as he cantered.

The moon was covered by a cloud. Draco disappeared into the darkness. We thundered on. The cloud sped across the moon's face, and a milky beam shone through its ragged edge, and then clear moonlight blazed down. Draco was trotting again. He was riding a tall, long-striding horse, as though he meant to go a great way in a short time, and his trot was almost as fast as Malachi's bouncing canter.

I saw him turn, and stand sideways-on to me, facing the swirling river. It was the ford. The river fanned out into broad shallows there, and ran over clean gravel. By day, in low water, it was nothing. It was a very useful short cut, saving many miles of road. Bright moonlight was nearly as helpful as daylight. Quite a lot of rain had fallen, but in the fine spell before, the river had been low, and it did not seem to have spated dangerously.

At any rate, if Draco crossed by the ford, I must cross by the ford.

I screamed again. It was useless. Draco, fifty yards ahead of me, might have been in John o' Groats. He patted his horse's neck, and they went down the broad path cut into the bank, and splashed into the water. The horse seemed quite confident, and waded strongly into the river, kicking up showers of water which the moonlight kindled into diamonds.

Malachi and I hurried on, and turned, and followed. We reached the ford when Draco was half way across. I kicked Malachi. He went cheerfully down into the water, and plunged along through it.

I shouted with triumph. I did not know what I was going to say to Draco, but I knew that I had caught him. Within seconds of climbing out on the other bank, I would be up with him, and he would stop, amazed to see me, and we would talk. I would find some tactful way to satisfy his pride and conscience, and still marry him. I reminded myself to be respectful, and careful, and treat him as someone of great importance . . .

It was just as I made this important resolution that the accident happened. I never knew what caused it – perhaps a flat slippery rock, scoured clean of gravel by an earlier spate: perhaps a rock brought down by floodwater. For whatever reason, Draco's horse, three-quarters of the way across, suddenly disappeared – fell sideways into the water with an enormous splash. I screamed, and urged Malachi forward. Draco's horse struggied at once to its feet. It was riderless. I thought it was unnerved but unhurt. It trotted towards us, sending up sheets of spray, swerved to avoid us, plunged past, and scrambled out on to the bank we had left.

Of Draco there was for a moment no sign in the moonlit water. Then a dark, limp shape surfaced a little downstream of the accident. He was stunned or dead.

Malachi jibbed, upset by the panic-stricken horse which had plunged by him. He wanted to get out of the water, and run back to the safety of his stable. He turned. Without reins or bit I could not straighten him. I screamed and kicked, aghast at the sight of the dark shape, like a log, being carried downstream by the river.

I jumped off Malachi. I tried to pull him through the water, to carry Draco home. But he reared, jerked the rope from my hand, and bolted off after the other horse.

I plunged through the shallow water, slipping and stumbling, knee-deep. To reach Draco, I had to step off the shallow bar of the ford into deeper water and on to a rocky bottom. I had long before lost my flimsy evening slippers. I hurt my feet on the rocks. I lost my balance, fell, felt myself being pulled downstream by the force of the water as the river narrowed. I rose, spluttering and panting, to find the water to my armpits. I thrashed my way towards Draco. All the while he was being sucked downstream. I could not see his face. The river was narrowing still, and approaching falls. With every yard the water was deeper and swifter.

I made a despairing lunge, and caught the toe of a boot. Soon, struggling like a madwoman, I had a handful of sodden coat, and then a handful of hair. I pulled Draco's face clear of the water. A cut on his forehead oozed blood, black as ink in the pallid moonlight, which diffused into a dark shadow in the water which covered his face.

'Please, dear God,' I screamed: and my prayer was answered, for Draco groaned.

I was standing breast-deep in water which plucked and

tugged at my legs, threatening every instant to pull me from my feet and whisk me downstream to the falls. Desperately I held Draco, one arm round his shoulders, one keeping his face out of the water. It seemed best to try to wade back to the shallow water of the ford, and thence to the bank. But wading upstream against the massive weight of the water was impossible. It might have been possible if I had had only myself to worry about; but I was burdened with the dead weight of Draco, his clothes heavy with water, his boots full of water. I could make no headway at all, and was constantly in danger of losing my balance again. So I started for the nearer bank. At once there was nothing below my feet. I had stepped into a deep hole among the rocks. I sank below the surface, Draco with me. I struggled madly to get my own head above water again, and his head. Without a footing, we were swept downstream. Still the banks narrowed, and the water was deeper and more rapid. There were rocks about us. I took my arm from Draco's head, and tried to seize and cling to one, but it was slippery, and the water foamed and battered round it, and I hurt myself on the rock, and nearly lost hold of Draco. Now we were going downstream faster and faster. I thought I could hear the roar of the falls over the boiling of the water round us.

The falls were a beauty spot, much visited by tourists in the summer. At one end there was a salmon-ladder. Above there was a long, swift stretch, a famous place for salmon, called the Minister's Pool. A Minister had been drowned there. He would have company tonight.

I was helpless now. It was all I could do to keep my own head and Draco's above water. Once again I prayed for a miracle.

Once again a miracle was granted me.

Something – a giant hand, somehow soft and flexible, yet powerful enough to hold us – stopped our helpless journey. It held us against the tearing current: it held us up. My foot became entangled in mesh. It was a net. I heard excited shouts from the bank. The moon was obscured. They thought we were gigantic fish. I felt myself being hauled towards the bank, going always downstream, but across, blessedly across, towards the land.

The moon came out from its cloud just as I reached the bank. Draco groaned again, lying full in the brilliance of the moonlight. I scrambled to my knees in shallow water, in a little bay which was out of the pull of the current. I was much hampered by my tight skirt, and by holding up Draco's head.

'Ma Goad,' said a terrified voice. ''Tis wha' they ca' a mairmed.'

'Ye ful,' said another and rougher voice. ''Tis the lassie frae the cassel. She'll infarm tae the polis or the laird, sae we maun—'

'Hoots,' said a third man, 'we'll du nae siccan thing.'

I said, as soon as I could speak, 'Will you help Lord Draco out, please?'

The first voice said in awe, 'Wha' an awfu' thing – tae pu' the laird frae the water wi' owr net . . .'

Of course they were poachers. One at least knew me. All, no doubt, knew Draco. He would know them too. Well, that was a problem for later.

Five men, very rough and roughly dressed, heaved Draco out of the river. They propped him against a rock near the bank, and looked at him in a puzzled way.

The moon went in for a moment, behind a small rushing cloud. When it came out I saw a sack by the rock, with a salmon half hidden in its mouth. I thought there were more fish deeper in the sack. By the sack was a big stoppered earthenware jug. I guessed at illicit whisky. Draco and I might have been better going over the falls, than falling in with these criminals. Every year, somewhere in Scotland, water-keepers were murdered by the salmon-poachers – and if they had illicit spirits too . . .

Yet there was something concerned about the manner of these men, about the way they stood staring down at Draco. Though their faces were as ferocious as any I had seen in the Glasgow slum, there was something gentle in their voices.

I said nervously, 'He has had an accident. He is all cold and wet. I think he should be warm. Do you think we could make a fire?'

There was a violent, whispered argument among the five. A fire would bring down every keeper on the Glendraco water. Yet here was the keepers' master, needing warmth.

Humanity won. I also heard mention of a reward.

Though there had been heavy rain earlier in the night, they somehow found dry twigs to start a fire, and branches to feed it. The warmth was like heaven. I crouched as near the flames as I dared, to warm myself and dry my sodden clothes. Meanwhile, with a kind of rough gentleness, the men pulled off Draco's coat and his boots, and dabbed at the wound on his head with a piece of rag.

He was conscious presently, and looked round with a dazed air, like a small boy waking up in a strange bedroom. He saw me.

I said, my heart almost too full for speech, 'We were drowning. We were saved.'

After a little his face cleared. When the moon next emerged from the clouds, he looked sharply at the five.

He said, 'Euan MacKay – you've been to gaol for poaching. Tod MacGregor, you were lucky not to go. I do not know your friends – unless that is Davie Ramsay, without a beard?'

'Ay,' said a giant with a stubbled but beardless chin.

'Thank you for saving our lives,' said Draco politely. 'And for lighting a fire, in spite of the risk to yourselves. My keepers may come. If I were you, I should roll up your net, and hide it under a stone. And what are these? Fresh-run fish? I'll buy them from you. Is there anything else I should see, or not see? That jug? Something to do with you, Tod MacGregor, I fancy. I have never tried the spirit from your still – it should be a fine tonic for a wet man on a windy night.'

'Yer Lordship wull tak' a dram?' asked Tod MacGregor nervously.

'I certainly will. Miss Drummond will also, if she'll be guided by me. I don't know if she'll appreciate the flavour, but she'll be better for the stimulant ... And now, Kirstie, will you explain why we have been bathing together?'

'I followed you. I had to talk to you. I still have to.'

'No. We have nothing to say to each other. You must see that. I had to leave when I did. I must do what I set out to do. Could you respect me, could I respect myself, if I did not? Am I a cheat, to compound that ancient fraud? Or a lapdog, to nuzzle round the skirts of an heiress? I cannot keep what is not mine –

you cannot expect me to. I cannot live on a woman's fortune – you cannot expect that, either. You must go back, I must go on. That is final. There is no more to be said.'

I sighed. It was exactly as I had supposed. Conscience, honour, pride – or, to put it more exactly, pig-headed masculine stupidity.

But I thought carefully before I answered him. Somehow I must persuade this proud, prickly nobleman to pocket his pride – convince him that he should ignore his conscience – make him see that he could keep both his fortune and his honour. I must use the utmost tact, the utmost diplomacy. I must show respect, always the deepest respect.

'Well, it comes to this,' I said. 'Either you promise to marry me, and stop talking pompous rubbish, or I will push you back into the river.'

After a long, silent, stupefied moment, and a black frown, and a furious glare at the attentively-listening poachers, Draco began to laugh. He spread his hands helplessly, still laughing. I knelt beside him, and took his hands; and he kissed me.

And we baked a fresh salmon, in a sheath of mud, on embers of the fire; and we toasted each other in the poachers' illicit whisky; and we plighted our troth before witnesses.

Jessica Stirling
The Spoiled Earth 95p

A powerful and exciting love story set against the loyalties and
oppressions, catastrophies and ambitions, of a nineteenth-century
Scottish mining community. This haunting saga traces the joys and
despairs of Mirrin Stalker, radical firebrand and tantalizing beauty, who
is unprepared for the directions which her passions take ...

'Jessica Stirling has a brilliant future' CATHERINE COOKSON

The Hiring Fair 80p

This magnificent sequel to *The Spoiled Earth* is set in the Scotland of the
bleak 1870s. With her father and two brothers dead in the Blacklaw
mine disaster, Mirrin Stalker, the restless firebrand of the Stalker family,
takes to the road. Through tinker camp and hiring fair she finally
emerges on the stage of the music-hall in its bright-lit heyday.